The Ultimate Sacrifice 6

Anthony Fields

Lock Down Publications and Ca$h
Presents

The Ultimate Sacrifice 6

A Novel by *Anthony Fields*

Anthony Fields

Lock Down Publications
P.O. Box 944
Stockbridge, Ga 30281

Visit our website @
www.lockdownpublications.com

Copyright 2021 Anthony Fields
The Ultimate Sacrifice 6

*This is a work of fiction. Names, characters, places, and incidents either
are products of the author's imagination or are used fictitiously. Any
similarity to actual events or locales or persons, living or dead, is
entirely coincidental.*

Lock Down Publications
Like our page on Facebook: Lock Down Publications @
www.facebook.com/lockdownpublications.ldp
Cover design and layout by: **Dynasty Cover Me**
Book interior design by: **Shawn Walker**
Editor: **Lashonda Johnson**

Stay Connected with Us!

Text **LOCKDOWN** to 22828 to stay up-to-date with
new releases, sneak peaks, contests and more...
Thank you.

Submission Guideline.

Submit the first three chapters of your completed manuscript to ldpsubmissions@gmail.com, subject line: Your book's title. The manuscript must be in a .doc file and sent as an attachment. Document should be in Times New Roman, double spaced and in size 12 font. Also, provide your synopsis and full contact information. If sending multiple submissions, they must each be in a separate email.

Have a story but no way to send it electronically? You can still submit to LDP/Ca$h Presents. Send in the first three chapters, written or typed, of your completed manuscript to:

LDP: Submissions Dept
P.O. Box 944
Stockbridge, Ga 30281

DO NOT send original manuscript. Must be a duplicate.

Provide your synopsis and a cover letter containing your full contact information.

Thanks for considering LDP and Ca$h Presents.

Dedication

This book is dedicated to my parents, Deborah Wiseman, and Thomas 'Brickey' Fields. May you both continue to rest in peace. It's been over a decade that you both have been gone. So, I guess this pain in my heart is forever.

Acknowledgments

In part five of Ultimate Sacrifice, I acknowledged a lot of people. Some who remain a part of my life and others who aren't. In the last book, I detailed how every book matriculated and each story grew while I was in a different prison. I wrote those acknowledgments as a man recently freed from years of incarceration. I was humble. I was driven. I was motivated. I was focused.

Then came impatience and disappointment. The urban novel game in 2016 wasn't what I imagined it would be. I imagined overcrowded book releases and signings at bookstores. I imagined Black Book Expos and events all-across the country specifically for black urban authors. I imagined books becoming movies and TV series. I imagined producing material for Netflix, Hulu, and BET. I imagined prosperity.

I never imagined that Wahida Clark would come after me for wanting to eat off my work that she wasn't paying me for. She sent an email to Amazon telling them that the Ultimate Sacrifice series was hers and I had no right to reproduce it. Amazon sent me an email letting me know that they were not going to make certain books available. After trying to rectify a bad situation, the realization kicked in, my imagination dissipated. I found ways to get around Wahida and Amazon, but the harsh reality was that I had simply come home too late. Physical books were becoming a thing of the past. Electronic books were the new normal.

Everything that I imagined was a thing of the past. Frustrated with basically no plan B, I started moving reckless. I burned a lot of bridges. I put one Timberland boot back in the streets, while trying to keep one suede loafer in the book game. Before long, I traded the suede loafer in for the other Timberland boot. In time, those Timberland boots became Gucci, Louis Vuitton, and Versace, foreign boots, shoes that rested on gas and brake pedals in foreign whips. My life became an urban novel and the feds got ahold of it. I wasn't home fourteen months before the ATF was on my line.

Eight months later, I was back in jail, charged with conspiracy to Traffic narcotics and possession of illegal firearms. I went to trial in 2019 three weeks later, I blew. It's now 2020 and I sit in Federal Prison writing the book that you now hold either physically or as an eBook. Everybody always asks me, *"Why did you do that to Khadafi? Why did you make him a rat?"* I did it because in every fictious story there's a degree of truth.

While Luther Fuller is a real person, Khadafi is a figment of my imagination. In my world, dudes who resemble Khadafi's Wanton, reckless nature, and desire for destruction for some reason they always become the rat in real life. The one that you never expected. The Byron 'Crud' Clarks of the world. Byron 'Crud' Clark had everybody fooled. Until he showed up at my trial and rocked the mic for the government. He lied on the stand for two straight days and cooked me. He was the only *street dude* to testify against me.

In a last-ditch effort to try and save myself and my co-defendant, I testified in my trial. I vehemently denied any conspiracy and anything else the government fabricated to get us. But people who don't understand defenses in court implied that I should have never done that. I want those who really know me to know that I have always honored and adhered to the codes of the streets. Always lived the Omerta. That will never change with me. *Never!* The death before dishonor lives within me like a star that shines bright.

Conflict, jealousy, unjust motivations have caused some to question my character. To those who question whether I am the same Buck, I say this, and Allah be my witness. I sat in the ATF headquarters for hours and never uttered a word. Never interviewed. Never debriefed. Never made any statement of any kind whatsoever. *Never!* My words on the stand implicated no one but were misconstrued by haters and suckers.

A good man told me, *"Slim, pay no attention to what people say behind your back. As long as they respect your presence."*

That made sense to me, knowing that no one would ever stand in front of me and disrespect my honor. They'd only do it while I wasn't around. I reclaimed my gangsta. I thank Antone 'Tone'

White for telling me that and believing in me. You gave me so many jewels and predicted so much that came to pass that I call you, *Tonestradamus*. I respect you and love ya like no other. To me, you are the best my generation has produced.

The good men will agree with me, the suckas gon' say, I'm dick riding you, and the haters gon' do what they do—hate. But they will never do it around me or you. Remember what I always told you, *"Heavy is the head that wears the crown."* You spent one half of your life earning your crown, you'll spend the next half protecting it. I pray that Allah grants you your freedom. To all the good men incarcerated in the BOP and beyond, hold y'all heads. I send my love and respects.

To all the good men here in Hazelton Pen, who've listened to me rant and rave, but understand that I care about my name and know that I remain unbroken, thank you. To Nehemiah Hampton, Cochise Shakur, Angelo 'Nut' Daniels, my brother. Marcus Martin, Twin- Kennedy Street, Mink, Poochie, DC-Trinidad, Andy Daniels, Bug and Greg, Denzel McCowley, Pete- Clay Terrace, Shelton Marbury, my cousin. Kenny Garmagoo, Griff, Wack, Big Mac, Eighty-Eight, Tay, John 'Buck' Rayner, Poo Poo, Dog, L, Henry, Veedo, Rico 'Suave' Thomas, James 'Rock' Smith, Sneeze, Wayne-Wayne, Berbeast, Gotti, Big Redds, Steve, Tony Roy, Zulu, Lips, Twin, Kenny, Big V, OG, Monkey D, Biggie, Tarzan, KQ, Loso, Face, Old Head Mummy and too many more to name.

Gotta give a special shout out to Delmont Player, Donell 'Fat Rat' Hunter, Cain and Scoop, Bernard 'Tapole' Johnson, Joe Ebron, Thomas Hager, Richard 'Babyface' Johnson, Dion Green, Zulu, Khalif A. Mujahad, Trey Manning, Moe Styles, Erron 'Son' Robinson,

To all my men who've made it out, Larry Moe, LA, Handsome, KK, Devon, NuNu, Vito, Tim-Tim, Timmy Smalls, Sean Branch, Rich Young, Khalid Abdullatif, Ducksauce, Marcus M. Brooks, Dave Bailey, Reggie 'Champ' Yelverton, Dave Battle.

To my cousin, Herb Austin. Thanks for everything, Slim. To my partner Richard 'Black Junior' Devaughn. I love you, ock, feasibullah and with dunyah love.

To Gloria 'Poochie' Mason and Pretina 'TT' Brown, I love y'all with all my heart. Thank you both for all the love and support. To my sister, Toi Wiseman, our bond is unbreakable forever. To Leshawn Wilson, thank you for everything you've done for me for the last twenty-three years. Although our bond is not what it once was, our friendship remains. I will always love you until they cover my face with my dirt. I love you!

To Angelina Scott, Cheri Johnson, Tontieta Virgil, Anett Snyder, Nacheshia Fox, Ikea Jones, Tina Grover, Tracy Rowe, and countless others. Thank you for all your support.

To my son, Kevin Grover, I am proud of the man you've become. Hold your head. To my daughter Aniyah Fields, you already know what it is with me and you, my twin. I love you with all my heart and soul.

To Nene Capri, Lashonda Johnson and Wayne Henry, thank you for everything.

Gotta give a special Rest In Paradise shout out to Dennis 'Dice' Hall, Mike 'OG' Jones, Theodore, Black Joe (Hov), Rose and Tricia, Antonio 'Nome' Price, Stuff, Paul 'Sloppy Top' Williams, Earl Edelin, Eric Weaver Jr. (Lil' Smooth), Cindy Holton, My nephews Tyquan and Lil' Buck.

To Cash and LDP, I appreciate everything you've done. Salute!

If anyone would like to contact me, I'm here. Take Care!
Anthony Fields #16945016
USP Hazelton
P.O. Box 2000
Bruceton Mills, W.V. 26525
One Love, D.C. Stand Up!
Buckey Fields

Anthony Fields

Chapter One
Nicole Brooks
June 2014: Three Weeks After Trial

Rene Regals walked into my office and sat in the chair directly facing my desk. I stopped what I was doing to give her my undivided attention.

"Hey, Rene. What can I do for you?"

"That's what I love about you, Nic, you're always working," Rene said.

"The bills gotta get paid, sista. What's up?"

Rene opened her briefcase and pulled out a file. She handed that file to me. I opened the file and started reading it.

"I'm working on a direct appeal for a guy named Anthony Phillips who lost in trial recently. A case about the ATF investigating a blue barbershop on MLK Avenue where drugs were alleged to be trafficked from. My guy was the head of the conspiracy. He was found guilty by a jury of constructive possession of narcotics found in the barbershop only because he had a key. He doesn't own the shop, nor did he lease it. The government used a cooperating witness named Byron 'Crud' Clark to put my client in the barbershop selling him drugs. The government—"

"What prosecutors?" I asked.

"Macaroni and Rose," Rene replied and smirked.

I nodded and smiled back. Chase Macchiaroli and Bill Rosen were notoriously known for prosecuting drug cases, conspiracies and gun offenses using shady witnesses. They were two prosecutors who'd lie, steal, cheat and kill to secure a victory in federal court.

"They used this guy Byron Clark knowing that he was giving a perjured testimony."

"Their usual," I commented.

"Right. My client swears that he doesn't even know the guy. In trial, the government presented evidence from my client's cellphone, but there were no text messages, calls or any contact info for Byron Clark. Yet, he testified that he purchased fifteen to twenty grams of Heroin three times a week for eight months from my client.

Clark also testified against Malik Hewitt recently. He's jumping from case to case providing false testimony for Macaroni and Rose. I need you to do two things for me. I need everything you can find *on and off* record about Byron Clark. Street name is *Crud*."

I wrote down everything Rene said. "And the other thing? You said two, right?"

"Right. In order to get my client a new trial, I have to argue that some 404-B evidence used against him at trial should not have been admitted, it should have been suppressed. Anthony Phillips was observed leaving a store called *Bob's* on Marlboro Pike months before his arrest. Officers allege that they stopped my client because Bob's is known to sell drug paraphernalia. I need you to go to Bob's and persuade the owners to let you take photos of the inside of the store. The store sells legitimate items as well. I need to show that to the appeals court to strengthen my argument that the officers who stopped my client had no probable cause or grounds for a reasonable suspicion."

"Persuade the owners of Bob's to let me photograph the inside of their store," I repeated aloud as I wrote it down. "Sounds easy enough."

"Well, it's not. The owners, black folks I might add, have been under investigation before for what they sell. They are a bit paranoid. I called and explained what I needed, and the person hung up on me. So, good luck."

"I don't depend on luck. I am the greatest salesman in the world."

Rene laughed. "You read the book, too, huh? By OG Mendino."

I nodded. "I did too, both of them in college. They inspired me to finish law school. Do you remember the scroll that was marked number three?"

"I will persist until I succeed. I will never consider defeat. I will remove from my vocabulary such words and phrases as quit, cannot, unable, impossible, failure, hopeless and retreat. For they are the words of fools. I will avoid despair. I will endure. I will ignore the obstacles at my feet and keep my eyes on the goals above my head.

I will always remember that where dry desert ends, green grass begins."

"Well said, sista girl. I knew that I could depend on you."

"Who's the best investigator in the world?"

"You are, Nicole Brooks," Rene said. "You're the best."

"You better know it. I'll get right on it and call you in a few days with an update."

About an hour later, I was reading some stuff I'd Googled, when a person appeared in my office doorway. I looked up and smiled for the second time that day. He was a gorgeous man, sexy as hell and free. He looked much better in street clothes, then the D.C. jail orange two-piece uniform.

"Antonio!"

"Hey, Nic," Antonio 'Ameen' Felder said softly.

My pussy instantly tingled. My heart rate quickened, and my body grew warm despite the air conditioner making my office feel like an igloo. I stood up and walked around my desk to meet him. Antonio's beard was perfectly trimmed and out low. His bald head glistened with oil. A half of Medusa's head design stretched across his muscular chest. The Versace T-shirt fit him like it was custom made for him. Antonio's jeans were fitted and looked expensive. A gold Medusa head jumped off the tongue of his high-top Versace sneakers that matched his shirt. I walked right into Antonio's arms as if I belonged there. He smelled of soap and fragrant oils.

"I missed you so much."

Antonio pulled me away from his chest. "I miss you, too. But I had to get my life settled before I could come here. Before I could see you."

"No need to explain," I said looking right into his eyes. "I understand all you went through over the last year. Trust me, I get it."

"Do you? Ever since I walked out of D.C. jail after I got acquitted, I been thinking about you. I probably wouldn't even be here if it wasn't for you."

"Antonio—stop."

"I can't stop, Nic. That's the problem. I love my wife with all my heart, but I also love you and want you. I make love to her sometimes, I think about you. Wish that it was you. I gotta keep quiet at times out of fear that I'll call out your name."

"Wouldn't want that to happen. I know exactly how that feels," I said nostalgically.

"You been with someone and wanted to call my name?" Antonio asked.

Letting Antonio go, I walked across the room and leaned on my desk. "I haven't been with any other man sexually since the day *we* did it inside my car. When I say I know how that feels, I was referring to you calling out a name that wasn't mine. One time I came to D.C. jail to sex you—it was the day you showed me the letters and asked me to go see Marquis Venable and Bayona Lake—we were in the attorney's room and I was up on the table. Skirt around my waist, legs wide open.

"You stood in between my legs holding a foot in each hand. You were fucking me so good. I remembered being turned on by the faces you made and the sounds that escaped your mouth as you pounded into me. My toes were painted red and each toe had the tiny initials A and F. I had let myself believe that you were really mine. Then you said, *"Damn, baby! Shawnay, your pussy is so good!"* I was hurt, I was mortified. Everything after that felt like rape. I left the jail that day and cried so hard in the car."

"Nic, I'm sorry—"

"You don't have to apologize. I'ma big girl. I knew what I was getting myself into. That was the day I knew I had to find your wife, you needed her."

Antonio turned and went toward the door. I thought he was leaving but he didn't, he closed my office door and locked it. Then in a blur, he was back in front of me, touching me and undressing me.

"Antonio—stop," my mouth said unconvincingly.

My body responded to his touch and my eyes beckoned for him to continue. Antonio knew exactly what I needed. My body was lifted from the ground and I was carried to my desk with one swipe of my arm. I knocked everything onto the carpeted floor. My two-thousand-dollar Macbook laptop included. Once my back touched the hard wood, I relaxed and gave in. Antonio removed my heels. His tongues licked at my toes like a cat famished for sweet milk. Then he moved up my legs and met my hormones in the center of me. When his tongue touched my clit, sparks flew, and a river flooded.

"Lift up, let me take these panties off," Antonio whispered.

I lifted my body and let him remove my panties. He tossed them across the room, then went back to his task. Antonio ate my pussy like he was forced to. He ate me greedily with purpose as if he was at gunpoint and trying to save his own life. He didn't take long before I squirted juices all over his lips and beard. I thought that he would stop then, but he didn't. Antonio kissed and licked my pussy until I had another orgasm.

"Shit! Antonio—"

Antonio lifted up and entered me and all seemed right with the world. He touched a place deep inside me that few had ever touched. His dick made me reckless, made me careless. I called his name, loudly.

"Damn, Nic—this pussy—" Antonio stammered.

"It's yours, Antonio. My pussy is yours!"

"Nic—Nic—"

"Antonio!"

Antonio held my legs tight, shuddered and came.

***

"So, what now, Antonio?" I asked, holding my panties in my hands.

"I'm leaving, Nic."

"Leaving?"

Antonio sat in the chair that Rene Regals had abandoned hours ago. He nodded. "That's what I came here to tell you."

"And here I thought you just wanted to fuck," I replied sarcastically. I was hurt. "Leaving how, Antonio?"

"I'm leaving D.C. I'm moving away from here. And I didn't want to leave without saying goodbye to you in person. It was never my intention to fuck you, Nic. Seeing you ignited something in me that I have been suppressing since I got out. I had to taste you, touch you, be inside of you. I'm sorry."

"Don't apologize, Antonio. I wanted it to happen. It takes two, right? So, you decided to leave the city, huh?"

"Yeah. Actually, it was Shawnay's idea. Then and now. She wanted to leave here after my daughter was killed but I couldn't leave. I was too consumed with guilt. I was consumed with revenge. I needed to punish everybody that had a hand in my daughter's death. I couldn't leave, wouldn't leave until I'd avenged Kenya. I did exactly that. I killed all the people that Khadafi said I did, Nic. All except one. But that's neither here nor there. I accomplished my goal, Nic. I avenged my daughter. It's time for me to move on, D.C. raised me after birthing me. It shaped me and sent me to prison. D.C. killed my daughter. D.C. has incarcerated all the dudes that I love. D.C. is a bitch that I been sleeping with for too long. It's time to part with her."

Tears fell from my eyes as I took a seat in my chair behind my desk. My eyes were on my shaking hands that rested in my lap. My heart was broken, and I wanted Antonio to see that, to feel that. "Leave, Antonio, I can't live my life waiting for you to be a part of it. I was a fool to fall in love with a married man. I need to get you out of my system. I need you to leave and let me heal."

"Nic, I'm sorry for—"

"Sorry doesn't heal wounds when they hurt. Leave, Antonio!"

"Nic, I—"

"Get the fuck out of my office, Antonio! Leave!"

I never looked up. I heard the office door unlock, open and then close. I laid my head on my desk and cried.

Chapter Two

Ameen

Leaving Nicole's office, I felt bad inside. I never meant to hurt her. The sight of her crying messed with my head. I drove through the city and let what I saw all around me fortify my position on leaving. D.C. was a different city. I was a different man living in a different time. I ended up at the cemetery, I kneeled at my daughter's grave and said a prayer. I stared at the smiling photo of Kenya affixed to her tombstone. In seconds, my tears started and rolled down my cheeks.

"Kenya, I miss you so much. I'm so sorry that this happened to you. I was supposed to protect you. Supposed to keep you safe. I failed you, baby. Badly! I pray that you forgive me. We're leaving, baby, moving away from here. Asia wants to go to Atlanta. Mommy wants to go back to Texas. I don't care where we go as long as we're together. Everybody misses you. Kay-Kay is getting bigger and Asia is a mini you. We will never forget you, baby. Never!" I reached out and touched the picture of my oldest child encased in the glass forever immortalized in my heart. "Until we meet again in paradise. I love you with all my heart. Bye, baby!"

***

"You have a prepaid call. You will not be cleared for this call. This call is from Angelo Daniels. To accept this call, press five now."

"Hello?"

"Ameen, what's up, slim? I'm glad you beat that case."

"Nut, what's up, big boy? I'm glad I beat that joint, too."

"That's fucked up what that nigga Khadafi did to you. After all you did for his sucka ass down Beaumont and beyond. He gon' rock that wood on you like that. That shit is crazy."

"It's cool, slim. Dudes like Khadafi are the narcissistic type. All they care about are themselves. He was loyal to no one, I knew that and still kept fucking with him. That error in judgement was on me. I'll never make that type of mistake again."

"Where his bitch ass at now?"

"I think he still over CTF on the fourth floor."

"I bet not ever catch his bitch ass in here, I'ma burn his ass up—"

"I feel you, slim," I said, cutting Nut off.

In his anger at Khadafi he was talking reckless on a federal government phone.

"Speaking of hot shit, bruh. What's this wild shit we been hearing about my man Buck?"

"*Buck?* Who Buckey Fields?"

"Yeah."

"Slim, niggas be hating on Buck. He didn't tell on that case. He was over the jail with me until they sent him to Warsaw. He got a codefendant named Lonell Tucker, a dude he grew up with. Buck was the one getting to the bag everybody else was hanging around. Buck came in and saw Lonell's name all over the discovery and *his* wasn't, he suspected that Lonell was a rat. He called to the streets and told dudes that Lonell was wicked.

"Buck had the biggest name, so the government wanted him. They offered Buck a cop to a hundred months. Since the people never got anything off Buck, he refused to cop. He never debriefed or made any statements. The government got mad and indicted five other dudes that were associated with the barbershop. Lonell, a dude named Lacy, and three dope fiend niggas that Buck was never supposed to be fucking with. They went to trial right before I did. Some bitch, nigga named Crud got on the stand and cooked Buck.

"Buck got on the stand to defend himself. His defense was that too many people had access to the barbershop for him to be charged with the drugs found in the shop. He said on the stand that everybody had keys but didn't implicate anyone. The people asked Buck who the barbershop belonged to and he answered, Willie Smith. Here's the thing though, slim. The people already knew the dude Will owned the shop. The dude Lonell was going to cart from

20

the street. He started telling everybody that would listen that Buck got on the stand and tried to put the drugs on the dude Will.

"That didn't happen. There were good men who sat in on the trial that I talked to. The dude Lonell was getting Buck back for putting the bad bone on him that he was hot. Then after they lost, a fuck boy, dope fiend nigga named, Foots another one of Buck's codefendants voiced to people that Buck should've copped and none of the other five would've gotten locked up. He got on Lonell's bandwagon and started talking that Buck being wicked shit. Ain't no truth to that shit, slim."

"That's good to hear, slim. No bullshit. You know I fuck with Buck."

"Me, too. I keep telling niggas running around with that bullshit. Buck gonna crush everybody who says that shit."

"I'm already hipped. All the good men send their love to you."

"Give all the men my regards as well. Where's Trey?"

"Trey Manning?"

"Yeah. I haven't heard nothing about him since I left the jail in twenty-twelve. He good?"

"Yeah. He's in Big Sandy chilling. Waiting to see the board."

"I gotta reach out to him, send him a few dollars."

"While you doing that, send me some, too," Nut said.

"I got you, big boy. I'ma get wifey to do it today. Call me tomorrow and let me know that you got it."

"I got you. I appreciate you, slim."

I disconnected the call and stared at my front door. The house in Arlington was home to us again and it felt good. I spotted Shawnay's rental car in the driveway and smiled. Then I thought about Nicole and what happened in her office. I sniffed myself and smelled her perfumed. My smile faded as I pulled off. I needed a shower, and I couldn't do it at home.

Chapter Three

Khadafi

I walked into the room and saw Ann Sloan and Detective Winslow sitting at the table. I took a seat across from them.

"I got good news and bad news," Ann Sloan said. "Which one do you want first?"

My spirit tanked immediately. The government was about to renege on their promise to me. I felt it. "C'mon, cuz, I did everything y'all asked me to do. I told y'all everything. I cooperated, got on the stand, and ratted. Now, here y'all come with this bullshit. The deal I signed said that my charges would be dropped. So, what can the bad news be?"

"Listen to me, you piece of shit rat. I know what the fuck your agreement said, I wrote it. Did I say anything about not honoring our agreement? I didn't, did I? So, shut the fuck up and listen. The good news is that I'm working to get another shot at Antonio Felder on some other stuff and you'll be able to help us with that. I can't lie and say that I'm not upset about Felder's acquittal, but it's not entirely your fault.

"I rushed to judgement with the speedy trial. That killed us. I never covered all the bases. The agreement you made with me is good. The bad news is that when I made the deal with District Attorney Delores Monroe, it was a deal with her. The decision she made to discard your charges didn't sit well within her office. She was forced to resign. Another person sits in her seat.

"A man named, Tom Dexter. He doesn't have to honor an agreement made by his predecessor, but chances are he will. But last week, and I just found this out, that guy you beat with the phone at Seven Locks has been clinically declared as brain dead. Tom Dexter is charging you with assault with malicious wounding. There's no way to get around that."

"Y'all tricked me. I can't believe it. I let y'all trick me like that."

"We didn't trick you, Khadafi. You tricked yourself. Since we still need you, I'm going to keep talking to the new DA and see if we can't get you into a diversion program or something. All is not lost. Give me some time and I'ma make it work out. Trust me."

I stood up and headed for the door. "I already did that once and look what that got me."

"Hold on—Khadafi, wait," Ann Sloan called out.

I stopped at the door but didn't turn around.

"Give me a few more days. If you know anything about any murders committed in the state of Maryland that would help your cause. I know you know somebody who's moving drugs across the Maryland line. Give me something to take to Tom Dexter and I promise that you'll be in the streets in a week. Help me to help you."

"You can't help me. I can't even help myself."

"Khadafi, be smart. Maryland is going to come and get you. You're facing up to ten years for the assault with malicious wounding. How long do you think you'll last in a Maryland penitentiary? Nobody likes a rat. You know that better than anybody. You're almost at the finish line, don't quit before the race is done. Give me some more murders, here and in Maryland."

"I don't have anything else to give." I opened the door and walked out of the room.

***

When I walked into my cell, I saw a dude putting sheets on the mattress on the top bunk. He turned around to face me.

"The C.O. downstairs told me to move here," the dude said.

I eyed the dude suspiciously, taking notice of all the tattoos on his arms, neck, and face. His head was shaved, bald and covered with ink.

"Where are you coming from?" I asked.

"The hole, I got caught with a phone."

"And what's your name, cuz?"

"Crud. Everybody calls me Crud."

***

Four Months Later

"Mr. Fuller, in light of your cooperation with the government in D.C. and your acceptance of responsibility in this case, I accept your plea. I hereby sentence you to three years to be served in the Maryland Department of Corrections."

Chapter Four

Khadafi

"That's fucked up/ You about to take the longest trip and can't do shit but suck it up/ Be strong as shit, handcuffed ankles to wrist in back of the bus/ Flashbacks of you back in the world, thinking about who in back of your girl/ Got her ass up, chilling in your crib, thinking about who raising your kids."

The sun rose in the Eastern skies like a person peeking over a wall. I sat by the window on the bus as the Beanie Siegel lyrics to *What Your Life Like* played in my head. It made me think about Mernie and who was fucking her and raising my kids.

"You ever been to WCI before?" I heard the dude next to me ask.

"Naw, cuz, I ain't never been locked up in Maryland before," I replied, still looking out of the window.

"Where you from, homes?"

"I'm from the city, from D.C."

"Me, too," the dude offered. "But my first charge was in Prince George's County. I did two years in Upper Marlboro and ten years in the Maryland system. I been to all of the joints, Eastern Shore, Jessup, Northbranch, Baltimore Pen and WCI. That's where we are going now—to WCI."

"How you know that?" I asked.

"I recognized the cops that are transporting us. I went home from WCI about nine months ago. I'm back on a thirty-six-month violation."

"What part of D.C. are you from?"

"Southeast. Wheeler Road, Wahler Place. All that area."

"Is that right? I'm from Southeast, too."

"That's what's up. What's your name, homes?"

"Redds."

"Okay, Redds. I'm Troy, Pastor Troy."

***

"Open your mouth and lift your tongue," a fat, pink faced C.O. ordered.

I knew the routine and complied.

"Lift your arms up, hands to the sky."

I lifted my arms, then instinctively turned, and squatted.

"Did I fuckin' tell you to squat?"

Turning back to face the C.O. with murder on my mind, I said, "My bad."

"Turn around slow and bend over at the hip, don't squat. Bend your entire body at the waist, spread your ass cheeks and hold that position."

Inhaling deeply, I did as I was told as anger rose inside me.

Pink face finally bellowed, "Good. Now get your ass in that line over there and get your clothes. The captain will be to see y'all shortly."

***

"Have you ever been sexually assaulted while in prison?" The Captain turned out to be a short, white man who reminded me of Danny Devito.

"Naw, never," I answered.

"Have you ever assaulted law enforcement?"

"Never," I lied.

"Is there any reason that I shouldn't put you in gen pop here at WCI?"

I had already decided that I'd deal with whatever came my way head on. I wasn't going to check into protective custody.

"Naw, I'm good."

"Where are you from, Fuller?" the Captain asked.

"I'm from D.C."

"Here, everybody from D.C. is murder one. You good with that?"

"I'm good with whatever."

The captain wrote something down on a notepad. "I run a tight ship here, Fuller. My staff is the biggest and toughest gang behind these walls. Respect them and we gon' be good. Don't give us no trouble and we won't give you any. Just do your time, don't let it do you. It says here that you have three years to do? Act right and you'll be home in two and a half years. Fuck up and you'll be in my lock up until you go home. You got that?"

"Got it."

"Good. You're going to D-3 Unit. Good luck, Fuller."

***

Processing us into the prison took all day. It was late by the time we walked into the housing unit. All the inmates were already locked down.

"Fuller and Stevens, y'all are in cell nine, over there," the C.O. directed us.

All eyes in every cell unit were on us as we went to our cell. Inside the cell, I told my celly, "You take the bottom bunk, cuz. I'll get up top."

"That's a bet," he replied. He was from Baltimore.

I made up my bed in a flash and climbed in it, but sleep didn't come easy. I couldn't help but wonder what tomorrow would bring.

The Next Morning

When the cell opened, I was ready for whatever. I was up, dressed and prepared to face my life. It didn't take long before I was approached by a group of dudes from D.C. none that I recognized.

"You from D.C., slim?" the ringleader asked.

I steeled myself for a sudden attack. Keith Bernett's situation on my mind. "Yeah, why? What's up?"

"What's your name, homie?" another dude asked.

"Redds."

"Where you from in D.C., bro?" a different dude inquired.

"I'm from Southeast."

"Cool, cool. I'm Jeezy from Hobert and these are the homies. Tarzan, KQ, Monkey D, Biggie, Face, and Loso from Choppa City. We got some cosmetics for you and some other shit. I'll be right back."

I took a bag full of stuff to my cell, surprised that nothing had happened. When they called yard, I went outside and stayed for hours. The rest of the day went by incident free. In the unit, that night a dude that slept in the cell not far from me, approached me.

"What's up, Moe? I'm Stone. When you get in your cell look under your mattress. I put something there for you."

Before I could respond, he turned and walked away. Inside my cell, I waited until my celly laid down before lifting the mattress on my bunk. What I found was a letter and a shank. I picked up the shank first and fingered the tip. It was sharp, there were ridges down the side. I picked up the letter, unfolded it and began reading.

In 2011, you killed a dude named, Greg Strong. Him and a dude named, Devan Horns on 3rd Street in SW. The dude Strong killed my mother in 2009. Allegedly she stole some drugs or money from him in a trap house on K Street. I was at the Ultra Max next door and couldn't avenge my mother. Her death destroyed me. My younger brother Deaundre went at Strong twice but didn't kill him. He put the police on my brother, testified against him and the whole nine. He's at the Feds doing ten years on an AWIK.

When I heard that he got killed, I cried tears of joy. For that, I am eternally grateful. By now, you should have figured out that I know who you are. Well, the homies in the block know who you are as well. They know you are Khadafi. The dude Troy that sat beside you on the bus ride here was in Seven Locks with you. He told everybody who you are and what you did to a dude named, Ameen.

They are trying to rock you to sleep. They heard about how you got down in the Feds and they're scared. But even cowards can kill. To be forearmed is to be forewarned. The move is supposed to happen tomorrow. On the strength you killed Strong, I had to give you a heads up and a fighting chance. In here, Jeezy is the head of the snake. Crush him and the others will hesitate out of confusion.

That slight hesitation might save your life. Flush the kite, keep the knife, and handle your business.

I balled the letter up and flushed it down the toilet. I gripped the knife and smiled, not believing my good fortune. The homies in the block thought I'd be easy prey. They had another thought coming.

***

The only thing that beats a good defense is an even better offense. As soon as the cell doors opened, I shot out of the cell like a bullet from a gun. It was a little after 6:00 a.m. and not everybody was up. A lot of people were still in their cells, except Jeezy. He was up, suited and booted, standing in front of a TV mounted to a beam near the wall. Him, Face, and Biggie watched videos on BET Jams. Half-naked women were dancing as Megan Thee Stallion rapped and twerked. Good for me, bad for them. I slid up behind the trio, knife already out. I attacked Jeezy first, with the briskness of a mountain cat. Stabbed him in the head trying to knock whole patches of dreads out. He tried to cover up, but I wouldn't let him. My knife found its mark in his neck and back.

"Aaarrrggg-gh!" he yelled. "Please—stop!"

"Shut the fuck up, bitch nigga!" I replied.

The white boy called Face and Biggie stood transfixed to their spots, paralyzed with fear. My attack on Jeezy was ferocious, unrelenting. When Jeezy dropped, I turned my knife on them, swinging with precision. I caught Face in the chest. Before he could run, I reached out and grabbed him. He screamed like a bitch. I hit him a few times and turned to Biggie, who took off running. I got right on his ass, stride for stride. He ran into the bannister of the stairwell and fell. He kicked his legs out and begged for his life.

"I wasn't with it, bruh!" he screamed.

"Yeah, you was," I said as I picked my shots and busted his ass good to the legs and body.

I heard feet, thought it was cops but turned to see other D.C. homies approaching with chairs, locks in a sack and knives out. I turned the knife blade down in my hand and met them in the middle. Always meet aggression with more aggression.

"What y'all wanna do? Let's work!"

Nobody moved, seconds later, the unit filled with Correctional Officers.

"Drop your weapon!" a lieutenant yelled at me with a can of mace in his hand.

The crowd of D.C. dudes with weapons backed away. I dropped the knife to the ground. The C.O.s rushed me and cuffed me. They led me out of the unit covered in them dumb niggas blood.

***

The demonstration that I put down in D-3 made me an instant celebrity at WCI. I was awarded a cell by myself in solitary. All the C.O.s told other dudes on lock up about my classic demo. After a week or so, the institution went on lockdown. It took a minute, but I eventually learned why. An inmate in D-3 unit was found dead in his cell, strangled to death. I learned that that cell was two doors down from my cell. The dead inmate's name was DeAngelo Stone, nicknamed Stone. It was the homie that gave me the letter and shank. He had aided and assisted me, and it cost him his life. I vowed to myself to find out who had killed him and pay their folks a visit on the street. I owed him that.

***

Like a genie in a bottle, I rubbed my hands together and got my wish. A dude named, Kito McMillan was snatched up and charged with Stone's murder. He was from Hobert, I found out and Jeezy was his childhood friend and codefendant. Talk had it that word got to Kito about Stone assisting me. Kito couldn't get to me, so he killed Stone. His cell was on the other side of the wall from mine. I dropped to the floor to do my customary push-ups and crunches. I added Kito's name to my list.

Chapter Five

Khadafi

Three Years Later

A gunfight with a cop who'd since died. Three different surgeries to save my life. Damn near killing a man with a telephone at Seven Locks. Copping to three years in prison for that assault, butchering three dudes my second day on the compound at WCI. The entire three years spent on lockup and here I was still standing and about to be released back into the world.

"Gimme your full name, date of birth, and Maryland Corrections I.D. number," the C.O. in the booth instructed me.

"Luther Antwan Fuller. Born seven-sixteen-eighty, nine-three-seven-one-one-two-one," I replied.

"He's good. Roll the gate, Ed."

The gate opened and I walked out of Western Correctional Institution a free man. In the parking lot sat a black Chevy Camaro with a young dude leaning on the passenger door. He was a little darker than me but his features were all the same as mine. His hair was cut into one of them nappy, bush, young nigga styles that I hated but it didn't matter. He was still my blood.

I embraced him. "What's up, lil' cuz? Was this joint hard to find?"

Marquette Lil' Quette Jennings, my uncle Marquette's only child smiled. "I put the address in the phone's GPS it brought me right here. Damn, it's good to see you out here, big cuz."

I couldn't get over how much Lil' Marquette resembled his father. I saw it in the photos he'd sent me over the years, but in person the resemblance was uncanny. He had the freckles and all.

"You look just like your father."

"When she ain't hating that's what my mother says."

"How is Tasca doing these days? Still fucking with the dude you wrote and told me about?"

"Yeah, she's still with that wild ass nigga," Lil Quette answered before walking around to the driver's side of the Camaro and getting in it.

I climbed into the passenger seat and noticed the hint of weed smell that permeated the cloth seats. "Where's the weed at?"

"Smoked it while I was waiting for you. I was outside for almost three hours waiting."

I reclined the seat and asked Lil' Quette about the dude who was fucking his mother. "Is the dude still beating on Tasca?"

Lil' Quette nodded his head and pulled off. After a long silence, he said, "I'ma kill that nigga one day."

I thought about all the people I wanted to kill, needed to kill.

"After him, I wanna kill the dude who killed my father."

"Too late, lil cuz. Already been done."

"For real?"

I glanced over at my seventeen-year-old cousin. "Real talk is all I know. I only lie to save my life or to trick a muthafucka. I never lie about the people I killed. A rack of muthafuckas died behind your father's death. He was my uncle, my blood. Vengeance was mandatory."

"So, it's true what they say about you, huh?" Lil' Quette asked.

"Depends on what they say," I answered.

"They say that you killed a rack of people in the streets."

"Killing is what I do, cuz. It's who I am."

"I also heard that you snitched on a dude before. I never said anything in my letters or over the phone because I wanted to ask you that face to face. Is it true?"

It was early with cloudy skies. The wind roared and kissed the glass windows of the Camaro as it ate the highway up. I listened to the wind as I watched the mountains go by in a blur. I thought about the best way to answer my cousin's questions, but then just settled on telling the truth.

"Yeah, lil' cuz, it's true. I dishonored myself and rocked that word against a dude named, Ameen. He saved my life twice and I still did it. I did what I did for reason that most niggas wouldn't understand. My life as I knew it was crumbling right before my eyes. I was powerless to stop it. I was facing a rack of time, but I needed to put things back together again. Couldn't nobody do that but me. So, I ate that cheese. I made a deal with the government that gave me immunity for a rack of murders I committed. I ain't gon' lie to you, cuz. I betrayed the code on some selfish shit, and every day I regret it. Every time I hear a muthafucka use my name and the word rat in the same sentence, it fucks with me. But at the same time, I reached my goal. With all the shit I did, I'm supposed to be under the jail, but I'm not. I'm free and I got a lot of scores to settle."

"Does that mean that you got a lot of people to kill?"

I nodded my head. "The dude who gave you this car—"

"Who, PeeWee?"

"Yeah, PeeWee. He's gonna be the first one I kill."

"Damn, big cuz. What did PeeWee do?"

"He violated my safe haven on some grimy shit. Went up in my house and robbed me out of all my shit. He's Godfather to both of my kids, bitch nigga betrayed me."

"Around me, he always spoke highly of you," Lil Quette added.

"He knew better to do anything but see, cuz, PeeWee don't know that I know it was him who robbed my house. He doesn't think I know he betrayed me. And betrayal is worse than slaughter," I said, sounding like Ameen. "I became a rat to be able to see this day right here. The day that I'd be able to repay dudes like PeeWee for what he'd done to me. That hot shit is my cross I gotta bear, cuz. I gotta carry that shit around. I did what I did for my own reasons. They were all wrong, I admit it, but I ain't going for nothing, cuz. I ain't tolerating no disrespect because of it. Even though I told I'm still the same muthafucka. I'm still an animal. Niggas can call me all the rats they want but I bet not hear about it, not even a whisper."

"I've never faced what you faced, big cuz. So, I can't judge you. You are my cousin and that's all I care about. I'm with you until the casket drops."

"I respect that, lil cuz. When we get near the city, take me to Aunt Mary's house. I need food, money, clothes, and some guns. In that order."

***

"The older you get the more you look just like your mother," Aunt Mary said as she freed me from her warm embrace. Next she hugged Lil' Quette. "And you are the spitting image of your Daddy." Aunt Mary's eyes welled up with tears. "Your mother and father. Mergie and Marquette. My younger sister and baby brother. I raised them the best I could. My mother, Mary Ann, y'all grandmother worked hard to give us a good life; worked herself into an early grave is what she did. On her deathbed, I promised her that I'd take care of my siblings. I tried to do that but they both got away from me. And now they are both gone. I buried both of my younger siblings and they were supposed to bury me. Standing here looking at both of you reminds me so much of them."

I didn't know what to say and neither did Lil' Quette because we remained silent.

"I couldn't save them from the streets," Aunt Mary said, wiping her eyes trying to compose herself. "Pay me no mind you two. I always get emotional in my old age. I cooked all y'all's favorite foods. You and Lil' Quette go in the kitchen and eat. I'll see you both in a little while. I need to gather my wits." Aunt Mary disappeared up the stairs.

"You hungry, lil' cuz?" I asked.

"You better know it," Lil' Quette responded.

"Well, let's go eat."

***

The sign over the building read, *EZ Storage INC*. I glanced at the papers that my aunt gave me. "This is the place, lil cuz."

"What's in there?"

"My shit. After PeeWee and 'nem went in my house, my baby mother moved out. I could never live there again. So, I had Aunt Mary sell the house. All the stuff that was inside the house, she put into storage. Here! C'mon."

Inside the storage unit, furniture, boxes, bags, and appliances were everywhere. Seeing the furniture instantly brought Kemie to mind and the day she purchased all of it nine years ago. I pushed thoughts of Kemie out of my head. It wasn't time to reminisce, it was time to kill.

"Help me move all this shit right here, lil' cuz. I need to get to the bed."

"Fuck—you tired or something, nigga?" Lil' Quette joked.

Ignoring my cousin, I started to clear stuff out of my path to get to the bed. Lil' Quette did the same. After a lot of lifting and moving, I reached the bed. Snatching the sheets off the bed, I flipped the mattress completely over until I could see the box springs.

"I need a knife, cuz."

The boxes were all labeled. It took another ten minutes to find what I needed. Inside a box marked kitchenware, I found a set of knives. I grabbed a steak knife and walked back over to the mattress. I felt around for the spot I was looking for, then plunged the knife into the mattress, cutting a large opening. I dug into the mattress and retrieved everything that I'd put there almost four year ago. Quickly, pulling a pillow out of its pillowcase, I used the pillowcase to put the money and guns in.

"Let's bounce, cuz," I announced and slung the pillowcase over my shoulders.

Once we were back in the car, Lil Quette asked, "Where to now, big boy?"

"I need clothes, shoes and coats."

"That's easy. Iverson Mall, Forestville or Pentagon City?"

"Neither one," I spat and eyed my cousin like he was retarded. "I'm thirty plus, cuz. Put Tyson's Galleria in your phone and let the GPS take us there."

Anthony Fields

Chapter Six

Rio Jefferson

On most days, no matter how much I tried, I couldn't remember why I became a police officer. People who grew up in Deanwood didn't become police officers. They either became drug dealers, drug users, or killers. Or a combination of all three. I'd grown up in Northeast, D.C. during the Murder Capitol days. As a kid, I saw a lot of things, experienced a lot of things. Drugs, sex, gambling, and death. In my neighborhood near Roper Jr. High School, it was nothing to walk into an alley and find a dead body.

For reasons I can't explain, I've always been drawn to the dead. I had a sick, morbid attraction to death. I stood over a dead woman once and watched as maggots feasted on her eyes. There had to be hundreds of them in her wide-open eyes. I remember wondering where maggots came from and why they feasted only on the dead. As I stood in the apartment on 3rd Street in Southeast, staring down at the bodies of a woman and two teenage children, I found myself asking myself the same thing. Where did maggots come from and why did they feast only the dead?

"These bodies have been in here for at least two days, Rio," Assistant Medical Examiner Yolanda James said to me. "The level of decomposition is consistent with the warm weather we've been having lately. Rigor mortis is livid. All the blood congealed at the end parts of the limbs. From what I can tell, it looks like the adult woman was beaten pretty bad near the face and head. She was also stabbed several times. I found puncture wounds to her neck, arms, and legs. She was probably tortured. But her cause of death was the gunshot wounds to her head. We have entry wounds here and here." Yolanda pointed. Then she lifted the woman's head. Her hair was matted with dried blood. "Large caliber handgun. I can tell from the exit wounds. Bullets went straight through and did a lot of damage. Looks like hydra shok ammunition damage."

"Hey, Ron!" I called out to the crime scene search photographer. "Get me a couple close ups of that tattoo on her chest.

The one on her wrist and the foot tattoo. She may have another tat on her leg. Yolanda can you check for me?" I turned to face the door, invading the dead woman's privacy less and less.

Minutes later, A.M.E. Yolanda Jones confirmed my hunch. "Good guess, Rio. There's a tattoo on the left leg that extends down the left ankle. Starts at the hip."

I walked over to the other two bodies both in close proximity to one another. Together in life, together in death. The two teenagers were good looking kids despite the holes in their heads. Seeing dead kids always made me question whether or not there was really a God. Some celestial being sitting on a throne in the heavens. A malevolent or benevolent deity that lets the worst things imaginable happen to the most vulnerable of his creatures.

On most days, I couldn't remember why I became a police officer, but I could remember all the faces of the kids I'd seen, their faces permanently set into a death mask. There were maggots in all their eyes. Yolanda walked over to me and stood next to me a little too close for my taste.

"The children got off a little easier but they still got dead. They weren't beaten or stabbed. Just shot. The girl looks to be around thirteen or so. About a hundred and ten pounds. Shot once through the temporal region on the side of the head. Death was instantaneous, she fell where she stood. Approximately twelve feet away from the woman. The boy could be a year older or a year younger. It's hard to tell. He was about five-eight, a hundred and fifty pounds, good musculature, probably very athletic. Also shot once in the head, through the occipitalis bone or back of the head. Possibly had different killers—"

"Two perps instead of one?" I asked, cutting her off.

Yolanda shook her head. "Not two, maybe three perps. Small caliber handgun was used on the kids. Evident entry wounds but no exit wounds."

"The condition of the woman says crime of passion to me. Her killer was definitely emotional when he worked her over and then killed her. Not so much the kids."

"Hey, Doug?"

Detective Doug Davis came over and joined us. "Yeah, Rio?"

"Have you been on site for a while?"

"Yeah, been here since the bodies were found and called in," Doug replied.

"Any signs of forced entry? Was the place searched?"

"Negative on the forced entry. Not sure on the search. CSI is dusting for prints as we speak."

"Thanks, Doug, I think—" I was interrupted by my cell phone vibrating in my hand. "Excuse me, Doug, Yolanda, gotta take this call." I walked out of the apartment, into the hallway and down the stairs where it was quieter. "Hello?"

"Rio, hey, it's me, Chuck Mosby."

"Hey, Chuck. What's up, buddy?"

"You asked me to give you a heads up when Luther Fuller was released from WCI. Well, here's your notice. He was released this morning."

"Thanks, Chuck. I appreciate that."

"Don't mention it, bud."

Disconnecting the call, I put my cell phone in my pocket and made my way back to Apartment 204.

"Judging by the look on your face, Rio, I'd say that either that call was bad news or you gotta take a shit," Doug said. "Which is it?"

"Bad news, Doug. You remember a man named, Luther Fuller?"

"Piece of shit that calls himself Khadafi? Of course, I remember him."

"Man fucking kills a decorated homicide detective, rats and gets off Scott free. He was released from a Maryland prison this morning,"

"You've gotta be fucking kidding me!" Doug exploded.

"I wish I was, Doug. I wish I was."

Chapter Seven

Marquette Lil' Quette Jennings

"These joints right here is that drip," I exclaimed as I picked up the solid black Givenchy shoe off the display stand. "Wet as shit."

Khadafi eyed the shoe with no obvious interest. "You like them?"

"Of course, I like them. Who wouldn't?"

"Well, get them. It's on me, I got you."

"Naw, big boy, I'm good," I said and put the shoe back. "You been in the pen for four years, you gotta get you. I'm straight."

Khadafi looked down at my sneakers before trying on the multicolored Christian Louboutins Red Bottom high-top sneakers. "You not straight, lil' cuz. Them Huaraches you rocking right now weak as shit. Get the Givenchys. I never got the chance to really look out for you before—"

"You got Pee Wee to give me a car. You don't call that looking out?" I interjected.

"Fuck that. All them cars on that lot mine anyway. I haven't even begun to look out for you. That punk ass Camaro some short shit. In a minute, you gon' be pushing some big boy shit. When I left the streets, you were thirteen and I had a lot of shit going on in my life. You said, I gotta get me. Believe me when I say that the streets gon' get me or die. I kill for bread and meat, if I didn't hunt niggas, I wouldn't eat. And I love eating, cuz. You are my only blood relative left besides Aunt Mary. I'm only doing what your father did for me. So, get the fuckin' shoes and pick out a few more pair that you like. Because we blowing all this shit in here." Khadafi pulled two bundles of big face hundreds from his pocket.

Hours later, we left Tyson's with loads of bags. I got on Interstate 66 East and headed back to D.C.

"Where to next?"

Khadafi pulled the pillowcase from under the seat. He reached inside and pulled out a gun. Popping the clip out, he checked it before slamming it back in. Then he repeated the same act with the second gun that he pulled from the pillowcase. He put both guns back in the pillowcase.

"I need to cop us some new cell phones. Then I need to go and see an old friend."

***

It wouldn't officially become Fall until another three or four days, but the temperature outside dropped and felt like it was already here. I rolled the windows up to keep out the cold air. My car was parked on New York Avenue across from Imperial Autos.

"I been here a rack of times," I informed Khadafi. "The first car PeeWee gave me was a Dodge Charger. I had to bring it back because it kept cutting off. Then he gave me an Audi A8, but that was fucked up, too. He gave me about five fucked up cars until he got it right with the Camaro. The two dudes walking around the lot are Remo and Polo. Inside the trailer, at the desk, there's always a broad sitting there. She bad as shit, don't know her name, though."

Khadafi sat back and listened without saying a word.

"There is a mechanic in the garage sometimes, an old nigga."

"Was PeeWee there every time you came here?" Khadafi asked.

I had to think about that one. "Can't remember. He was here at least twice when I came, I'm sure. I talked to him personally both times. Other times, I dealt with the dude, Polo."

"Okay, cuz. Listen up. Here's exactly what I want you to do."

Chapter Eight

Khadafi

I sat in the car across from the car lot that I started and watched everything. Lil' Quette disappeared inside the trailer with a fat dude on his heels. Minutes later, he walked out alone and called my phone.

"It's only three of them here. The fat nigga Polo, Remo and the pretty broad at the desk. I told Polo that I wanted the mechanic to look at my engine. He said the mechanic left for the day. PeeWee was here earlier, but he left, too. What you want me to do?"

"Just chill out, I'm coming over," I told him and exited the car.

***

"What type of car are you interested in, bruh?" the fat, curly haired dude asked me as I walked onto the lot.

"A Hell Cat. Y'all got one on this lot somewhere?" I asked but kept walking toward the trailer.

The fat dude laughed. "We don't stack HellCats. Them joints like eight bands, but we got Charger SRTs, Challengers, Camaros, and a rack of other shit."

Lil Quette stood in front of the trailer looking at his phone. I nodded as he looked up, and entered the trailer. fat boy was right behind me.

"How ya doing, baby girl?" I said to the woman sitting at the desk. "I'ma need you and fat boy to go in the back with me right quick." I turned to face him.

"Go in the back?" the woman asked quizzically. "Go in the back for what? And who are you?"

Pulling both guns from my waist, I pointed one at fat boy and the other at the woman. "Who am I? I'm the Grim Reaper. PeeWee is using my old office still, right?"

"Khadafi?" Fat boy and the woman said in unison.

I nodded my head. "In the flesh. My old office, PeeWee still using it?"

"He is," the woman said.

"You gotta key to it?" I asked.

The woman nodded.

"Good, go and open the door. Step inside and sit down on the floor," I told her. "You, too, fat boy."

Lil' Quette walked into the trailer then. "Go and get the other dude and bring him in here." Inside the office, I looked around. PeeWee had redecorated the place. It looked good, brighter, bigger.

"Why are we sitting on the floor?" the woman asked. "And what's this all about?"

"You'll know in a minute," I told her.

Minutes later, the trailer door slid open. The second dude called out, "Myra?"

"Answer him," I instructed. "Call him back here."

"We're in here! In PeeWee's office! C'mere."

"Why is everybody in here?" the dude asked as he appeared and took in the whole scene. "Why are y'all sitting on the floor?"

I pointed the gun at him. "Because I told them to sit there. Get your ass over there and sit beside fat boy before I blow your shit off."

The second man was tall, light-skinned with a bald head. As he sat on the floor, he said, "We don't keep large amounts of cash in here at night."

"It's not cash that I'm looking for per se. It's PeeWee that I want. I don't feel like looking for him. So, I'ma need one of y'all to call him and get him here. But you can't tell him that I'm here. It's a surprise."

"He said you were his friend," the woman said.

"I am. We been friends for over thirty years."

"So, what are the guns for?"

"To help me get my point across. You got PeeWee's number?"

The woman nodded. "Of course."

"Call him and tell him there's an emergency and you need to see him here as soon as possible."

"My phone is on my desk."

I motioned to Lil' Quette, who stood in the doorway. "Get the lady her phone, would you, cuz."

***

From my position on the side of the trailer, I watched the new model Cadillac truck pull onto the lot and park. I watched PeeWee get out of the passenger seat, a dude I didn't recognize exited the driver's side. The sun had set, and a cover of darkness hid my position. When PeeWee and the dude entered the trailer through the sliding door, I was left open. I quickly crept through the door behind them. PeeWee entered the office, the dude with him stood in the doorway. I aimed the gun and blew his brains into the room and his body fell forward.

"What the fuck?" PeeWee exclaimed.

I appeared like an apparition and stepped over the dead body. PeeWee's eyes focused on me and filled with fear.

"Khadafi?"

"What's good, cuz? Happy to see me?"

"Slim, let me talk—"

I put the barrel of the gun to my lips and shushed PeeWee. Lil' Quette sat on the desk with a gun aimed at the three people sitting on the floor.

"Cuz, go outside and close the gate. Put the closed sign up. Secure the gate if you can. Go!"

Lil Quette passed me the gun as he left the room.

PeeWee's skin bleached. "Come on, Slim—"

"Come on, what?" I asked PeeWee. "You had to know that I'd come. All the shit you pulled while I was in jail. It's time to answer for the disrespect, cuz."

"I never disrespected you, Slim. You know that. Come on, Redds."

Shaking my head, I shot PeeWee in the leg. *Boom!*

"A-a-r-r-rg-g-h-h-h!" PeeWee screamed and grabbed his wounded leg.

"What's my name, cuz?" I asked.

"Redds—no Khadafi. It's Khadafi."

"Listen, cuz, I ain't mad at you for ducking my calls—"

"I never ducked your calls."

"Cut me off again and I'ma drive to your mother's house and kill her. Like I was saying, I'm not mad about you ducking my calls. I'm not mad about you showing your dick to Marnie or throwing the money at her like she made her living on the pole. I'm fucked about you putting a gun to her head and robbing my house."

"You wrong, Slim! It wasn't me. I would never do no shit like that to her or to you. You know me, Slim. I'm not crutty like that."

"Liar, liar, pants on fire!" I teased as I smiled. "It was you. You know how I know it was you? Because you were the only person who knew I had all that weed in my house. All them pounds of skunk we took from Black Woogie's spot on Canal Street. Nobody knew it was there but you. You didn't know that, though, cuz. Your stupid ass mentioned the weed specifically when y'all ambushed Marnie at the door. You knew I had money in the house. You asked about the money. You knew we had more than one child. The problem is, you talked too much that night. When Marnie told me what was said, I instantly knew it was you. I just never let you know that I knew. And the fucked- up part about it is that you are the godfather to my kids, and you took food out of their mouths. That's foul, cuz."

"Khadafi, you got it all wrong, Slim!" PeeWee protested.

"Do I? Where's my money, PeeWee?"

"I don't know where—"

I shot the tall, light-skinned dude in the forehead. The woman screamed.

"Bitch, shut the fuck up. You've seen worse than that on TV," I told the woman. To PeeWee I said, "I'ma ask you again and I want you to think about these two dead muthafuckas before you lie to me again. Every time you lie, somebody's gonna die. I know you robbed the house. I don't even wanna know why. All I want is the money you took and the money for the weed. Where is it?"

The fight completely left PeeWee's body as blood from his leg stained his pants and left shoe. "I spent all the money. Gambling! I spent my last money on that Benz you made me buy Marnie. I went in the house because I had to. It was either that or sell this lot. I got about sixty racks in the safe over there."

"Open the safe and get it. If there's a gun in there and I see it—"

"There ain't no gun in there. Just money," PeeWee answered defeatedly.

"Get the money. If you try anything, I'ma kill everybody left in here."

PeeWee hesitated to move, so I shot the fat dude in the face. His brains and blood coated the wall behind him. The woman opened her mouth to scream again, but my eyes found hers and quieted her. Tears rolled down her cheeks as her body shook violently. The last display of barbarity moved PeeWee across the room to the safe like he had skates on. He had the safe opened in seconds. I spotted a plastic Harris Teeter shopping bag with something in it by the desk. Grabbing it, I dumped out its contents and handed the bag to PeeWee.

"Put all the money in the bag, cuz."

PeeWee did as I instructed and then tossed me the bag.

"The night that you robbed my house, there was somebody with you. Who was it?" When PeeWee didn't answer, I aimed the gun at the woman.

"Please-please—no! Don't kill my sister. That's my father's youngest daughter. She ain't got nothing to do with none of this shit. Let her go, Slim! Please."

"Who was the dude with you that night?" I asked again.

"Meechie. Meechie was with me."

"Southwest Meechie?" PeeWee nodded. I shot his sister in the face. "She saw me kill three people, cuz. I had to kill her."

PeeWee dropped to his knees and put his bloody hands to his face. I was completely unmoved by his tears.

"I let you eat off my plate. I handed you a way to get out of the streets and fed your family. You in turn, crossed me in the worst way. Just like Tee did when he set up Damien Lucas. Just like Bean and Omar did when they fucked Kemie. Like Creeko did. Like Devon and TJ. I showed you the tattoo that I got across my chest right before I killed Tee. Remember it, cuz? The one that says, *God Protect Me From My Friends. I Can Handle My Enemies.* In life I realize that God doesn't always answer a thug's prayers. Because all my fuckin' friends here crossed me."

"Don't kill me, Slim! I can make it right. I can get you all your money back. Just give me some time. I can—"

"It's too late for that, cuz. You died the day you decided to put a gun to Marnie's head and walk into my house. All you've been missing was a casket. I'm here to make sure you get one." I emptied the rest of the clip into PeeWee's head and body. Putting the smoking gun in my pocket, I pulled out the cellphone.

"Lil' cuz, go to the garage and find some gas. Look for a gas can. There's one in there somewhere. Find it and bring it to me."

The security system was the same one that I installed when I opened the car lot. Instead of removing the disc from the RDU, I disconnected the wires and picked up the whole mainframe and set it on the desk by the door of the trailer. I went back and rifled through the file cabinets until I found all the paperwork relating to the black Infiniti QX60 SUV parked on the lot. I'd seen it while sitting in the car across the street. It took me a few more minutes to find the temporary paper tags. I found them and filled out a set for the Infiniti. I was outside putting the paper tags on the Infiniti when Lil' Quette walked up, gas can in hand.

"I don't know how much gas you need but it's about a quarter full," he said.

"Sit it down and leave, I got everything else from here," I told him.

"What about your bags in my car?"

"I almost forgot about them. Go get 'em, sit the bags right here next to the truck." I walked back into the trailer and searched for the keys for the Infiniti.

I found the key hanging on a hook near the desk and grabbed it. After unlocking the doors to the truck, I pulled directly up to the trailer. Lil' Quette came across the lot, hands full of shopping bags.

"Put the bags in the back of the truck, cuz." I went back into the trailer and picked up the security system mainframe. I loaded it in the truck, then went back for the money. Lil' Quette was walking across the lot when I came out of the trailer.

"Hey, cuz, come here."

"What's up, big boy?"

"That pillowcase under the passenger seat got about twenty grand in it. It's yours, a gift from me."

"Stop playing, big cuz. You for real?"

"I play a lot of games at times, lil' cuz, but money games ain't one of 'em. I told you earlier I'ma do for you what your father did for me. In a minute or two, you gon' have more money than you can spend. I got you."

"Thanks, big boy. I really appreciate you. I love you, big cuz."

"Love you, too, youngin. Be safe, I'll call you tomorrow."

I waited until Lil' Quette's Camaro was all the way gone from the scene before picking up the gas can and going back inside the trailer. I searched all the pockets of the dead dudes and pocketed all their money.

"Y'all won't be needing it," I muttered.

I poured gas on all the bodies and all over the trailer. Grabbing some papers out of the office, I made a wick, then lit it. In seconds, the office was aflame. I walked out of the trailer and hopped in the Infiniti truck. When the entire trailer became engulfed, I pulled off the lot.

***

"Damn, baby, it's been a long time," Erykah said as she hugged me. "You look good as hell, too." I palmed her phat ass. "What's that smell?"

I knew exactly what smell Erykah was referring to but played coy.

"Why do you smell like gas?"

"I was pumping gas into the truck and wasn't paying attention when I pulled the pump out. Gas spilled all over my pants," I lied. "I was looking at some lil' young, big, booty chick. Shoulda been paying more attention."

"Is that right? Big booty chick, huh? I got your big, booty chick right here. Take off them clothes and take a shower. I'ma show you a big booty chick."

***

Erykah was a bad muthafucka and she knew it. Her Instagram followers totaled over a hundred thousand. She was the self-professed selfie queen. I thought about all the pictures she'd sent me over the years. Her presence in my life had helped keep me sane while I was on lockup at WCI for those three years. She laid on the bed, dressed only in a sheer tank top and matching sheer panties. I could see the piercing in her clit and pussy lips from where I stood in the doorway.

Erykah's hair was dyed two tone burgundy and black. It would've looked clownish on someone else, but Erykah pulled it off with ease. Her caramel complexion and flawless skin shone almost as bright as the diamonds affixed to the tennis bracelet she wore on her right ankle.

"Put your phone down and put your fingers inside your panties for me. I wanna watch you play with that pussy."

Keeping her eyes on me, Erykah did as I requested. Her facial expressions changed as I stood there rubbing my manhood. I slid out of my boxer briefs. At the sight of my rigid dick, Erykah's fingers moved inside her more vigorously, purposeful. I stroked myself.

"I'm about to cum, Khadafi! Damn! Shit, I'm cumming!" Erykah moaned and did exactly that. "Look what you made me do," she said and pulled her fingers from her panties and licked them clean.

"When you used to do that for me on the phone, I pictured it being exactly like I just saw it."

"Can we talk about that later?" Erykah said, then lifted up and pulled her panties down, and off. Her tank top came off next. "It's been four years since I last had you. I need you now. Your beard is turning me on like shit. I love that look."

"Before I put my mouth and dick on you, tell me who you been fucking."

"I ain't been fucking nobody in a long time," Erykah answered.

"How long is a long time?"

"Over a year, it's been over a year."

"You're lying, E."

"I'm not lying. The nigga I was fucking, I stopped fucking him last year in like July or something. Too much drama. That's on my father's grave."

I crawled on the bed and touched between Erykah's legs.

"Stop teasing me, Khadafi," Erykah purred.

Throwing caution to the wind, I turned her to face me. Her toes were light blue. I kissed her toes and made my way up her leg. I focused strictly on her soaking wet center with my tongue. I locked her legs in my embrace and there was no escaping me. Erykah screamed out in ecstasy.

Several rounds of sex with Erykah was intense. It was sweaty. It was exhausting. I laid in her bed next to her, my eyes closed.

"You talked to Mousey lately?"

"A couple of days ago. He called here ranting about me not answering his fuckin' emails in corrlinks. I be too busy to keep up with all that shit. Whenever he and I talk, we don't do nothing but argue. Mousey been in jail for what, fifteen years? I was a little ass girl when he went to jail. I'ma grown ass woman now. And he can't accept that."

"That's my man. I gotta send him some bread."

"Your man?" Erykah said as if she tasted shit in her mouth. "Boy, bye. I know you mean well and all that, but James Carpenter is not your man. Not no more. Sorry to be the bearer of bad news, baby, but Mousey don't fuck with you."

"You told him about us?" I asked, a little disturbed.

"Fuck no. Why would I do some stupid shit like that? I can hold water. But according to him, you can't. His beef with you ain't got shit to do with me. He said something about you being a rat. You got on the witness stand and told on some dude named, Ameen and all this and that.

The dude helped you beat a murder in Texas. That's all he talked about for the last couple of years. You betrayed the code. You did the same thing that the dude Keith did to him. You can't ever come back to the feds. They gon' kill you like you did Keith Barnett—"

"Mousey said all that?"

"His words exactly. I got tired of hearing all that shit."

"Why didn't you tell me all that on the phone over the years?"

"You were going through enough shit out Maryland. I didn't want to add to it."

"Damn," I said, incredulously. "That's how cuz really feels about me, huh?"

"Yep. I can't even remember all the other wild shit he said about you. I told you, that's all he talked about for months at a time."

I laid there fucked up in the head about what I'd just heard. Silence became my solace. Shaking my head, I thought about the Washington Post article that had come out about me in 2013. Everybody in the BOP had to know about what I'd done.

"Fuck what a nigga say and feel about me," a voice in my head said.

"All rats feel like that," another voice said.

"Fuck that shit," I said aloud.

"Fuck what?" Erykah questioned.

"Fuck that shit Mousey talking and fuck him. Talking that shit gon' get his mother killed. He hipped to me. Tell him what I said."

"I ain't telling him shit. I ain't thinking about no Mousey, right now."

"Is that right?" I asked Erykah. "Who you thinking about?"

"I'm thinking about you. Fuck Mousey."

"That nigga in the joint talking reckless and I'm out here fucking his bitch, and he don't even know it. The jokes on him."

"I'm not his bitch," Erykah said, offended.

"You right. Not no more you ain't. You my bitch, now."

"Fuck you, Khadafi." Erykah turned over and put her back to me.

I snuggled up close to her after turning on my side. "Naw I'm about to fuck you. Again!" I slid my dick into her wetness from behind. In the throes of passion all was forgotten.

Anthony Fields

Chapter Nine

Detective Corey Winslow

"Gasoline was used as an accelerant," Arson Specialist Jamar Davies said as he smelled pieces of debris.

I looked at the burned out remains of what used to be a double wide trailer. "The fire was set intentionally then, right?"

"Had to be," Officer Davies surmised.

Detectives Anderson Collins and Terrell Preston walked over to us.

"Skeletal remains of at least five people were found," Detective Collins announced.

"M.E. says that all the skulls have bullet holes in them," Detective Preston added.

"Which makes them homicides," I uttered, inhaled and then slowly exhaled.

"You betcha," Jamar Davies said. "Somebody killed five people and then torched the place to cover it up. Good luck finding out who that was. You gentlemen have a nice night." Jamar Davie left the scene.

"No missing persons calls yet?" I asked.

"Not that I know of, but I'm not surprised. It's still early," Collins said.

"And nobody's come forward?"

"All of this," Terrell Preston waved his arms. "Is only about nine hours old. We had to let the place over there cool off before going in."

I looked around the car lot, the garage and at the burned-out trailer. "I've been here before, but I can't remember when. And who the hell kills five people nowadays?"

"Khadafi," a voice behind me said.

I turned around and came face to face with Rio Jefferson. "Did you just say, Khadafi?"

Rio nodded. "I walked up just in time to hear what you said and the question you asked. I answered your question about who would kill five people nowadays. And speaking of Khadafi, Moe Tolliver thought Khadafi was here at this lot back in twenty-eleven when he wanted to arrest him. He called for backup and all of you, myself included, diverged on this location that night. But Khadafi wasn't here. Captain Dunlop blew a gasket that night, remember?"

"You're right, I remember now. This car lot used to belong to Khadafi."

"He still owns it," Rio stated.

"Are we talking about Luther 'Khadafi' Fuller? That Khadafi?" Collins asked.

"The one and only," I replied.

After consulting his notepad, Terrell Preston said, "But this lot is owned by a Mary Henderson according to the Department of Consumer and Regulatory Affairs."

"Khadafi's aunt," Rio informed him. "It's always been registered to her. Everything that Khadafi owns is in her name. Before going to prison, Khadafi installed James Smith also known as PeeWee to run the place. That was a part of Moe's investigation. As soon as I heard Imperial Autos, fire, and possible dead bodies, I rushed right over."

"The bodies were burned beyond recognition. All that remains are skeletons. Bullet holes in the skulls. All five of them. Any idea who they might be?" I asked Rio.

Rio button up his peacoat, then coughed into both hands. "Can't say for sure, but I'd wager and say that at least one of them is PeeWee Smith. And if one of them does turn out to PeeWee Smith, I'd place another wager that I know who killed him."

I turned to Terrell Preston. "Press, get on the phone and find out everything you can on a James 'PeeWee' Smith."

"On it," Preston said and pulled out his phone.

"And if one of the victims is PeeWee Smith, who do you think is responsible for this?" I asked, but already knew the answer.

"Khadafi."

I knew it. "He's home, huh?"

Rio nodded. "Got released from Western Correctional Institution this morning."

"Time sure does fly. It's been three years already?"

Terrel Preston disconnected his call. "Chris is going to text me everything he finds on Smith. And I hate to be the square pig trying to fit into a round hole in all of this. But who in the hell is Khadafi?"

"Khadafi is the street name of Luther Fuller," I started.

"The most prolific killer this city has ever seen," Rio finished. "The muthafucka that killed my friend and fellow detective Maurice Tolliver. The man that Corey and Ann Sloan made a deal with to close cold case murders. They put him back on the streets."

Instantly, I got offended at Rio Jefferson's words. "They? Me and Ann Sloan? Does it look like I work for the got damned U.S. Attorney's Office, Rio? I had nothing to do with that deal and you know it."

Rio Jefferson stood at least three inches shorter than me. He walked up to me within inches of my face. "When we were at that meeting in District Heights three years ago, when it was announced that the U.S. Attorney's Office was making a deal with Khadafi to close murder cases—your murder cases—I never heard you protest. In fact, you never said one word as long as I was there. But I did, I was against that deal. It was a smack in the face to Moe Tolliver and I expressed that to everybody present. Even Chief Laney. Got myself kicked out of that meeting that day. Remember that?"

"Hold on," I spat and pushed Rio out of my face. "What you tryna say?"

Anderson Collins and Terrell Preston both quickly stepped in between Rio and me.

"Cool it you guys," Collins said. "We're all on the same side here."

"Naw, fuck that," I persisted. "Maurice Tolliver was a friend of mine. Something like a mentor. We weren't as close as you two were, but I still considered him a friend. I had nothing to do with that deal Ann Sloan made with Khadafi."

"You never did or said anything to stop it!" Rio hissed. "So, that makes you just as guilty. And no matter how much you wash your hands tonight the people that died here today their blood is on your hands. Yours and Ann Sloan's. Khadafi is a free man and he's going to kill again. And again! It's all he knows. For homicide cops like us it's about to be a long winter. So, remember to dress warm." Rio turned and walked away.

"What if you're wrong, Rio? What if it's the other way around? What if we find Khadafi's remains instead of PeeWee's?"

Rio stopped and turned around. "For your sake, Corey, let's hope so."

***

Rio Jefferson's words got in my head and messed up my sleep. Groggy, but anxious, I ended up in front of the U.S. Attorney's Office building on 4th Street at a little after 8:00 a.m. and I called Ann Sloan.

"Good morning, you," she cooed into the phone.

"Are you busy, right now?" I asked.

"I got several meetings lined up but the first one isn't until nine. Why?"

"I need to speak to you in private. Can you come down?"

"Sounds important and serious. You're out front, I take it?"

"I'm out front in the Tahoe."

"I'm coming down." She hung up.

As soon as Ann Sloan was in my truck with her door shut, she asked, "What's got you all serious sounding, requesting an impromptu meeting at eight a.m.?"

"A car lot was set on fire last night."

"*A car lot?* A fire? Why is that important—"

"It's not the car lot I'm concerned about. It's the five people that were killed there and who the car lot belongs to," I asserted.

"*Five people killed?* On a car lot? Who does it belong to?"

"Think about it, Ann. Imperial Autos. The most notorious murderer—"

"Oh, my gawd!" Ann Sloan gasped as the light in her head turned on. "Khadafi! He's out?"

Nodding my head, I told her, "Yep. Got released yesterday morning. And by yesterday evening five people were killed. On his lot on New York Avenue. He's making good on what he told Monica Curry and Bayona Lake."

The color drained from her face, Ann Sloan leaned back in her seat and closed her eyes. "Refresh my memory, Corey. What did Khadafi tell Monica and Bay One?"

"I had to pull up the transcripts online but according to both women's testimonies at Antonio Felder's trial, and I'm paraphrasing, *He wants to get home to kill people. He said when he gets home everybody is gonna pay.* It makes sense, Ann. Khadafi gets released that morning, kills five people that evening. It's his style. In the file that Moe Tolliver compiled on Khadafi, he suspected Khadafi of killing at least two people and setting their bodies on fire. Do you understand the importance of what I'm telling you?"

"I'm not slow, Detective. I'm the fucking United States Attorney, so don't patronize me. Do you have anything to prove that Khadafi was even there at the lot? Something other than the fact that he owns it?"

Deflected, I exhaled. "Nothing tangible, no. Just a lot of speculation and conjecture. And to be honest, I wasn't the one who put all of this together. Rio Jefferson did. I had totally forgotten about Khadafi until last night. Three years went by too quickly."

"I agree. The last time I saw Khadafi was two years ago. I went to WCI to see him, hoping he'd connect some more dots for me. He was in solitary for stabbing three people his second day there. I asked for his help, I told him I could get him out early."

"You never told me that. What did he say to you?"

"He called me a conniving, cracka, bitch and told me to suck his dick." Ann smiled. "Luther Fuller always had a way with words. I told him to get out of the hole and go and suck his cell mate's dick."

I laughed at Ann and she turned to face me. "I'm gonna go upstairs and cancel my first meeting, then I'm coming back down here. All this talk about sucking dick has made me horny. I need a little stress reliever now that I've just realized that I put a serial killer back on the streets. Anacostia Park should be damned near deserted this time of morning, right?"

"I believe so, yeah. Why?"

"You'll find out when we get there. I'll be back in a few minutes."

***

At Anacostia Park

"Corey, your dick feels so good," Ann Sloan moaned.

We were in the backseat of the Tahoe, my arms under Ann's as I gripped her shoulders and forced her down onto me, up and down, side to side. I leaned back and laid her down on my chest as I guided into her deep. Ann bit down on her lip. The fuck faces she made had me ready to bust for the second time that morning. I had to control my desire to cum. I wanted the moment to last for as long as it could. But it was hard. I couldn't get rid of the image of her mouth on my dick, sucking me until I busted in her throat earlier. Ann Sloan was one nasty woman. She could deepthroat me, and she swallowed my seed. I couldn't believe my good fortune. A poor kid from the projects in Southeast D.C. had grown up to be a detective. A detective sitting in the backseat of his SUV fucking the United States Attorney for the District of Columbia. Go figure.

***

"On a serious note," Ann said as she fixed her clothes in the front seat. "We have to take this Khadafi mess serious. It's a longshot but I'll look for a legal loophole that will allow me to have him researched. Nobody needs this homicidal maniac loose in the city, killing people without compunction. We gotta protect the city from him."

Ann's last comment was like a craw in my side. It irked my soul. Rio's accusation about me not stopping the deal came to mind. "Why did you make that deal with him, then?"

"Come again?" Ann said defensively.

"We—you and I and a lot of other people all knew how dangerous this guy was back in twenty-thirteen. He admitted to more murders than the Columbine school killers and John Wayne Gacy combined, and we ignored the threat he posed. You put that deal together and granted him immunity for all his past crimes, knowing that one day, that sociopath would be released back into these streets. So, why make the deal?"

Ann Sloan thought for a minute, then shrugged her shoulders. "It seemed like a good deal at the time." Without a backward glance, she exited the truck.

Chapter Ten

Lil' Quette

The news about the murders and fire at Imperial Autos had been on the TV all night long. I saw it broadcasted on Facebook. Somebody posted the Fox News clip about it and several people reposted. Five people dead, shot and burned beyond recognition. I read all the comments people left about it. One person mentioned that it had been years since five people had been killed at one time in one place. Not since the seven people had been killed on Alabama Avenue in 2013. Another wrote, remember when all them people got killed on that basketball court in 2013? A person commented, on and on it went.

My mother and her boyfriend began to argue and physically fight. Then fucked and acted like nothing had ever happened. To drown out their voices, I let the music from Pandora play off my phone through the TV speakers. What would I do without Bluetooth? I laid across my bed and thought about PeeWee and the dude with him who got his brains blown out in the doorway. Maybe it was the violent video games I played or the movies I watched on Netflix but witnessing my first real murder hadn't bothered me at all.

My cousin Khadafi was the real deal. A natural born killer. Everything that the streets had said about him was true. His killing game was legendary. My eyes wandered over to the pillowcase near my dresser. It was filled with money. I looked at the Newman and Saks Fifth Avenue bags with all my new clothes, belts, and shoes in them.

Then I heard Khadafi's voice in my head, saying, *"I'm just doing for you what your father did for me."*

My father Marquette Delshawn Henderson. My eyes traveled up over the dresser to the 10X12 photo of my father that I had on the wall. He was handsome, fly and looked very alive. His smile was a mirror image of my own. I remembered the day that my mother picked me up from school. Her eyes reddened from crying.

She took me downtown to Chuck E. Cheese's and ordered pizza for us both. As I ate, she broke the news to me.

"My eyes are red from crying, Lil Quette. I been crying because I heard some bad news today. Your father is dead. Somebody killed him."

I remember my nine-year-old eyes filling with tears. My pizza suddenly tasted like Play Doh. The one man who loved me with all his heart was gone. My whole life changed after that day. I stopped caring about school, my friends, and my life at home. I became rebellious and indifferent to the men in my mother's life who tried to replace my father. My life became a reality show.

A never-ending episode of Love, Hip Hop and Stupid Shit. I often dreamed about finding the person that killed my father, although I didn't know who that was. When I thought about my father, I often remembered the days he'd visit me and Khadafi was with him. After my father's death, I didn't see Khadafi again. But the streets spoke his name like an audiobook. I found out from my Aunt Mary that Khadafi was in jail a few years ago. I decided to write him a letter, then he called me.

Someone on Facebook posted that they knew who the five people were that was killed at the car lot, even though the police hadn't released any names. I wondered who that could be. I looked at the news clip on Facebook one more time and it made me think about the first time I went to Imperial Autos almost two years ago, weeks later, I'd gotten my driver's licenses. I walked into the trailer, the pretty woman behind the desk asked me how she could help me.

I told her, "I need to see PeeWee about a car."

Minutes later, I was in his office.

"What's up, lil' man? What can I do for you?" PeeWee asked.

"My cousin sent me here. Said you'd give me a car," I told him.

"How much money you tryna spend with me?"

"I don't have any money."

"You don't have any money? You got to be kidding me. and you said your cousin sent you here for a car?"

"Uh huh. He said that you would be happy to give me a car."

"Is that right?" PeeWee asked and laughed. "Your cousin said that?" I nodded. "And your cousin is who?"

"Dirty Redds, but everybody calls him Khadafi."

PeeWee's whole demeanor changed right before my eyes. He looked at me closely. Then as if seeing me for the first time, recognition set in. "Lil Marquette?" Again, I nodded, but kept quiet. "How could I have missed that? That's crazy you look just like your father."

Thirty minutes later, I was pulling off the lot in a Dodge Charger. A loud crash broke my reverie.

"Jomo, get the fuck off me!" my mother yelled.

Whack!

"Calm your ass down then, Tasca, before I fuck you up in here."

"One day, Jomo. One day," I muttered and called my girlfriend Shakira.

"What do your lying ass want, Quette?" Shakira spat into the phone as soon as she answered.

"What did I lie about this time, Sha?"

"Where were you all day yesterday?"

"With my cousin, I told you that already."

"You lying, Quette," Shakira accused. "Don't no man spend no whole day with no fuckin' other man. Not even his own cousin."

Ignoring Shakira, I said, "I'm 'bout to get in the shower and put on my clothes. I'll be over there in a few."

"Yeah, right, Quette. Bye."

Shakira Simmons was insecure and feisty as hell, but I loved her. We'd been together since we were twelve years old. I thought about the fact that when I got to Shakira's house we'd argue, then fuck and that made me smile. I thought about my mother and Jomo doing the exact same thing. All I could do was shake my head.

"Somebody gotta break the cycle," I told myself.

I took off my clothes from yesterday. Then the phone fell out of my back pocket. It was the Samsung Galaxy phone that Khadafi bought for me, the perfect match to his own. His phone number was programmed into my phone. I pressed send.

After three rings, Khadafi picked up. "What's up, lil cuz?"

"Just wanted to check on you. Aunt Mary looking for you. She sent me about six text messages."

"I spent the night out. She probably worried about me. I'ma call her, right now. Other than that, you good?"

"I'm more than good. You looked out for a nigga too proper yesterday. I appreciate it, no bullshit."

"That ain't shit," Khadafi replied nonchalantly.

"To me it is. Where you at?"

"I'm at Walgreens picking up some pictures I gotta send to an old friend. Then I got a few errands I need to run. After that I'ma need to meet up with you."

"Whenever, wherever, whatever. Just holla."

"A'ight lil' cuz. Be cool."

"You do the same."

Chapter Eleven

Khadafi

"I have been trying to reach you all night. Why didn't you call me and give me your new cell phone number if you bought it yesterday?"

"I'm sorry, Aunt Mary—"

"Forget sorry," my aunt blew. "I was worried sick about you."

"I was with my lady friend—"

"I don't care. The police called me last night to inform me about a fire at the car lot. They said someone's remains were found in a burned-out trailer. I thought it might be you in there dead."

"That's crazy!" I said, feigning alarm. "I gotta call PeeWee and make sure he's good. Make sure he knows—"

"Imperial Autos has been on the news all morning. Trust me, he knows. If that ain't him they found. I never like him, Luther. Never did understand why you left him in charge. You are gonna have to figure out what you want to do with the insurance people. But we can talk about that later. I'm just glad to know that you're okay. Thank God! Even though I don't like him much, I sure hope that's not that PeeWee guy dead in there."

"It's him." I wanted to say but couldn't. "Let me call him. I love you, auntie. Sorry that I had you worried. I promise to call you every day from now on."

"You do that," Aunt Mary said and hung up.

"Sir, your pictures are ready," the kid at the picture counter said.

I walked to the counter and put a few things down on the counter. "Can I pay for these right here, too?"

"Sure," the kid said.

He handed me the photos and I flipped through them. Erykah was asleep in the photos. She had no idea I had taken them. There was a sheet wrapped around her but that's it. It was subtle enough to figure out she was naked under it. I had photos of me lying beside her with my hands all over her. There were photos of me inside her apartment holding a picture of Mousey. I had photos of Erykah's panties and tank top in a heap on the floor. I took photos of Erykah's diamond tennis anklet. There was no denying that it was Erykah and pretty much what had happened. If there was any doubt the final photo quelled it. The photo showed Erykah's face with fresh cum on it. I was proud of myself for that one. Smiling, I remembered how I had masturbated and skeeted on her that morning. Erykah never woke up, never even stirred.

I opened the pack of ink pens and took one out, then opened the greeting card and began writing.

Watch what you say out your mouth, cuz. If I hear one more person say that you got my name in your mouth on some disrespectful shit, I'ma visit your mother in the Wingates. Then I'ma go see your sister on Dorrington Street. Say, hi to your nieces and nephews. You know how I get down, cuz. So, stop playing with me. Keep my name out your mouth and I might keep my dick out of hers.

See the pictures enclosed.

Take Care!

I put the photos inside the card, put it in the envelope and sealed it. Mousey was in McCreary so I had to Google the address. I wrote it out along with Mousey's name and Fed number. My next stop was to the Post Office to mail it off.

***

Crossing my fingers, I dialed a number that I knew by heart, hoping it hadn't changed.

"Speak on it," A male voice said.

"Cuz, what's up?" I asked.

"Who dis?"

"Khadafi."

"What the fuck is up, bruh?" Bosco exclaimed.

"Just got out, I need to see you."

"You know where I'm at, big bruh, same place."

"That's what's up but check this out. Your hood is about what ... three blocks from Hobert?"

"Four, but who's counting? Why, what's up?"

"You hip to a dude named, Kito McMillian?"

"Of course, I'm hip to him. He went on a rack of murders out Maryland. We grew up together and went to Bruce Monroe as kids."

"Cool. He looked out for me when I was out Maryland and I wanted to repay the favor. I wanna take his people some money. I know they live on Hobert but I can't remember where."

"I'll ask and find out then I'll let you know."

"And what about his co-defendant, Jeezy?"

"Know him, too. Same deal, grew up with them."

"Bet. I need a line on both of their folks so I can drop the bag off to them."

"I got you, bruh," Bosco assured.

"As for the other thing, I'll hit you when I'm on my way."

"Sure thing, bruh. One love."

I tossed the phone into the passenger seat and eyed the sign above the clothing store. Islamic Sportswear Originals. Ameen's store hadn't changed in years. The only thing different was the clothes on the mannequins in the windows. I sat in the parking lot of the bustling strip mall and watched people move around inside the store. I couldn't tell if Ameen was inside but so far, I hadn't spotted him.

Ameen was the single greatest threat to my survival, and I needed to eliminate him sooner rather than later. Killing PeeWee first was born out of convenience and principle. Ameen's death was a necessity. The two handguns in my lap were geeking to be let go. I could sense it and I vowed to myself to put all thirty bullets into Ameen's corpse.

After an hour or two, I left Ameen's store with another destination in mind. In my hand was a hit list with several names on it. I drove to Forestville Health and Rehab Center with the third name on that list on my mind. My heart rate sped up as I drove through the parking lot hoping to spot Marnie's Benz. I'd seen enough pictures of the car to spot it out of a line up. I didn't see it anywhere. Maybe she had a different whip. I parked and walked around the corner to the entrance.

"Can I help you, sir?" The woman behind the counter asked.

"Yeah, I'm tryna locate a friend of mine. Does Marnie Curry still work here?"

The woman's face lit up. "I wish, but no. Marnie was cool as shit. She been left here right after she got married to that fine ass, grey eyed dude. Sorry."

Married? Marnie had gotten married. My heart broke and my anger rose.

"After the wedding, I saw her a few times, but since then I've lost contact with her."

"Do you know where she works now?"

"Sorry, I sure don't. Can I help you with something else? My cell number perhaps?"

The woman's name tag read, *Sherita.* She looked like a brown-skinned Muppet baby. "Sure, baby girl," I said and slid my phone across the counter. "Put your number in my phone."

Muppet baby programmed her number into my phone and slid it back to me. "Call me, your freckles sexy as shit and I love your beard."

"I'ma call you," I lied and left the building.

Inside the Infiniti truck, I sat back and thought about what I had just learned. Then it all made sense to me. Marnie wasn't mad about the hot shit. She had met another dude and wanted to be with him. That's why she abandoned me. To eventually get married. I couldn't believe Marnie had done it, moved on with her life knowing that I'd made that sweet deal with the government. She knew I'd be home in a few years, but yet, she chose to move on as if I'd never get out of jail again. My initial shock at learning that Marnie was married turned to confusion. Her actions were baffling. Marnie knew me better than anyone in the world. Her cutting me off, I could accept. But keeping my children away from me and some other dude playing father to them, I could not accept.

"Stupid, bitch," I said out loud as I started the truck. "She know I'ma kill her. Her husband, too. Why would she do something so stupid?" I laughed. I wanted to kill Marnie. I needed to kill. A face that wasn't Marnie's appeared in my head. I picked up my phone and called Lil' Quette.

"What's good, big cuz?" Lil' Quette answered.

"You know where Walker Mills Road is?"

"Yeah."

"Good. There's a small strip mall right where Walker Mills meets Addison Road."

"It's a McDonald's right there, I'm hip to it."

"Meet me there, right now, cuz."

***

"I'm over by the Chinese spot, lil cuz. My truck parked in the parking lot in front of it. You see me?"

"I see you I'll be right there."

Minutes later, Lil' Quette climbed into the Infiniti. He looked around. "Damn, I like this joint."

"I need you to go in that store right there called Islamic Sportswear Originals. Here." I passed Lil' Quette a couple hundred-dollar bills. "Buy something and ask the dude with the beard in there where Ameen is. Make up something about y'all being family or something."

"Ameen?"

"Yeah. He owns the store. I need to find him like yesterday."

"So, I'm looking for Ameen who owns the store and we're family?"

"Yeah. As a matter of fact, use Ameen's government name. Use Antonio, Ameen. Say your last name is Felder."

"Felder?"

"Yeah, Felder. You're Marcus Felder, you're looking for your big cousin, Antonio. That's believable, try to get a line on him."

"Got you," Lil' Quette replied and hopped out of the truck.

I watched him casually walk into Ameen's clothing store.

"Where are you, Ameen? I need to kill you."

Chapter Twelve

Lil' Quette

Having seen the sign above the door and walking into a place that smelled of prayer oils, I easily figured that people inside the store were probably Muslim. Living next door to a Muslim family for the majority of my life and being close friends with the twins Rahman and Rasheed, I knew a lot about Islam.

"Assalaam Alaikum," I greeted as I entered the store and spotted a brown-skinned dude behind the counter wearing a Jalabiya and multicolored kufi.

"Walaikum Assalaam, ock," he replied.

A female came out of the aisle and asked me what I was looking for.

"I like jogging styled sweatsuits. Like the one on that mannequin with the Allah in Arabic on it. Let me see that joint in black, grey and beige."

"And you would be—what? A medium?" she asked.

"I guess."

"Well, what I'll do is bring out a medium and a large in the colors you requested."

"Okay, sis. Thank you."

"I'll be right back." The woman disappeared into the back room.

Who is Ameen? And why does Khadafi want to kill him? I thought as I moved around the store looking at jeans, jackets, hats, and shoes.

"Here's the black ISO jogging suit in medium and large. Try 'em on. The fitting rooms are right back there."

In the fitting room, I decided that the medium sweatsuit fit better. I also rehearsed the spiel I was about to spit to the brother behind the counter. I walked out of the fitting room.

"I need all three in the medium please."

The bearded brother behind the counter folded all three sweatsuits before putting them in a bag. "That's gon' be two-hundred and fifty dollars, plus tax, ock."

"Aye, ock, I'm looking for my cousin. He owns this store," I said to the brother.

"Your cousin? Who's your cousin?"

"Antonio. My aunt Cheryl told me where this store was. I was hoping to see Antonio in here."

"Why didn't you ask for Antonio when you first walked in?"

"I didn't see him, so I figured he wasn't here. I saw the sweatsuit on the mannequin and had to have it. So, I grabbed a few of them first."

"If Ameen is really your cousin, you might can get these sweatsuits a little cheaper. What you say your name was?"

"Marcus. Marcus Felder. I been trying to catch, big cuz."

"Hold on for a minute let me try and reach him." The brother pulled out a cell phone and dialed a number. "No answer, ock. Sorry, looks like you gotta pay full price."

I pulled out the money that Khadafi gave me and counted out $275.00. I passed it to the brother. "My people told me that Antonio is always here, so I stopped by."

"They said he's always here, in this store?" I nodded. "Well, whoever told you that lied, ock. Ameen ain't never here. I run this store. He opened another store out of town. He hardly ever comes here. But if I talk to him, I'll be sure to let him know that you came by." The brother pushed the bag across the counter to me. "Be safe, ock. Assalaam Alaikum."

"Walaikum Assalaam and Shakran, ocki," I replied, grabbed the bag, and left.

***

In the truck, I relayed the whole conversation between me and the bearded brother word for word. "You think he was hip to me and shut me some bullshit?"

"Hard to tell," Khadafi said. "Your story sounded good. Ameen probably did open another store somewhere else. I can see him leaving the city after his trial. I'ma get somebody to try and Google him and see what comes up. Damn, I was hoping to find cuz and finish him off. It wasn't meant to be, though. It's all good. I need some weed, cuz. Where the good shit at?"

"That's easy, my man on Talbert Street got the best loud in the city. That San Fernando Valley O.G."

"You got his number?"

"Yeah, I got it."

"Call him and tell him you need a pound of that," Khadafi ordered.

"Got you." I pulled out my phone, called my man and placed the order. "He said it's already on deck. We just gotta go get it."

"A'ight. Go get your car and I'ma follow you over there."

I was about to hop out the truck when Khadafi stopped me.

"When you picked me up, you asked me about the hot shit, remember?" he asked.

"Of course, I do. It was just yesterday."

"You said that you heard it. Where did you hear that from?"

"My man Adrian's father knew me, and you were some kin. So, he always mentioned it like he was tryna get under my skin. Said it was all over the newspaper?"

"Your man Adrian? Who's his father?"

"A dude named, A.D."

"Adrian Wade?"

I nodded. "His son is Adrian Wade Jr. You know him?"

"Yeah, I know him. What part of the SW do you hang in, lil cuz?"

"I'm reppin' first and P. 106 and Park all day."

"Meechie still hanging out down there?"

"Yeah, he the big homie. Him and his brother Carlton. Carlton be where we be at, but Meechie hangs on Half Street by the corner store."

"Cool. I'ma need you to make sure that you don't mention to anybody that I'm home. Hopefully, you haven't told no—"

"I haven't. Why would I?" I blurted out.

"Good. I'ma holla at Meechie and A.D. real soon, so I'd like to keep the element of surprise on my side. You feel me?"

"I feel you."

"And you were never at that car lot yesterday, right?"

"What car lot?"

"That's what I'm talking about. You're a smart kid. Let's go get that weed. But before we go, tell me everything you know about Meechie, A.D. and your mother's boyfriend."

"A'ight, my mother's boyfriend's name is James Tolliver but everybody calls him Jomo—"

Chapter Thirteen

Ameen

Tallahassee, Florida

"Time for a pop quiz, kid," Coach Don Jones told Kashon. "You ready?"

"Always ready," Kay-Kay answered.

"And why are you always ready?"

"Cause when you're always ready, you ain't gotta get ready."

"What's your style of boxing?"

"Southpaw."

"What does it mean to be a Southpaw?"

"It means that I lead with my right hand."

Coach Jones smiled. "And why is that?"

"Because I'm left-handed and that's my power hand. I lead with the right hand to set up my big left hand. All my combinations come off the lead right jab."

"Is that right? So, what is your one hand?"

"Straight right jab."

"Your two hand?"

"Left straight hand."

"Three?"

"Right hook."

"Four?"

"Left hook."

"Five?"

"Right uppercut."

"You sound like you're ready to train. We gon' start with the mitts."

Sitting on the stand at ringside in IMPACT gym, I watched my stepson go through his drills and smiled. I felt so much love for Kashon despite the way I felt about the man who he resembled. Last year, while watching the 2016 Olympics in Beijing, I caught Kashon behind me with his eyes glued to the TV as the boxing events unfolded. After that, any time boxing came on, he'd be stuck in place watching. Then out of nowhere, the precious seven-year-old cornered me in the kitchen.

"Dad, I want to box," Kashon said.

"Are you sure that that's what you wanna do?" I asked him.

"I'm positive, boxing is all I think about."

"Being about to box is one thing, getting hit repeatedly is another."

"I don't care about getting hit, I can take it."

I went to his mother and despite Shawnay's strong protestations, I found him a gym. In the end, I think Shawnay realized that her son being a cinnamon colored, pretty boy with reddish brown, curly hair and freckles would make Kashon easy prey for bullies. I laughed when I thought about young boys thinking that Kashon was soft, then found out the hard way that he was really an animal. In the fourteen months that Kashon has been boxing, everyone, even his mother discovered that the kid was a natural. I watched Kashon get his hands wrapped, then put on eight-ounce boxing gloves and spar a kid twice his size. This bigger kid didn't stand a chance. Kashon was smooth, his punches calculated, and crisp. His combinations were fluid, concise and quick.

"Keep your hands up at all times, Kay Kay," Coach called out. "You gotta always hold the phone. Snap your punches out and bring 'em back. That's right. One, two—one, two."

***

"Where you tryna get something to eat from?" I asked Kay Kay as I maneuvered the Buick Lacrosse through the streets.

"Um—pizza," Kashon answered. "Pizza from Manny's and Helga's."

"Pizza it is then, champ."

"I ain't the champ, yet, but one day I will be."

"I believe you. When you get rich, I wanna Bugatti."

"I'ma buy you two of 'em. You can give Ma one."

I laughed at that. "Who's your favorite boxer? Floyd Mayweather?"

"I was on the Money Team but not no more. I like Errol Spence Jr. and the Cherlo Twins."

"You know what you know, youngin. You know what you know."

***

When I pulled into the driveway, Asia's Nissan Maxima was parking on the street in front of the house. She got out of her car at the exact moment that me and Kay Kay exited the Buick.

"Hey, Kay Kay. Hey, dad," Asia said and tried to hurry past me.

"Ain't no, hey, dad. Where you been all day? School lets out at three-forty-five. It's—" I looked at my watch. "—it's sixteen after eight.

"Dad!" Asia said exasperated. "That's not late. You act like it's midnight or something. I was at Michelle's house with her and Tionna. I needed some help with my Calculus homework. Michelle is a math genius. We did our homework and chilled."

"Did the chilling part include teenage boys?"

"No, Dad. Our chilling didn't include any boys."

"Okay, now, don't make me get on my aggressive Dad stuff, Asia. You already know how I get. I ain't playing no games about my baby."

Asia hugged me and kissed my cheek. "Dad, your baby is seventeen and almost grown."

"I don't care if you're forty. You will always be my baby," I reminded her.

"I know, Dad, and I do not want you to become penitentiary Ameen. So, no boys until after college. Okay?" Asia reached out and tried to hug Kashon.

Kashon held his gym bag and the box with the extra large pizza in it. He shied away from Asia. "I'm too big for all that, Asia."

"I'll catch you later by yourself. You showing off in front of Dad."

We walked in the house and instantly smelled food cooking. It smelled like fried chicken. I looked at Kay Kay and he looked at me, we shared a smile.

"You gon get in trouble," Kay Kay said and laughed.

"I didn't know that she was gonna cook," I defended myself.

"Ma is gonna say that you should have called," Asia added.

I turned back to Kashon. "Why you ain't call your mother from the gym?"

"Duh—I'm only eight," Kay Kay said and passed me the pizza. "Not my responsibility." He laughed again and darted upstairs.

He'd left me holding the bag literally. I looked at my daughter for help.

"You're on your own, Dad," Asia said, then called out, "Hello, Ma," to her mother in the kitchen.

"Hey, baby," Shawnay called back. "Be ready for dinner in ten minutes."

"Okay, Ma," Asia replied and went up the stairs.

I walked in the kitchen carrying the pizza. "Damn, you look good, baby."

Ignoring her words, Shawnay's focus was on the pizza in my hand. "I know you ain't brought no pizza up in here when you know I was gonna cook?"

***

"What are you doing?" Shawnay asked.

I looked up from my laptop and stared at my wife. She stood in front of the mirror on the dresser with a towel draped around her body and one wrapped around her hair. The smell of fruit scented soap and or shampoo filled the room.

"I'm on Corrlink responding to emails from my men."

Shawnay closed our bedroom door and let her towels. My dick responded immediately, I was drawn into her sexiness. At thirty-seven-years old, Shawnay was as young looking and as beautiful as she was at seventeen. Even after birthing three children, burying one and a lot of pain and heartache. She sat on the bed and rubbed lotion into her flawless, caramel skin. Her toes were polished a bright orange that matched the designs on her nails. Shawnay shook her hair out and let her dreads fall down her back.

"You tryna start something," I told her and smiled.

"Why do you say that?" Shawnay replied. "I'm just lotioning up."

"Yeah, but you're doing it naked."

"Is there any other way to lotion up after a shower?"

"You know what I mean. Do me a favor and lock that door."

"And why do I need to lock the door?"

Powering down the laptop, I closed it and set it on the dresser. I walked around the bed until I stood in front of Shawnay.

"Because Kay Kay will walk right in here and you know that." I leaned down and kissed her, put my lips on her neck and then her nipples.

"Let me go and lock the door."

After locking the door, Shawnay got on the bed on all fours. She looked back over her shoulder and said, "We can get back to the foreplay later. Right now, I need to be fucked real good, but quiet."

"I can do quiet," I said as I undressed. "But the question is, can *you* do quiet?"

"I can as long as I put my face in the sheets and bite down on them."

I got behind Shawnay, eased into her wetness and handled my business.

***

The Next Morning

"How is everything going with the store?" Shawnay asked, getting ready for work.

"Everything's good, I got Roshene and Sicario opening and closing. Ever since I switched the Islamic theme to the D.C. flavor, business has skyrocketed. I guess it ain't a lot of Muslims in Tallahassee."

"Well, that was smart changing it up."

"I put Hugo Boss on the mannequins in the window with the New Balance tennis shoes and that swag brought 'em in. The store stays packed. In a minute, I'ma start looking for a second location."

"That's really good to hear. Especially since I might end up working in one of them," Shawnay said.

"Girl, stop. Ain't nothing gonna get you outta of hospitals. You been in the healthcare industry all your life."

"I know, right. I guess I'm just getting a little burnt out. I might be experiencing a midlife crisis."

"At thirty-seven?" I said and grabbed Shawnay in a warm embrace from behind.

"I'll be thirty-eight soon. That's old enough for menopause nowadays."

I kissed her neck after moving her dreads.

"Antonio stop, don't kiss me, right there. My legs open automatically when you kiss me right there."

"My bad, I was having an early morning crisis. My dick keeps getting hard every time I see how phat your ass looks in them slacks. Or that camel toe."

Shawnay turned to face the mirror and lifted her blouse. "Is there really—my slacks ain't—I don't see no camel toe."

"That's because you used to seeing it and so am I."

"Boy, bye. Did Asia tell you that she wants to attend Howard University next year?"

I shook my head. "Naw, she didn't. Did she say why Howard?"

"No, and I didn't ask either. Do you think she just wants to get back to D.C.?"

"Maybe. Maybe not. You know how fickle she is. In a month, she'll want to go to Spellman again. I think she should stay close and go to Florida A & M. It's a great school from what I hear and it's a HBCU."

"Well, we'll see what she decides. Ultimately, it's her choice. Just wondered if she'd told you and how you'd feel about her being in D.C.?"

"She can go if she really wants to but I'd definitely be worried about her. I do still have a rack of enemies there."

"I know. We'll cross that bridge when we come to it. And just for the record, I'm still against my son being the next Sugar Ray Leonard. Boxers get killed in the ring all the time. The rest take so many punches to the head that their speech gets slurred as they get older."

"Kay Kay is a natural, bae. James is teaching him the Pernell Whitaker style defense. That Floyd Mayweather shit, roll your shoulders, never get hit shit."

"Coach better do something because as soon as my son starts talking Reddick Bowe, I'm fucking one of y'all up."

We both had to laugh at that.

***

I was in the store hanging up the EAT shirts when Fargan called my cell phone.

"Assalaam Alaikum, ock. What's good?"

"Walaikum Assalam, Ameen. Everything is good here, alhamdulillah. I just wanted to pass on some info to you. A youngin came in here a couple of days ago and said that he was your cousin. Asked me where you were, he was tryna see you."

"A youngin? Said he was my cousin?"

"Yeah, called you Antonio and y'all both share a last name."

"What was his name?" I was confused.

"Marcus Felder, he said. Said y'all are first cousins."

"I don't have no young cousins. And not no cousin named Marcus. Whoever shorty was, he was welling."

"By Allah, I figured that. He gave himself away when he said that somebody in y'all family told him that you are always here in the store. When he said that, I said this store. To make sure I heard right. He said yeah, this store. I thought to myself, if he really

Ameen's cousin, then somebody had to tell him that Ameen don't even live in D.C. no more. You been gone what, three years now? How can he be a first cousin and not know that?"

"I'm hipped. What did he look like, ock?"

"Light skinned, reddish brown hair, cut low, waves, freckles—"

"Freckles?"

"Yeah, freckles. About my height, jive slim. Typical young nigga. Came in and copped a couple sweat suits a size too small. Asked about you, paid and left."

"What did you tell him?" I asked.

"Nothing just that you opened another store and moved out of town. I told him that when I talked to you, I'd tell you he came looking for you. You know me, I'm naturally suspicious of people I don't know. Him saying anything overloaded my bullshit meter. When he left out, I looked out the window.

He got into the passenger side of a black Infiniti truck. The same Infiniti truck that I saw sitting in the parking lot earlier that day. You know I'm hip to you, ock. How you get down and all that. I think somebody from the past is tryna find you and it ain't to wish you well."

"I can dig it, ock. You might be right. I appreciate the call and you putting me on point. I need you to call me asap if he comes back, okay?"

"Insha'Allah. Everything good with you down there?" Fargan asked.

"Everything is great. Call me if you need me. Jazakellah."

"Wahiyakem," Fargan said and hung up.

The description Fargan gave of the young dude who came in the store looking for me made me smile. He could have been describing Kashon as a teenager. Khadafi was home and he was looking for me. He'd sent somebody from his family into the store to ask for me while he waited in the Infiniti truck. Khadafi's uncle Marquette has a son but his name wasn't Marcus.

It was Marquette after his father. That I knew for sure from all the conversations I had had with Khadafi at Beaumont before Keith was killed. The youngin' had lied to Fargan. He wasn't my cousin, he was Khadafi's cousin.

My mind went back to September of 2014 when Rudy Sabino called me and told me that Khadafi was sent to Western Correctional Institution to do the three years, he'd been sentenced to a few weeks before. I did the math in my mind. It had been three years exactly. Khadafi's first order of business was to find me and I knew why. Because I was his biggest threat. One natural born killer against another.

"I'm tryna chill out, Khadafi, but if you continue to shake the tree looking for a cat, a lion is going to come down. Live your life while you can because if you push me, I'll come for you," I said to myself with great conviction.

Putting the phone in my back pocket, I went back to hanging shirts.

Chapter Fourteen

Nicole Brooks

United States Penitentiary, Hazelton
Bruceton Mills, W.V.

"Ma'am, step right in there and have a seat. The inmate will be out shortly," the visiting room C.O. instructed.

The legal room inside the main visiting room at the prison was small. It was bare except for one small table and two chairs. One on either side of the table. I chose the chair closest to the wall and sat down, pulling out a writing pad and ink pens. About ten minutes later, a brown-skinned man with tattoos on his face walked into the room.

He was dressed in tan khakis and beige Timberland boots, Tony Glenn looked younger than his forty years. His long dreadlocks were pulled back into a ponytail that dropped almost to his waist. I stood up, reached across the table, and shook his hand.

The pain in my side hit me hard again, but I ignored it. "I'm Nicole Brooks. Thank you for agreeing to talk to me."

Tony Glenn smiled. "It's cool. Anything for Dice."

"Glad to hear that. As I explained to you on the phone, the Supreme Court has recently made a decision that affects hundreds of thousands of convicted killers, all around the country, state and federal. I work for the lawyers who represent Anwar Dice Beckwith. He's been at the D.C. jail for over a year waiting to go before Judge Harold Sullivan for resentencing. The Supreme Court ruled that you can't give juveniles a life sentence due to underdeveloped brain function. They ruled that to give a juvenile life is cruel and unusual punishment.

Anwar was sixteen when he was sentenced to life in nineteen-ninety-four. He's been in prison for almost twenty-five years and we think that's long enough. Judge Sullivan is big on reform, though. He pays close attention to what a person's done since his incarceration. So, naturally, he's concerned about a riot and serious assault that Anwar was charged with.

Anwar says that you were in USP Pollock with him in two-thousand-nine and that you can attest to the fact that, one, Pollock was a very dangerous place in two-thousand-nine and that the stabbing he was involved in was done in self-defense. I'm here to take your statements. If his lawyers decide that they need you in court at the hearing, you'll be writted back to D.C. Okay, let's start with the dangerous atmosphere at USP Pollock in two-thousand-nine."

"I arrived at USP Pollock in 2007 after leaving Beaumont Pen. My second day there, I exited the chow hall early in the morning after breakfast. As soon as I walked out of the door, I saw one group of black dudes approach another group of black dudes with prison made shanks. The two groups, both from the state of Louisiana started fighting and stabbing one another. A scene straight out of the movie Gladiator. There were over twenty dudes injured. A couple months later, D.C. inmates and Florida inmates went at it the same way over a flag football game. Then came the race riot—"

I wrote as fast as I could to jot down every word Tony said. "Did you say race riot?"

Tony Glenn nodded. "Yeah, a full-scale race riot. A dude named Jay stabbed two white inmates early in the morning, injuring one and killing the other. Another white boy stabbed Jay and killed him. Word spread around the pound quickly because the C.O.s walked the white boy past the kitchen, which was full of blacks. As he walked by the white boy inmate called out to his friends nearby. *He said, "I just killed one of them niggers!"* The blacks took off on the whites and it escalated."

"Did anybody else die?" I asked.

"Nobody else did, but there was a rack of severe injuries on both sides. And that was the second time in a number of years that that happened. USP Pollock became what Beaumont Pen used to be. The Staff found two dudes dead on the same day in two separate housing units. Then C-Dog, the Crip shot caller got killed walking to chow. A five-percenter dude got killed on the steps of C-building. After that Chino, a Mexican got killed by two Mexicans in the SHU. I can go on and on—"

"By all means please do. This is good stuff and it should help Anwar."

"The whiteboys went to war. The Texas ABs and the independent white boys—"

"Independent whiteboys?"

"Yep, that's what the white boys who are not part of any gang calls themselves. They usually be from all over the country and they ban together to fend off the white prison gangs like the Aryan Brotherhood. The independents ran all the racist white boys off the yard. Then after that it was DC inmates warring with Louisiana. DC versus the Crips, DC against the Muslims, it was crazy."

"Sounds like DC inmates get into it with everybody, huh?" I asked.

"Pretty much, we are the most hated dudes in the whole federal system. Always have been, always will be. It's gotten a lot worse since Lorton closed in two-thousand-one and sent everybody to the Feds. Over the years, dudes from DC have gone to war with every geographic location and gang in the BOP. We've warred with the GDs, Crips, Bloods, Vice Lords, Latin Kings, Netas, all the Mexican gangs, but mostly the Surenos, Abs, ACs and the natives, everybody. All the states, New York, Florida, Texas, the Bay Area, Ohio, Philly, Baltimore, the Carolinas—you name it, we warred with it."

"I never knew that," I told Tony. "Why do DC inmates beef or war so much?"

"Your guess is as good as mine. All I know is that we ain't going for nothing and we ain't even no gang. I think our water might've been fucked up for a long time because destruction is all we know. In the last few years, though, all the murders in the BOP have been DC inmates on DC inmates, like I said, shit's crazy."

"Damn, that's fucked up."

"I know, right?"

"Okay, you've detailed for me the dangerous nature of USP Pollock in two-thousand-nine. Now, I need to know about the riot and Anwar's role in it."

"It wasn't his fault. He didn't have nothing to do with the dispute between the New Orleans dudes and a homie name Box. Dice—Anwar just went to try and squash the beef. When talks broke down, one of the New Orleans dudes took off on Anwar with a knife. Anwar fought the dude off and took his knife. He stabbed the dude with his own knife. Anwar was not the aggressor. What was he supposed to do? Let the dude kill him? After Anwar got the knife and the dude off him, he could've killed him, but he didn't, it was self-defense."

"Let's hope that the courts and judge Sullivan see it like that. I think I've got enough to amend our motion. If there's anything else I need, I'll come back to see you, or we'll have you *writted* back to DC. Is that cool?"

"Of course, it's cool. When you see Dice give him my love and respect."

Gathering my things, I replied, "As soon as I see him, I'll do that. Thanks again for talking to me."

"My pleasure. Have a safe trip back to DC."

"I will, God willing, I will."

***

"Little boy, didn't I tell your little bad ass to sit down?"

"Mommy! Mommy! Mommy!" my son hollered, ignoring my mother.

I ran to my son Antonio and snatched him up into my arms. "Hey, A.J.! How's mommy's little man?"

"Gamma mean, Mommy! Gamma mean!"

"Gamma mean, shit. I'ma mean your little bad ass you keep it up. I don't care if your mother here or not," my mother said.

"Ma, you better leave my son alone."

"Chile, I will whip both of y'all asses at the same time."

"I know that's right, Mommy De La Hoya. We don't want no smoke, right, A.J.? Tell her. Gamma, we don't want no smoke."

"Gamma, we don't want no smoke," my two-and-a half year old son said.

My mother laughed. "How was West Virginia?"

"Scenic, full of mountains. Was Antonio really that bad?"

Miranda Brooks smirked. I'd seen that smirk too many times to count. "You know your son. I don't know where he gets that wild Banshee shit from because it wasn't you. At his age, you were a perfect child."

"You told me that a thousand times," I said aloud, but in my head, I thought, *Antonio gets the wild shit from his father. His father has killed more people in DC than Fentanyl.*

"You over there looking all spaced out. What you thinking about?"

"Antonio's father wondering if my son gets his mean streak from him."

"Why don't you find him and see?" my mother suggested.

I don't have to find him. I know exactly where he is. "I would if I could, Ma. I don't know where to begin to look for Antonio. My son was created out of a one-nightstand filled with mind blowing sex. Afterward, I knew I was pregnant because that man sexed me and touched my soul."

"Have you ever heard the term *too much information*?"

"Have you? All the stories you done told me about you and my father."

"Well, that's different. Just wanted you to know how you got here."

The relationship between myself and my mother was great. More sister to sister then mother to daughter. That's why I couldn't understand why I always lied to her about my son's father. I guess I didn't want to disappoint her because she wanted the best for me. She lived her life deferred, so that mine could be better. I initially felt like I failed her by getting pregnant without being married or in a relationship. She'd always told me how hard it was for her to raise me without a father around. In my heart, I knew that I had repeated the cycle and it hurt her. I didn't want to compound her heart by admitting that I was fucking a married man and had fallen in love.

I couldn't tell her that on the day my son was created that married man told me that he was leaving me. It was easier to lie. Safer. I often thought about Antonio. What he was doing. How life was treating him. My friend Mock out at Quantico had found him easily. Antonio was in Tallahassee, Florida. He owned a nice house with his wife and a store called District Culture. When I really miss Antonio, I'd Google Earth the address. I had to see their house and whether I could spot Antonio leaving or coming.

Then I'd take to Social Media, Antonio didn't have a Facebook or Instagram page, but further research revealed that his daughter did. I trolled Asia Dickerson's Facebook, IG, Snapchat, and Twitter for any sights of her father. The recent pics she'd posted of her and Antonio were screenshotted to my cell phone. I cropped out the daughter just to stare at Antonio. I always felt like a stalker, but I didn't care, love makes you do crazy shit at times.

"Nic?"

"Ma, I'm right here," I said and spent Antonio Jr around.

My son giggled hysterically.

"I can't tell, I was talking to you and felt like I was talking to myself."

"What were you saying?" I asked.

"See, I knew you weren't listening. I was telling you about the stuff coming out that our Mayor is gay. I knew that bitch Mary Bowser was a lesbian, I knew it. But nobody listens to me anymore. Now, the shit done come out—"

I covered my son's ears. "Ma, can you please watch your language and content around my son. I don't want him repeating all the foul shit you be spewing."

"Girl, bye. What I just said was mild. You should hear the shit I say to his little bad ass when you ain't around."

"I can only imagine. You gon' mess around and get your grandma privileges revoked. Keep it up."

"*Grandma privileges?* When you ain't around, I tell Tonio that I'm really his aunt. Ain't that right, baby boy?"

"Gamma mean," Antonio Jr. said and laid his head on my shoulder.

"Look at him pouting. But damn, that little nigga fine."

"You should see his father," I said and smiled.

"A one-nightstand with a gorgeous nigga can be excused. Especially if you get yourself pregnant. It could've been a lot worse. You could've been drunk and liquor has a way of making a ugly nigga look good. Then you would've been standing here holding a baby that looked like Lil' Wayne with his baby dinosaur looking ass."

I cracked up laughing. "Ma you're terrible. Always joneing and shit." Then a sharp pain shot through my body and I almost dropped my son. "O-o-o-w-w-w!"

"Nicole," my mother said, rushing by my side in an instant. "What's wrong? You okay?"

I straightened up and grabbed my side. "I'm good, Ma. I keep getting this excruciating pain that starts in my side and then shoots all throughout my body. Sometimes, it gets so bad that I get light-headed. My periods have been unusually heavy for the last few months. I been meaning to go and see my OB/GYN Doctor, but I been busy."

"Gimme Tonio, you go and lay down for a little while. When the food is ready, I'll bring some to you."

I handed my son to my mother and went to lay down.

Anthony Fields

Chapter Fifteen

Detective Corey Winslow

"The ancient Egyptians were the first civilization dental records," Pamela Steinberg, Chief Medical Examiner for the District of Columbia told me as I stood inside her office. "All the victims burned in the fire had to have had dental work done at some point in their lives. We were able to identify all five victims." She passed me a list of names on a piece of paper.

I read the list of names. "Thank you, Doc. As always you've been a great help."

"Don't thank me, detective, thank the ancient Egyptians."

I called Captain Dunlop and let him know the names on the list.

"Get the list to Duncan. He'll notify the next of kins," the Captain said. "Keep me posted on anything else you find out. The chief is on my ass about this one."

My next call was to Rio Jefferson. "Rio, it's me Corey Winslow."

"Corey, I want to apologize for the way I acted the other night—"

"Don't mention it, Rio, it's water under the bridge. I know how you get when it comes to Khadafi. Speaking of the other night, that's why I'm calling. You were right about PeeWee. Just left the M.E.'s office with a list of names of the victims from the fire Monday night. James Smith's name is at the top of that list."

"I knew it, Corey. I knew it. Do you have the list in front of you?" Rio asked.

"I do. You want me to read you the names?" I replied.

"Yeah, I wanna see if I recognize anybody else on it."

I read off the list of names to Rio.

"None of the other names sound familiar. The rest were probably just employees at the car lot."

"I figured as much, but why kill them? His beef was with PeeWee."

"Leave no witnesses. That's why he killed everybody who probably saw his face. I read Moe's file on Khadafi. You did too, right? Okay. I also read what Moe had compiled on Tyrone T.J. Carter and Antonio Felder. Their motto was never leave witnesses. It's a damn shame, buddy. Khadafi killed four innocent—"

"Rio, let's be objective here. What if it wasn't Khadafi?"

"It was him I know it was. And he killed four innocent people to cover him killing one piece of shit. When you can, I'm gonna need you to text me a copy of that list so I can try and find out who those other four was. Maybe there was a reason why he killed them."

"Good idea, I didn't think about that. Be sure to share what you find out."

"I will, you already know."

"Listen, Rio, I know how you feel about Ann Sloan and I get it completely. I talked to her about these new developments. She's regretful that she made that deal. She assures me that her office is trying to find a way to put him back in prison. A legal loophole—"

"*Prison?* Put Khadafi back in prison?" Rio spat as if the words tasted like shit in his mouth. "Who said anything about prison? Luther Khadafi Fuller doesn't belong in prison. He belongs in a grave. A shallow one with no marker. I promised myself and Moe—"

"Rio, be careful what you say."

Rio paused for a minute. "Corey, check the house on Montrose Avenue. Contact the aunt Mary Henderson and interview her. She knows where Khadafi is; she might even provide an alibi for Monday. Have Ann Sloan's people threaten her about all the shit Khadafi buys and puts in her name. It's the least Ann Sloan can do since she's so contrite all of a sudden."

"I'll talk to her about it. What about the baby mother, Monica Curry?"

"Two steps ahead of you; I looked her up already and can't find shit. I think she decided to disappear after helping Antonio Felder in court. Going against Khadafi took a whole lot of guts on her part. He has to want to kill her."

"If we can't find her, then neither can he," I told Rio.

"You're right about that, but that won't stop Khadafi. If he really wants to find her he'll find a way."

"She's the mother of his kids."

"Even more reason to kill her. If she's disappeared, he can't see his kids. That probably fucks with him more than anything. Khadafi is like a family pit bull that turns one day and bites the kids. All you can do is take him in the woods behind the house and put him down. If I ever get the right chance—"

"Everything you say can be used against you in court of law—"

"I remember having a conversation like this with Moe before his shooting happened. He was talking like me and I was the voice of reason like you. I can still hear Moe say, *Locking up a dude like Khadafi is pragmatic but not really the answer. We have to find a way to end Khadafi's terror on our streets.* People like Ann Sloan only care about politics and case closure rates. No real human lives, Corey. Getting rid of Khadafi would be my contribution to mankind. It would be my sacrifice."

Before I could respond the line went dead.

Chapter Sixteen

Lil' Quette

Shakira's eyes found mine and held them. I couldn't help watching her as she sucked my dick. The hungry sucking sounds, her moans while sucking, her eyes always on mine, the way she twists her fist as she holds me in her palm. There was no better feeling than getting head when you get up in the morning.

"Damn, Sha! Shit!"

In response to my words, Shakira popped me out of her mouth, spit on my dick and rubbed it all over the length of me. Then she put me back in her mouth and damned near sucked my soul loose. I couldn't hold back any longer. I exploded in her mouth and watched her swallow my seed. I closed my eyes. "Sha, I'm starting to wonder about you."

"Wonder about what?" Shakira asked, wiping her mouth, and getting up off her knees.

"Where the hell did you learn that shit from? Every time you give me head it gets better and better. Your shit Superhead on the low."

"I'm addicted to sucking your dick and watching porn. I watch Pornhub, X videos, the old movies on Youtube by Vanessa Del Rio, Sinnamon, and Janet Jacme. I watched Kim Kardashian eat Ray J. I watched Eve and Stevie J. I watched MiMi eat Nico. I done watched all the celebrity sex tapes and a lot of them nerdy star bitches be cold blooded whores on camera. I see, I learn, I do it to you. What you think I'm doing? Sucking these neighborhood niggas off when you ain't here?"

"I think you know better than that. I ain't no killer but don't push me."

"And what's a sweeter joy than me giving you this pussy?"

"You giving me that head," I said and smiled.

"You keep talking crazy about starting to wonder and all that, you won't be getting it. Talking about I'm Superhead on the low. That ain't cute."

"To me it is. Just like you, baby." I looked at Shakira as she moved around the room dressed only in a t-shirt and panties. She would never be the prettiest girl in the room or the baddest body wise, but she wasn't ugly.

Her hair stayed done, she dressed well and the braces on her teeth looked sexy to me. All the dudes I know called Shakira a swubby, because she was thick and because she had a slight pudge in her stomach that matched her thick thighs and large breasts. I loved Shakira, everything about her was pleasing to my eyes.

"Everything about you cute to me."

"Say that shit, then, nigga. I know I'm bad."

"Yeah, everything except your feet," I joked.

Shakira stopped in her tracks and looked down at her feet. "Ain't nothing wrong with my feet, Quette."

"Naw, not if a muthafucka like pig feet and pork skins."

"You make me sick! Always tryna be funny," Shakira said and rushed me.

After throwing a few punches that I blocked easily, Shakira wrestled me on the bed. I overpowered her and turned her over. Then I pulled her panties to the side and entered her.

"Quette! Stop!"

***

An Hour Later

"Quette, I know you ain't out there selling that shit again."

I bent down to tie up my shoes.

"I know you hear me, nigga. Are you back out there hustling again?" Shakira nagged. "You know what happened the last time you had dope boy ambitions."

"I'm not hustlin', shit too slow."

"And you, too goofy. Go ahead and say that. Got chased your first day out there and had to throw all the work. Then you couldn't find it. I had to give you my hair and nail money to help you pay Meechie back. Goofy ass."

"Stop calling me Goofy. Kelly Price lookin' ass."

"Fuck you, Quette. If you ain't hustling, what the fuck you doing to get all this money then?" Shakira held up the bank roll that was in my pocket.

"Give me my shit." I snatched my money from Shakira. "And stop going in my pockets with your nosey ass."

"Whatever, you better be glad I ain't find no condoms or nothing like that. Cause I would've really been in here fucking your ass up. Where you get the money from and all them fly ass shoes and shit if you ain't hustling?"

"My cousin. He bought me a rack of shit the day I took him to Tyson's when he first got out. Then he gave me a rack of money, too."

"Is that right? Did they used to call your cousin Dirty Redds?"

"Yeah. Why?" I asked.

"Because my friend Shanell got a brother named Scooby. Scooby told Shanell that you got a cousin named Dirty Redds who changed his name to Khadafi. He said your cousin used to be the man, had all foreign whips, a rack of money and his guns had killed a rack of people. Then he shot a police dude and went to jail but instead of manning up and doing his time, he told on a rack of murders to get home. Scooby told Shanell that his men 'nem locked up out Maryland said that Khadafi is home now and that he just got out. So, I figured that he had to be talkin' about your cousin Khadafi—"

"Tell your friend Shanell to tell her brother Scooby to stop running his mouth because if his words get back to my cousin, he gon' crush Scooby shit. Flat out," I said with a little too much venom.

"Damn, don't kill the messenger," Shakira said sassily. "I'm just telling you what Shanell told me. That's your cousin. I don't care if he snitched on niggas or not. I'm not in the streets. Dag getting all mad and in your feelings."

"I'm not in my feelings. Whatever that man did that's on him. I'm just trying to help her brother since you said Shanell is your friend. My cousin is a cold-blooded nut and he tryna see anybody that got his name in their mouth. That's all I'm saying. If Shanell loves her brother, she better tell him to keep my cousin's name out of his mouth. That's it."

"That's it. That's it, okay, cool. I'll tell her, but if you ain't in your feelings. Why are you getting so defensive about it?"

Shakira was starting to get on my nerves. "I'm getting defensive about it because that's my blood cousin and I love him. And niggas be doing and saying the most, but they be faking. I know who Shanelle is and I know her brother Scooby. He talking all that code shit and bad mouthing my cousin, but he on the K Street side hanging with a rack of rats. Every crew on every block gotta Henry Hill in it—"

"*Henry Hill?* Who the fuck is Henry Hill?"

"This famous rat nigga from the movie Good Fellas. Real talk, though, at the end of the day, niggas in the hood accept hot niggas as long as the nigga either bring money to the table or bust his guns. Look at Anthony Chandler."

"Zinc?"

I nodded. "Yeah, Zinc's hot ass. Dove Carson running around, call himself screaming on hot niggas and Zinc his man. Dooby be with him, he *hot.* Manny in the wheelchair. Willie Cobb, Black Gene Byars, Yuself—all them niggas fucked up and niggas out there fucking with them. What's the difference? It's a rack of gangstas in the streets waiting to tell, they just ain't got no reason to yet. They can miss me with all that—" My cell phone vibrated interrupting my rant. It was Khadafi. "What's up, big cuz?" I answered.

"Where you at?" Khadafi asked.

"At my girl's house, but I'm about to leave. What's up?"

"I'm sitting in front of your house in a black Kia Optima, pull up."

"A'ight, I'm coming right now."

***

I was in the car with Khadafi for over twenty-minutes and he still hadn't said a word. He appeared to be in deep thought. My cousin was like an urban novel. You never knew where the story was going, but the read was exciting. "Where we going, big cuz?"

"It's my first Friday home in four years, so I gotta go to Jumah. I gotta offer the prayer and make dua. After that I got a surprise for you."

"A surprise for me?"

"Yeah, a surprise. Just chill out, you gon' love it."

Chapter Seventeen

Khadafi

"I don't really like surprises."

"Well, you gon' like this one. I promise. You ever been to a Masjid?"

Lil' Quette shook his head. "Heard about them. I know what it is and all that, but naw I ain't never been to one."

"How you know what a Masjid is?" I asked curiously.

"I grew up next door to a Muslim family. My men—the twins— Rasheed and Rahman taught me all about Islam. I spent many nights in their house. I fasted with them before. Ate the meal after Ramadan and a rack of other stuff. I know that they attend Jumah every Friday at the Masjid, but I never went."

"Well, today, you get the chance to go. When we get in there just take off your shoes and find a seat in the back. It should be chairs in the back for guests."

"A'ight, I hear you, big boy."

The masjid sat on the corner of Larchmont and Central Avenue on the Maryland side. It was a little smaller than Masjid Al-Islam on Benning Road, but no other Masjid was as big as the one on Benning Road. I thought back to the last time I'd been to that Masjid—

When we stepped out of the Masjid, I noticed that the ground was wet. Umar and Boo were debating something Islamic when I saw the metallic silver Hummer H2 sitting on 24-inch rims. The black caravan was the same caravan that the dude drove who tried to kill me on MLK Avenue at the traffic light. I pulled my gun and pushed Umar to the ground.

"Boo, it's a hit, cuz!" I shouted.

The dude trying to kill me had a choppa inside a tennis racket case. He fired the choppa and mowed down everybody in its path. Boo and I returned fire but our handguns were no match for the choppa, so we ran. Fourteen people, fourteen Muslims had been killed that day and several other injured.

I was so guilt ridden about the innocent lives that were lost, that I never returned to the Masjid on Benning Road. There were so many cars in the parking lot that I had to park on the street a block down from the Masjid. As we got out of the car, I heard a bump noise near the truck.

"Did you hear that? That noise?" Lil' Quette asked.

"Wasn't nothing, something moved around when we stopped. C'mon."

Inside the Masjid, Lil' Quette and I separated. He found a seat at the rear of the Masjid and I went to make Wudu. In the bathroom, I looked at myself in the mirror, I looked older. My beard had a couple of grey hairs, but I felt young and I thought young. I washed my hands, put water in my mouth, up my nose and all over my face. Then I ran my wet hands over my head, beard and last my socks. In the gallery, I found a place to sit on the rug, in the ranks of other Muslims. I could feel eyes on me, but I looked straight ahead. My mind focused on the Imam who was on the member giving the Khutbah.

***

After Jumah after we exited the Masjid, I could see all the streets dudes that I know staring at me, ice grilling me. I ice grilled them right back. Under my grey Jalabiya I had two handguns in each front pocket of my shorts. I expected all eyes to be on me. I knew they would be. I could read eyes. The ones on me said, *"This hot ass nigga back on the streets."* The so-called stand-up men hated it. But there was nothing they could do about it but take me to war. Ninety percent of the dudes standing around in front of the Masjid didn't want my kind of problems. I locked eyes with Cateye Kay Kay from Barry Farms and Black Junior from Lincoln Heights. Two formidable opponents whose faces were a mask of distaste as they eyed me. I could feel their hatred toward me.

I lifted the Jalabiya until both guns were visible. I smiled at them, then mouth the words, "What's up?"

Neither responded, I kept it moving.

"Aye, big cuz, was it me or was everybody staring at you back there?"

"It wasn't you, cuz. They were looking at me. Probably wanted to do something to me, but everybody know I'm wicked with them pistols. I came here for two reasons. One was to pray, but the other was for everybody to see me. I want the whole city to know that I'm back. I want them to know that I'm accessible. If anybody wants to see me about what I did to Ameen, they can line up and come on. I'm ready for whatever."

When we got to the Optima, Lil Quette asked, "Who's car is this?"

"A friend of mine, she let me push it."

"I'ma have to cop Shakira one of these."

Inside the car, I put on my seatbelt and told Quette, "It's time for your surprise."

Anthony Fields

Chapter Eighteen

Lil' Quette

The old public auto auction area near Blue Plains was abandoned. Khadafi parked the car in the most remote area I'd ever seen. Trepidation overtook me as I looked around, I was totally baffled.

"My surprise is down here?"

Khadafi looked at me. "Why you look so shook? The surprise is in the trunk. I had to come down here in order for you to see it. Appreciate it." He opened the door and stepped out of the car.

"In the trunk?" I repeated to the air and followed Khadafi to the rear of the car.

The trunk opened as we approached. I peered inside, my mother's boyfriend Jomo laid in the trunk on his side, bound and gagged. His terrified eyes looked in on mine.

"You can never let anyone violate your family, cuz. And according to you, this nigga been violating your mother for years. Well, guess what? It's time to make your bones. First, you gotta earn your self-respect and then other niggas will respect you—"

"Niggas respect me, big cuz—"

"He don't," Khadafi said, pointing at Jomo. "If he did, he would never put his hands on your mother. Our aunt May is the safest woman alive. You know why? Because niggas wouldn't dream of hurting her. Not nobody who knows who she is. You know why? Because her nephew is a killer. I do the worst shit to people to make them understand who and what they're dealing with when they fuck with me or something that I love. When you picked me up and I asked about this nigga, I did that because I knew months ago that I was gon kill him. But yesterday, I decided that I'ma let you kill him. You said you wanna kill him, right?"

"Yeah—but—I—" I stammered.

"Ain't no buts, Lil' Quette. I told you before, I laugh and joke, but I don't play about killing and my family. Jomo violated you by hurting your mother, so he violated me. I snatched his ass last night before he could go into your house. Your mother been blowing up his phone all night and day looking for him." Khadafi pulled out a cell phone and handed it to me.

It was Jomo's phone, I recognized it immediately. I could see that he had over fifty missed calls and text messages from my mother.

"It's time for you to get some blood on your hands, literally. It's time for you to get that look in your eye."

"Blood on my hands? Look in my eye? What look?"

"It's a look that all killers have. We can all identify each other. I can spot another killer from across the room if I can see his eyes. The soul reflects life and death. Come on, help me get his ass out the trunk."

Together, Khadafi and I lifted Jomo out of the trunk and dropped him on the ground. Khadafi pulled a bag out of the trunk, from the bag he produced a big ass knife. One of them Michael Myers knives that he killed with in the Halloween movies. He handed the knife to me.

"Kill him," Khadafi said as casually as if he'd just told me to eat all my vegetables before I leave the dinner table.

Jomo's eyes widened at the sight of the knife in my hand. He tried to scream, but his cries were muffled by the gag in his mouth. He was a frightened cat in fear of being mauled by a pit bull. The ground beneath Jomo became wet with fresh urine, his pants were stained as well. I looked at Khadafi one last time to see if he'd smiled and tell me he was just playing, he didn't. The look on his face was to the contrary. He was dead serious. I stood over Jomo with the knife, paralyzed with fear, I had never taken a life before.

"This nigga been beating on your mother for years, cuz. And you scared to kill him?"

"I ain't scared," I lied.

"Well, go ahead and kill him, then. I got other shit to do."

I summoned the images of Jomo beating my mother to my head. I could hear her cries. I thought about all the days I vowed to myself that I'd kill Jomo one day. I bent over and plunged the knife into his side. He squirmed around on the ground like a fish out of water. His muffled screams filled my ears, but my mother's screams overrode

112

them. Now in a daze, I stabbed him over and over again. Warm blood splattered my hands, arms, and face after I stabbed Jomo in the neck. I never even noticed that he had stopped moving. I continued to plunge the knife into his body. Then I felt the bloody knife being pried away from my hand.

"That's enough, lil cuz, he's dead. You did good. Look at me."

I looked into Khadafi's eyes.

"It ain't there yet. Your next murder will put it there for sure."

"*My next murder?* What next murder?"

"You'll see when it's time. I'ma make you heartless. Now take off that jacket and that shirt. I don't want you getting blood all over the car.

***

"What kind of car does your mother drive?" Khadafi asked when he pulled in front of my house.

I looked around for it. "A Honda Accord, it ain't out here. She's gone to work."

"Good, go in the house and get cleaned up. Get rid of everything you have on right now. Even them fly ass shoes you got on. I'ma get rid of your jacket, shirt and Jomo's cellphone. Take a shower and clear your head. Once you've done all that, get dressed and call me. I'ma come back for you. We gon' go and get some food."

"Okay," was all I could say.

I opened the door and got out of the car.

***

I was in need of a bath, not a shower, so that's what I did. I sat in the tub and soaked my body for an hour. What I had done replayed in my head like a horror movie. I couldn't get Jomo's terrified eyes out of my head. when his face faded away, his eyes stayed to haunt me. His eyes went from complete terror to a look of pleading for mercy. I had shown none. Then I thought about my mother. She would be beyond hurt when she learned that the man she loved was dead. I looked at the clothes and shoes strawn across the bathroom floor. I needed to get rid of them, because it would crush my mother even more to learn that her man was killed by her only son. I couldn't let that happen.

***

Khadafi was no longer driving the Kia when he pulled back up outside. He had switched back to the Infiniti truck. "What's in the bag?" he asked as I hopped in.

"The clothes I had on earlier. I gotta get rid of them somewhere but not at my house."

"I'ma pull over somewhere and you can throw 'em out then."

After getting rid of my clothes, we ended up at RuthChris Steak House in Virginia. Khadafi parked the truck and rolled a jay of weed. He hit the weed a few times and passed it to me. I inhaled the weed and almost coughed up a lung.

"Gimme my fuckin' weed," Khadafi hissed and snatched the jay from my hand. "Wasting my shit, coughing and shit."

I was high as hell from that one pull of the weed. Silence filled the truck as Khadafi finished off the weed.

"I'm hungry as hell and RuthChris got this stuffed chicken breast entrée that's good as shit. In a few minutes we gon' go in there and crush some shit, but first I need to talk to you and tell you about my life. So, that you will understand exactly who I am and who I want you to be. You feel me?"

"I feel you, big cuz. I feel you."

"My mother was killed when I was seven-years-old. By two drug dealers in our neighborhood named Rick and Moody. They thought my mother, who was strung out on drugs at the time, had stolen their stash. They came to our apartment and beat her to death. I was home when they did it, hiding in the closet. I watched them kill her. I was terrified, I couldn't speak.

I couldn't move. I didn't want them to see me and hurt me. They left my mother motionless on the floor. I knew that she was dead. So, I stayed in the closet, afraid to come out. I didn't eat or move for a whole week. I pissed and shitted in the closet. As I recovered from that trauma and grew older, I vowed to myself three things. I vowed to never be that afraid again ever in life. I vowed to never cower in the face of adversity and not help someone that I love if they are being hurt and I vowed to kill Rick and Moody when I got older.

Your father was the one who raised me. Him and his friend named Damien Lucas. Your father taught me to hustle and be a man. Damien Lucas taught me to kill and become heartless. At thirteen-years-old, I killed my first man, Rick. I shot him, then stood over him and emptied my gun in his face. Then a year later, I caught Moody and killed him, too. It felt good to avenge my mother's death. While I loved your father with all my heart, secretly, I detested the fact that he didn't have the heart to kill the men that killed his sister. So, I idolized Damien.

Your father was my uncle, but Damien Lucas was like my father. When I was sixteen years old, Damien got killed. One of my childhood friends named Tee set him up to be killed. When I found that out, I went to my real father's barbershop and killed Tee in front of everybody. I got locked up for Tee's murder. I pled guilty and was sentenced to ten to thirty years.

In prison, I was just as vicious as I was in the streets. I had a partner named Mousey. His co-defendant told on him on some murders and got Mousey sixty years. I promised Mousey that had I ever caught his co-defendant Keith Burnett, I'd kill him. In two-thousand-seven, at Beaumont Pen, I caught Keith and killed him. What you did to Jomo wasn't shit. I chopped Keith's body up with a homemade hatchet. Ameen took the beef—"

"Ameen? The same Ameen that I went to the store asking for the other day?"

Khadafi nodded. "The same one."

"I thought you were looking for him to kill him?" I asked.

"I was, but that's a whole 'nother story. A story for a later date. Where was I? Yeah. When I came home after doing ten years, I didn't have shit. Your father was up, but he didn't want me depending on him for money. He wanted me to have my own. So, one day, he took me to a restaurant on Southern Avenue called White Corner. There was a dude inside the restaurant that your father did business with. That day, he decided that it was time for Fat Sean Bundy to pay his taxes. I will never forget what he told me that day.

He said, *"In these parts, ain't no muthafucka tryna give a nigga shit. I'm the same way, nephew. Don't get me wrong, I'm glad you home and all that shit, but I ain't gon' make a bed hustler out of you. I know you tryna eat, feel me? I could throw you a few dollars and a fish dinner right now, but then you have only eaten for one day. But if I show how to fish and take you where the fish swim, you can feed yourself for a lifetime."* Without directly saying go in there and get Fat Sean, he's food for you.

I knew exactly what your father was saying. And that day I became a fisher of men. The streets became my lake, and my gun became my fishing rod. I ran in that restaurant and killed Fat Sean then took his car keys. In the trunk was a rack of money and dope. Your father took all the dope, and I kept the money. After that we became a team. He lined dudes up and I knocked 'em down. But eventually, it caught up to us and one of the dudes that your father lined up figured that it was him who'd crossed him up. That's what got him killed—" Khadafi paused for a long time as if he was reliving the past.

I was high when Khadafi began the story but hearing about my father was having a sobering effect on me.

"The dude who killed your father was named, Money. Me and my partner Boo ambushed him outside his P.O.'s office. I held him at gunpoint while Boo went to his house and got the drugs and money. When Boo got back with the stuff, instead of letting Money go, I shot him in the head twice. Somehow, he lived. Both bullets went in his head and exited without any damage. Because he was on our ass almost immediately, he put two and two together and came up with your father, then me.

When your father got killed, I never thought it was Money because I thought he was dead. I killed a rack of niggas that I thought had something to do with your father's death. I eventually learned that it was Money who'd done it and that he had survived the two shots to the head. I killed both of Money's parents. He retaliated by killing Boo and then his whole family. I got mad, went to the cemetery where Money was burying his parents and killed him in front of everybody."

"Damn," I said, shaking my head.

"Damn, is right, cuz. I was fucked up in the head about my uncle—your father. But I reveled in the fact that the dude who'd killed him was dead. I had a domestic incident with my girl at the time and went back to prison for a year. When I came home, I discovered that your father's girlfriend, Liyah—remember her?"

"Yeah, I remember her. She lived with my father."

"I discovered that she had a nigga living in your father's house. I killed her and the dude in the house."

"Damn, Liyah's dead? I had no clue," I commented.

"She had to go. I don't play that shit. Fuck her! Anyway, lil' cuz, you was a kid then, but now you're a man. I gotta do for you what your father did for me and that's provide you with a means to get money. Real money! But once you start getting money, niggas gon notice and get jealous. Then you gon' become food in their food chain. Unless I give you, what Damien Lucas gave me. The desire, the will, the proclivity to kill.

You gotta make niggas so afraid to move against you that they never try it. You gotta be ruthless and you gotta be heartless. You have to be able to kill man, woman and child without a second thought. You gotta kill niggas, dogs, cats, pet birds, all that shit. When niggas know that you are a different kind of killer, they sidestep you. Niggas like me, they sidestep. Why? Because they know I'ma kill everybody in their family. Now this is not an exact science because every now and again, you gotta make examples out of niggas.

For me, that example was PeeWee. PeeWee ran up in my house and robbed me because he thought I was never coming home. After having a shootout with that cop everybody thought I was washed up. PeeWee played checkers. I was playing Chess. My next example is gon' be Meechie."

"Meechie? My big homie, Meechie?"

Khadafi nodded. "You sound alarmed. You fuck with him?"

"Of course, I do. Him and his brothers, Squirmy and Carlton raised us."

"Meechie was with PeeWee when they went in my house. Meechie hipped to me. He knew better."

"So, what you want? You want him to give you what he took back?"

"Naw, cuz. It's too late for that. I want him to die."

"Well, fuck it. He violated. He dies. I don't care."

"Good. Cause I might let you kill him. Let's go eat."

Chapter Nineteen

The News

D.C. Police are investigating a fatal shooting today in Southeast involving a police officer. At 10:12 pm, metropolitan Police responded to a call about a man waving a handgun on the 4500 block of C Street, near Plummer Elementary School. Officers arrived on the scene to find Emmitt Little, age thirty-three displaying a gun. Little was ordered to put down the gun but refused. Two officers fired their weapons but only one actually shot Little. Little was shot once in the chest. He was rushed to nearby P.G. Community Hospital where he was pronounced dead.

In other news today, three people found dead in an apartment on Third Street in Southeast have been identified. The badly decomposed bodies of Kiera Clark and her two children Keyma and Brian were discovered after family members went to the apartment to do a welfare check. Keyma Clark was thirteen years old and her younger brother Brian Clark was only eleven. Authorities believe that the three victims, who'd all been shot to death were killed because of Kiera Clark's husband Byron Clark's assistance given to law enforcement that has led to the convictions of over thirty different people in D.C. Courts.

Lawyers for notorious Kingpin turned government informant, Rayful Edmonds, have filed motions in Federal Court yesterday to have the former Kingpin's life sentence commuted to time served. Edmonds was convicted in 1989 after a lengthy trial here in D.C. on RICO and continuous criminal enterprise charges. Edmonds was the youngest major supplier of cocaine that the District of Columbia has ever produced. In 1994, while still in federal prison, Edmonds was charged with Federal Drug Trafficking in the state of Pennsylvania where he allegedly ran and operated a drug ring and orchestrated the sale of hundreds of kilos of cocaine to local drug dealers in the District. According to the indictment laid out then Edmonds acted as an intermediary between Colombian Cartel members, incarcerated with him to several individuals in D.C.

It was then that Rayful Edmonds became a government informant, cooperating with Federal authorities to convict his Colombian connects at Lewisburg and his associates in the city. Edmonds has been in prison for nearly thirty years and according to petitions filed in Federal Court, he has been cooperating with law enforcement for over twenty years. Edmonds was last seen in the District in 2002 when he testified in the trial of alleged Murder Inc. leaders, Kevin L. Grey and Rodney Moore. Edmonds told a jury that Moore and Grey had committed multiple murders for him in the eighties.

D.C. Police have also released the name of one of the men killed on Birney Place over the weekend. That man has been identified as thirty-five-year-old Scorpio Phillips. Mr. Phillips was shot and killed in broad daylight during a block party. He was a known confidential informant and discovered to be wearing high tech audio and video equipment at the time of his death. Police have also released the names of the five people killed at a local car lot. Their bodies were burned beyond recognition. The victims had to be identified by their dental records. The victims were identified as James Smith, Paul Williams, Deontay Jackson, Ramon Pitts, and Jamya Smith.

Chapter Twenty

Bay One

Secure Female Facility, Hazelton

Crystal James walked into my cell holding a magazine. "Got something I think you need to see, Bay."

"What's that?" I replied without looking up from the Sudoku puzzle I was stymied with.

"This new magazine called State Versus U.S. It's new, but I said that already."

I glanced at the magazine in Crystal's hand. "And who is that on the cover?"

"That's the chick that put the magazine out. A Baltimore chick named Tia Hamilton. Calls herself Ms. Komoiseur. Magazine is a good mag, got a lot of good articles in it, a few bad model bitches, shit like that. But it's mostly a magazine where they interview a rack of jail muthafuckas and let them tell their stories."

"Is that right? I'm in jail and got my own story. So, why do I need to see this particular magazine?"

"Because it got somebody in it that I know you wanna see. Look!" Crystal opened the magazine and handed it to me.

I looked at the face on the page and couldn't believe my eyes. "Get the fuck outta here!"

"Same thing I said when I saw her."

The smiling face of Gloria Dunbar stared back at me. "They glamorize rat bitches in this magazine?"

"Not from what I read. All the dudes, mostly from Baltimore or somewhere else in Maryland seem official. I don't know how that bitch ended up in there. She must know somebody."

I read the article in the magazine. It mentioned all the murders Gloria was suspected of in D.C. The murders she got convicted of in Maryland and the fact that she'd beat the death penalty for murders in Virginia. Nowhere in the article did it mention that Gloria Dunbar had told on me. I thought back to the day I told Gloria that I was going to kill Mytika Lemens. She was the only person I told—

"I need to holla at you, Gloria."

"What's up, Bay?"

"Listen, I'ma kill, Tika," I told her.

"What? Bay, why would you do that? I'ma get her ass, I'm just waiting for the right time."

"Not gon' happen. You already facing the death penalty out Virginia. I can't let you go out like that. I'ma take this one for the team."

"But why? When you can potentially get out after trial?" Gloria asked.

"What can I say? I'm bored. Plus, I'm sick of that bitch, Tika."

"But—how do you plan on doing it without getting caught?"

"You just fall back and let me handle this. See you in the morning."

I assumed that Mytika Lemens was the person that was dropping notes to the C.O.s at CTF about me selling drugs. The C.O.s were always in my cell searching for shit and I blamed Tika, unjustly. As it turned out, the rat was Gloria. After taking back my cop on T.J.'s murder, the government dismissed the case. I was already indicted on Mytika's murder anyway. Instead of facing Gloria Dunbar at trial, the government's star witness, I copped to ten years for killing Tika with almost five years already in prison. I only had three years remaining on my sentence.

"Hot bitch," I uttered and gave the magazine back to Crystal. "I'ma kill that bitch if I ever get the chance. I put that on my daughter."

Someone knocked on the cell door, then stepped in the cell, it was my homegirl, Shawntay. "Bay, they calling you for a visit."

"Okay, thanks, Shawntay." Shawntay left the cell. "We need to write that bitch on the cover—"

"Tia Hamilton."

"Yeah, her. And tell her that she featured Gloria Khadafi Fuller in her magazine."

Crystal laughed. "Bay, you crazy as shit. Gloria Khadafi Fuller, though?"

"They both killer rats. Fuck em."

***

"Ma'am, I need to look in your mouth," the female C.O. told Lisa. "Then I need to look in your mouth, Lake, before y'all kiss."

Lisa's face screwed up instantly. "What the fuck? When y'all start—"

"They just started this last week, baby. They tryna make sure you don't spit nothing in my mouth," I told Lisa. "Let her see inside your mouth."

"Stupid ass shit," Lisa muttered, then opened her mouth.

The C.O. looked in. "Okay, now you, Lake. Open wide! Move your tongue. Thank you."

I grabbed Lisa by her ass as I hugged and tongued-kissed her.

"There's children around, Lake. Keep it rated, PG," The C.O. said.

"What the fuck is up with these crackas in these mountains?" Lisa asked as soon as we were seated. "They took all the food out of the machines. They put a sign up that says, *Visitors Can No Longer Buy Inmates Food or Beverages.* How in the hell are y'all supposed to eat?"

"They got food trays for us in the back where I came in at. We gotta drink water out of the fountain, I guess. All of this is to stop drugs from hitting the compound via the visiting room. They misguided, though. All the drugs come in through the cops in here. It'll change back in a minute. Fuck 'em. Other than that, how are you?"

"I'm good. Running on life's same treadmill as everybody else but ain't getting nowhere. Work is work, everybody in the family is good. I just need you to hurry up home."

"Shit gon' get better. We gon' be together soon. These last few years gon' fly by. You can hold everything together for a few more years, right?"

"Of course, I can. I just get lonely sometimes, that's all. I get my moments of weakness. Missing you like hell. But I'm good, though. My shit built for this, ride or die."

"That's what I'm talking about. That's my girl."

"Oh—before I forget, I was at RuthChris last night with Toya, Crissy and Josette. And guess who we saw?" Lisa was suddenly animated.

"Who?"

"Khadafi."

"Get the fuck outta here!"

"Bay, I'm serious, he's home. We was at the one on Alexandria eating and drinking when he walked in with a youngin' that looks just like him. It was him, I'm sure of it."

"Are you sure it was him?" I asked.

"I met him at your house when he came home in 2008. And how many times have I met him to get shit for you? It was him, Bay. Same walk, swag—all that shit. He got a little more muscular and he rocking a big beard."

"Damn, they really let him out. Although Ameen got acquitted, becoming a rat in the case freed Khadafi."

"You still beefing with him?"

"Beefing with him? That implies some sort of action. I feel nothing for Khadafi. When I talked to him in the cage at CTF and he crushed my heart, that was it. That dude doesn't exist to me. Morphing into a rat to get back at Marnie for fucking a nigga and wanting to kill PeeWee is—"

"Damn! That's crazy that you just said that. I never even made the connection."

"What connection?" I asked, befuddled.

"PeeWee's death. I never even—"

"Wait—PeeWee's death? PeeWee's dead?"

Lisa nodded her head. "Yeah. Him, his sister and three other people got killed at that car lot that PeeWee owns."

"That wasn't PeeWee's lot. It was Khadafi's. He let PeeWee run it. Damn, PeeWee's dead. Khadafi came home and killed PeeWee."

"Yep. Don't forget about his sister. Some girl named Jamya and the other three dudes. Shot them to death, then set their bodies on fire."

Shaking my head, I digested what Lisa had just told me. Khadafi was a vicious muthafucka.

"If it was Khadafi who did it," Lisa continued. "Why kill the other five people when all you beefing with is one person?"

"Because they were weaknesses—I mean witnesses. He couldn't leave them behind."

"*Witnesses?* So, why not wait until you catch PeeWee by himself? What was the urgency to kill him there?"

"That's just how Khadafi is. You gotta know him to understand him. It was his whole mission. He became a rat to get home, just to kill PeeWee and Marn—oh shit!"

"What? What's wrong?"

"Marnie, she's in grave danger. Oh-my-gawd—would he?" I rose from my seat. "Baby—I love you, but I gotta go—"

"You gotta go? Fuck you mean you gotta go?"

"I gotta warn Marnie. Let her know that Khadafi is out. He threatened her. He's gon' kill Marnie, Lisa. Just like he did PeeWee."

"How do you know that Marnie doesn't already know?"

"She might, but I'd doubt it. I gotta find out, warn her and—"

Lisa became irate. "I drove two and a half hours up here in these fuckin' mountains to see you and you wanna cut our visit short so you can go and call another bitch—"

"Another bitch? You better pipe your ass down, Lisa."

"Lake," the C.O. started. "Sit down."

I reluctantly sat back in my seat. "Baby, you gotta understand that Marnie is not some broad I used to fuck. That girl is like a daughter to me. She was best friends with Esha growing up. Her life is in danger, baby, and that's real. What have we been talking about? Khadafi and how ruthless he is, right? Well, he's worse than that. And if he said that he's gonna kill, Marnie, he means it. I gotta find out if she knows he's home. I gotta warn her. My warning might be the difference between her life and her death. How do we know Khadafi ain't sitting outside that girl's house, right now?"

"You said she moved to Virginia, right?"

"Not far enough. Khadafi traveled to New York to kill a muthafucka."

"Damn!"

"That's what I said. Marnie done got married and had a baby. She testified in court for Ameen, just like I did. To Khadafi, we betrayed him. If I was home, he'd be gunning for me, too."

"You think so?"

"I know so. I know him. At the end of the day, relationships, friendships, kinship, love, bonds—none of that means anything to Khadafi, if he thinks you've betrayed him. Damn near all the people he's killed was once his friend. The only reason that Marnie is still alive is because Khadafi hasn't found her yet. When he finds out about the baby that will seal her fate."

"But Marnie has his kids, too."

"Khadafi is a wicked, heartless, vindictive, dangerous muthafucka. He won't care. I gotta go and call Marnie. I can't sit here and enjoy our visit wondering if Marnie is alive or dead."

Finally, Lisa capitulated. "Fine, go and call her then. At least I did get to see you and get a hug and kiss. I'm coming back next weekend and I'm staying nearby so I can visit Saturday and Sunday."

"I'ma be looking forward to it."

"Make sure you call my phone after you talk to Marnie. Now I'm geeking to know if she's seen Khadafi or not. Promise me you'll give me all the tea."

Smiling, I stood up. "You nosey as shit but I got you. We gotta go and tell the cop you're leaving so I can get my kiss goodbye."

***

"No running on the compound!" the loudspeaker announced.

I knew that the C.O. in the tower was referring to me, so I stopped running and walked fast to my unit. Once the C.O. let me in, I beelined straight to the phones. Knowing Marnie's cell phone number by heart, I dialed quickly. The other end started ringing.

"Come on, Marnie. Answer the phone." My spirits tanked.

Then finally, she answered. "Hello? Bay?"

"Damn, it's good to hear your voice," I told Marnie.

"Bay, we talked a couple weeks ago."

"I was worried about you. Praying that you were okay."

"Why? Bay, what's wrong? Why wouldn't I be okay?"

"Because evidently you haven't heard the news. Khadafi is home."

There was a prolonged silence on the other end of the phone.

"Hello, Marnie?"

"I'm here, Bay. Are you sure that he's out? How do you know?"

"That tells me that you haven't been talking to nobody from around the way and you haven't been watching the news."

"And?"

"Lisa just left here. She saw Khadafi last night at RuthChris in Alexandria. Said he was with a young dude that looks just like him. Khadafi ain't got no grown kids, do he?"

"Not that I know of."

"She's sure it was him. Said he's more muscular and has a big beard now. And I mentioned the news because PeeWee has been all over it, Lisa said. She said that somebody killed PeeWee, his sister and three other people at the Imperial Auto Lot. Then they set the place on fire to cover up the murders. Lisa didn't know, but I know exactly who did that. You know, too."

"You right. Shit I forgot all about the three years he got out Maryland. And damn, it's been three years exactly. I can't believe I gotta deal with this crazy—"

"Khadafi fucked up in the head. Have you talked to him at all over the years?"

"Nope, not since I went to visit him at CTF and practically begged him not to tell on Ameen. When he refused to case up, I changed my number and told my mother to not accept any calls from him."

"Shit, Marnie. That man hasn't spoken to his kids in three and a half years?" I asked, shocked.

"Don't judge me, Bay. You acting like I never told you that before."

"Maybe you did, but I guess it didn't sound as bad when Khadafi was doing a bid. But now that death walks upon us with that same name, it sounds bad."

"I was going through a rack of shit mentally, the home invasion, Khadafi's infidelity, then his gangsta turned rat routine, it was a lot. Then on top of that Cree was fucking the shit out of me. I was weak. I wanted to hurt him. There was a lot of moving parts to why I decided to keep my kids from talking to him."

"Marnie, do you think he knows that you're married and have another child?"

"I don't see how he could."

"When he finds that shit out, that man is gonna see all red. You and Cree ain't no match for that crazy, red nigga. Y'all lives are in danger. Khadafi came straight home and killed PeeWee and four other people with him. It's only a matter of time before he shows up at your front door. Woodbridge Virginia ain't far enough to deter him. Marnie you know that like I know that. Do you remember when he went all the way to New York to kill—"

"I remember, Bay. T.J. and some Spanish bitch took him up there. He told Esha about it and T.J. told Reesie. They both told me. The New York dude is the one that penned Khadafi to the gate for Ameen to stab him. Khadafi couldn't get to the New York dude, so he went to New York and killed his brother."

"After he killed the dude's baby mother out Maryland at a restaurant. He never forgets a perceived slight and he always seeks revenge. You betrayed him Marnie. We betrayed him. He's not going to forgive us."

"Damn, Bay, I know you tryna warn me and all, but you are really not helping me, right now. Keep talking about what I've done to him and what he's gonna do. You think I don't know what I'm dealing with—wait, the baby's crying. I gotta go get her. I appreciate the call, the heads up. I gotta think about my next move. I love you, Bay. Call me back tomorrow, okay?"

"I will. I love you, too, Marnie. Take the family and get as far away from D.C. as y'all can. I don't want nothing to happen to y'all. Real talk. You gotta take this shit serious. Please take it serious!"

"I will, Bay. I gotta go. Bye!"

Click!

Slowly, I walked to my cell. I had been so angry at God for allowing T.J. to kill my daughter that I stopped praying. But under the circumstances, I decided it was time for me and the big guy upstairs to get reacquainted. I needed him to protect Marnie from Khadafi. Marnie and her husband. After putting the towel over the window on my cell door, I dropped to my knees and prayed.

Chapter Twenty-One

Marnie

What were the thoughts of a small child? Did they have dreams and nightmares? I looked down into the face of my thirteen-month-old daughter Creation and wondered. Her tiny fist closed around my pinky finger as I held her bottle of milk and rocked her back to sleep. I silently prayed that her world as an innocent child was better than mine. Bay One's call continued to rattle me. Knowing that my real life BoogeyMan was somewhere nearby scared the hell out of me. Khadafi was home and not even thirty miles away from me.

"Woodbridge, Virginia ain't far enough," Bay One had said.

She is absolutely right Woodbridge was a suburb out of Washington, D.C. that boasted history, million-dollar homes and neighborhoods thriving with Federal workers and politicians. That made the commute into D.C. every day. It was thirty minutes away by car. There was the Metro Subway rail that linked Woodbridge to D.C. no Woodbridge was not far enough at all.

"Somebody killed PeeWee, his sister and three other people at the Imperial Auto Lot. Then they set the place on fire to cover up the murders. Lisa didn't know, but I knew exactly who did that. You know, too."

After what he did to me by pointing that gun at me and invading my house to get Khadafi's drugs and money, I hated PeeWee. I never really liked him growing up in Capers, but I didn't wish such a tragic death on him. Bay One was right, I did know who had killed PeeWee and those other people. Without a doubt in my mind, I knew the culprit was Khadafi. He had promised to kill PeeWee and he had.

I shook my head and inhaled, then exhaled and repeated the exercise. I always knew that one day, Khadafi would get out of prison. I had heard all about his three-year sentence in the Maryland system. I knew the threat he presented, but back then I didn't care. I was too busy building a new life for myself and getting sexed wonderfully by Cree along the way didn't help.

"Y'all lives are in danger."

My life and my husband's life were definitely in danger. I agreed wholeheartedly. I thought about Cree Summers and tears welled up in my eyes. He was not only my husband and daughter's father Cree was my whole life. I love that man in a way that I have never loved another human being before. I remembered the days, I thought I loved Khadafi like that. I used to believe that I couldn't live without Khadafi in my life.

Cree changed all that. He showed me what love really was. In my three years and counting with Cree, I had been reborn. I was a brand-new woman. All Khadafi had done was take, take, take. All Cree did was give. He gave good advice, direction, love and affection, facials, foot rubs, massages, and the best head in the world. He'd also given me the beautiful, grey eyed little girl in my arms.

I walked back to her bed and laid my daughter down. I wiped at the tears in my eyes. I wondered what type of drama, trouble, and danger the future held for me—for us—for my family. I couldn't help but stare at the pictures in Creation's room. Pictures of her four-year-old brother Khamani holding her. Pictures of her seven-year-old, Ms. Grownie Pants sister Khadajah kissing her. Both mini replicas of their father.

Their father who is eventually going to come for me. Their father who is never going to accept that I have a different life that doesn't include him. Their father who surely wants to kill me. Then a thought crossed my mind as I paced the carpeted floor. It was a phone call I had received a few days ago but brushed it off. Rushing to my cell phone, I scrolled my call history until I found the number that I needed. I touched the number and pressed send.

"Hello, Marnie?"

"Rita, when we talked a few days ago, you said something about someone looking for me at Forestville Health, right?"

"Yeah, it was the reason why I called you. But I guess you were kinda busy."

"I'm sorry, Rita, but I was busy as hell that day. Listen, I just thought about it and I need you to describe the man that came by looking for me. Do you remember?"

"Of course, I do. Um—let me see—he was fine as shit. I remember that. Brown eyes, cinnamon complexion, low-cut taper waves spinning, taller than me—about five-ten or eleven, he looked like he was in good shape, freckles and a big ass, reddish brown beard with tattoos all over his arms."

Khadafi, I knew. "Do you remember what he said to you?"

"Not really, just asked if you still worked here. When I told him no, he asked did I know where you worked now. I told him no. He said y'all were friends and that he was at your wedding—"

"At my wedding, he said that?" I asked.

"Yeah, after I told him you left Forestville after you got married. He paused for a minute then said he was at the wedding."

"Okay, thank you, Rita. Let me go, I need to get the baby."

"Is everything, okay, Marnie? Did I say something wrong?"

Yes, you should have kept your fucking mouth closed, I thought. "No, girl, everything is good. I was just trying to figure out who it was. It's all good. Thanks for calling to tell me."

"No sweat, Marnie. Anytime, you be safe."

I dropped the cell phone from my hand. It was official, Khadafi was home and he was looking for me.

"Y'all lives are in danger."

My hand started shaking uncontrollably. It took me a while to compose myself, but I had to make the next call.

"Hello? Baby, what's up? Y'all okay?" my husband asked.

"No, I'm not okay, Cree. I need you to stop what you are doing and come home."

***

I moved my pacing to the living room. That's where I was when Cree walked into the front door twenty minutes later. The look on his face was one of concern.

"What's going on? Where's the baby? Is she okay?" Cree asked looking around.

"The baby's upstairs asleep. She's fine, it's nothing like that," I told him.

"So, what's the emergency? You know I do yoga and the gym on Saturdays."

"Mani and Dada's father is out of prison and he's looking for me."

"So, what's the big deal in that? Probably just wants to see his kids."

"Cree, it's not that simple," I explained. "When things between us started happening, I wasn't completely honest with you. I only told you that me and their father had broken up and that he was in prison. I never told you why he was in prison, why we broke up or who this man really is, what he really is. I should have told you—"

"Marnie, please get to the point. You weren't honest when we first met, I get that. But why did you summon me home like the Ebola virus is out front?"

"It's funny that you used that analogy because the man I'm trying to tell you about has probably killed as many people as the Ebola virus. You said get to the point, right? Here's the point. I just found out today that Khadafi is home. Must've come home in the last week or so. I'm not sure, but I'm sure he's home. He went to the nursing home in Forestville looking for me. You're right about one thing, he does want to see his kids. Have you ever noticed that he's never called—they've never communicated with him? No letters from jail, no pictures—nothing?"

"I thought that he didn't want to reach out to them. I thought—"

"No, Cree, that wasn't it. I changed numbers and addresses. I instructed my mother to not take his calls. I eliminated all avenues that led to his kids. I kept them from him, him from them. And now he's home and looking for me. Not them, me. He wants to kill me—"

134

"Kill you? Marnie, don't you think you're being a little melodramatic, right now? Come on, now. Being mad at you is one thing, wanting to kill you is another."

"Melodramatic, huh?" I said and smirked. "Let me make sure you understand something. Luther Fuller's nickname was Redds until he turned thirteen-years-old and started killing people. He killed with such skill and ruthlessness that his nickname changed to Dirty Redds. At sixteen-years-old he killed his friend in his father's barbershop while his father cut the dude's hair. He went to prison and did ten years. But he almost didn't make it out of prison.

You know why? Because he killed another inmate and dismembered his fucking corpse. He changed his name to Khadafi before coming home in two-thousand-eight. Our relationship started then, although we'd known one another as kids. He was in love with an old friend of mine named Kemie and I was his side chick. I knew I was his side chick, but I didn't care. I just wanted him, I thought I was in love with him. I ended up getting pregnant and had Dada in twenty-ten. The former friend that I just mentioned, the one that Khadafi loved, ended up getting killed in twenty-eleven.

I think that opened the door for him and I to become a couple. I moved into his house and we acted like a family. Shortly thereafter, I got pregnant with Khamani. Khadafi was a great father at home, I give him that, but in the streets, he was the Barbaric Plaque. Everywhere he went, he left dead bodies behind.

The police could never arrest him for the murders because he made sure to kill all witnesses. One day, a homicide detective confronted Khadafi at his aunt's house. Alone. They shot each, the cop died and Khadafi lived but went to jail for the shooting. That's when I met you. Do you remember the day we met? You saw the car I was driving and said—"

"Not many nurses drive a new model Mercedes Benz. I remember."

"Well, Khadafi made his friend PeeWee buy that car for me because he felt PeeWee had disrespected both of us. Now, I don't know if that was why PeeWee did what he did next or was it for other reasons, but he ambushed me outside my house one night.

Actually, it was the night of our first date. Two men ambushed me, at the time, I didn't know it was PeeWee but I knew it was someone that knew both me and Khadafi because of some things he said. They took me in the house at gunpoint and searched and took all Khadafi's money and drugs he had in the house. That's the night I ended up sleeping with you and that's why I moved out of the house in Tacoma Park.

When I told Khadafi what happened, he was livid. He figured out that one of the robbers was PeeWee. I was so traumatized that I told Khadafi about you and that I'd had sex with you. That pushed him off the deep end, mentally and physically. He threatened to kill me and PeeWee. I thought his words were just empty threats until he made his next move. Then I knew just how serious he was about getting out to kill PeeWee and me.

Khadafi hates weaknesses, homosexuals, and perverts, but what he absolutely despises is snitches. He loathes rats. The Omerta and the Death before Dishonor were the codes that governed his entire life. I knew that Khadafi was serious about his promise to kill when he did the unthinkable. He made a deal with prosecutors to snitch on one of his friends to get out of jail. Nobody thought that he'd actually go through with what he promised to do in his deal with the government in D.C., but he did.

He took the stand and ratted on his man another stone-cold killer named Ameen. Then to add insult to injury, I helped his friend beat the case. I got on the stand and said that Khadafi was lying on Ameen and why. Me and my homegirl, Bay One both helped Khadafi's friend. In his eyes, I betrayed him. I made the decision after that to discontinue the communication Khadafi had with his kids.

"Where was I when all this testifying in court happened?" Cree queried.

"Where else? At work. I never told you where I was going or what was going on. I kept all of that from you. Now, let me finish. While at Seven Locks, the detention center in Montgomery County, Khadafi beat a man damned near to death with the phone receiver. Maryland dropped all his charges pertaining to the cop that he'd shot but pressed on with the assault with the phone. Khadafi got sentenced to three years. He did the three years and now he's out. And like I said earlier, he wants to kill me."

"But Marnie, how can you be sure that that's what he wants?"

I walked over to the couch and sat down, suddenly exhausted. "I'm sure, Cree. I threw it in his face that I fucked you. I betrayed him, I abandoned him. And I cut him off from his kids. I got married to you and I have another child—I'm sure."

"I hear you, but still, can you be one-hundred percent sure that these are his intentions? How can you be that sure?"

"Because I just spent twenty-minutes giving you his background. That means I know him. He's vindictive and he's evil. He doesn't let shit go and besides he's fulfilled one half of his promise already."

"He what?"

"He killed PeeWee, Cree. PeeWee's dead. I told you I just found all this out today. Right before I called you. I googled his name, and the news clip came up. PeeWee's government name is James Smith. He ran a car lot for Khadafi—"

"Wait, I thought you said he robbed Khadafi?"

"He did."

"And that Khadafi knew it?"

"He does, but evidently he never told PeeWee he knows. On Monday, someone went to that car lot, killed PeeWee and four other people, and then set it on fire. The police don't know who did it, but I do. It was Khadafi."

"You can't be sure it could all be just coincidental."

"Cree, are you not listening to me or are you just being naïve and in denial? My current situation with you is gonna add fuel to the fire and Khadafi is gonna come here. It's only a matter of time."

"So, what exactly are you saying to me?"

"That I'm dealing with a narcissistic maniac who wants to kill me. My life is in danger and so is yours. We have to leave here. In the next few days for our family's safety."

"Have you lost your mind—gone insane?" Cree exploded.

"I'm not insane, Cree," I responded. "I'm a realist, you don't understand what we are up against."

"Can't we just involve the police and tell them what you just told me? About Khadafi killing PeeWee."

"No, Cree. We can't do that. We don't have no proof that Khadafi killed anyone. What am I gonna say? He told me three-years ago that he was gonna do it? That's not an option."

"Not an option and picking up and leaving to go God knows where in the next few days is? Just because your homicidal ex is out of prison. You are insane if you think I'm going for that. I'm not leaving my home and my job on a whim like that, Marnie. You are my wife. We have a family. Khadafi or whatever his name is just gonna have to understand that and get over it."

"Have I been talking to the wall for the past thirty minutes, Cree?"

"I can protect my family, Marnie. I can buy a gun. He doesn't know me. You have a different job. He doesn't know where we live. Your name hasn't been Curry in years. So, if he looks you up online, nothing new will come up. I think you're overreacting. I'm not ready to go to Def Con one over this guy getting out of prison. I'm not leaving my home, and neither are you. If you decide to not go to work that's your decision. I make enough money to take care of our family. But all that *let's leave now* talk is nonsense. End of story."

"*End of story?* Cree, you're not listening to me. You—"

"I am listening," Cree emphatically stated. "I'm just not hearing you the way you want me to hear you. I'm not afraid of this guy. I believe in a higher power."

"Babe, please don't start this higher power stuff. The higher power can't save you or me from that man. He's not going to go away. Not as long as I have his children and won't let him see them.

"Well, let him see them. I would probably feel the same way if you kept Creation away from me. Let him see his kids. Give them to your mother and—"

Dropping my head, I said, "It's not that simple, Cree. As long as I am happy with a man that's not him, he's gonna be upset. He wants the kids, but he's mad at me for what I did. If I wasn't with you, then I could probably—who knows. All I'm saying is, it's not just about the kids. You come from a different place, a different world. You have no clue—"

"So, now I'm clueless because I didn't grow up in the projects in Southeast, Washington, D.C.? Because I had both parents in my house and they didn't raise me to be a killer? I'm from a different world, is that a good thing or a bad thing in your eyes?"

"Come on, Cree, this is not a socioeconomic conversation. This is about a real sociopath. A man who cares nothing about two parent households, degrees, good jobs or how well you've raised his two kids in his absence. This man that I'm telling you about is the devil disguised as a Muslim. All he wants to do is kill, steal and destroy shit."

Cree picked up his gym bag and slung the strap over his shoulder. "And what does that say about you as a person, Marnie? You know his whole life story and still laid down and brought two children into the world with him."

"Cree, that's not fair!" I shouted, offended.

"Life's not always fair, but we still gotta play the hand we were dealt. I'm through talking about your ex. I'm going upstairs to kiss the baby. Then I'm going to work out. Later, I'll stop by your mom's house and pick-up Mani and Dada. Tomorrow, I'm going to buy a gun."

Cree turned and left the living room. He was making the situation into a pissing contest. His manly pride wouldn't allow him to be afraid. No matter what I said to him, nothing would get him to understand just how dangerous Khadafi is. There was nothing else I could say or do.

Anthony Fields

Chapter Twenty-Two

Khadafi

Bosco Davis looked sixteen but was actually thirty-eight-years old. His profession was guns and he'd had a helluva run selling them.

"Tell me exactly what you need, slim."

I pulled the two Ruger P. 89s off my hips. "I need to get rid of these two joints. And get some brand new shit."

"No problem. Hey, Tuff, come get these," Bosco called out to a dude standing by the fence. The dude came and got the guns. "I got new Rugers if that's what you prefer. If not, I got Tauruses, Sig Sauers, Glocks, XPSs, FNNs, and Smith and Wessons. Got 'em in all flavors. Revolvers, Autos, Semi-autos, whatever. I got nines, tens, forties, four fifths, three eighties and all them joints come in black, black and silver, chrome and camo. I got legs, dicks, and money nuts that hold thirty, fifty and a hundred. Got them big bamma joints, too. Keys, SKs, HKs, Dracos, Minis, Subs, Pistols, and all the trimmings."

"You got muffles or sound suppressors?" I asked.

"For certain joints, yeah. Everything don't come equipped to fit attachments. What you got in mind?"

"I need like three hand joints and that baby Draco I been hearing about. I need suppressors for the handguns. What you got that fit 'em?"

"Glocks. You need extendos, dick and balls?"

"Naw, that's all that young nigga who ain't tryna nothing shit. Shit too tip drawing. Ten to seventeen is enough for me. I don't waste shells."

"In the Glocks, you prefer nines, forties or four fifths?"

"All of 'em fitted for the suppressors?"

"Naw, just the nines and forties."

"Gimme the forties and boxes of hydra shocks for all of em."

"Hey, Rocko, come here!" Bosco called to a second man also standing by the fence. The dude named Rocko walked up. "Go get me three Glock forties, brand new. Get three of them *be quiet* attachments for them, too. Grab me one of them new baby Dracos and boxes of ammo for everything." Rocko left.

"What's the ticket for that?" I asked Bosco.

"Eighteen for all three Glocks. A stack for the Drake, five hundred for the ammo and we'll call it even for the suppressors since you gave me the two used Rugers. That cool with you?"

My answer was to pull out a wad of money and peel off thirty-three hundred dollars and pass it to Bosco. "Any news on that other thing I asked you about?"

"What thing, bruh? Remind me."

"The info on Jeezy and Kito. So, I can drop this bag off to their folks."

"I forgot, bruh. Real talk. But I'm on it, right now. I'll hit you when I get the info."

***

I didn't have info for Jeezy and Kito, but I did have info on Meechie and it didn't take me long to find him. I watched Meechie sell dope hand to hand on Half Street and shook my head.

"The cemetery got a gate around it, cuz. Because niggas is dying to get in. Look at Meechie over there. He don't have a clue that today is his last day on Earth. But he's about to learn today." I spent the cylinder suppressor onto the Glock .40 and reached for the door handle.

"Wait, big cuz," Lil' Quette said suddenly. "Hold on for a minute. You been gone for a few years. Shit done changed since you left. You can't just be hopping out and crushing shit no more. Not in broad daylight without no mask or nothing. Look up at the sign over the corner store. See that camera right there?"

I looked where Lil' Quette directed my attention. "I see it, cuz. I see it."

"There's one on the building across from the corner store. One mounted to that lamp post right there on O Street, there's cameras everywhere."

Seeing all the cameras, Lil' Quette pointed out, I whistled. "Damn, it's a rack of them joints out here."

"And they got that shotspotter technology, too. Once you fire a gun—"

"The police know exactly where the gun was fired from. I'm hip to that. So, I came prepared," I said tapping the sound suppressor. "Here, take this." I grabbed one of the Glocks and gave it to Lil' Quette. "That's yours. You ever bust a gun before?"

Lil Quette popped the clip out of his gun and slammed it back in. Then he cocked it back to put one in the chamber. "In the air, but yeah, I did. A few times, never had my own joint, though."

"Cool," I said, only half listening to Lil' Quette. My focus was back on Meechie. I had waited almost four years to get back at the man who had violated Marnie, my home and me. One man was already dispatched to the next life. There was one more to go. I unwrapped the Keffiyeh around my neck and tied it around my face. It covered my nose all the way down. I grabbed a baseball cap out of the backseat. "I gotta get him, lil cuz. Watch my work. I'll be right back." I hopped out of the truck.

I was in great shape, so covering the distance between me and Meechie was nothing at full speed. By the time, he looked up and saw me coming, it was too late.

Pfft! Pfft! Pfft! Pfft! Pfft! Pfft! Pfft!

***

"I'ma go and get rid of this truck, lil cuz," I told Lil' Quette as I pulled in front of his house. "I appreciate you riding shotgun with me. I'ma call you later. One! Be safe."

"You might've just started world war three, big cuz."

I laughed. "I like war, cuz."

"You wild as shit but you be safe, too. Hit me," Lil Quette said and left the truck.

***

I decided to lay in all day Sunday just to relax. I had basically accomplished a lot of my goals in the one week, I'd been home. Both of the dudes that robbed my house were dead. There were several other people that I planned to kill but they could all wait. Since I was in the house, having dinner with my Aunt Mary was mandatory. She cooked fried turkey chops, home fried potatoes, garlic buttered bread, corn on the cob and green beans with smoked turkey in them. I was at the table smashing shit when Aunt Mary started with the questions. Just like I knew she would.

"Have you talked to that girl and seen them babies, yet?"

I forked food into my mouth and shook my head.

"That's a gotdamn shame, Luther. How in the hell you gon' have three children and don't ever get to see any of them? I don't get to see them."

"What you want me to do, Auntie? Their mothers ain't messing with me. I been in jail. They both got married and moved on with their lives. I don't even have contact info for either one of them."

"The girl, Monica, that used to live with you got married, too?"

I nodded. "Yeah, I just found that out a few days ago."

"Dayum!" Aunt Mary replied and stopped eating her food. "You gotta change your life, baby. I done heard all the things people say about you. I read all the articles the newspaper publishes about you. I don't be attending none of them trials you be in, but I hear about what be going on. Killing people and whatnot. I'm aware of your lifestyle, I just don't ever say anything.

I mind my business and let you make your own decisions, good or bad. But now, I feel like I gotta say something, gotta try to reach you. Talk some sense into you. You are thirty-seven-years old and still a rolling stone. Wherever you lay your hat is home. How long are you gonna continue to live like that, huh? Do you even want to change? Live a more stable, normal life. Like a normal person?

A life that doesn't include guns, drugs, fast money and loose women? You ain't tired of that shit yet? Going back and forth to prison, getting stabbed and shot every other year? Fighting for your life each time? When is enough gonna be enough for you? Right before you face your maker? You are financially well off, the money from your house is in the bank acquiring interest. You'll get insurance money from the car lot. You're a wealthy man, you can be anything you wanna be, legally. Ain't no excuses for you now. And what the hell was PeeWee into to make somebody kill him and all them other people at that lot like that?"

I drank the last of the fruit juice in my cup before speaking. "Aunt Mary, you've been in my corner my entire life and I appreciate everything you've done for me. There's no one in this world that I love more than you. And I hear everything you're tryna say to me, I do. Let me answer your questions. I'll start at the bottom and work my way up. I have no clue what was up with PeeWee and why someone would do that to him and all those other people. But what I do know is just like everything else, the cops are going to eventually blame me first. Just like they do everything else my name comes up in. The Metropolitan Police Department ain't gon never forgive me for that detective dying—"

"But you didn't kill him. A viral infection did."

"They don't care, they still blame me. So, they're gonna blame all kinds of stuff on me. You can't believe any of it or any of the stuff you read and heard in the past. I went to that lot and got money and that truck from PeeWee and left. That's it, as for me changing my life, being financially stable and all that, you're right. I promise you I'ma change, Auntie. I'm just figuring things out, right now.

I only been home seven days, give me a minute to figure things out. And I hope to find a good woman one day, settle down and have more kids. As for the ones I have now, I love my kids and it hurts me every day that I haven't seen them and can't be the father to them that I wanna be. In time, hopefully the situations will change and both of us will be able to spend time with them. I'm tryna get everything on track. That's all I can tell you and you gotta believe me when I say that I'm tryna do better. No more jail, beefs, none of that stuff. I'm tryin, Auntie."

"Then I guess that's gonna have to be enough," Aunt Mary answered. "You got a lot on your plate, but I believe you can get it together. I'm rooting for you, boy. God knows, I am. I love you so much. You know that, right?"

"Of course, I do. And since I'm your favorite nephew who's tryna change his life, I need a favor."

"What do you need?"

"The truck that I got from PeeWee broke down already and I ain't tryna keep wrestling with no used cars. I wanna get something new off the showroom floor. I need you to put the car in your name."

Aunt Mary got up and grabbed both of our empty plates. "I can do that. When do you wanna go and get one?"

"Tomorrow, when you get off work."

"Done."

***

I was in my room doing push-ups when my cell phone vibrated. It was Erykah.

"Hey, sexy. What's up with you?" I cooed into the phone.

"Don't' hey, sexy me, Khadafi. Why the fuck did you do that shit?"

The pictures had landed in USP McCreary, I smiled to myself. "What I do?"

"Don't play, nigga. You know what the fuck you did. You sent Mousey pictures of me and you in my bed. Pictures of me, pictures of my place. You holding his fuckin' picture. And a muthafuckin' picture of me with cum on my face. Really though? After I stuck by you and—"

At first, I thought the shit was funny, but then the switch in my head flipped and I got upset. "Cuz, don't ever in your life think you can call me and question me with venom in your voice. Who the fuck do you think you talkin' to like that? One of them suckas you been fucking with? Calm your ass down and remember who's on the other end of this phone. Yeah, I sent Mousey the pictures.

I was fucked up about what you told me he said. I took two pics while you were sleep. I wasn't trying to hurt you. I wanted to hurt him, in hindsight, I knew it was wrong. I shouldn't have done that to you. But when you told me that he wished death on me, that fucked me up. I'm an impulsive nigga, E. It was either that or I was gon' go and kill his mother. Which one would you have preferred I'd done?"

"He told me that you threatened to kill his mother, his sister—"

"And I will. He knows it and you know it. Running his mouth—look, E, I appreciate you being there for me the last few years and I fucks with you the long way. I didn't mean to hurt you. Sending the pictures was a bad idea, but I'm glad he knows about us. Fuck him. I thought you said he's just a voice on the phone? Why are you so bent out of shape?"

"Yeah, I said that he's become like a voice on the phone, but I never said that I didn't love him anymore. Mousey is my first everything. I'm bent out of shape because I didn't want him to find out about me like that. He didn't deserve that shit."

"Aye, E, please don't sit here on this phone and preach to me about what Mousey don't deserve. I took care of that man like he was my blood brother for years and as soon as—" The connection broke.

Erykah had hung up on me, I couldn't do nothing but laugh. I thought about calling her back. I thought about catching an Uber to her house. Then another thought hit me. Thinking about the pics that I'd sent Mousey aroused me. I went through my phone's contact list, found the number I wanted and pressed send.

After a few rings, a female voice answered, "Hello?"

"Did I catch you at a bad time?"

"Um—naw, I just had to figure out whose number this was."

"Did you figure it out?" I asked.

"I did figure it out, yeah."

"You busy?"

"Naw. Why? What's up?"

"I wanna see you, need to see you."

"Is that right?"

"Yeah, that's right. I've been thinking about you for days," I lied.

"That's what's up. I'm texting you my address, pull up."

"I can't pull up, I had to put my truck in the shop. You pull up."

"Text me your address and I'll be right there."

***

"Damn, Rita. This pussy good as shit. Tight as hell."

Sherita 'Rita' Simms, the Muppet baby with the bangin' body was up on all fours on her bed, looking back at me over her shoulder.

"I ain't been fuckin' nobody, but I had to give your fine ass this pussy. Fuck me, baby! Fuck me!"

I did what she asked, I fucked her.

Chapter Twenty-Three

Ann Sloan

"Today, we're here for a suppression hearing, correct?" Judge Allen Dampier asked. "For Mr. Roman Jones?"

"That's correct, your honor. Ari Weinstein on behalf of the government."

Rudolph Sabino stood slowly. "Rudolph Sabino, your honor, behalf of the defendant, Roman Jones, who is present."

"Okay, let's get started. Let the record reflect that everyone of interest in the matter of the United States Versus Roman Jones is present. Counselor Weinstein, why don't we start with you."

"Thank you, your honor. The defendant has been charged in a two-count indictment with unlawful possession of a firearm by a convicted felon and possession of one kilogram of cocaine hydrochloride. The defendant seeks to suppress the evidence that was obtained from a vehicle he was operating on March fifth, twenty-seventeen. According to the defense's motion, the investigation stop by D.C. Police Officers was non consensual and supported by any reasonable, articulable suspicion, unlawful violations, traffic or otherwise or by probable cause. The government disagrees.

Law enforcement officers do not violate the fourth amendment by merely approaching an individual on the street or in a public space by asking if he or she is willing to answer questions voluntarily. The crucial test for determining whether police conduct crosses the threshold from a consensual police-citizen encounter to a seizure or forcible stop is whether, taking into account all of the circumstances surrounding the encounter. The police conduct would have communicated to a reasonable person that he was not at liberty to ignore the police presence and go about his business. This court's analysis should take into account all the objective circumstances of the encounter—"

I sat in the gallery and listened to Ari present the government's case to the judge, but my focus was on the defense attorney,

Rudolph Sabino. The elegantly dressed, intelligent, black defense attorney had beaten me in every case I tried against him. Three cases total and that fact irritated me to no end. When Ari Weinstein informed me that this suppression hearing was coming up, I stepped in and prepared the government's arguments personally. I needed to beat Rudy Sabino at something, even if it was a lowly suppression issue. Roman Levar Jones was one of the major players in the cocaine trafficking business in the Nation's Capital. He was a smart son of a bitch but an error on his past had given the government a good chance to take him off the streets.

"Defense Counsel Sabino, it's your turn," Judge Dampier announced.

"Thank you, your honor," Rudy Sabino stood and said, "The evidence in this matter was adduced from MPD Officer Calvin Roberts, but I'll get back to our esteemed Officer Roberts momentarily. Roman Jones and another man, Jordan Lucas were sitting in a new modeled Porsche Panamera parked in the area of the one-hundred block of Yuma Street in Southeast. Mr. Lucas was in the driver's seat and the defendant was in the passenger seat. It was seven p.m. and dark outside. Officer Roberts—"

***

Judge Dampier called a short recess to go over both sides of the suppression issue. I called Ari Weinstein out into the hallway.

"How did I do?" Ari asked me.

"You did great. Argued it just like we planned."

"Good, hopefully, Judge Dampier—"

"Ari, I called you out here about another matter. Do you remember, Luther Fuller?"

"Luther 'Khadafi' Fuller? Of course, how could I ever forget him?"

"My sentiments exactly. Listen, he's out and some officers at MPD believe that he might be back in the killing game. At the moment, it's all just assumptions, but if it's not, I need to find a way to toss out that deal we made with him and possibly put him back in jail. Charge him with something that he's already admitted to. Something! You are the brightest mind we have at Triple Nickel. I need you to look into it for me. Help me put Khadafi's ass back in prison and for a long time and I promise you you'll sit in my chair when I'm done."

"I'm on it, Ann, as soon as I leave here today."

"Good, let's get back inside and see what Judge Dampier decides."

***

One-Hour Later

Busboy & Peets Restaurant

"You look like somebody has pissed you off, Counselor," Corey Winslow said as I approached his table.

"That fucking, Rudolph Sabino beat us again." I sat and pouted. "I swear that man has a golden horseshoe stuck in his ass."

"He beat you in trial?"

"No, on a motion hearing to suppress evidence. I know there was a little wiggle room for the defense to get in, but I figured that the staunchly pro-government, conservative, Republican Allen Dampier would overlook a few deficiencies in our case and rule in our favor. I crafted the motion myself, worked all day yesterday and half the night on it. I thought it was pretty strong. I guess I was wrong. But what I hate most is the little self-righteous, smug smile Sabino gives me every time he beats me in court. I'd like to wipe that smile right off his fucking face."

Corey picked up his drink and sipped it. "The Antonio Felder case is still a thorn in your side?"

Ignoring Corey's question, I said, "Why detective, is that alcohol you're drinking at one-fifteen p.m., while you're still on duty?"

"It is alcohol and it's really good. You can always complain to my supervisor or file a report, ma'am."

"What is it?"

"A watermelon Mojito."

"Sounds delicious, order me one," I told Corey and pulled out my phone. I had several missed calls from family members, my office and two from my husband. Corey ordered my drink and it arrived at the table minutes later. I sipped it. "Wow, that is delicious."

"Not as delicious as you."

"Can we get through a meal, please detective, without you trying to get me wet?"

"I'm sorry, just trying to get my mind off of what I told you about the other day."

"Khadafi?"

Corey nodded. "Over the weekend another body turned up. On Half Street in Southwest. A guy named Clifton Brown, also known as Meechie got himself killed. He was shot seven times in the head and face. A couple detectives in the unit know Meechie well. Turns out that Meechie and one of the victims of the car lot murders, James 'PeeWee' Smith, were buddies. And before you ask, no, I don't have anything to prove my hunch, but I think this last murder was Khadafi's work, too."

"Corey, we can't suspect Khadafi of every murder that happens since he's been home. You do that and you lose sight of other possible suspects."

"I agree, but Ann, Monica Curry said that two men ambushed her at her home and robbed it. PeeWee was one of them, I think Meechie was the second person. Given PeeWee and Meechie's history of committing crimes together. I think Khadafi figured that out and meted out his personal brand of justice. All head and face shots is his MO."

"Still a stretch, I need something more concrete to help you," I said. "Besides the man has been in prison for the last three years. What if Khadafi has had a change of heart? A religious conversion? Maybe he found Christ—"

"I never knew he was missing—but on a serious note, I'd doubt it. He's a Muslim, hence the name Khadafi."

"Well, Allah, then. Or whatever he might worship. These murders can be committed by someone other than Khadafi."

"I know, I know, but let's not forget that we're talking about a man who wasn't home for one hour in two-thousand eight before he killed a woman and her three-year-old daughter all because he suspected her son of being a rat. Him coming home and getting right back to killing is not a far-fetched idea."

"Has anyone tracked him down yet?"

Corey finished his drink. "Not yet, he could be anywhere. About to do anything."

"I got someone in my office looking at that plea agreement I made with Khadafi. I'm trying to find a way to lock his ass back up, but until then, all we can do is wait. Wait until he slips up and gets caught with a gun or doing something like committing a murder. We can't violate his constitutional rights, a federal judge reminded us of that in court today."

"Understood," Corey acquiesced. "Can I see you later."

"I wish. I gotta go home and spend time with Sol. He's been acting a little strange lately. Neglected. I've been working really hard and not paying him much attention. He might be sexually frustrated."

Corey laughed. "You're not giving him any?"

"You're sort of a hard act to follow, detective."

"Ann, you gotta—wait, you said he's acting strange? Think he's onto us?"

I thought about my husband for a minute. Solomon Sloan was docile. An academic mind, a doctor, a researcher. "I doubt it, he's a GW—at the hospital or University so much, I doubt it if he even— I don't know. He never really talks to me about us. It's just that when he's home, when we're alone—he's different now. Maybe I'm overthinking it. He took the day off today, maybe I'll surprise him, put on something sexy and rock his world. That's sure to make him happy."

"Lucky him, that sure would make me happy."

"I bet it would. Has anyone ever told you, you look like Omar Hardwick?"

"Let's get out of here. You feel like showing me Anacostia Park, again?"

"Sure, it's beautiful this time for year."

Chapter Twenty-Four

Lil Quette

"Twenty, one hit coming out," Gunplay called out.

"Bet, I got you," Delow said.

"Anybody else?"

"I got a hundred, you lose," Big Pat challenged.

"Bet." Gunplay rolled the dice. An eight came up, he picked up the hundred at Big Pat's feet. "Bet back, Big Pat?"

"Bet back."

"Delow, bet another twenty, one eight."

"Bet."

"What's up, Quette? You with me on the eight or against me?"

"I'm with you," I told Gunplay.

"Bet a hundred he lose," Big Pat said. "Since you with him."

I pulled out some money and dropped two-hundred-dollar bills on the ground. "Bet a hundred he hit the eight and a hundred he hit six eight."

"Bet it." Big Pat dropped his money.'

"Let me get some of that," Juvey said and dropped two hundred.

"Me, too," Willbo added and dropped his money. "Gunplay's janky ass ain't gon' back no numbers."

Gunplay got on his knees and shook the dice, then threw them out. He rolled a six, four times before the eight came.

"Fuck y'all niggas talkin' bout. Gimme my fuckin' money," Gunplay said as he collected his money.

I picked up all the money on the ground except the pile under Big Pat's foot. His Timberland boot was on top of the money. "Move your foot, Big Pat."

"I ain't moving shit," Big Pat fumed. "I don't like the way Gunplay swirl the dice when he rolls. Bet's no good."

"Let me get my money, Big Boy," I said.

"You heard what I said, little nigga. Bet's no good."

In a flash, I whipped out my Glock that Khadafi had given me. "Ain't nobody gon' take nothing from me."

"You know how to use that, Lil' Quette?" Big Pat asked.

I upped the gun and pointed it right at Big Pat's head. "If you don't get your foot off my money, I'ma show you. Your brains gon' be all over the sidewalk behind you."

Big Pat's foot rose off the pile of money.

"That's right, Quette," Gunplay said. "Fuck that nigga playing with?"

Juvey and Delow whipped out guns. "Y'all old head niggas think this sweet with us youngins, huh?" Juvey said.

"Big Pat, you better get the fuck on before your shit be on a candlelight vigil out here," Willbo added.

I reached down and picked the money up off the ground. Big Pat turned and walked away.

"I don't know what the fuck done got into you, Lil' Quette, but I love it," Gunplay said breaking the tension and everybody laughed.

"Ain't nobody taking nothing from me," Juvey mocked.

"Young nigga sounded sweet when he told that nigga, *your brains gon' be all over the sidewalk behind you,*" Willbo teased.

"Fuck Big Pat's bluffin' ass. Fuck he think he Debo or something?" Delow said. "If he ain't like Gun's roll. Why he ain't try that shit with him?"

"Because—" Gunplay beamed. "All the old heads around here know that I ain't having none of that shit. They know what I'ma do. I'ma fuck they asses around. Big Pat know not to play with me."

"Aye, LQ?" a voice called out from behind us.

There was only one person in the hood that called me LQ. I turned to face him. "What's up, Cee?" I said and tucked my gun back in my waist.

"I know this nigga ain't about to say nothing to niggas about, Big Pat?" Gunplay said. "Cause his ass can get it, too."

I walked away from my crowd of friends and met Carlton in the street. "What's up, big homie?"

"Ain't shit, youngin. How you?"

"I'm good considering," Carlton said.

"I can dig it. I'm sorry about Meechie, slim."

"Yeah, me too. What you know about that shit, LQ?"

I feigned ignorance. "Me? I don't know nothing about what happened. How would I?"

Carlton was almost twenty-years older than me, but he was younger than Meechie. He was well-known and respected in our hood for putting in work and getting to the bag.

"Muthafuckas telling me that you been riding around in a black Infiniti truck like the one that pulled up on my brother. Is that true?"

"My cousin got a Nissan Armada. Them joints look just like the Infiniti truck."

"Your cousin?"

"Yeah, my cousin Gary. He from Rock Creek Road, uptown."

"A'ight, Lil Homie. I'm just checking with you because of the whispers."

"As you should, but don't pay no attention to these niggas out here talking like broads."

"I feel that, but make sure you spread the word for me, lil homie. If I find out anybody from this hood backdoored my brother and lined him up for what happened to him, I'm killing mothers and grandmothers. You got that?"

"I got that, big homie, loud and clear."

"Good. Now what the fuck Big Pat talking 'bout all the youngins just whipped out guns on him?"

"He tried to take my money at the crap game. And I ain't going like that. Me or none of my men. Big Pat needs to recognize that."

"You 'bout that life now, youngin, huh?" Carlton asked.

"Been 'bout it, homie. Niggas just didn't know it until now."

Carlton eyed me with a look that I couldn't decipher. "I can dig it, catch you later, youngin. You be safe out here."

"You do the same," I said to Carlton's back as he walked away.

***

Shakira walked around her room straightening up and knocking into things, huffing, and puffing.

"Sha, what the fuck is up with you?" I asked her.

"Ain't nothing up with me, I'm good," she replied.

"I can't tell you good. You acting all moody and shit with tears in your eyes. I know you ain't crying about Meechie?"

"Crying about Meechie? Fuck I'ma be crying about Meechie for? That's my girl's father but I barely knew him. You sound stupid. Gon' ask me some stupid ass shit like that."

"Sha," I said and sat on the bed. "You throwing me off."

"I'm throwing you off, huh? You really wanna know what's up with me?"

"I wouldn't be asking you if I didn't."

"I'm pregnant, Quette. That's what's up with me. I'm pregnant!"

"Get the fuck outta here with that shit," I told Shakira.

"Fuck you mean, *get the fuck outta here with that?* How am I supposed to do that?"

I looked at Shakira and noticed that she was crying. She was serious. "Damn, Sha, I thought you were playing. What are you gonna do about it?"

Shakira walked over and sat beside me on the bed. "I don't know, yet. I'm only seventeen, my mother is gonna kill me."

"No, she ain't, Sha. It ain't she don't know we fucking. And that's how babies get here." I hugged Shakira and wiped her eyes. "Whatever you decide, I'm with you."

"I'm not ready to be nobody's mother, Quette," Shakira said with her head laid on my shoulder.

"Neither am I. I ain't ready to be nobody's mother either," I joked.

"Stop playing, Quette. This shit is serious. I haven't had a period in two months."

"Make an appointment with your doctor and we'll go together."

"I already did, we go tomorrow."

***

"Ms. Simms, Doctor Littlejohn wants you to give a urine sample," the nurse said to Shakira and handed her a cup.

Shakira got up and went to the bathroom. Minutes later, she returned with the urine sample in a plastic bag and handed it to the nurse. Thirty minutes later, the doctor called Shakira into an observation room. I played video games on my phone until she returned.

"It's official, I'm pregnant, ten weeks."

Chapter Twenty-Five

Khadafi

"—he used to call me from the joint until he ran out of change/ when he called collect and I heard his name/ I quickly accepted/ but when I reached the phone/ he's talking reckless/I can sense deceit in his tone/I said, damn dog, nine weeks and you home/ he said main man, you think shit sweet cause you're home/I just sat/spat no more speech through the phone/ them crackas up there bleaching your dome/ you reaching—"

"Aye, lil cuz, turn that music down for me," I told Lil' Quette.

Lil Quette looked all over the middle console for a volume button. "How the fuck you do that? I don't see no volume button or nothing."

"Oh, my bad, cuz. That shit is voice activated. I forgot, turn the music down a little."

The music volume lowered.

"Oh, yeah, big boy," Lil' Quette said and smiled. "You gon' shine on me like that?"

"Never that, I forgot that this big, bad muthafuckin' S550 ain't got no buttons. Everything in here is controlled by voice or remote. What I'ma shine on you for?"

"Yeah, right, but it's cool, though. I'ma get my weight up."

"I'ma see to it that you do," I told him.

"What you do with the truck?"

"Got rid of it like I said I was gon' do."

Lil Quette reclined his seat and stared straight ahead, preoccupied almost. "So, what do you think I should do?"

"Do about what?" I asked.

"About Shakira being pregnant?"

"You ready to be a father, lil cuz? You 'bout that diaper life?"

"If she decides to have the baby, I'ma have to be. Ain't got no choice."

"You always got choices, cuz, remember that."

"Sayless. What about the other shit I told you about?"

"Which one you talking about, Big Pat or Carlton?"

"Both."

"What did Meechie's brother say to you, again?"

"Told me that niggas told him they seen me in an Infiniti truck just like the one that dude was in that killed his brother," Lil Quette explained.

"And what did you tell him?"

"That the truck was a Nissan Armada, not an Infiniti, but they look alike. I told him the Nissan truck belonged to my cousin from Uptown. Then he said that shit about if he finds out anybody from the hood lined his brother up, he gon' kill them and their mothers and grandmothers."

"Did you feel disrespected?"

"Yeah, I did, I ain't gon' lie."

An alert on my phone got my attention, it was a video text. I opened the phone and viewed the video mail. It was from Sherita the Muppet baby. She was in the shower and she'd soaped up her body, then stopped to play with herself. *"Wish you were here,"* she said in the video and then it ended.

"And you asking me what you should do?"

"Yeah."

"You sure you wanna ask me? You ain't gon' like what I say."

"Let me be the judge of that," Lil' Quette replied.

I watched Sherita's video again. "I think you should kill them both."

"Kill them for what?"

"The dude Big Pat for even playing with you like that and Carlton because somebody pointed him in your direction. He's gonna be like a pit bull who smells blood. If he gets it in his head that you were with it, and I think he already does, he might decide to kill you just to temporarily sate his appetite for revenge. I heard that Slim will bust his gun and if not him, his man Cutty gon' do it for him. So, if you ask me and you did, I say launch a preemptive strike and kill him, I would."

Lil Quette closed his eyes as if he were asleep for several minutes. I sent Sherita a text responding to her video and then put the phone down.

"Why are we sitting right here? You about to visit somebody in that jail?"

I refocused my attention to the parking lot adjacent to the Seven Locks Detention Center. The staff parking lot, I looked at my watch. A few minutes before four p.m. "I'm looking for somebody, cuz. Wanna see if he still works here. I'm hoping that not only does he still work here, that he also still works the same shift. The four to twelve shift."

"You looking for one of the C.O.s?"

I nodded my head.

"You gon' kill him or her?"

"Him?" Again, I nodded.

"What did he do to you?" Lil' Quette asked.

"Slammed me on the ground and fucked up my shoulder."

"And why did he do that?"

"Because I told him to suck my dick."

"You're a savage, Fuller. A real sociopath," Quebecky said. "You beat that guy like that because he wanted to use the phone. That's a crying shame. If that poor guy dies, I hope they give you the needle. And what's crazy is—heck, I don't even know you and I hate you. You shot that fuckin' cop and it looks like you're gonna get off on that. God bless that guy's family. The big man upstairs doesn't like ugly and everything about you is ugly. Ugly and rotten to the core. I can smell it. Them Baltimore boys don't like you D.C. boys. So, when you get to the UltraMax or WCI, they probably gon' kill you anyway. At least that's what I hope happens. Come on, Fuller," Quebecky said as he unlocked the chain that secured me to the bench I was sitting on. "To the hole you go and please, please make my day by giving me a reason to slam your ass to the ground and stomp it. Please make my day."

"Fuck you, cracka," I told him. "You can suck my dick."

"Cuz, you wild as shit," Lil Quette said and laughed.

"I guess I made his day because that big cracka and his team fucked me up. The other C.O.s did some slight shit, but this cracka did the most. I promised myself that if I ever made it home, I was gonna kill Quebecky. And I'm—wait, is that—there he go, right there, Cuz."

Lil' Quette moved closer to the window. "Where, where he at? Which one?"

The big, white boy that just got out of that bamma ass pick up truck. See him?"

"Yeah, I see him. That nigga looks like one of them wrestlers."

"When I finish with his ass, he gon' look dead."

***

I dropped Lil Quette off to his car and drove back to Seven Locks. I ate Chick-Fil-A in the Benz and talked to Sherita. I tried to call Erykah but she wasn't answering my calls. At some point, I dozed off, when my eyes opened next it was fifteen minutes to twelve. As soon as I spotted Quebecky exiting the detention center, I pulled out of the visitors parking lot and parked on the main street. Minutes later, I was behind Quebecky's truck. Tailing the big ass GMC pick up was easy, I made sure to stay a good distance behind him to not arouse his suspicions.

When the scenery turned a little more rural, I closed the gap between us. He took the exit for Elmhurst Avenue and so did I. He drove about fifteen minutes on Elmhurst until he reached Elmhurst Way. I watched the pick-up turn onto a gravel driveway and descend to a house tucked away and surrounded by woods. A silver, old fashioned mailbox set near the entrance to the gravel driveway. The metallic numbers read 2103 Elmhurst Way. From the street, I could see Quebecky entering the house.

"I got your ass, cracka," I muttered and made a U-turn.

Twenty minutes later, I was parking outside of Sherita's apartment building.

"I'm outside," I called and told her.

"Come on in, the door is unlocked," she replied.

My dick got rock hard just thinking about fucking her funny looking ass.

***

The Next Morning

"Alex, it's been a long time," I said as I walked into the office at Prestige Motors in Greenbelt.

The Middle Eastern owner of the car lot looked older, but still the same. "Khadafi! My man, it's good to see you again, ock," Alex replied.

Alex extended his hand, and I shook it. "I need you, ock."

Glancing over my shoulder through the glass window, he spied the Mercedes. "Is that your S550 outside with the paper tags?"

"It's mine but I didn't cop it, my people did. But look, I'am come back and fuck with you. You know how much I love SUVs. Right now, I just need something off your small lot, the used section."

"Anything for you, my man. What do you need?"

"I need one of them cargo work vans. Like that Chevy Express Cargo van at the end of the line over there, the black one."

Alex's eyes found the van I spoke of. "No problem, I got like five grand in the van. I can do seventy-five."

I pulled out a wad of big faces. Alex's eyes settled on the cash. "I spent hundreds of thousand of dollars with you, Alex. And like I said, I'ma come back in a minute and spend probably another hundred grand on a few whips. Remember how I did with the Rovers? Copped one for me and one for my girl. I been in prison for the last three years. Just got out a week ago. I got a new girl now and she'll go crazy over that 650 Convertible BMW you got over there."

"That's a nice car, my man. For you, good price."

"I'm sure it is and I'm sure you will, but right now, I need the van and I ain't about to pay no seventy-five."

"You win, Khadafi, my man. Give me the five racks it got in it and it's yours." I peeled off five grand from my bank roll and passed it to Alex.

"Whose name do you want the paperwork in?"

"Sean Taylor, the best safety to ever play the game of football."

***

Lil' Quette drove the van to the window tinting spot. While the van's windows were getting tinted, I looked over at Lil' Quette and said, "The maturation of Marquette Jenkins is about to begin."

"The matur—what?" Lil' Quette asked confused.

I laughed. "Your little goofy ass should've stayed in school," I said. "Maturation it's the action word for mature, means to grow up."

"Is that right? Maturation, huh?"

"Yeah, it's gon' be a beautiful thing."

"I'm ready," Lil' Quette informed me.

"We gon' see. When they finish with the van, I got a few items I need to pick up. What size overalls you need?"

Chapter Twenty-Six

Khadafi

Opening the screen door, I knocked on the house door. 2103 Elmherst was a beige brick, story home with dark brown shutters and a brown door.

A middle aged, white woman with blonde hair and workout clothes opened the door. She reminded me for Pamela Anderson Lee. "Can I help you?"

"Yes, ma'am, I'm Clark Construction. We're working nearby on Pinehurst Avenue and we experienced a water main crack. The pipeline comes directly to all the homes on Elmhurst Way, so we're checking to see—well ensure that none of the homes are experiencing water distribution disruption."

Looking at her watch, Blondie said, "At this hour? It's after six in the evening."

"If your home's water supply is being disrupted, we'd like to fix it before it gets any worse. There may be no disruption, it'll just take a minute to check the water gauges in and outside your home. Then we'll be on our way."

"Well, I guess an ounce of prevention—come on in."

As soon as I was inside the house, I pulled the gun and smacked Blondie in the back of the head. She dropped to the floor like a sack of potatoes, holding her head.

"Gullible bitch," I muttered.

Blondie turned over and looked up at me with a terrified look on her face. "Why?"

"How many people are in this house, right now?" I asked her. "Lie and they all die. How many?"

"J-j-just three of us, my mom who's sick and my son. A special needs kid, please—please don't hurt us!"

"Who are you to Quebecky?" I asked her.

"Which Quebecky? We are all Quebecky's," Blondie replied.

"Quebecky, the Correctional Officer at Seven Locks Detention Center."

"That's my brother Percy. Please—my son has spina bifida—"

"I don't give a fuck about your son. I'm here for Percy, we're old friends." I opened the door all the way and signaled for Lil' Quette to come in.

He walked in dressed in all black overalls that matched mine, his gun out and by his side.

"Get up," I told Blondie, then waited until she stood on her wobbly legs, before continuing, "I need everybody in one room. Cooperate and you live, make me mad and you all die. Understood?"

Blondie nodded, with tears falling down her cheeks.

"Cuz, move the van around the back out of view. Then come back inside and lock the door." Lil' Quette left the house. "Where is everybody?"

"Upstairs, they're both upstairs," Blondie answered.

"Well, upstairs we go."

Ten minutes later, Lil' Quette and I had all three Quebecky's tied up in one room. Both women in tears and gags in their mouths. The special needs kid was small, his eyes were dry and attentive.

"Now what, big cuz?" Lil' Quette asked.

"Now we wait, Quebecky gets off at twelve."

***

From the window, I watched the headlights on the GMC pick-up truck go out, I heard the engine shut off. The living room lights were out, I hid on the side of the stairs. In minutes, keys turned in the locks on the front door. In stepped Quebecky, he turned and locked the door, as soon as he turned back around, I shot him.

"Aw—shit—what—the—fuck!" Quebecky said as he grabbed at the wound in his stomach.

His fingers bloody, Quebecky looked in my direction, his mind was trying to understand what happened. Light coming from outside made it possible to see me, I leveled my silenced .40 at his face.

"You're injured, not dead. Walk up the stairs to your mother's room. Do anything stupid and your family dies."

Slowly, Quebecky climbed the stairs, stopping to glance back at me once. I was a few stairs behind him. "Keep moving, cuz."

In the mother's room, the light was on and it was the only one on in the house. Quebecky walked in and surveyed the scene. All three of the Quebecky family members lay on their backs, hands tied behind them, legs bound, and mouths gagged. Lil' Quette leaned on the wall by the bureau.

"Get on your knees, Quebecky," I ordered.

"Please, whatever you want, I will get it. Don't hurt anyone, please!" Quebecky pleaded.

"On your knees, cuz. Now!" I repeated.

Quebecky dropped to his knees. "I'm bleeding bad, I need an ambulance."

"Turn around, cuz and face me."

On his knees, Quebecky turned his whole body toward me and his eyes grew large.

"Looks like you remember, huh?"

Quebecky nodded. "C'mon, Fuller—"

"Remember what you did to me, cuz? What you said to me?"

"Please—I'm sorry for what I did—what I said. I'm losing too much blood."

"I waited over three years to see you again, Quebecky."

"What we went through—what I did—c'mon, Fuller. It ain't worth dying over."

"Says who, cuz? You? I disagree, you slammed me on my head, fucked up my shoulder. You kicked me and stomped me. I can't forgive you for that. You told me that the Big Guy upstairs didn't like ugly. Since you know so much about the Big Guy upstairs, today you get to meet him." I shot Quebecky in the stomach again. Then I turned to Lil' Quette and said, "Lil' Cuz kill his mother while he watches."

"No—please!" Quebecky screamed.

"Kill her, cuz. Now!" I said again to Lil' Quette.

Lil Quette raised his gun and aimed it, but still didn't shoot. I aimed at Quebecky's mother and fired the gun, killing her instantly. Blondie screamed a muffle scream, Quebecky sobbed openly.

"Lil cuz, you're disappointing me, right now. I need you to focus. These muthafuckas don't care nothing about us or people who look like us. They are racist crackas, kill the other woman. Kill her now, cuz."

Lil' Quette stiffened his resolve, eyed the woman I called Blondie, aimed his gun and shot her repeatedly. Bullet holes appeared in her forehead; she was dead.

"Good, cuz, be heartless. Kill with no conscience, you killed the kid's mother. Now kill the kid."

Lil' Quette looked at me, eyes pleading, he didn't want to do it.

"Heartless, cuz. Be heartless, kill him."

The gun in Lil' Quette's hand coughed again and hit the kid, but he wasn't dead.

"Finish him," I demanded.

"No-o-o-o—o!" Quebecky cried in a horse tone.

"Do it!"

Lil Quette stood over the special needs kid and shot him several times. His body lay still, the kid was dead.

"It's your turn, Quebecky, you did this to your family." I shot Quebecky in the head. Then emptied my clip in his ass. "Let's go, cuz."

I turned to leave but didn't hear any footsteps behind me. I turned around, Lil' Quette hadn't moved. He was riveted to where he stood, his eyes on the people he'd just killed.

"You did it, cuz. Tonight, you grew up. Tonight, you became a cold-blooded killer. Let me see your eyes."

Slowly, Lil' Quette looked up at me, his eyes on mine.

"It's there, cuz, I see it. The look in your eye right now will never go away. C'mon, lil' cuz, let's get out of here, our work is done."

We left the house and climbed into the van out back. All the way back to D.C. even as I dropped him off, Lil' Quette never said a word.

Chapter Twenty-Seven

Nicole

Montgomery County Family Laid To Rest

Four members of a Clarksburg family were laid to rest yesterday. Seven days after their bodies were found shot to death in their home. Percy, Matilda, Patricia and Jonathan Quebecky were memorialized at the First Baptist Church of Clarksburg. Then laid to rest at Greater Harmony Cemetery in Clarksburg. Authorities are still stymied by their lack of leads in this case. Last week, Clarksburg Police were called to do a welfare check on Percy Quebecky, a Correctional Officer at Seven Locks Detention Center, after he'd missed two days of work without notifying his supervisor.

Officers went to the home in the 2100 block of Elmhurst Way and discovered a 2016 GMC Sierra pick-up truck that belonged to Percy Quebecky parked out front. After several attempts to get someone inside the home to answer the door were unsuccessful, police then forced their way into the home. They discovered all four members of the Quebecky family upstairs in one bedroom shot to death. According to sources close to the scene, three of the victims were bound and gagged. Clarksburg Police Chief, Donald Pentz released a statement denigrating the senseless and barbaric act.

One of the victims killed was a ten-year-old child with special needs. Chief Pentz vowed to use all the resources available to his department to track and arrest the person or persons responsible for the murders. An investigation is ongoing, but authorities have yet to identify any suspects or any motives.

"Nicole Brooks?" a nurse called out.

Hearing my name, I closed the Metro Section of the Washington Post Newspaper and put it and the rest of the paper on the table. The waiting room was full of people, mostly young mothers with little kids that were out of control.

I stood up. "I'm here."

"Right this way, ma'am. Doctor Collins will see you now."

***

"At your last visit we did an ultrasound since you complained about pains in your stomach and side. I also had you submit a urine sample. That's where I'll start. Your urinalysis revealed the presence of Creatinine in your urine. High levels of Creatinine, Creatinine is a bad protein that the kidneys excrete to let the body know that something is putting pressure on your kidneys. We have to run more test to find out what that something is. You say you have a family history of Hypertension and diabetes.

"Yeah, my mother has type one diabetes. She's insulin dependent daily."

"I see, your lab results revealed that your blood glucose levels were a little high. I'm gonna order another round of lab work and check that again," Doctor Collins said and typed into his computer. "You might be developing type 2 diabetes."

"I don't eat a lot of sugar, though. How can—" I started.

"Most people hear diabetes and automatically think sugar, raw sugar. Then they think of sweets, candy, cookies, cakes, and sugary soft drinks. That's a misconception, you never have to eat any of the things I just mentioned and still develop diabetes later in life. Which is basically what type 2 diabetes is. It's not from sweets, it's from starch, when you eat a lot of pasta, potatoes, corn, they are mostly starch. Guess what? Our bodies convert starch into sugar to digest it. Type two diabetes occurs when the pancreas doesn't produce enough insulin to regulate high levels of sugar in the blood."

"I had no clue—"

"Most people don't, in your case it may not be type 2 diabetes. You might be prediabetic, the blood work I'll request will tell me more and I'll be able to tell you more at the next visit. That's two things so far, the creatinine in your urine and your high glucose levels, the third and most important concern I have is that your ultrasound revealed a mass near your cervix. I'm scheduling you for an MRI and a few other tests. So, make sure you go downstairs to the lab and get the blood drawn. Give another urine sample, too. Here are the orders for the other tests as well." Doctor Collins wrote out some stuff on some papers, signed them and handed them to me. "I'll see you back here in about three weeks or so. Okay?"

"Okay, thanks for seeing me, Doctor Collins. I hope that everything is okay."

"Me too, Nicole. Take care and enjoy the rest of your day."

"I'll try, Doc, I'll try."

Anthony Fields

Chapter Twenty-Eight

Lil Quette

"Your mother has been calling my phone since yesterday. She wants to know where you are and why you're not answering your phone. I can only tell her you're sleep so many times. What do you want me to tell her?"

"I'ma call her," I told Shakira.

"When, Quette? Because I'm tired of her blowing my phone up."

I reached down, picked up my phone off the floor and powered it on. As soon as it came on, pings in rapid succession alerted me to Facebook posts, Instagram messages, missed calls and unanswered texts. I also had several voice messages, all from my mother. I saw that I had missed calls from my mother, a few of my men and a few from Khadafi. I decided to call my mother first.

She answered on the first ring, "What the fuck is wrong with you, Marquette?"

"What do you mean? I been here at Shakira—"

"Without calling? Bring your ass home! Now!" My mother demanded and hung up the phone.

"Ooohhh—you in trouble," Shakira teased.

"*Trouble?* I'm grown, I can't get in trouble," I said defiantly.

"Having a baby on the way doesn't make you grown, Quette."

I began to dress. "Whatever, Sha."

"Don't whatever me, nigga. You know I'm right. That's why I'm not having no baby by you—"

"Good then don't. I don't care," I said and grabbed my car keys. "I'm out."

***

I walked through the door at home and the first thing I saw was my mother sitting at the dining room table. Her hair was disheveled, and she'd been crying. A half empty bottle of Hennessy set in the middle of the table and a glass with the brown liquor in it in front of her. She heard me come in but never looked up in my direction.

"I called you. I have to tell you in person that Jamo is dead."

I know that, I killed him. "What happened to him?"

"Somebody stabbed him to death," my mother answered.

Silence filled the air in the room.

"They found him yesterday, down Blue Plains. They said he'd been there for a week or more. Ever since he went missing. That's fucked up what they did to him. I saw the pictures of the crime scene. I identified him. That man ain't never hurt nobody."

"He ain't never hurt nobody? Stop it, Ma. He hurt you," I told her.

"We hurt each other. People do that sometimes when they love each other."

"I love Shakira and I never beat her like he did you."

"You'll understand better when you get older."

"I understand it now, Ma. You called me here to tell me about Jamo in person? Why? You know I don't fuck with that nigga. I never did. He probably deserved that shit."

The next thing I know, the Hennessy bottle whizzed inches past my head and hit the wall behind me. The bottle exploded on impact and sent broken glass and liquor everywhere.

"How are you gonna say that shit to me?" my mother hissed. A maniacal look etched across her face. "That man was like a father to your ungrateful ass!"

I couldn't help but laugh at that. "That man wasn't like a father to me. He was a friend of my father's that waited until after my father died to push up on you. He never liked me, and he never did shit for me. He never did shit for you. You took him in and took care of him."

Eyes with tears, my mother looked at me and said, "He was a better man than your father. In every way, believe that."

"He was a rat," I started out, now upset. "Everybody in the streets knew that. He told on a dude named Keith Young back in the day. My father was a real dude. A stand-up dude that everybody loved and respected. He had the bag, clothes, money, cars, women and all that shit. James Tolliver wasn't half the man that my father was."

"A rat?" My mother repeated and then laughed herself. "Ain't that about a bitch. You gon' stand here and call Jamo a rat? Oh, so, is that a bad thing? Because if it is, what does that say about you, Quette? Huh? You been hanging with your cousin Khadafi every day since he been home and he's a rat. He's one of the most notorious rats ever. Like Rayful, like Alpo Martinez and everybody in the streets knows that. Did you?" When I didn't reply, she trudged on, "He been all in the newspaper and shit, front page of the Metro. If Jamo deserved to die because he was a rat, then why is Khadafi's ass still alive?"

I decided not to answer.

"What's wrong, grown muthafucka? Cat got your tongue? Yeah, that's what I thought. The grass is always greener on the Henderson side of things. Your ass is getting too big for your britches. Talking slick, cursing and shit to me in muthafuckin' house. Where I pay all the bills at. I think it's time for you to be on your own, whole grown man. Get your shit together and leave. When I get home later on, I don't want you to be here. I need to be alone. I need to mourn my rat ass boyfriend who deserved to be stabbed and left abandoned for an entire week."

My mother got up, crossed the room, and disappeared up the stairs. On the way to the basement, my mother's words replayed in my head. Everything she'd said about Khadafi was true and everything I'd said about Jamo was true. They were both rats and the streets knew about them. I knew about them. I thought I hated rats, but I loved Khadafi. My life was a constant battle of good and evil and right and wrong. I was starting to feel like a mouse trapped inside a maze, a maze with no way out.

***

Nine days after we killed four people in a house in Montgomery County, I still hadn't talked to Khadafi. My phone wasn't charged, and I left it that way. I was playing Assassin Creed 2 on the XBOX when Shakira came in the room.

"I told my mother about being pregnant," Shakira announced.

"And yet you still live," I answered.

"She wants to know what we plan to do about this, Quette."

I paused the video game and dropped the controller on the bed. "I thought you said you didn't want no babies with me? Didn't you tell me you were getting rid of it?"

Shakira's eyes watered immediately. "Don't be trying to put that on my head. I say a rack of shit when I'm mad."

"Well, you need to stop doing that because that shit is confusing. Days ago, you acted like I ain't have no say in the matter. Now, I do, huh?"

"I don't know, Quette." Shakira was crying now. "Somedays I feel one way and then other days I feel different. I love you with all my heart, but the biggest question in my mind sometimes is what type of father would you be? Can you answer that for me?"

I looked at the floor and stared at my socks, clueless.

"See, that's what I mean. How can I bring a child into this world based on the unknown? Then, on the flip side, I can't bring myself to get an abortion. We created this life inside me, who are we to say that it can't live? I can't, I'm not a killer."

I am! "I hear everything you're saying, Sha, and you're right to feel the way you do. All I can say is that I love you. I've always loved you. And I don't know if love will be enough to get us through, but as long as I live, I'll be there for you and the baby. As long as I breathe, you and I will be together, and we'll raise the baby together. So, I guess that's what you gotta tell your mother. Tell her that we laid down and made the baby, so we've decided to raise it. Tell her that."

"I love you so much, Quette," Shakira said and hugged me.

"I love you, too. Now can I finish my game?"

"Yeah, after you put all them stupid ass bags you brought in here up in the closet. Then you can finish your game. And you still haven't told me why you left home."

"I'll tell you about it later," I told Shakira.

"You better. Put them bags away."

***

I woke up in a cold sweat, it was the fifth time that happened to me. The kid I'd killed haunted my dreams. The news reports said the kid was only ten-years old. In my dreams, he looked younger. His face wouldn't leave me alone. As I began to rise, Shakira burst in the room.

"Get up," she emphatically stated. "Somebody wants you downstairs."

A scowl crossed my face instantly. I reached under the bed and grabbed my gun. "Somebody like who?"

Shakira eyed the gun in my hand and the color drained from her face. "Quette, you gotta gun in my house? Are you fuckin' crazy?"

"Not, right now, Sha," I replied and got up. "Who wants me downstairs?"

"Why do you have a muthafuckin' gun in here, Quette?"

"Did you hear what I just said? Not right now!"

"I don't give a fuck what you just said. Go and see what your cousin wants and then get that gun outta my—"

"My cousin?"

"Yeah, your cousin. He's outside on the front porch."

"How in the hell does he know where you live?" I asked.

"How the fuck do I know? Get that gun out of my house, Quette. I'm not playing."

I dressed quickly and went downstairs. I opened the door and there was Khadafi standing on the curb leaning on his Mercedes. He was dressed in a Balenciaga sweater and matching hat. On his feet were black print Balenciaga boots. His ability to find people was mind boggling.

I walked down the stairs and out to meet him, we embraced. "What's up, big cuz? What are you doing here? And how in the hell did you know where my girl lives?" I asked in rapid succession.

Khadafi just smiled.

Anthony Fields

Chapter Twenty-Nine

Khadafi

"Relax, cuz. I ain't your enemy. Your mother told me where to find you."

"My mother?"

The uneasy look on Lil' Quette's face was priceless. He was uncomfortable. "Yeah, I pulled up on her this morning as she was leaving the house. Told her I hadn't heard from you in almost two weeks and I was concerned. I asked were you in the house. She gave me a look that cut through me, major attitude, and the answer to my question. She told me you moved out after a dispute with her—"

"She put me out because I told her Jamo deserved to be killed."

"You actually told her that?" I asked. Lil' Quette nodded. "Fuck it, then. She told me where you were and gave me the address. Here I am. You gotta problem with me coming here, lil cuz?"

"Problem?" Lil' Quette repeated.

"Yeah, problem. You got a problem with me knowing where you laying your head?"

"Of course not. Why would I? It's just that it was unexpected, that's all. What's up with you?"

"Naw, cuz, what the fuck is up with you? We put in some work and then you stop answering your phone for weeks. You good or do I need to be worried about you?"

"Worried about me?" Lil' Quette asked and scowled. "It ain't been no two weeks. And fuck you mean? Do you need to be worried about me?"

I saw the look on my cousin's face and respected it. The look in his eyes spoke to me. It told me that he was a killer just like me. It was the look I needed to see. "Forget I said that, cuz. I'm trippin' you just threw me off with your silence. We good? I need you to take a ride with me. You strapped?"

"No doubt, the attachment too."

"Cool. Get in the car, I gotta go see a guy."

***

The sign above the door read, *Pal's Mini Mart*. It was still early in the morning and not a lot of people were at the convenience store. I watched the door.

"Before I forget, lil cuz. I caught A.D. loading on Housing Place a few days ago and pushed his shit back. Walked right up on his car and wore his ass out."

"I heard about it. Shakira's mother grew up with him. Somebody called and told her," Lil' Quette said. "She was crying and all that shit. I figured it was you who did it."

"When I tell you I'ma do something, I'ma do it. I been fucking this bitch named, Sherita so much that I needed a break. Finding and killing A.D. was my break. I wanted you to do it, though."

"Why because I told you that his son is my man?"

I nodded. "Amongst other reasons."

"I already know. You tryna make me heartless."

"You got it. Now, your man can pay for his father's funeral. Anyway, back to this nigga right here. The one that owns that store right there. His name is Fat Moochie and he's a cold-blooded piece of shit. He's from Potomac Gardens. Came up with your father, Asay, Red Ronnie, Wayne Perry, and them niggas. His brother Martin used to be with my man Damien Lucas back in the day. We had his ass lined up before your father died, but after Unc got killed, I forgot about Moochie.

When I was out Maryland, some niggas on the tier was talkin' about him. How he getting all this money and this and that. I heard about all the shit he moving in this store right here that he hangs in. I feel like it's time for the big fella to pay his taxes. I'm here to collect them. I know he's in there now because that's his black Benz truck parked out front. There should be at least two or three other niggas in there, too. I been watching this spot for the last few days. When we get in there, I need you to be the eyes in the back of my head. I'll do the rest. Got it?"

Lil Quette screwed the suppressor onto his Glock .40. "I got it, let's rock.

***

When I walked into the store with Lil Quette on my heels, a bell chimed to alert the people in the store that someone had just entered. I noticed the cash register and counter to my right. On the wall to my left were shelves stocked with food that had to be refrigerated, cases that held items that needed to be cold or frozen. The man behind the counter eyed me as I moved slowly through the store. I upped the silenced Glock instantly and shot him in the face twice.

His body dropped to the ground, getting the attention of the man behind the grill in the rear of the store. Eggs and bacon cooking had the store smelling good. My stomach growled as I moved toward the man at the grill. His eyes focused quizzically on his fallen coworker or friend. Then he looked at me, I closed the space between us in seconds and shot him repeatedly. When he dropped, I stood over him and ended his existence.

I turned back to Lil' Quette. "Go lock the door, cuz."

Standing where I was, I watched Lil' Quette lock the door and flip the sign from *Open* to *Closed*. When he was beside me, we walked into a corridor, there were two doors to the left and one to the right. I turned the knob on the first door, and it opened to a closet. Then I tried the door on the opposite side, it was locked. When I reached the third and final door, I saw that it was shut but not all the way. It was slightly ajar. Inching it open, I could see Moochie's fat ass behind a desk writing on a notepad. I pushed the door open and walked into the room.

"Moochie, what's good, big boy?" I called out.

"Khadafi?" Moochie said, alarm on his face. His eyes on the gun in my hand. "Damn, slim what's this all about? Guns and shit, what's up?"

"What does it look like to you?" I asked.

"Two niggas with guns out for no reason. Me and you ain't never had no beef. Your uncle was my man."

"We still ain't got no beef, big boy. I just got home, and I need a few dollars. I—"

"You need a few dollars? That's all you had to say, slim. All this guns out shit—"

I quickly tired of the charade. "I think I misspoke, cuz. I meant to say, I need a lotta dollars and you got em. I need all the money in your safe and wherever else you got it and all the drugs, too. You know how I get down, bullshit the baker, you get a bun. Bullshit me and you get a closed casket, your choice."

"I'm hip to you, slim. Just be easy, I'ma open the safe. You can have the money, just be easy. Moochie got up and went to what looked like a flatscreen TV mounted to the wall. He swung the TV outward to reveal a wall safe.

"Open the safe and back up, big boy. If you got a gun in there, that might tempt you to be heroic, open it and step back."

Moochie did as instructed. Once the door to the safe opened, he backed up and turned around. "Now what, slim?"

"You moving a lot of dope in the hood, I hear. I want some. Where is it?"

"Over there in that black bag by the wall. It's two bricks of Afghanistan in there. My man Dick should be here any minute to get it."

"Then, I'll have to kill Dick. Empty your pockets, too," I ordered.

Moochie complied, he dropped money and two cellphones to the ground.

"One more question and then I'll leave. Where's the security camera's mainframe?"

"Over there by the table. It's mounted inside the cabinet. Just open the door."

"Thanks, cuz. You've been a big help," I said and shot Moochie in the chest twice, then his face. I made sure that he was dead. Leave no witnesses. "Cuz, get all the money out of the safe and put it in the bag over there with the dope. I'ma get the security camera hookup."

As we walked through the store, I stopped and put the security camera equipment down on the floor. I stepped over the dead body and looked at the grill. On a piece of foil sat fried eggs and several pieces of turkey bacon.

"What are you doing, big cuz?" Lil Quette asked. "We gotta bounce."

"Hold on, cuz. This food smells good and I haven't ate yet. I'm making a sandwich."

"Man, you lunchin' like shit," was all I heard behind me.

"They ain't gon' be needing it." I put the sandwich in my pocket without wrapping it up. I picked up the security unit and followed Lil Quette out of the store.

***

"What if a muthafucka try to bring us a move, right now?" Lil Quette asked. "You got our hammas in a fuckin' Nike bag."

"Look in the back seat," I told him.

Lil Quette saw the Draco lying on the floor in the back.

"Damn! That's a bad muthafucka right there, cuz. That's a baby Draco, right?"

"You better know it, holds about seventy in the clip."

"I saw a white dude busting one of them joints on YouTube before."

"You like that joint, huh?" I asked.

"Love it." Quette was like a kid in a candy store.

"Well, it's yours and tonight you get to put some work in with it."

"Tonight?"

"Yeah, while you were on hiatus, pouting and shit about killing that sick kid, I was still working. My Capers homegirl, Lil Keisha told me that there's a celebration of life party going on at the Bliss Nightclub for Meechie. MoneyBagg Yo and Blacc Youngsta is gonna be there. Think about it if there's a party for Meechie at the Bliss. Who do you think is gonna be there?"

"Shit, my whole hood gon' be there."

"But who in particular?"

"Meechie's brother, Carlton gon' be there."

I nodded my head. "Correct, ain't no better time to kill him than tonight. It's out of the neighborhood and it'll look like anybody could have done it. Nobody will suspect you."

"Sounds like a plan, then. I'm with it," Lil Quette said.

"Good, but cuz, you can't keep doing what you just did. Flaking out on me after a kill. I told you before, killers kill whoever, whenever, wherever. You gotta be able to keep your head in the game. You can't be ignoring me for days and weeks and shit. You feel me?"

"I feel you, big cuz. I feel you."

"That's good because—" My cell phone vibrated. "Hold on for a minute," I answered the call, it was Sherita. "What's up, boo? I was just about to call you."

"Is that right? Well, I beat you to it. I cooked dinner. You want some?" Sherita asked.

"I told you I don't eat pork or beef, right?"

"I remember, I made barbecue chicken."

"And what else?"

"Spinach, mac and cheese and rice pilaf with fresh biscuits in the oven."

"I'm there and I hope you made enough for three."

"Three?"

"Yeah, three. My little cousin Quette is with me."

"I made enough, bring him through."

"We're on our way." I hung up the phone. "That's the bitch that keeps sending me naked pics and videos that I told you about."

"The funny looking joint with the banging body and good pussy?"

I nodded. "That's her, she cooked us a meal. Let's go eat."

***

After we ate, I tossed Lil Quette the black bag with the money in it. The one we'd taken from Moochie. "I'ma go in the back and fuck shorty right quick. Count that money for me."

"I got you, big boy. Have fun," Lil Quette said.

"I will believe that."

***

"Here, take this," Sherita said and tossed me something.

I caught it in the air and looked at it. It was Astroglide lubricant gel. "What's this for?"

"I'm full of good food. Now, I wanna be full of good dick. But I wanna do something different this time."

"Different like what?" I asked.

"I want you to put that dick in my ass."

"I don't know about that, I don't really—"

Sherita wiggled out of her jeans, then her pants. She pulled her shirt over her head but left her bra on. "Come on, boy, I got you. You gon' love it."

"How you know I'ma love it?"

"Because this ass is so super tight."

"I bet it is."

She laid down across her bed on her stomach. Then opened her ass cheeks. "You gon make me cum hard as shit. I know it. Come on, start slow, until I get used to it. Then I'ma need you fuck the shit outta me."

Anthony Fields

Chapter Thirty

Lil Quette

I was on Facetime with Shakira when Khadafi came out of the back room. Telling Shakira that I'd hit her back, I saw that Khadafi was walking funny.

"Fuck is wrong with you?" I asked.

"Cuz, this bitch is an animal. She made me fuck her in her ass until she squirted all over the bed. Then she did some Karmasutra shit on my dick. Put me in some weird positions, I think I'm in love."

I busted out laughing.

"You laughing, but I'm dead serious. That bitch's ass is so good, I started crying while I was in it."

I continued to laugh and couldn't stop.

"I was hitting the ass from the back and started crying. She asked me what was wrong. I told her that I loved her. You keep laughing me out, I'm gone. I'ma go hop in the shower, then we gon' be out. How much money was in the bag?"

"A hundred and eighty-six thousand," I told him, still in awe of seeing and touching that much money.

"While I'm in the shower, separate it. Put the three keys and eight in my bag. The hundred—hold on, naw, I'ma give that bitch something to hold them keys for me." Khadafi walked into the kitchen and came back with a plastic Safeway bag. He handed it to me. "Put sixty and the three keys in the black bag it came in. Put twenty racks to the side and put the hundred racks in the Safeway bag. Can you remember that?"

I nodded. "Got you."

Khadafi turned and left.

Twenty minutes later, he returned. "Cuz, give me the bag and the twenty racks."

"What you gon' put the twenty racks in?" I asked him.

"Here, put it in this." Khadafi handed me a wet towel.

I put the twenty bands in the towel. He picked it up in one hand, in the other hand was the black bag.

"I'll be right back," he said and disappeared.

A few minutes later, he was back. "Come on, cuz, let's bounce. We gon' go and get the van, it's more inconspicuous then the Benz. Bring the Safeway bag."

***

Cars started to arrive in the parking lot of the Bliss nightclub. I sat in the van and thanked God that the seats were comfortable because we'd been there for an hour or so, waiting and watching.

"You said Carlton drives a G-Wagon, right?" Khadafi asked.

I knew that he asked me something about a G-Wagon but didn't hear everything. "What did you say?" I asked pulling the wireless earbuds out of my ears.

"Cuz, how are you gonna hear me wearing ear buds?"

"My bad, big cuz."

"What you listening to?"

"The Migos new shit."

"The Migos? Let me hear it."

I passed Khadafi one of the ear buds, he put it in his ear. Khadafi listened for a few minutes, then handed the ear bud back.

"Straight trash, cuz. I hate all this trap, young nigga music. You said that Carlton drives a silver G-Wagon, right?"

I nodded my head. "Yeah, he got that and a big boy Lexus, it's burgundy. For an event like this, he gon' bring out the G-Wagon. But that's only if he's driving. He might be riding with Cutty. Cutty gotta mint green Jaguar truck. So, we looking for either one of them."

"Bet," Khadafi said and fell back.

***

"What time does this shit let out?"

I looked at the time on my phone, it was 1:47 a.m.

"Bliss on Saturday nights be lit, especially with Money Bagg in there. It ain't over till like three, but people gon' start coming out in a few tryna beat the traffic."

The silver G-Wagon was parked across the parking lot on some VIP parking shit. An hour and a half ago, it pulled into the spot reserved for it. We watched Carlton, Cutty and V Dot exit the truck and enter the club. Now we were waiting for them to leave.

"If they going back down the West, they gon' take New York Avenue to two-ninety-five, two-ninety-five to the South Capitol Street exit. If they do that, they gotta stop at the light on M Street. We baking their asses right there. I'm on the driver's side where V Dot is, you're on the passenger side where Carlton is. Cutty is in the backseat. You hit Carlton and the backseat, let me take care of V Dot and please try not to shoot me."

"I won't, big cuz. Like you always say watch my work."

***

Everything happened just as Khadafi had predicted. V Dot left the Bliss and took the exact route that Khadafi said he would. At the intersection of South Capitol and M, the G-Wagon was stuck behind other cars waiting to turn left onto M Street. The van was about four cars behind the G-Wagon.

"I love it when a good plan comes together," I said to Khadafi before hopping out of the van with the Draco in hand.

I never saw Khadafi hop out, but I knew that he was on the other side heading toward the G-Wagon like me. In my haste to crush shit, I forgot to cover my face. It wouldn't matter because everybody in that truck that knew me would die tonight. Using the briskness of a cat, I got to the truck and let the Draco spit, the bullets ate through glass and metal as if it was paper. I heard tires screech nearby that brought me out of my zone. I ran back to the van, Khadafi was already inside waiting for me. He pulled out of the line of cars, two wheels in the street and two wheels up on the curb. The whole move took less than three minutes.

***

Somewhere near Aunt Mary's house, Khadafi pulled the van next to my Camaro.

"You did good, lil cuz. I respect your gangsta. To me, it seems like you're a natural. Killing has come easy to you. He reached in the back and grabbed the Safeway bag with the hundred racks in it and handed it to me. "Here take this with you."

"You want me to hold it?" I asked, confused.

"Hold it if you want to or put it up for the baby. It's yours," Khadafi said.

I couldn't believe it, never in a million years would I think that I'd have a hundred racks before my eighteenth birthday. I still have most of the money that Khadafi gave me in the pillowcase the day he killed everybody at the car lot. I wanted to reach over and hug my cousin, but didn't, because I wasn't up on the proper thug etiquette. I didn't know if killers did hugs.

"Thanks, big cuz. I don't know what to say."

"Don't say shit, just take the money and bounce. And drive carefully because it's early in the morning, the police is out here geeking. Put the Draco and the money in the trunk. You got your driver's license, right?" I nodded. "Registration and insurance handy?"

"Yup."

"Cool. You should be good. I'm going back to Sherita's. Call me when you get to shorty's house."

"I'ma do that, love you, big cuz."

"Love you, too, youngin."

***

The Draco stayed in the trunk, but the bag of money went with me to Shakira's front door.

"It's late as shit, Quette. My mother gon' start bitching about you coming in her house so late," Shakira complained as we climbed the stairs.

"I got something for her that's gonna make her feel better."

"Something like what?"

"This dick," I joked.

"Boy, don't play with me like that. And what if she heard you?"

"Then I'd really have to give it to her, that's all."

Shakira turned and punched me in the chest. "I said don't play with me like that."

Inside her bedroom with the door shut, Shakira saw the Safeway bag in my hand. "What's in the bag?"

"Something for you and the baby," I told her.

"Oh yeah? What is it? Let me see."

I opened the bag and dumped all the big face hundreds onto Shakira's bed. Her eyes got large, her hand flew to her mouth, she covered it.

"Oh—my—God!"

"Listen to me, Monday you go to the bank—any bank that you choose and open a savings account. You gotta put under ten grand in there at a time. Then go back and make deposits with their ATM. Make as many trips as it takes to put all the money in the bank."

"Where in the hell did you get all this money?" Shakira asked. "Did you rob a bank or something?"

"No, my cousin gave it to me. That's all I know, that's all you know."

"You're scaring me, Quette. Something about you has changed since your cousin has been hanging with you. You carrying guns and shit. Did you get rid of that gun like I told you to?"

"Yeah," I lied.

"I don't want anything to happen to you."

"Nothing's gonna happen to me," I assure her. "What you got on under that T-shirt."

"Nothing," Shakira answered and flashed me her naked body.

"My cousin stopped over one of his chick's house today and she gave him some butt. When you gon' give me some?"

"Give you what? Some ass! As in anal sex?"

"Yeah, all of that."

"Never."

"Never."

"Never, that hole back there is for shit exiting only. It ain't made for nothing entering back there. Sorry, but you gotta get that from the next bitch."

"I got your permission to do that?"

"If you don't wanna live past eighteen, you do."

"I'm good, I don't like that way that sounds."

Shakira pulled the T-shirt over her head and off. "I thought you'd see things my way. Hurry up and take your clothes off. I got something for you better than ass."

"And what's that?"

"Head—Superhead."

Chapter Thirty-One

Rio Jefferson

Scorpio 'Fat-Fat' Phillips, Jamar Reed, Birney Place—Open! James 'PeeWee' Smith, Jamya Smith, Dontay Jackson, Paul Williams, Remon Pitts. Imperial Autos Murders—Open. Clifton Brown, Half Street, Southwest—Open! Adrian Wade, Housing Place Southwest—Open! George 'Geo' Dunn, Doris Vinson, Layton Shaw. 7th and 1st Street Southwest—Open! Carlton Brown, Lavelle Nichols, South Capitol Street, Southwest—Open!

The homicide board on the wall reflected our ineptitude. A compilation of abysmal failures that ate at my core. Ours was one of the most decorated police agencies in the country, yet Metropolitan Police Department suddenly could not close murder cases. I sat on top of my desk and stared at the board that troubled me. Pieces of a puzzle formed in my head and made something stick out. Of the last seven cases recorded on the homicide board, four cases involved a victim associated with the Southwest area of the city.

The Clark Family murders happened on 3rd Street in Southeast. The triple homicide on 7th and 1st Street happened on the Southeast side of the Southeast/Southwest line. The Fat-Fat Phillips case was also in the Southeast. James 'PeeWee' Smith was killed in Northwest at the car lot, but he was from Capers and associated to Southwest through Clifton 'Meechie' Brown who was killed days later on Half Street in Southwest. Adrian 'AD' Wade was killed on Housing Place hours before a candlelight vigil for Meechie. Carlton Brown, the younger brother of Clifton Brown and Lavelle Nichols had been killed the night before. Southwest—Khadafi.

"Hey, Pete, come here for a minute. Bring Doug and Leo with you," I called out.

Minutes later, Pete Sandoval, Doug Davis and Leo Jacobs walked over and stood around my desk.

"All of you guys are familiar with the Capers, Potomac Gardens, and James Creek area, right?" I asked.

"Of course," Doug said.

"Definitely! That's my neck of the woods," Pete chimed in.

Leo Jacobs remained silent but nodded his head.

"I need to know if any one of you see what I see. James Smith killed the same day Khadafi gets out of prison. Him and four other people, including Smith's sister. James Smith ran Imperial Autos for Khadafi. He was close friends with Clifton Brown. Our computer records show that PeeWee and Meechie caught a case together in two-thousand-four. And ironically, it was a home invasion case that got dismissed due to insufficient evidence."

"Was Meechie friends with Khadafi?" Leo asked.

"I don't know," I admitted. "But what I do know is that Meechie getting killed on Half Street days after his friend PeeWee wasn't by happenstance. It wasn't coincidental. The Adrian Wade killing doesn't add up either. There's no connection to PeeWee for him, but an association with Meechie."

"Adrian Wade?" Doug said. "Why is that name ringing bells within me?"

"Because we locked him up ten years ago for killing Paul Heart. He beat that murder. Then we arrested him again three years later for killing Paul's brother, Daniel Heart. He beat that case as well," Pete told him.

"I remember him now. Karma's a bitch, huh?"

"Meechie's brother getting killed last night has to figure into the equation some kinda way," Leo Jacobs added. "Carlton also known as Lil C and Lavelle Nichols also know as V Dot, might be connected to whatever is going on. V Dot is rumored to be a shooter for Lil Cee. Him and Marthell Simmons, was also in the SUV with Brown and Nichols when they were shot. He was shot as well but survived with non-life-threatening injuries.

"Marthell Simmons? Cutty?" I stood up. "Why wasn't I told that Cutty was in that SUV last night? Where is he now?"

"You weren't told because—uh, we investigate homicides, not AWIKS. He survived, so his name isn't on any of our board."

"He was injured, right? Where is he?"

Leo Jacobs pulled out a notepad and looked at it. "He's at UMC."

I grabbed my coat and ran out of the room.

***

At the United Medical Center's Information counter, I flashed my badge to the pretty, young nurse with blue hair to match her navy-blue scrubs. "I'm detective Rio Jefferson. Can you tell me what room Marthell Simmons is in?"

"Marthell Simmons, you said?" the nurse replied.

"Yeah. Came in, in the wee hours of the morning, gunshot victim."

Fingers flew across the keyboard in front of her, then the nurse said, "He was in room two-o-one on the second floor. He had emergency surgery to stop the bleeding in his leg. His femur artery was punctured, he was also shot in his wrist, forearm, and ankle. Doctors put him in a soft cast. Sometime this morning, he disappeared. Must've just walked right out."

"Disappeared?" I asked, confused. "Walked out? He could do that? Have the ability to just walk out after surgery?"

"It must be possible, detective, because he did it. And believe it or not, that's actually a more frequent occurrence then people may think. Hospitals provide care, not security. We can't force a patient who's injured to stay here. No matter how badly injured they may be."

"Damn!" I exclaimed. "Thank you for your help. I appreciate it."

"Anytime you have a nice day."

***

"No luck with Simmons, huh?" Pete said as soon as I walked back into the office. "I could've told you he wasn't gon talk. It's a little thing that these assholes have called Omerta. As in the Italian Mafia Omerta."

"He wasn't there," I sulked. "Walked out after surgery. Disappeared is what the nurse said."

"Guy must be Superman without a cape. Did you see that fuckin' Benz truck? Someone swiss cheesed it and Simmons just walks away from it and the hospital. Can't believe some people's luck. Nevertheless, come with me, Rio."

I followed Pete to one of the interrogation rooms. In the two-way glass, I could see Doug Davis sitting in one chair across from a short, chubby man, while Chris Logan, another detective sat in another chair.

"Who is he?"

"Anthony Chandler, the streets call him Zinc. He's on the payroll."

"He's on whose payroll?"

"Ours, and he happens to be from Southwest. Chris called him in, we think he might be able to connect some dots for you."

"Is that right?" I said. "Well, let's see." I walked into the room, followed by Pete Sandoval. Grabbing a chair, I sat close to Zinc. "Doug, Chris, pardon the intrusion." I turned to Chandler. "Hey, big guy. Zinc, is it?"

"Yeah, I'm Zinc," the man answered.

"Do you know a man by the name of Luther Fuller?"

"Luther Fuller. Naw, the name doesn't sound familiar."

"What about his street name, Dirty Redds or Khadafi?"

Zinc's face lit up with recognition. "You talking about shorty from Capers? Marquette Henderson's nephew? His father old man Fuller owned the barber—"

"Khadafi just came home a few weeks ago and I believe that he's declared war on your hood. I'm not sure but I think he killed his friend PeeWee and Meechie. Maybe even AD and Meechie's brother Lil Cee. Know any reason why he might wanna kill all of them?"

"Not right off hand, naw," Zinc answered.

"Did you know James 'PeeWee' Smith?"

"Yeah, everybody knew PeeWee."

"Was Meechie still hanging out with PeeWee before they were killed?"

"No doubt, PeeWee was Meechie's man."

"Did PeeWee and Meechie hit licks together?" I asked.

"All the time," he replied.

"Have you ever heard anything about them robbing or invading a house that belonged to Khadafi? While Khadafi was in jail?"

"A few years ago, they hit a big lick and came off with a rack of weed. Recycled weed is what we called it. That might have been it."

"Recycled weed, what does that mean?"

"The dude Khadafi and some other dudes went into a spot owned by Black Woozie years ago on Canal Street. Killed a rack of people and took off with guns, money, coke and like three or four hundred pounds of weed. The weed was from Arizona, the best in the city. Word got back that it was some dude named TJ and Khadafi. Black Woozie and his men went to Capers to talk and never came back. They all got killed by the rec up there."

"I remember that massacre," Chris Logan said.

"I do, too," Doug Davis added.

"Well, the Arizona weed ended up back on the streets. Word around town was that Meechie had it, him and PeeWee. They probably got it from Khadafi's crib. If Khadafi was in jail, I can see Meechie and nem doing that."

"Is there a connection there with AD? Was he with the weed lick?" I asked Zinc.

Zinc shrugged his shoulders. "I don't have a clue."

"Well, I think there is. I need you to be vigilant. Call Chris or whoever your contact is if you hear anything or see anything that has something to do with Khadafi Fuller. Okay?"

"Okay."

I rose to leave but another thought came to mind. "Has the streets said anything about Lil Cee's murder, yet?"

"Other than that fact that he went to the Bliss nightclub to party with MoneyBagg Yo and Blacc Youngsta? It was a celebration of life for his brother. Him, V Dot, and Cutty were together in the G-Wagon, coming and going. They said that a black van followed them—"

Doug Davis said, "When you said that earlier, it caught my attention. Let me check something, I'll be right back. Chill for a moment, Rio." He left the room.

"Zinc, what about a Southwest power struggle? A beef between AD and Meechie?"

"I doubt it, and I'd know if it was. I'm the unofficial ambassador of the whole Southwest."

The door of the interrogation room opened. In walked Doug Davis and Corey Winslow. The room was getting crowded.

I hugged and fist bumped Corey Winslow.

"Don't mind me, just here to observe," Corey said and leaned on the wall.

"Rio, you might be onto something, buddy. It's the black van," Doug answered.

Befuddled I said, "The black van! What black van?"

"The black van is the connector," Doug explained. "Corey, you got a lead on the Adrian Wade murder, right?"

Corey Winslow nodded.

"What did your witness say?"

"There was gonna be a candlelight vigil for Meechie. The second one in a matter of days. Adrian Wade was parked on Housing Place, just sitting in his car when the black van pulled up. A man got out of the driver's seat, walked up to AD's car, and shot him repeatedly."

"All that from an eyewitness?" I asked.

"Yep," Corey replied. "Said she saw the gun and the sparks come out but didn't hear any gunshots. Described it as weird."

"Perp used a muffler or sound suppressor to circumvent the shotspotter. There's been an uptick in cases where suppressors are used. Did she describe the man who shot AD?"

"No clear ID. Just described a man dressed in black with something like a scarf covering his face."

"The same thing the killer was wearing on his face when he killed Meechie," this came from Pete Sandoval.

"The connector, a black van seen at AD's murder on Housing Place and a black van seen at the Lil Cee and V Dot murders last night," Doug Davis added.

"So, we're looking for a black van and a black SUV?" Corey Winslow asked.

"It looks that way, a man in a black SUV gets out and kills Meechie, face covered by a scarf or some kind. A man gets out of a black van and kills AD, face covered with a scarf of some kind. Black van pulls up, someone gets out and floods Carlton Brown's Mercedes Wagon with bullets, killing him and his friend Lavelle Nichols. I think it's Khadafi."

"Could be but might not be. Do we know what kind of black van we're looking for? Caravan, Passenger van, Conversion van, cargo van, minivan, what?" Doug asked.

I looked at Zinc, who I'd forgotten was in the room. "Did anyone say what kind of black van it was?"

"I never asked," Zinc answered. "But I'll check, asap."

"Good, we sure can't stop every van in the city because it's black," Pete Sandoval commented.

"We only do that to black people. It's called driving while black," Doug Davis, the lame white detective in the room joked.

Everyone in the room looked at him crazy.

"Just kidding. Damn! Touchy, today," Doug replied.

Chapter Thirty-Two

Khadafi

I don't want no paint-over job, cuz," I vehemently told the dude at the paint shop. "I need y'all to sand it down, prime it and remove all traces of black paint. Then I want it painted silver."

"I got you, homes," the Mexican man in paint covered overalls replied.

I called out to the other dude in the shop, the lone black guy. "Aye, cuz, come here for a minute." The black dude walked over. "What's your name again?"

"Jug, everybody calls me Jug."

"That's what's up. Aye, Jug, I'ma need you to detail this joint real good. And put them racks and the ladder you was telling me about on it."

"You got that, moe," Jug replied.

"How much is everything gonna run me? Paint job, detail and racks?"

"That's gon' be like seventeen-hundred for everything," the Mexican man said.

I pulled out money and counted out seventeen-hundred dollars. I passed it to Jug. "How long before she's ready to be picked up?"

"Shit, you paid the entire amount in cash, so it's a priority. Pedro and nem can have the whole paint job done by tomorrow. Time to dry and then detail, plus ladder and racks installation. I'd say—it's Monday. You can pick her up on Wednesday."

"Bet, good looking, cuz."

***

It was warm for an October afternoon, so I pulled off my Versace jacket and tied it around my waist. I walked across St. Barnabas Road and headed for the IHOP, where I'd order some food and wait for Lil Quette to pick me up. I walked on the sidewalk in front of a small strip mall. A nail salon sat right next to a hair salon.

Coming out of that nail salon was a familiar face. Smiling I headed her way.

"Lisa, what's good, bro?" I said getting her attention.

The look on her face as she stared at me was one of trepidation. "Khadafi? Hey!"

"Hey, yourself. You still with Bay One?" I asked her.

"I'ma always be with Bay One. Why do you ask?"

"No reason, just asking."

"Cool. So, since we're asking questions. I got one for you," Lisa said.

"Okay, shoot."

"Are you following me? If so, why?"

I thought Lisa was joking, but judging by the look on her face, I could see that she was serious. "*Following you?* Why in the hell would I wanna follow you?"

"I don't know, but I know this—I don't have nothing to do with you and Bay One's beef. I know how you get down and all I'm saying is, I don't have shit to do with anything."

Lisa was starting to irritate me. "You throwing me off. I already know that you ain't got nothing to do with me and Bay. I just dropped my truck off down the street to get painted and decided to walk to IHOP to wait on my ride. I saw you just now and I decided to say hello. Innocent. Coincidence! So, why would I be following you?"

"I said that because I just saw you in RuthChris a few weeks ago. That's twice in twenty days, I'm just saying—"

I smiled. "I was there with my little cousin Marquette. My uncle Marquette's son. We went to get a meal. I never even saw you."

"Well, I saw you and the young boy together. I asked Bay did you have a grown kid because the young dude looked like you."

"Oh, so you already told Bay that you saw me? What did she say about that?"

"Does this color pink look good on my nails and toes?" Lisa asked, dodging my question.

I looked at her nails as she waved them in front of me. The polish was hot pink with something that looked like tiny diamonds on every other finger. My eyes fell to her feet and my dick twitched and woke up. There was no way that Lisa could know about my insane foot fetish. Her toes were pedicured and polished the same color pink as her nails. They were gorgeous toes.

"Yeah, it's proper, I like it."

"That's good. You said you were on your way to IHOP, right?"

"Yeah, I'ma order some food and wait on my ride."

"Is your ride a bitch?"

"Naw, it's my cousin. The one who was with me at RuthChris."

"Great, because I suddenly feel like some breakfast food, on you."

I had to laugh at that, Lisa went from thinking that I followed her, to wanting to follow me, all in five minutes. "You got that, Lisa, c'mon."

***

Pancake syrup coated Lisa's lips like gloss and every time she licked them, I got more and more aroused. We sat in a small booth in the back of the small IHOP. My chicken tenders and waffles were half eaten, the rest on my plate was getting cold.

"I didn't speak to you at RuthChris because I didn't really know if it was right or wrong to speak given the situation between you and Bay One. I know all about the ill feelings between y'all and I get it. I just don't want to be in the middle of it. Me and you always been cool, but Bay is the love of my life. I think that y'all need to talk—"

"Bay One made the decision to cut me off. I love her, but I can't live my life thinking about how much I disappointed her."

"Bay One is old school. You know that better than me. I needed to get here. I needed to make—"

"Things right," Lisa interjected. "I already know that Bay told me that when I last went to see her. She thinks you killed PeeWee and all those people at that car lot."

"That's what she thinks, huh?" I said and smiled.

"Yep. And that shit eating grin on your face makes you look guilty."

I laughed a throaty chuckle. "Is that right? What else does Bay One think?"

"She thinks that next you're going to kill your baby mother, Marnie."

Bay One had raised me, she knew me better than most. It didn't surprise me that she knew what I had planned. But I was a little disturbed that she voiced all her fears to Lisa.

"Bay trippin'! Lunchin' like shit. I didn't kill PeeWee or nobody else. And I would never kill the mother of my children."

"Have you seen her or your children?" Lisa asked.

I cut a piece of cold waffle and forked it into my mouth. "Naw, not yet."

"That's crazy, and you been home for how long?"

"Almost a month, today makes four weeks."

"I know your ass been out here fucking like shit, haven't you?"

My eyes found Lisa's and held them. Her sly grin spoke words that her mouth didn't.

"I got some pussy a few times, but I wouldn't say I been fucking like shit. Guess I haven't found the right woman to release the three years of freak shit I got pent up inside me."

"Ditto that, other than some plastic, I haven't had no dick in about eight years. So, I guess we're kinda in the same boat."

"Didn't know you even liked dick, plastic or otherwise," I told Lisa.

"There's a lot you don't know about me, Khadafi."

"Like what, Lisa? Tell me what I don't know."

"I'ma do you one better. Call your ride and tell him that you gotta ride. My car is parked near the nail salon. Go with me to my place and I'ma show you better than I can tell you."

As if they had a mind of their own, my fingers speed dialed Lil Quette. I told him exactly what Lisa had said.

***

Lisa reminded me of the chick Deelishis, the model from Flavor of Love. Her body was flawless. I stood by the wall and watched her undress.

"You gotta be gentle with me. I was dead serious when I said that I haven't had no dick in eight years, except plastic. The first nut is on you. Everything after that is on me, I promise you that."

I stripped down to my boxers and walked over to the bed.

"See, that's why we here. Versace down to the drawers, you sexy as hell and all them tattoos and war wounds. Like that zipper on your stomach, turns me on. The quintessential bad boy. Ever since I first met you, I wondered about you. Wondered why all the young bitches wanted to fight over you. You like piercings?"

"Love that shit, cuz. Them piercings in your nipples look good as shit."

"Wait until you get close enough to see the one in my clit and pussy lips," Lisa said salaciously.

My dick threatened to bust out of my boxers, so I freed it.

"And you toting," Lisa said, her eyes on my dick. "Triple threat."

"Triple threat, what's that?" I asked.

"You're fine as fuck, fly and got a big dick. Don't get no better than that."

"Yes, it does," I told her. "Let me show you."

***

Man did we get to it, I licked every inch of Lisa's body. I put my tongue inside her as far as it would go and let her cum on my lips and moustache. I licked her ass, her toes, inner thighs, her navel, and all her piercings. Then I fucked her like a porn star, for hours. I had been fucking Sherita so much that I was almost drained, but I still performed for Lisa out of pride alone. True to form, I fucked her all over the apartment.

***

Lisa had a vaping pen that you put pure THC wax into and smoke it. I inhaled the smooth smoke once and passed the pen back to Lisa. I was high as hell, laying in her bed next to her, I closed my eyes. I felt like I was floating in outer space.

"I still can't believe I did this, with you," Lisa said. "But I don't regret it not one bit. You gave me exactly what I needed, multiple orgasms. We call them moregasms and that shit was long overdue. I can get myself to one, maybe two orgasms, but like five or six in one session is unheard of. I'm still shaking and shit. Dick was good as shit all that fake dick shit is in the way."

I laughed at Lisa.

Lisa giggled, too. "I ain't lying." She grabbed my hand and put it between her legs, on her soaking wet pussy. "Feel that shit? It's still tingling. I can feel my heartbeat down there. Feel it?"

"I feel it," I said, surprised that she was telling the truth.

"Had I known that your dick game was this lethal, I would have—"

"Gotten us both fucked up. Bay One loves you like no other."

"I love Bay, too with all my heart. But a bitch got desires, you know? If Bay ain't here—what she don't know can't hurt her. You agree?"

"Definitely," I answered.

"Damn! This shit is crazy. I swear it is. Me running into you, sharing a meal, then climbing on top of you, riding you. Laying next to you, wanting you again. After all the wild shit I done heard about you. Horror story shit, I can't believe it."

"My life is an urban novel everyone wants to read."

"I heard that. Is all that stuff I've heard about you true?"

"Naw, you know how muthafuckas always hyperbolize shit. I'ma regular nigga that likes to chase the bag and foreign shit, clothes and whips."

"I don't expect you to tell me the truth, Khadafi. But let me say this, you can't expect to be killing people and think that niggas ain't gon put the police on your ass. I'd hate to see you and that dick back in jail."

"I ain't never going back to jail if I can help it. I'm holding court in the street, I'd rather be carried by six, then deliberated by twelve. I'm chilling, though. You can't be listening to Bay One and whoever else be talking about me. I didn't kill PeeWee and them other people. That was my car lot. Why would I set my own shit on fire? I could've caught PeeWee anywhere and killed him if that's what I wanted to do."

Lisa inhaled the pen again, coughed and exhaled. "That's what I said. I told Bay that, but she says otherwise. She thinks that Marnie getting married and having a baby is some shit that you can't get over."

"Marnie had a baby?" I asked.

"You acting like you ain't know that," Lisa said and giggled.

"I didn't know that. I knew she got married, but not about no baby."

"Damn! Me and my big mouth. I thought you knew. Marnie been had that baby. The little girl—her name is pretty as shit—Creation. She's over a year old. Her name is not as pretty as her though, she got grey eyes. Marnie and Bay One communicate, Bay snuck the pictures of their family in the visiting hall and showed them to me."

Suddenly, an inferno raged inside of me, but I smiled and remained calm. "You and your big mouth, huh? I can think of something you can do with it to make sure you don't blurt out no more secrets."

"Yeah, I bet you can. I hope it doesn't include me sucking your dick? Because I don't give no head," Lisa stated. "I don't know how."

"Is that right, you sure about that?"

"Positive about that."

"Okay," I said and got quiet. Then started thinking and planning.

"That's what you like, huh?" Lisa asked.

"It's the key to my heart."

Lisa got up and onto her knees and got between my legs. She grabbed my dick and kissed it.

"I thought you said you don't know how to suck dick?"

"I don't, but I never said I wasn't coachable."

"That's what's up, let me coach you."

***

Later That Night

I thought about what Lisa told me. Marnie had had another child. I never imagined that her betrayal would run that deep. There were days when I felt like I needed Marnie to balance out my crazy life. I had days when I yearned to be in her life, loving her, forgiving her. To come home and find out that that was no longer possible was a crushing blow to my heart and ego. Getting married and having another nigga's kid was the gauntlet that slammed down on the wooden desk in a show of finality. The curtain had definitely closed on the stage that represented a life, a love between her and I. I never really realized how deep I must have hurt Marnie. I looked at the digital clock on Lisa's dresser. It read 12:17 a.m., I had spent the entire day with Lisa and hadn't meant to. It was time to bounce.

I tapped Lisa's shoulder. "Lisa?"

"What? I can't fuck no more. My pussy's sore and now my jaws ache. Go back to sleep," Lisa said sleepily.

I laughed. "Cuz, I ain't trying to fuck. I'm just letting you know that I'm about to leave."

"You leaving?" Lisa turned and looked at the clock. "At this time of night?"

"It's still early to me. I can't sleep and I need to prepare for tomorrow,"

Lisa laid back on the pillow and closed her eyes. "Prepare for what?"

"You nosey, ain't you?" I asked.

"Whatever, I hope that you're not preparing to kill nobody?"

"I'm not."

"Good. Let me get up and put my clothes on. I'll take you home," Lisa said and rose up a little.

I reached out and stopped her. "Don't bother, Union Station is nearby, I'ma catch the train home. I need to exercise."

"So, was this a one-night stand or can I see you again?"

"I need to see you again. Feel you again. I need to put your number in my phone," I said and got out of the bed to grab my pants.

"It's already in there," Lisa said.

"*It's already in there?* How?"

"I put it in there while you were in the bathroom earlier."

"You went into my phone and did that?"

"I did."

"What else did you do?"

"Scrolled through your text messages."

"And?"

"I saw all the video texts that that funny looking bitch sent you. She must've been a sympathy fuck or some bitch that did the bid with you. Not your type at all, looking like Ms. Piggy in the face. You need to do better."

All I could do was crack up laughing.

Chapter Thirty-Three

Khadafi

When I stepped out of the building, the crisp, cold air hit me in the face like a punch. But as I started walking, I began to ignore the cold. It was dark outside, and life in the big city was still dangerous, but I wasn't afraid at all. I wasn't alone, the Glock .40 in my waist was all the companion that I needed. Lisa's condo in a newly built high-rise building in ROMA wasn't far from Union Station. I popped my collar and headed in that direction. My mind was full of thoughts of Marnie.

"I'm going home, Marnie, for good. I wanted to tell you face to face."

"You're going home?" Marnie repeated. "What exactly does that mean?"

"Come on, Marnie. You know what the fuck that means."

"Naw, I don't, enlighten me, boo. Please!"

"I'm going back home to Kemie."

"Oh," she said. "You're going home to Kemie. Okay, I get it now. So, where exactly does that leave me and us?"

"Cuz, you know how I feel about you, I—"

"Didn't I tell you about calling me that, cuz shit? And please don't assume I know shit. Tell me what's up. Tell me exactly how you feel about me. And tell me why you've decided to go back to Kemie? I want—"

"You just don't understand," I told her.

"Don't patronize me, you muthafucka. Talkin' 'bout I don't understand. Make me understand, then."

"We got history. It's—complicated, something happened—"

"What? Speak up, nigga. You babbling. What did you just say?"

"Look, cu—Marnie, I'm sorry if I led you on. I love you, but I gotta—I still love Kemie, too. You know that."

"You still love her?" Marnie said to herself.

"She proved—she—she—I can't say how, but she proved—she showed me that she—she proved herself to me. We got history, almost twenty years—she proved herself."

"And I haven't, is that it? What has Kemie proved except that she can shit on you while you're in prison and you'll take her back? What has she proved other than the fact that she'll fuck your friends, cross her own friends, fall in love with the next nigga? Keep fucking him after you come home and prove that she can lie good as a muthafucka? Me, I haven't proved but two things. That I will always be there for you and that I love you—"

That Kemie had just killed Phil and I convinced myself that I was better off with Kemie than Marnie. I could hear her voice in my head.

"I will always be there for you—I will always be there for you!"

The day I killed Devon and Strong, I was wounded in the leg and back. I went to Marnie's apartment. She cleaned me up and patched up my wounds. She was there for me.

"I will always be there for you!"

I thought about me being at D.C. Jail days after that. Marnie took care of everything for me. She retained a good lawyer, paid the lawyer, made sure I had everything I needed and although separated by thick partitions of fiberglass in the visiting room, I still felt her presence, I felt her love. I remembered her telling me—

"I'm your woman, well one of 'em. Not your buddy in the streets. Respect me as such. I'll never leave you. We are bonded by blood, a child and sacrifice."

Bonded by blood, a child and sacrifice. These were the words she used. Ironic that she'd mentioned the word sacrifice. After the knife fight with me and Ameen, Marnie was the first person to visit me at D.C. General Hospital. She cried over my body, her tears coated my cheeks and lips. Then she kissed me, and I felt her presence. I opened my eyes and smiled. She left me that day and went to broker the peace between Ameen and me, which led the way to Ameen saving my life the night Lil Cee caught me slippin'.

"I will always be there for you!"

I dug my hands deep into my pockets, another conversation I'd had with Marnie came to mind.

"Why does it seem like trouble and death sticks to you like flies on shit?"

"That's the way my life is," I explained to her. *"I can't explain why I always end up with blood on my hands. Death is always lurking around every corner for me, always has been. I don't know why, but I do know that this life—my life is what you signed up for. This is the life you wanted. The life you chose."*

"It was the life you chose," I said to myself as I pulled my hands from my pockets and blew into them to warm them. "You chose my life, Marnie. I didn't force it on you."

"I was there for you, Khadafi, when nobody else was. But that doesn't mean shit to you. I have been the only good and constant force in your troubled world!"

Marnie's words reverberated in my head like a bomb going off. For years she had been the only constant good in my life.

"Don't talk, let me. This is what I signed up for, remember? I love you so much, Khadafi, that sometimes I feel like I can't breathe without you. I have never felt like that for no other man in my life. Whatever it is that's going on with you, we gon' deal with it. Together! No matter what I'ma ride with you. Whether it's one year or life in the pen. You know how I'm built. Plus, we got lawyer money, so fuck the police."

I felt so much love for Marnie that night, but then twenty-four hours later, things went horribly wrong. I went to Aunt Mary's house and was confronted by Maurice Tolliver. I almost died, got charged with a rack of shit. Marnie found out about Erykah, then PeeWee and Meechie robbed the house and I became a rat. Instead of talking to Marnie, I let her find out my betrayal to the code from the Newspaper. Then she'd come to visit me at CTF. It was the last time I'd seen her and my kids. Her pleas for me not to become a rat came to mind.

"What are you talking about? What am I doing now?"

"You talking to them people about Ameen. Luther, I know how you feel—"

"You can't possibly know how I feel. Nobody knows how I feel. Because you ain't never been in my position."

"I thought you were dead. I wanted to die too to be with you. I didn't care about either of our children. All I cared about was you and finding you in the afterlife. I was gonna kill myself to do it. You ain't never been in that position. So, don't preach to me about nobody knows how you feel and I ain't in your position. I have to be in your position because as long as you're in here, we're in here with you. I told you on the phone that I have another man. I don't, I was hurt about bumping into Erykah and I wanted to hurt you. I know you wanna get at PeeWee and you wanna get back at me. I know that's how you feel and that's what made you cooperate with them people."

I thought about my responses to Marnie that day and how I tried to justify my decision to tell on Ameen to regain my freedom. I thought about how weak and unSuperman like I must've sounded. In the end, here I was upset at Marnie for what I deemed as betrayal, but in all actuality, she had kept it gangsta and I hadn't. I was the one at fault, not her. She'd fallen in love with Khadafi and everything that was Khadafi. Deciding to snitch on Ameen wasn't a Khadafi move. It was a seven-year-old Luther move.

"You're a different man now and I don't know if I can continue to love the one you've become."

Those were Marnie's last words to me. I looked up and saw that I was a block away from Union Station. The more I reminisced and walked, my desire to kill Marnie dissipated. I had violated the code, not her. I had become someone that she couldn't love. A weaker man. I had to respect that. But I could never respect her decision to alienate me from my kids. That was her most egregious cardinal sin. One that couldn't go unpunished. Someone close to her had to pay for her sins. Someone had to make the ultimate sacrifice.

Chapter Thirty-Four

Lil Quette

"Four chicken wings, mumbo sauce, French fry!" Mama-San called out from behind the thick bullet proof glass in Leo's carryout.

I walked up to the counter and paid for my food. Mama-San put the food in the turn style for me to get. I grabbed the bag and inspected my food. Steam rose off the chicken wings, moving over to the counter on the wall, I added salt and pepper to my French fries. The door to Leo's opened and in walked several of my friends.

"Quette, what you doing in this death trap spot by yourself, boy?" Gunplay asked.

I popped a French fry into my mouth and chewed it. Then I lifted my coat to show him the Glock on my hip. "I ain't never by myself."

"Nigga," Willbo said. "You keep flashing that weak ass Glock, mediocre ass joint."

Blue Black pulled out a pistol and said, "This that new Desert Eagle, ten shot. Step your game up, moe."

"Both of y'all niggas out here bullshittin. He got sixteen and you got ten in that big, stupid ass DE. It's gon take five minutes to pull that dumb ass joint."

Everybody laughed, especially Blue Black.

"This is what you need for these mean streets," Gunplay continued and pulled out a compact Heckler and Koch S20 with air holes in the short muzzle and a clip that was see-through. "The clip stores bullets beside one another. There's seventy-five in here and you can't even tell."

Everybody gathered in Leo's stared in awe at the futuristic weapon that Gunplay held. I couldn't even tell if it was some sorta hybrid sub machine pistol. I wanted one just like it.

"Let me take a pic of that joint. I gotta show that joint to my cousin," I said, then pulled out my phone and snapped a picture. "That muthafucka like that."

"Ain't it past your bedtime, Quette?" Willbo asked.'

"Why you ask that?" I replied, eating my chicken.

"Because we all know that Shakira's mother ain't gon' have you outside this time of night. And Shakira will mess around and put hands on you for being out so late."

"Shakira gon' put hands on who?"

"The nigga behind you," Delow teased.

I was by the wall and knew that there was no one behind me. "Ain't nobody putting hands on me, slim. Nobody."

"Ain't nobody putting hands on you?" Gunplay said. "Your mother's boyfriend used to put hands on you. Remember that day we was in front of your house—"

"I forgot about that, but he won't be putting hands on nobody else in this life."

"I heard that somebody killed that nigga," Blue Black said.

"Killed who?" Delow asked.

"Quette's mother's boyfriend, Jamo. Wild ass old head nigga, closet cake smoker," Gunplay told him. "Somebody shot—"

"Stabbed," I corrected.

"Stabbed what? Jomo? I thought he got shot?"

"Naw, he got stabbed, I know because I stabbed him."

"Nigga, you welling!" Gunplay said and laughed as others followed.

I didn't, I continued to eat my food.

"Damn, homes, you put the knife in that nigga?" Gunplay asked.

I nodded. "Got tired of him hitting my mother."

"As you should've," Blue Black stated. "I'd have put that Lorton knife on his ass, too."

"Nigga Lorton closed in two-thousand. You ain't never been to Lorton," Willbo said.

"Man, fuck Lorton. Lil Cee was down Lorton and look what that got him and Meechie," Gunplay commented.

"And A.D.," I added.

"Did Cutty and nem get into something at the Bliss?" Delow asked.

"Andre told me that nothing happened inside the club. He said they turnt up the whole time in VIP. So, whatever happened had to be some street shit," Willbo told them. "Cutty is always in some shit and Lil Cee be doing a rack of wild shit with that dope he was selling. He probably beat a nigga and he came back."

"Put that chopper on their asses," Lil Mike-Mike said.

"I wonder how in the hell Cutty survived that shit? Did y'all see the G-Wagon on the news? Swiss cheese," Blue Black said.

"Nigga gotta horseshoe up his ass," Gunplay replied. "Mama-San, let me get the fried Tilapia special with Coleslaw and fries."

***

"Gunplay, I got thirty-five dollars," Michelle said, producing crumpled bills from her bra. "Can I get a fifty?"

"Go head with that shit, Michelle. Every day you come short. A fifty is fifty dollars, not thirty-five," Gunplay replied.

"Please, Gunplay! I need you to fuck with me one time. Please!"

Gunplay eyed Michelle's phat ass in her jeans and large breasts. Before he said a word, I already knew what the next play was gonna be.

"A'ight, I got you. C'mere for a minute, though, let me holla at you about something."

Smiling to myself, I watched Gunplay walk off with Michelle to the second building where the hallway lights never worked.

"That nigga about to trick with Michelle," Delow said and bust out laughing.

I couldn't help but laugh, too.

"Gun wrong as shit," Willbo said. "He gon' fuck Mike-Mike's mother like that."

"Dirty nigga, there—" I started but got cut off by Delow.

"Who dat, right there?" Delow asked. "Stumbling and shit."

All our eyes followed the direction Delow pointed in. A man was staggering around, holding onto the gate of the sidewalk.

"Go and see who that is," Blue Black demanded.

Red Ronnie took off down the street and then back to where we were. Winded Red Ronnie said, "That's Big Pat, he must be drunk."

I watched Big Pat steady himself and enter an alley nearby.

"I'ma get with y'all tomorrow," I announced to my man. "I'm tired as shit."

I pulled out my phone and pretended to call Shakira. Told her to come and open the door. After giving all my men a soldier hug, I headed toward Shakira's house. Once I was out of the eyesight of my men, I ran down the street and crossed over. Then I ducked behind some cars for a minute. I crossed back over to the other side of 1st Street and hit the same alley that Big Pat had stumbled into. I spotted his big ass barely able to get down the alley. He had to repeatedly stop to gather himself. From inside my dip, I pulled out the suppressor attachment and screwed it onto my Glock. Then I slowly walked up to Big Pat.

"Hey, Big Pat!" I called out.

"Who's there, who dat?" Big Pat stammered.

"It's me, Lil Quette."

"Quette?"

I was right in front of Big Pat now. "Yeah, you remember when you tried to take my money the other day?"

"What? What you talkin' 'bout, youngin?"

"You tried to take my money. I pulled my gun. You asked if I knew how to use it. Remember that?"

"I was just playing, youngin," Big Pat said.

"Well, I wasn't," I told him, raised the gun, and fired.

***

The phone vibrating on the table next to my head woke me up. I looked around for Shakira, but she was gone and her side of the bed was warm. I grabbed the phone and saw that the caller was Khadafi.

"What's up, big cuz?"

"You, cuz. You up?"

"Yeah, I'm up now. What's up?"

"Meet me for breakfast, I gotta breathe on you."

"Cool. Where at?" I asked him.

"Meet me at the Ben's Chili Bowl on U Street," Khadafi responded.

"They got breakfast in there?"

"Hell yeah. Turkey half smoke, egg, and cheese. Good as shit."

"A'ight, let me get up and get myself together. Gimme about thirty minutes and I'm there."

"A'ight, bet, see you then." Khadafi hung up.

As if on cue, Shakira walked into the room, mad. "I'm glad you're up. I was just about to wake you up anyway. I thought I told your ass about bringing that gun in my house? You hard- headed as shit."

Damn, I forgot all about the gun in my pants pockets on the floor. I usually hid it from Shakira, but last night I was so tired from that food and the weed I smoked with Gunplay that I forgot to hide the gun when I got in.

"Look, my bad. I meant to leave it in the car, but I was rushing."

"Rushing? Rushing to do what, Quette? You didn't get in here until almost three o'clock this morning. So, whatever you was doing, it wasn't rushing. And I already told your ass twice about coming in here so late. My mother gon' fuck around and put both of us out on the street. And if she walks in here and sees that gun on the floor—boy—" Shakira shook her head in disgust. "Your head hard as a brick wall."

Before I could answer her, my cell phone vibrated again. It was Gunplay. "Gun, what's up?"

"Somebody crushed Big Pat last night," Gunplay said.

"I'm already hipped."

"Sayless. When you coming out?"

"Later, I gotta take care of some stuff."

"I don't know what the fuck has gotten into you, but I love it. Get at me later, peace."

I disconnected the call.

"Uh-uh—where the hell you think you going? What you gotta take care of?"

I got all the way up and headed for the shower.

"I know you hear me talking to you, Quette," Shakira nagged.

Once in the bathroom, I relieved myself, and hopped in the shower. Shakira was still talking on the side of the door, I laughed her out.

***

Khadafi was sitting in a booth at the rear of Ben's eating.

"You didn't order me nothing?" I asked as I slid in on the other side.

"Ain't know what to order you. You ain't about to be crushing no pork and shit while I'm sitting right here. I ain't tryna see nor smell that shit, right now."

"I don't see why not. That pork bacon good as shit," I said smiling.

"Lil cuz, just because you putting in work, don't mean I won't beat that ass. You think my gun game mean, wait till you see my knuckle game."

"Okay, big fella, I hear you. But just so you know, I killed the last muthafucka who threatened me."

Khadafi laughed. "Oh, yeah. Who threatened you, cuz?"

"That nigga, Big Pat from my neighborhood. The one who tried to take my money. I took your advice and smashed his ass."

"When?"

"Last night, caught him slippin' and nailed his ass to the ground."

"That's right, lil cuz. Spoken like a true killer, I'm proud of you."

"I learned from the best. You heard about South Capitol Street, right?"

"Saw it on the news," Khadafi said and bit into his sandwich. "One survivor, huh?"

I nodded. "The nigga Cutty was in the back. Bitch nigga made it out alive."

"You think he saw you?"

"I don't know," I said honestly.

"Has anybody seen him, yet? At the hospital?"

"I don't know, streets ain't talking."

"Well, just give it a few days and we'll see what happens. Go order your food."

I went to the counter and ordered turkey sausage, scrambled eggs with cheese and French toast. While I waited for my food, I thought about Cutty. I'd heard a lot of stories about Cutty's gun game. He was a loose end that needed to be tied up. The night I ran up on the G-Wagon with the Draco replayed in my head.

"Do you think he saw you?" Khadafi had asked a few minutes ago.

"I don't know," I replied because I really didn't know.

I saw the scene in my head and tried to remember Cutty's exact movements.

I searched my mind to see if there was a chance that he'd seen me. It was dark out, I was wearing black, but my face was uncovered. I had moved quickly from the van to the G-Wagon, unloading the Draco as I moved. The probability that Cutty had seen me was slim to none. My food appeared in front of me quickly. I grabbed it and went back to the booth where Khadafi sat. I noticed that he had finished his food.

"Damn, you was hungry as shit, huh?"

Khadafi leaned back in his seat. "I been fucking so much—I might got somebody pregnant. My shit stay hungry."

"That funny looking joint draining you, huh?"

"Jive like, but lately it ain't her. I gotta dyke joint that's fucking the shit outta me, cuz. Remember the other day when I dropped the van off to be painted? You was supposed to come scoop me from the IHOP?" Khadafi asked.

"I remember," I told him and started crushing my food.

"I bumped into this bad dyke bitch that fucks with somebody I know. We ended up eating together at IHOP and then I ended up eating her. Still don't know how it happened. Said she hadn't had no dick in years, and I guess she decided she wanted mine. That's why I called you and told you I didn't need the ride."

"A dyke, though?"

Khadafi nodded. "Not one of them dominant man-bitches. Lisa is the feminine one in the relationship. Bad as shit, piercings everywhere, pussy a torch. We been fucking nonstop for the last two days. The funny looking joint been blowing my shit up, texting me, leaving threatening voicemails and shit."

"Threatening?"

"She don't know no better. I been ducking her, so she's mad at me. On some real live shit, cuz. I'm tired of fucking for real. I been fucking either one of three bitches every day since I been home. I'ma have to get some Cialis or Viagra or something. No bullshit. Fucking and killing, that's all I do. I need to ease up."

"You can't ease up," I said.

"One day, I will, when all the people that's on my list is dead."

Chapter Thirty-Five

Khadafi

"I feel you on that."

I leaned in close to Lil Quette. "Do you really, cuz?"

Lil' Quette nodded his head.

"You gotta list, cuz?"

"Yeah," Lil Quette replied.

"How many people on it?" I asked.

"Just one and that's Cutty."

Seeing the look of a stone-cold killer in my cousin's eyes made me proud. I knew that he meant every word. "Speaking of my list, I chose this spot to eat breakfast for a reason. Not too far from here, I need to go and send a message to a man in prison. I can't touch him, so I gotta touch someone he loves. You got to be my wing man. My car is parked down the street in one of them all day pay to park lots. I'ma hop in the whip with you, take care of business and then you gotta take me to get the van. And I'ma need that Glock on your hip so that I can meet up with my man and swap our guns out. This joint on Hobert is gonna be my last body for my two joints. I should've told you to bring that Draco."

"Bring the Draco for what?"

"To get rid of it, it got bodies on it," I answered.

"That's a no go, big cuz. Hell Rell stays with me."

"Hell Rell? Who the fuck is Hell Rell?"

"That's what I nicknamed the Draco, Hell Rell. It's with me do or die."

I laughed at Lil Quette, he was still young, and it was customary for young dudes to get attached to their guns. I could've put my foot down and demanded that he get rid of the assault rifle, but I decided quickly to let it ride. The bodies on it were his to claim, so if he wanted to keep the weapon used in a double homicide, so be it.

"Cool, cuz, keep it. Let's bounce, so I can go and take care of this business.

***

"Do you see any cameras on the houses that I don't see?"

The house that I wanted set on the left side of the street. The 700th Block of Hobart Street in Northwest was as residential as D.C. could get. There were no manicured lawns, but the houses in close proximity to one another looked expensive. An occasional person walked up or down the street, but at that early hour, it was almost deserted. Good for me, bad for my victim. I looked at the address texted to my phone and stared at the red brick house to my left, 714.

"Naw, big cuz, they ain't got none. Unless they hidden smart cameras or something," Lil Quette said.

"You know what, cuz?"

"What's up, big boy?"

"I fucked up when I did that rat shit, cuz. Real talk. Most times I hate myself for that shit. Even though it worked out for Ameen because he beat that shit. I fucked my whole legacy up with that shit. I should have never agreed to that shit. But I was blinded by emotion that was too much for me to shake. In my mind, I convinced myself that it was my only option.

When I got out Maryland in twenty-fourteen, some niggas was plotting on me, to bring me a move. Probably would have killed me, but that wasn't what Allah wanted. A dude who I didn't know from nowhere named DeAngelo Stone saved my life. He knew I had dishonored myself by telling on Ameen, but unknown to me, one of the bodies I caught was on a dude who had killed his mother. He overlooked the hot shit and wisened me up about the move. And he armed me, gave me a big, pretty ass knife.

The next morning, I took off on the floor and put that knife all in them niggas. Damned near kilt Jeezy. They locked me down on lock up tight as shit. A couple days or so later, the CO's found a dude dead in his cell, stabbed to death. It was the dude D. Stone that saved my life. Somebody, probably his celly, told the homies, namely, Jeezy's codefendant, Kito, that it was D. Stone who warned and armed me.

They killed him for it, I promised myself that when I got home, somebody in Kito and Jeezy's family would pay for their actions. I owe that to DeAngelo Stone. He would be alive if I never did that hot shit and Kito's people would still be alive if that had never happened." I screwed the suppressor on the end of the Glock and exited the vehicle. I walked around the Camaro and up to the red brick house bearing the numbers 714. I knocked on the door.

"Who is it?" a female voice called out from inside the house.

"Donnell, a friend of Kito's."

I could hear the locks turning and then the door opened. A middle-aged woman stood in the doorway. She was pretty with salt and pepper, layered, straight hair falling down her shoulders and back.

She smiled. "Did you say that you're a friend of my nephew?" the woman said.

I nodded my head.

"Well," she continued. "You do know that he's locked up, right?"

"Yeah, I was locked up with him. I just came to send him a message," I said.

"And what message is that?"

From behind my leg, I produced the gun, stepped back, and fired. When the body dropped, I stepped up closer and put more bullets into the woman's face and chest. Overkill, message sent.

***

"Damn, big cuz. This look like a totally different van, ladder on the back door, rack on the roof and a different color. I like it," Lil Quette said as soon as he saw the van.

"Good, then you drive it. I'ma take the Camaro. We going to Aunt Mary's house," I told him, then got behind the wheel of his car and pulled off.

At the light on St. Barnabas Road, I pulled out my cell phone and called Bosco.

He answered on the second ring. "What's good, homes?"

"You, I need to come and see you later," I told Bosco.

"Hit me when you ready, I'll be ready."

"A'ight, cuz, I appreciate you."

"Don't trip, slim, you good."

"Bet, later."

***

"Gimme your hammer."

Lil Quette pulled out his Glock and the attachment and dropped it in the Harris Teeter bag I held open. My two Glocks and attachments were already in the bag.

"I'am call you once I cop the new joints and give you one."

"That's a bet, make sure you do that. I feel naked."

"As you should. I got you, cuz, before the end of the day."

***

//: I'm outside in the parking lot! I pressed send on my phone

Seconds later, I got a returned text from Sherita.

//: I'm on my way out.

Five minutes passed and finally Sherita exited the side door that led to the parking lot of Forestville Health and Rehab. Her multicolored scrubs and crocs reminded me of Marnie. Sherita's hair was in a ponytail. Her face was heavily made up and her lips were covered with gloss. She climbed into the passenger seat of the Benz.

"I like this," she said as she looked around the car.

I pulled out of the parking lot on Marlboro Pike. "Where you tryna get lunch from?" I asked her.

"Somewhere far," Sherita said, then reached down and pulled off her crocs.

"Somewhere far?" I repeated.

"Yeah." Sherita climbed over to my side, unzipped my jeans and pulled my dick out. "So, that I can suck this dick all the way there and all the way back."

It took everything inside me to focus on the road while Sherita's head bobbed up and down in my lap.

***

All I could do was shake my head and smile as I watched Sherita walk into the building at Forestville Health and Rehab. True to her words, she ate my dick to and from the Carolina Kitchen off Branch Avenue. Her ass had an extra sway to it, confined in her scrubs. I thought about the day she forced me to sex her anally. Before pulling off, I read an incoming text from Lisa.

//: *Just got home. Stop by!*

Pulling out of the lot, I stopped at the first gas station I saw.

"Gimme one of them Mojos and a silver Rhino 500," I told the guy behind the glass at the Amoco. "Oh, and a Kiwi Strawberry Nantucket."

In the car, I popped the Mojo pill and Rhino together. I needed both of the sexual stimulant pills to handle both Sherita and Lisa. I drowned the entire twenty-ounce fruit juice.

***

"Khadafi! Oh, shit! Khadafi!"

Lisa's butter pecan skinned ass was phat and jiggly. As I slammed repeatedly into her tight, wet pussy. I couldn't help but stare at it. It had a perfect heart shape. Lisa was on her bed on all fours, her pants, and panties at her ankles. The blouse she wore had ridden up to where most of her back was exposed. My hands held her waist as I pounded, then grinded, pounded then grinded myself into her.

"Shit, I'm cummin'! I'm cummin' again!" Lisa moaned.

"Cum on that dick for me. Cum all over that dick!" I told her.

Lisa grabbed the blanket on her bed and screamed a loud muffled scream into it. She kept screaming into the blanket until I finally came, then pulled out.

"Nigga—what the fuck?" Lisa said, looking at me over her shoulder. "Fuck you took, an E-pill?"

I rubbed my now soft dick in between Lisa's ass cheeks and laughed. Seconds later, I got hard again, so I fucked Lisa again and again.

***

Bosco told me to meet him at a complex called the Cloisters on Michigan Avenue near Children's Hospital. When I pulled into the complex, he flashed his lights to let me know that he was there. It was dark out, but there were lights attached to the buildings that surrounded us. I parked the Benz and walked over to his car. He exited a silver four door Porsche as I approached.

"What's up, cuz?" I greeted.

"That's fucked up what you did, homes," Bosco said in return.

"What you talkin' 'bout, cuz?" I asked but knew exactly what he was referring to.

"You lied to me, slim. You asked me for Kito's people address because you wanted to drop off some bread. I got that info for you and text it to you. Hours later, you go to the man's house and kill his aunt."

"Aye, cuz, you barking up the wrong tree," I warned.

"Naw, I'm not, homes. When you knocked on the door, Kito's aunt came to the door, but there was a little boy behind her. When you hit the aunt and turned to leave, shorty saw you. He told his people that the man with the big beard killed his auntie. Kito's people called him on his cell phone, the jack he got in the joint. Shorty told Kito not the cops that the man at the door said he was a friend of Kito's. Then he shot his aunt and that the man had a big beard.

Kito called my man E-Goody and told him that it was you, and that y'all got—correction you got into something with Jeezy. You stabbed Jeezy while y'all was in the joint together. He said that a dude named Stone armed you and sent you at Jeezy. So, he killed

Stone. E-Goody called me and told me. But nobody knows that I'm the one that gave you the address. Had I known that you—"

As Bosco talked, I eased the suppresses Glock out and shot him, right in the face. Then I walked over to his car prepared to kill whoever was inside, but the Porsche was empty. I walked back to Bosco and searched for his keys. I found it in his coat pocket. I pressed the button and opened the trunk. Inside the trunk was a large duffle bag. I opened the bag and peered inside. It was full of guns and ammunition. I lifted the bag out of the trunk and walked back past Bosco.

"Stupid ass nigga. You talk too much," I said and shot Bosco again.

I tossed the bag into my backseat and drove off. I drove from there to Hayas Point near the water. I stood by the railing and tossed both of my Glocks into the water. Then I tossed Lil' Quette's Glock in too. Next went all the suppressors.

***

"Big cuz, what's good with you?" Lil Quette said.

"I'm outside," I replied. "Come on out for a minute."

Minutes later, Lil Quette opened the passenger door and climbed into my car. I handed him a Smith and Wesson .45 with a slightly extended clip that held thirteen instead of ten.

"Thanks, big cuz."

"That ain't shit, cuz. I'll holla at you in the a.m."

"In the a.m.," Lil Quette said and left the car.

Chapter Thirty-Six

Nicole

"Your Honor, I call to the stand, Nicole Brooks," the prosecutor announced.

I rose from my seat in the gallery and walked up to the witness stand. It was a peculiar feeling having to be a vessel for the government. I worked for defense attorneys in defense of street niggas. That's the path I chose when I started my investigation service. But Bernard Grimes was one of the attorneys who paid me well to work for him, so when he asked me to come to his defense, I had to, I had no other choice.

"Please state your name for the record."

"Nicole Brooks."

"And who are you employed by, Ms. Brooks?"

"I am self-employed, I own my own private investigation business, but I contract my services to several attorneys with private practices. I also do CJA work for public defenders here in the city."

"How long have you been an investigator, Ms. Brooks?" the prosecutor asked.

"For about sixteen years," I answered.

"Okay, let me take you back to two-thousand-twelve. Were you an investigator then?"

"I was."

"Do you remember who you did investigator work for in two-thousand-twelve?"

"I do. There were four attorneys that I worked for. Nicki Lotze, Renee Reynolds, Mark Robinson and Rudolph Sabino."

"Do you know why you have been called here today?"

"Yes, I do."

"And why are you here?"

"For an evidentiary hearing. A former client of Bernard Grimes, Andre Dalton has filed a motion claiming ineffective assistance of counsel."

"And according to Mr. Dalton, Bernard Grimes did not call his defense witnesses, nor did he do a pretrial investigation in his case. Do you still work for Bernard Grimes, Ms. Brooks?"

"I do not."

"Any particular reason why not?"

"No ma'am, I have other contracts now."

"Is it fair to say that you have no invested interest in Bernard Grimes, his past or current cases?"

"That's a fair assessment."

"In two-thousand-twelve, when you did investigative work for Bernard Grimes, did you have the opportunity to meet with Andre Dalton?"

"I did, I went to D.C. Jail and met with Andre Dalton at least ten times over the course of twenty-seven months."

"On any of those occasions while at D.C. Jail visiting Andre Dalton, did he give you any names of potential defense witnesses? Anyone that he wanted to call at trial?"

"He did not. We talked at length about his case. Especially about any potential witnesses that could help him. His case was a murder case. One that happened at approximately three fifty p.m. while Cardozo High School was letting out for the day. There were people everywhere when the murder was committed. I repeatedly asked Andre Dalton if anyone he knew who was on eleventh street that day could say that the person who committed the murder wasn't him. He replied in the negative. I repeatedly asked him about an alibi or any alibi witness. He had none."

"Did you take notes in this case, Ms. Brooks?"

"I did and I still have them. I made them available to this court."

"Anywhere in the records that you have, did you see anything about a man named Cedrick Black?"

"No."

"What about Donald Christopher?"

"Never heard of him."

"Never heard of him? What about Angela Dalton, Andre's sister?"

"Andre Dalton never gave me those names."

"Okay. When you were doing investigative work for Bernard Grimes, were you the only investigator that did work for Mr. Grimes?"

"No, I was not. There was another guy, Michael Pollins."

"Did you and Mr. Pollins work together on Andre Dalton's case?"

"We did. Although the city of D.C. has been gentrifying for years, it's still a dangerous place to work and live. There were still high crime areas that white male investigators wouldn't be safe in. Mike Pollins could not go to Garfield Terrace, the projects across from Cardozo High and ask questions, but I could. Mike investigated the staff inside Cardoza, the crime scene and questioned law enforcement officers. I beat up the pavement on and around eleventh street to include Garfield Terrace and Clifton Terrace."

"So, a pretrial investigation was done?"

"A thorough pretrial investigation was done."

"Thank you, Ms. Brooks. No further questions, Your Honor."

After the hearing, I stood in the hallway outside of the courtroom and started to feel lightheaded.

"Andre Dalton is doing forty years in prison and he will say and do anything to get out of his situation. Judge Sullivan knows that, and we know that. Nicole was pretty convincing in her testi—"

"Nicole!"

I hadn't even realized that I had passed out and was on the floor until I opened my eyes and saw Bernie kneeling over me calling my name. Paula Sorenson, the prosecutor, kneeled beside Bernie, holding my hand.

"Stay with me, Nicole. An ambulance is on the way," Paula Sorenson said.

Suddenly I was very exhausted and dizzy. I closed my eyes and drifted to a very dark place.

***

Two Days Later

I opened my eyes, and everything seemed different. I was no longer in the hallway at Superior Court. I was inside a hospital room, hooked up to an IV drip. My mother slept in a chair beside my bed.

"Ma," I muttered.

My mother awoke and exclaimed, "Oh my gawd, baby, don't ever scare me like that again."

"Ma, what happened? Why am I here?"

"You fainted at the court building. You don't remember?"

Shaking my head, my eyes watered, and tears rolled down my cheeks. "What's wrong with me, Ma?"

"They don't know, Nic. You wouldn't wake up. They've been running all sorts of tests on you. That's all I know."

"I know my body. I knew that something was wrong. I been feeling really weird lately."

"You're gonna be fine. Nothing is wrong with you. You've been working hard for months. You're probably just stressed out. And your diet of mostly carryout food hasn't helped."

"Ma, people who are healthy don't faint and go to sleep for— what day is it?" I asked.

"Today is Friday," my mother replied, concerned.

"I've been out for two days. How can I be fine?"

"Your body was tired, baby."

"Maybe, but I was feeling lightheaded all-day Wednesday. I was—"

The nurse walked into the room, an older black woman. "Glad to see that you're finally awake. I'll get Dr. Chung." She turned and left.

Minutes later, an Asian doctor walked into the room.

"Ms. Brooks, good to have you back with us," the doctor said.

"What's wrong with me, doc?"

The doctor looked in my mother's direction. I recognized the look.

"It's okay, doctor. My mother can hear whatever it is that you have to say."

"Actually Ms. Brooks, it's hard to say at the moment, but my guess is that you are suffering from some sort of virus or disease—"

"*Virus? Disease?* I haven't had sex—"

"No, not a sexually transmitted disease or virus like HIV. I can't say for sure until your lab work comes back, but whatever it is, it's serious. Your blood pressure was through the roof when you were brought in. You were minutes away from cardiac arrest. We found blood in your urine and stool. Something is definitely amiss inside you and I assure you we are working diligently to identify exactly what it is. You were unconscious and that befuddled us because we could find no immediate cause for it.

The fact that you are now awake gives me hope that everything is okay and maybe you experienced some sorta forty-eight-hour bug. We've been giving you antibiotics intravenously and pain medicine to make you comfortable. Your vitals are better but not stable enough for us to release you. So, you'll have to stay with us until we can get all the lab and test results back. If there is anything you need, hit the call button, the nurse will come running. I'll leave you and your mom alone now. I'll be back tomorrow to check on you, okay?"

"Okay, doc and thank you," I said.

"Thank you, doctor," my mother repeated.

"Ma, where is Antonio?"

"With Sheila, I just talked to him."

"I'm scared, Ma," I said and closed my eyes.

"Don't be, everything is gonna be fine."

***

Turns out everything wasn't fine. The test results came back on Monday. Dr. Chung came to my bedside to discuss my condition. The dire news was written all over his face.

"Nicole, I hope you don't mind me calling you, Nicole?"

"I don't."

"I'm sorry to have to tell you this but you have stage four cervical cancer. Which is why you've been experiencing the pains in your side. The cancer has spread to all your major organs, including your brain. That's why you fainted and went into a semi-comatose state. Your dizziness, lightheadedness, all of that is a direct result of the cancer. Had your condition been caught and diagnosed sooner, it could have been aggressively treated and the prognosis would be different, better. We can do chemo and radiation therapy but that will only prolong the inevitable. It would be like treating a gunshot wound with a peroxide. Frankly put, you are at the end stage, Nicole. The medical term is terminal. I fucking hate cancer, but it's here and it's not going anywhere until the people way smarter than me develop a cure."

"Are you telling me that I'm dying, doctor?" I asked in disbelief.

Dr. Chung simply nodded his head.

"No! No! No! No! No!" my mother bellowed.

Tears rolled down my cheeks. I choked up but still asked, "How much time do I have left, doctor? Do you know?"

"From the CT scan, X-Rays and lab work I've been studying all morning. I'd say that maybe you have six to eight weeks left to live. I will give you and mom some time to come to—"

I could see Dr. Chung's lips moving through my tears. I could see my mother's tears and her mouth open, but for some reason I couldn't hear anything anybody was saying.

Chapter Thirty-Seven

Marnie

"Good morning, Mrs. Dunleavy," Doctor Lillian said.

"Good morning, Ms. D," I followed.

Patrease Dunleavy was seventy-years old and basically abandoned at the hospital. She had no family to speak of and was content to watch TV all day. She looked up as we approached her bed but did not return our greetings. Doctor Samantha Lillian, the residential doctor for the fifth floor and myself, the head nurse, were used to most elderly patient's dispositions.

"Mrs. Dunleavy, recent tests revealed some enlargement of the heart middle to late-stage kidney disease. Probably the result of your long history of hypertension. We also found edema and congestion of the lungs. You smoke, right?"

Mrs. Dunleavy nodded her head. "For more than fifty years, three packs a day."

"Well, that explains the lung damage. Other than that, everything else looks good. Nurse Summers is going to take your vitals. Are you feeling okay? Regular bowel movements? Uninterrupted urine flow?"

"I'm fine," Mrs. Dunleavy admitted. "Just living waiting to die, is all."

"If I have any say in the matter, Mrs. Dunleavy, that won't be for many, many more years from now," Doctor Lillian responded and made her exit.

"Let me get your blood pressure, Mrs. D."

I wrapped the wrist monitor around her wrist. "One-forty over one-hundred. That's a little high, Mrs. D. We need to bring it down."

"It doesn't matter, child, what my blood pressure is. I'm not long for this world, no matter what that lady doctor says. I can feel myself getting closer and closer to them pearly gates."

"Don't speak like that into the universe, Mrs. D."

"Well, it's true, gotta face the truth."

***

It's been at least a month since I found out that Khadafi was home. Yet, I still haven't heard not one word from him. That scared me more than anything. I knew that it would be hard for him to find me, but we still had mutual friends. He could've easily gotten some type of message to me, a threat, a summons, something. I knew that he wanted to see his kids, but still, he'd said nothing.

"Maybe, he's decided to leave you alone," the voice inside my head said.

"He'd never do that," I said out loud.

Luther Khadafi Fuller would never concede defeat. He'd never willingly give up access to his children after giving up his rights to his oldest son, Kashon to Shawnay. Naw, that was out of the question, which brought me to the conclusion that Khadafi was up to something. He was planning something. Not knowing what that something was made me lose sleep at night. Khadafi was my own personal boogeyman. One that could strike at any moment. I drove home on the Capitol Beltway listening to music and a song came on the radio that reminded me of Khadafi every time I heard it. Erykah Badu's song was a Khadafi favorite and it coming on the radio while I thought about Khadafi was another sign for me, he was coming.

"What you gonna do when they come for you/ Work ain't honest, but it pays the bills/ What you gonna do when they come for you/He gave me the life that I've come to live/Do I really want my baby/ Brother tell me what to do/I know you've got to get your hustle on/So, I pray/ I understand the game/Sometimes/And love you strong—"

I remembered all the days that I had sung that song to Khadafi as if I was Erykah. I remembered how it always seem to captivate him. The look in his eyes as he listened. I was filled with so much love for him then.

"What we gonna do when they come for you/ I know I can't spend life without you/Me and baby got this situation/See, brother got this complex occupation/And it ain't that he don't have no

education/Cause I was right there at his graduation/I ain't saying that this life don't work/ But it's me and baby that he hurts/ Because I tell him right, he thinks I'm wrong/ But I love him strong—"

A nervous chill ran through my body. I wondered if Khadafi knew about Creation. He probably had and the news of my third child must've pushed him close to the edge. It had, too. Scary! Scary! Scary! As one song on my radio switched to another, I thought about the pain Khadafi must feel. His anger, his appetite for blood, his reckless desire to kill. The streets of D.C. had to be raining blood and it would continue to do so until Khadafi found me. Another chill ran through me again, God help us all.

***

"Ma, it's your move," I told my mother.

"Okay, I can't be the bank *and* focus on my properties, too. Where am I?"

"You're still on St. Charles Place, roll the dice."

My mother rolled a seven and moved her wheelbarrow one too many.

"Stop cheating, Ma. Go back one, you landed on utilities. I own that, roll one dice and see how much you gotta pay me."

"Damn, Marnie. You worse than them damn Jews that own Hollywood."

"What's Hollywood, Mommy?" Khadejah asked.

"It's a place in California where all the movies are made, baby," I explained.

"Who are the Jews?" a precious four-year-old Khamani asked.

"A bunch of stingy, rich muthaf—"

"The Jews are a nationality of people, Mani. Rich people from Israel," I interrupted, giving my mother the side eye.

Tawana Curry just laughed.

"Was Frozen made in Hollywood, Mommy? And Cars? Was Lion King made there?"

"I think so, Dada. And come on, it's your move."

Khadejah rolled the dice and moved her piece. Go straight to jail.

"You gotta go to jail, Dada," my mother teased.

"That's okay, Nana. Maybe I'll get to see daddy."

"Daddy's not in jail, Dada. He's at work. Right, Mommy?" my son asked.

"My daddy is in jail, boy! And so is yours. Our daddy is in jail. Cree's at work, he's not our daddy, dummy!"

"You a dummy," Khamani whined. "Dummy, dummy, dummy. Cree is my daddy! My daddy, your daddy, and Cree'a's daddy. Dummy!"

I listened to my two children go back and forth and it broke my heart.

"Stupid little boy, your father's name is Khadafi. He's in jail, you should know that stupid."

"You stupid!" Mani hollered.

"Hey! Both of you quit it! Now before I get my belt," I demanded.

"Mommy, is my daddy named Khadafi in jail?"

I nodded my head. "Your sister is right, Mani. Your father's name is Khadafi and yes, he's in jail."

Khadejah licked out her tongue. "Told you, told you!"

"But, Mommy, you said—"

"Mani, I never told you that Cree was your daddy. He's a father to you, but he's not your daddy. There's a difference. Your daddy is and always will be Luther Khadafi Fuller. Okay?"

"Okay, Mommy," Khamani said pouting.

"Now, move your car after you roll the dice. It's on you," I told him.

Khamani had to reach across me to get the dice. I grabbed him and kissed him over and over.

"Stop it, Mommy!" He giggled and blushed.

"And I never want to hear you two insulting one another and calling each other names ever again. Neither one of you are stupid or dumb. Do I make myself clear?"

"Yes, Mommy!" Khadejah and Khamani said in unison.

Khamani rolled the dice, counted the black dots on the dice and then moved his car five spaces. He landed on Marvin's Gardens.

"Uh, that'll be me, Mani," my mother said. "Pay me one-hundred and twenty dollars."

"Mommy, which color money is one-hundred twenty-dollars?"

Everybody at the table busted out laughing.

***

My daughter decided that she wanted to stay up for a while so my mother held her and fed her a bottle in the kitchen, while I did the dishes.

"I didn't say nothing then, but that little scene at the table was a little crazy, huh?" my mother said.

"I know, right. And it's crazy that it happened for the first time tonight. At a time when Khadafi is home and I'm scared to death of what havoc he's gonna wreak."

"Hopefully, none. But it's clear that Dada really remembers him. She spent the most time with him. Even though she was really young, those years are the most impressionable on a child. Mani was an infant the last time he saw Khadafi so it's understandable that all he knows is Cree."

I stopped washing a plate and turned to face my mother. "I know all of what you just said. My heart nearly broke in half out there in the dining room. Dada is seven and she wants to see her father. I've been keeping her away from him based on some twisted loyalty I felt to the streets and a code that I don't even follow. Ain't that some wild shit?"

My mother shifted Creation to where my daughters head lay on her shoulder. She softly patted her back to burp her. "You said it was about their security back then and it made sense. To both of us, but I guess in hindsight, it wasn't a great idea."

"It wasn't if it hurts my daughter. And I never really knew it did until today. She's never even mentioned him before. Do you think their hearts are connected to the point where she knows he's home? Somewhere nearby?"

"Could be, baby. Stranger shit has been proven to be true."

"I'm in a catch twenty-two, Ma. Damned if I do, damned if I don't. my daughter wants her father, and I can't continue to deprive her of a father's love. She'll resent me when she's older if I do, but—"

"In life there's always a but, baby."

"Khadafi probably hates me for abandoning him, denying him his rights to be with his kids, getting married and having another child."

"Khadafi knows about Creation?"

I took a deep breath and then exhaled. "I'm not sure but I have to assume that he does. How can I just contact him and say, 'I'm sorry, your daughter needs you without him killing me?"

"I get it, Marnie. It's a tough spot to be in and usually I try to be the voice of reason. This time you have to decide what to do on your own. The only person who can figure this out and answer the questions in your mind, is you. Good luck. Here, take Cree'a and put her to bed. I'm late for Bingo."

"You and that damn Bingo. Do you ever win?" I asked.

"More than I lose. Don't hate, congratulate."

I grabbed my daughter from my mother. "Be safe, Ma. I love you."

"I love you, too, baby."

***

The shower curtain opened, startling me. Cree stepped into the shower. I ran my eyes all over his nude, chiseled physique, yoga, pilates and weight training definitely did the body good.

"Hey, Mrs. Summers," Cree whispered in my ear from behind me.

"Hey, Mr. Summers," I replied and leaned back into him.

Cree's manhood started to rise, so I grinded my ass all over it. His presence was making me horny.

"What did you do all day?"

"Chilled with the kids and my mother."

Cree kissed me on the neck and made my legs weak.

"Did you stop in and check on Cree'a?" I asked Cree.

"Of course, I did. She's sleeping like a baby," Cree replied.

"I wish I could sleep like her."

"Why can't you?"

"Because I'm worried about that crazy ass man I used to love. He's out there somewhere and I don't know what he's going to do."

"I don't want to talk about him," Cree whispered and licked on my neck. "Not, right now."

"Okay, but you keep that up and you're gonna start something."

"That's exactly what I'm trying to do."

Cree entered me, then took my mind off everything but ecstasy.

Chapter Thirty-Eight

Tawana Curry

"How many times do I gotta tell your crazy ass that I ain't writing no niggas in jail? That shit played out. What the fuck are we, teenagers? In our second childhood?" I said to my best friend Sherry as we talked on Facetime while I drove home. "We did that shit in the eighties when Lorton was open, remember?"

"Of course, I remember those days, but Tee, you fifty-five-years old. I hate to be the one that bust your bubble, boo-boo, but you ain't getting no younger and you need a man. Not more nights of Bingo. Donzell McCauley is about to come home. The man been in jail since 1990, that's twenty-seven years. He fine as shit, in great shape, and he got a clean bill of health. He's only like forty-nine. You can be the smart one and snag him now."

"Snag him now? Bitch, time done already done that. Fuck I'ma do with a fifty-year old nigga that been in prison almost three decades? Who was the president back then? Bush the father?"

Sherry laughed. "What does that have to do with anything? I'm tryna put you down with a good man, a good returning citizen and your ass talking 'bout presidents."

"It ain't about the president. I said that to say, 'the nigga is old'. He ain't tryna learn no new tricks. Like how to live life according to the rules of Tawana Curry. You said he been locked up since 1990. Fuck he do?"

"His name is Denny he was a real live street nigga. Something happened and he killed a rack of muthafuckas. That's what I was told. I'ma text you a picture of him and Peanut. You gotta see him. Then you'll recognize the beauty in fucking with a real nigga like him."

It was tough, driving, laughing, and looking at my phone but I managed it. "Recognize the beauty—bitch that sounds gay. And how the hell do I know that he ain't been in jail recognizing the beauty in other men? Naw, I'm good, I'll pass."

"You gotta point there, but Peanut wouldn't endorse no nigga living foul like that. Besides all I'm asking you to do is fill out the visiting form and fly to Louisiana with me to see him and Peanut. Ain't no harm in that."

"I'll think about it, if I go Donzell better have some swag."

"Swag? Girl, swag today is tight ass outfits and shoes that cost more than both of our rents. If that's what you looking for, bitch, stay home."

I cracked up laughing at Sherry. "I'm pulling into a space out front of the building, I'll call you before I get in the bed."

"Yeah, you do that. I'ma need a few of them Bingo dollars to cop me some more of them weed edibles Paula be selling. Call me, bitch, bye."

***

Inside my apartment, I hit the light switch, but no lights came on.

"That's strange," I said to myself and flipped the switch up and down. "Fuck is up with this stupid ass light?"

"I took the fuse out," a male voice said, scaring the shit out of me.

The balcony curtain was open, light from outside illuminated the living room enough for me to make out the silhouette of a person on my couch.

"Who the hell?"

"Since you live on the ground floor, I took the liberty of letting myself in. Hope you don't mind?"

Immediately, I recognized the voice. I hadn't heard it in years, but it was a voice that was unmistakable. Speaking of the devil. "Khadafi?"

"Surprised to come home and find me here, huh?" he said.

"I am! But why did you break in and fuck with my fuse? I'm confused."

"I guess some old habits are hard to break."

It was then that I noticed that my apartment looked ransacked. I squinted to adjust my eyes to the little bit of light and make sure. "How long have you been here and why does it look like my shit been searched?"

"I been here about two hours. I got bored, so I looked around a little. Wanted to find something with Marnie's address on it, pictures of the kids, that type of shit. Didn't find shit. Now I'm mad. Again, I hope you don't mind."

"You hope I don't mind?" I sat my purse on the table and walked closer to Khadafi. "You keep saying that shit. Of course, I mind you breaking in my house and going through my shit."

"I'm sorry to hear that. I would probably be pissed off if somebody broke in my shit and—wait somebody did break in my shit. They put guns to your daughter's head and took all my shit. But I didn't care about what they took. I cared about the fact that they disrespected Marnie. They violated her, that's why I made decisions I made.

To be able to punish the people who violated her. And I've done that, both of the men responsible for violating her are dead. I tried to get her to understand that I needed to right the wrong. But she couldn't understand that and evidently neither could you. Because you could've continued to take my calls despite Marnie obviously telling you not to. You knew the relationship I had with my kids and yet you said fuck me—"

"I couldn't go against Marnie's wishes. I couldn't take sides against her."

"I understand that and that's what makes you just as responsible as her. Both of you kept my kids away from me."

I didn't like the direction the conversation was going in. How was I responsible for the decision that my daughter made? I suddenly thought about the fact that an angry, scorned, certified killer was sitting in my living room in the dark and decided to not say anything. I decided to just listen.

"No reply to that, huh?" Khadafi said. "That ain't cool, Ms. Tawana."

"What do you want me to say, Khadafi?" I asked meekly.

Khadafi stood up, I could see the shadow of the gun in his hand, the barrel elongated. My heart rate quickened.

"I want you to tell me where I can find my children. That's what I want you to say. Tell me where Marnie is."

I was very afraid, but there was no way I was going to tell the deranged man in my living room where my daughter lived. Or give him info that would lead to his children. There was no doubt in my mind that Khadafi would kill Marnie. I couldn't let that happen. I could never live with myself knowing that I had led a mad man to her front door.

"I don't know where Marnie lives. She moved away years ago, I haven't spoken to her in years."

"Liar, liar, pants on fire," Khadafi said in a child's sing-songy voice. "But I respect that, cuz. I expected you not to tell me. Reminds me of another mother that I killed years ago. I was looking for her son after he killed my uncle. Her and her husband refused to tell me where I could find their son. I begged them both to just call him and they refused. Like you're doing right now.

Let me tell you what I did." Khadafi laughed a low manic laugh. "I raped the mother. I put Crisco oil on my dick and fucked her in her ass. Until she got hoarse from screaming. All while her husband watched. After I busted a nut in her ass, I had to recover for a while. Then I fucked the father in his ass until I came again and I ain't even gay. But I was so mad that they wouldn't tell me where their son was that I lost my sanity. After that I shot both of them dead and set their bodies on fire."

"Just like you did PeeWee and his sister?"

"I didn't rape them, though."

"So, is that supposed to be my fate, too? You gon' rape me?"

"Naw, I got too much respect for you to do that. Besides, you might enjoy it."

"You are a sick, perverted muthafucka."

"Sticks and stones will break my bones, but words will never hurt me," the sing-songy voice appeared again.

I thought about something Marnie told me about Khadafi. He never left witnesses that could testify against him. By admitting to me that he killed PeeWee and the fact that he was standing in my living room with a gun, I had unwittingly become a witness against him. That's when it dawned on me that I wasn't going to make it out of the situation I was in alive.

"Marnie understood your decision, Khadafi. But she worried that someone looking to hurt you would hurt her and the kids. That's why she left, that's why she kept the kids away from you. She didn't make a bad baby mother decision. She made a smart, grown woman and mother decision. To protect her children. Even if that meant protecting them from their father's decisions."

"Is that why she got married? And had another child? To protect my kids from my sins?"

"Like I said, she made grown woman decisions. What was she supposed to do, huh? Wait for you?"

"Since you put it like that, I guess not. It's cool, though. Her moving on with her life, that's on her. But keeping my kids from me is making me angrier and angrier. Where are my kids, Ms. Tawana?"

"With their mother, wherever that may be."

Khadafi laughed again, for a long time. Then he said, "I gotta respect you, Ms. Tawana, you thorough. A real southeast chick, morals and principles. I respect that. You're courageous. Even after I just told you what I did to the last mother and father who refused to give me the info I needed. You still refuse to tell me where my children are. That's some gangsta shit."

Chapter Thirty-Nine

Khadafi

"Here you are staring death in the face and you refuse to fold. Gangsta shit." I clapped my hands together with the one with the gun in it. "My beef wasn't necessarily with you, although I do feel like you are just as responsible as Marnie. I was going to spare you, but your refusal to reunite me with my kids is an act of war. That makes you my enemy. And I kill all of my enemies."

"I don't have anything to do with what's going on with you and my daughter," Tawana Curry pleaded. "I am not your enemy, Khadafi. Please don't kill me!"

I crossed the room until I was standing only about a foot from Marnie's mother. "I remember this book I read while on lock up recently. It was called *In The Blink Of An Eye*. In the book a woman accused an innocent man of a murder that her baby's father committed. The innocent man did eighteen years in prison. He came home and befriended the lady's daughter just so that she could lead him to the mother.

It worked, right before he killed everybody daughter included, he told the daughter who believed that he loved her, *'Sometimes the sins of the parents are revisited on the children.'* I never forgot that line because it made sense and it sounded fly. In this case, the sins of the child is revisited upon the parent. I'ma kill you, then Marnie's husband. Too bad you won't get the chance to warn her."

I upped the gun and blew Tawana Curry's brains out. I continued to shoot her even after her lifeless body dropped. The black latex glove on my hands irritated my skin. I scratched under the gloves but kept them on. After tucking the gun, I rummaged through Tawana's purse until I found her cellphone. It was the new iPhone 7S Plus. You needed a fingerprint to open it. I put the phone down low and pressed the dead woman's thumb to it and that opened it.

First, I scrolled through her list of contacts. I saw phone numbers for Marnie's cellphone and work phone. Under Marnie's name was someone named Cree Summers. Phone numbers were listed as well. On a hunch I pressed the contact number for the person named, Cree and the phone rang.

After a few rings, a man answered, "Hello? Hello? Ms. Tawana?"

I disconnected the call.

Minutes later, the phone rang. It was the Cree person calling back. I let it ring. Then a minute later, another call came through. Marnie's number came up on the screen. I smiled. Cree was Marnie's husband. I imagined them in bed together, both curious as to why Tawana Curry wasn't answering her phone.

"She's dead," I said aloud as I continued to rummage through the purse.

When Tawana didn't answer, Marnie called again and again. I picked up the phone and pressed ignore. Then I scrolled through the photos on the phone. There were hundreds of photos of my children. Some from that day that they'd been taken hours ago. I sat in one of the chairs at the dining room table and stared at Khadejah and Khamani. They'd both gotten bigger, older. My daughter was beautiful, an exact replica of my mother when she was younger.

Khamani was a mini me. Him and Kashon could be identical twins. I couldn't take my eyes off my children. Then I saw a toddler. In various stages of growth. A little girl with light grey eyes. She was beautiful. The baby looked like the man who held her, Cree. There were photos of Cree holding my children. Photos of him with Marnie. Him and all the children. All of them together, selfies. Pics from various trips. So, many pictures of Marnie.

While my world had stopped, hers continued. Several times while viewing the photos, Marnie tried to Facetime her mother or call back. I pulled out my phone and took pictures of the contact info for Cree and Marnie. Then I group text photos from the iPhone to my burner phone. Careful to delete all traces of what I had done, I put the phone back in Tawana's purse. Satisfied that I'd done what I had some to do, I left through the balcony door, the same way that I come in.

***

I laid on Lisa's couch with my head in her lap as she rubbed my face. The phone was in my hand. I scrolled through the photos I'd taken from Tawana Curry's phone.

"Your children are beautiful, Khadafil," Lisa said.

"Thanks, cuz. I appreciate that," I replied.

"Marnie sent you the pics, huh?"

"Naw, I got them from her mother."

"That was nice of her."

"Yeah, it was."

Chapter Forty

Detective Rio Jefferson

The parking lot of the complex was filled with cops. I spotted a man in the parking lot behind yellow crime scene tape comforting a hysterical woman. I killed the engine of my Impala and exited the vehicle. I had to fasten the top button on my peacoat to ward off the cold. Throngs of crime scene personnel filled the hallway of 4820. I spoke to friends and coworkers as I made my way to apartment 3G. The apartment door was open, Doug Davis was already on scene.

He looked up, saw me, and walked over. "Howdy, buddy?"

"This murder is obviously out of our jurisdiction. Why are we here? We got enough murders to solve in First District," I said.

"We're here because of the deceased. A lady named Tawana Curry. Does the name ring any bells?"

I tossed the name around in my head but drew a blank. "Naw. Should it?"

"Dispatch gets a call from a frantic woman saying that her mother is dead. Officers respond to the scene and encounter a woman who leads them here to this apartment where they discover a woman shot to death. Multiple shots to the head and face. In her anguish about her mother, the woman mentions a name. One name, Khadafi. Cops all over the city know the name, Khadafi. They question the daughter who clams up immediately. But the cat is already out of the bag. Fred Perry calls me, and I come over. I see the daughter. Guess who she is?"

Suddenly, it hits me like a ton of bricks. "Monica Curry, Khadafi's baby's mother."

Doug nods his head. "Correct, you just won every Teddy bear in Six Flags."

I couldn't believe it. Thoughts of the night Moe Tolliver was shot by Khadafi in the backyard of the house in Montgomery County came to mind.

"Hey, Detective Jefferson? Can you come over here for a minute?" the young, Montgomery County Officer called out.

I walked over and the officer explained to me that the lady in front of him was looking for her boyfriend and feared that he might've been the person involved in the shooting behind the house on Montrose Avenue.

"My name is Detective Rio Jefferson with the D.C. Police Department. What is your boyfriend's name?"

"Luther Fuller, his name is Luther Fuller. He's driving that black Caddy truck over there."

I thought that Moe Tolliver was going to die I was afraid. I was upset, I had tears in my eyes. I wanted Khadafi to be dead so bad, I hoped that if I spoke it into the universe, it would really happen.

"I'm not supposed to do this because a next of kin hasn't been notified but I understand your situation. Khadafi is dead. He was pronounced dead at nine-thirty p.m."

I remembered the woman fainting and us calling an ambulance for her. I remembered her name, Monica Curry. I thought about later that day at the hospital when I saw Monica again. She was with a woman who looked like an older version of her. I knew it had to be her mother. Monica walked up to me in the emergency room lobby.

"Excuse me," she said tapping my shoulder. "We met earlier today on Montrose Avenue."

I looked her up and down. "I remember you. What can I do for you?"

"You lied to me earlier today and I wanna know why."

I was upset that Moe was in surgery fighting for his life. I was angry that Khadafi hadn't died and irritated that his girlfriend had the audacity to confront me in public and question me about him.

"You're Khadafi's girlfriend, right? Your boyfriend has killed more people than smallpox and you have the temerity to question me about him. Well, since you asked, I'll tell you why I told you he was dead. That is the lie that you're referring to, right? Me telling you that Khadafi was pronounced dead at nine-thirty?"

"That's right."

"I told you that because I hoped that I could speak his death into existence. I thought that if I kept saying it, it would really happen. I prayed that it happened. But my prayers weren't answered. I couldn't speak his death into existence. I guess that means I won't be putting any money in the church collection plate this Sunday. You win, I lose. Congratulations!"

"I don't need your congratulations and I don't care—"

"You're going to need something or someone, Ms. Curry. You're Monica Curry, right?"

"That would be me."

That would be me. I walked over and lifted the sheet to get a look at the deceased. I could tell that the woman on the floor dead was the same woman at the hospital that night four years earlier.

"You think Khadafi killed her?" Doug Davis asked me.

"It's hard to say. Why would he kill his children's grandmother?"

"Beats me. According to Fred Perry and the cops here, Monica Curry let it slip that she thinks he did it."

"Tell me everything you've learned thus far about this murder."

"Only been here like ten minutes before I called you, that's forty-five minutes, tops." Doug called over a young, white, uniformed cop. "Officer Wilks, give Detective Jefferson the rundown on what you know so far."

The cop pulled out a notepad and read from it, "Call came through dispatch about an hour ago. Daughter gets a call on her cell phone from her mom's cell phone. Daughter calls back several times, but Mom doesn't answer. Daughter suspects foul play, rushes here from Northern Virginia and uses her key to get in. She finds her mom shot to death. She calls it in.

We get here and confirm that her mom is dead. The daughter's name is Monica Summers. Crime scene search says that the perp broke in through the balcony door. Probably surprised the deceased. It appears to be some ransacking, someone was looking for something. Maybe a crackhead looking for money or drugs or anything valuable. They're still dusting for prints, but there are none on the balcony door. The perp wiped the door clean. Uh, that's all I have."

"Scratch the crackhead angle. Crackheads don't shoot people in the face and head multiple times. This feels personal," I said before turning to Doug and asking him, "Has anyone tried to talk to the daughter again?"

Doug shrugged. "Can't say, Fred Perry says that she doomed up after letting Khadafi's name slip. She's outside with her husband."

"Husband?"

"Yeah, didn't you just hear Officer Wilks say her name is Monica Summers? Apparently, she's gotten married. She's no longer just Khadafi's baby's mama. You're welcome to go talk to her, see if she'll talk to you.

"I think I'll do that. Do me a favor, Doug. Call Corey Winslow and see if he can get down here."

"I'm doing that now," Doug replied, pulling out his cell phone.

I left the apartment and walked outside. The crisp, night air gripped me and chilled me to the bone. I looked at my watch, 1:51 a.m. I glanced to my right and saw a man consoling a woman. The same two I'd noticed when I pulled up. I couldn't see her face, but I knew that the woman was Monica.

When I was inches away from the couple, I said, "Monica Summers?"

The woman looked up at me, recognition crossed her eyes. "You!"

Chapter Forty-One

Marnie

"You!" Was all that I could think to say when I saw the detective who had just said my name. I wiped tears from my eyes and remembered the night I'd met him. There were specks of grey in his curly hair, but he still resembled Shemar Moore. "I remember you."

"I'm sorry about your mother. I remember that she was with you the night you confronted me at the hospital."

My mother had always been there for me. The detective's words provoked images of my mother with me at the hospital. It was she that found out that Khadafi wasn't dead. It was her who had saved my life when I tried to end it.

"Marnie! N-o-o-o-o-o!"

Before I could seal the deal, the gun was yanked out of my mouth. Then it was wrestled away from me. Everything happened so fast, but the next thing I know, I was on the floor of the closet looking up into my mother's face.

"What the fuck was you about to do, huh?" my mother questioned. On her face was a hurt and wounded look that I'd never seen before. Tears fell down her cheeks. "Answer me, gawd dammit! What was you about to do, kill yourself?"

My lips moved but no words came out of my mouth. I couldn't speak. I didn't have the courage to tell my mother the truth.

"You selfish, stupid ass bitch!" my mother exploded. "You wanna die?"

My eyes watched as my mother's hand that held the gun in it came up and was aimed directly at me.

"You wanna die? Kill yourself about that nothing ass nigga? I should kill you myself. You selfish muthafucka! I can't believe your stupid ass. You got a beautiful two-year-old daughter that loves you and needs you and this is what you wanna do to her? Fuck the rest of her life up, having to grow up knowing that her weak ass mother killed herself. Because her father got shot? Bitch, you really are

crazy. Answer me! Sitting there looking all stupid and shit. Like the cat ate your tongue. You wanna kill yourself."

"Yes," I muttered, then covered my face in shame.

My mother stooped low and smacked at my hands that covered my face.

"What did you say? I couldn't hear you. Say it again! Uncover your damn face and look at me. At least be woman enough to do that. You was just woman enough to stick a loaded muthafuckin' gun in your fuckin' mouth, be woman enough to face your mother."

I remembered the hurt look on her face and what she said next stayed with me ever since.

"What if I wouldn't have come back here? What if I hadn't left Dada's bag over there by the bed? I would have lost my only child. Killed by her own hand. Did you ever stop to think about me, huh? What about me? You have no right! No fuckin' right to kill yourself.

You didn't create yourself. You didn't give birth to yourself. You didn't carry yourself for nine months. Or change your own diapers. You didn't nurse yourself when you got sick. You didn't take care of yourself as a child. You didn't work two jobs to feed and clothed you and make sure you had toys and shit. I did! I did all that shit for you.

I gave up my dreams, my goals, my life to be there with and for you. When your father left us, I was devastated Marnie. I was beside myself with grief and despair. I was fucked up mentally for a long time, but I never put no muthafuckin' gun in my mouth. Why? Because of you. I couldn't leave you by yourself. As sure as my name is Tawana Curry, I have it rough. There's a lot of shit that you don't know.

Things that I had to be able to do to take care of you. Fucked up shit, but I did it and never complained. Did I? Did you ever hear me complain while I was raising you? I have loved you, Marnie, since the first time I felt you move inside my stomach. And you know that. So, how could you decide to kill yourself and take yourself away from me? From your daughter? And—"

My tears started anew, and my knees buckled. Cree held me in his arms and stopped me from falling to the ground.

"I have loved you, Marnie, since the first time I felt you move inside my stomach."

The detective reached out and shook Cree's hand. "Detective Jefferson, I'm sorry for your loss. Your wife and I met in twenty-thirteen after her boy—after Luther Fuller and a friend of mine, Detective Maurice Tolliver shot each other."

"Marnie told me about the incident."

"And I'm assuming she also told you how we met?"

"You're the detective that told her, her ex was dead."

"And he wasn't, but I wanted him to be. That would be me."

"Now, I wish he would have died that day. My mother would still be here," I said through tears.

"Monica, listen, if you believe that Khadafi did this, you gotta tell me," Detective Jefferson said.

"I just did, didn't I?"

"But do you have any proof?"

"No," was all I could say.

"Look, I know you're grieving, but I need to catch the person responsible for doing that to your mother. I know who you are and what you did to help Antonio Felder. I was in the courtroom the day you testified for him and went against Khadafi. I remember what Bayona Lake said on the stand. She said that Khadafi wanted to get home and kill people. PeeWee and whoever your new man was. You told the court that Khadafi told you that people would pay when he got home.

I have dedicated my whole career—what's left of it to taking down Luther Fuller. I hope that you and I can work together to bring him to justice if it was him that killed your mother. Khadafi has been killing people since he walked out of Western Correctional Institution on September seventeenth. I could see Khadafi doing this to hurt you. So, I'ma ask you again, do you have any proof that Khadafi is responsible for your mother's murder?"

"I can't believe that I'm standing here discussing my mother's—the day I met you and you told me Khadafi was dead. I went home that night and tried to kill myself. My mother stopped me. She gave me back my life, my will to life. She sent me to see a therapist who made me understand that I really didn't love Khadafi the way I thought I did. I can't believe she's gone—I can't believe it!"

"Marnie, let's go home," Cree urged.

"Okay but let me finish what I've been saying. My mother was everything to me, to my kids. We just spent the day together. You wanna know if I have proof that Khadafi killed my mother. I do not, but I know it was him. I can feel it inside me. He couldn't find me, so he got frustrated. I moved to Virginia. I cut off all communications with him. I told my mother not to take his calls. He always knew where she lived. But I never imagined that he'd hurt her. I never thought that he'd go this far. Khadafi knows how hurt I am, right now. He knows that she was the closest person to me—"

"It was him," Cree interjected. "He dialed my phone from her cell phone. He—"

"He did what?" Detective Jefferson said, his disposition lively.

"My cell phone rang and it woke me up. I saw that the caller was Ms. Tawana. I told Marnie that her mother was calling me and then I answered. The call disconnected. I called back and got no answer. Then Marnie started calling and texting. Fearing the worst, we came here to check on her. That's when—" Cree damn broke as if the reality of what happened finally hit him. Cree collapsed against me and it was my turn to hold him tight.

"I got my mother killed," I said in disbelief.

"Monica, please, you can't blame yourself for this," the detective said.

"I can and I do. Life is funny like that detective. My mother never did anything to anybody and now she's gone. My best friend Reesee never hurt a soul, but she's dead. Esha, Bayona Lake's daughter never hurt anyone—dead. My friend Daunt—dead. PeeWee's sister Jamya—dead. Never hurt or killed anyone. All dead! But Khadafi, he's killed so many and yet he's still here. Why do you think that is, detective?"

"I wonder the same things sometimes, a lot actually."

"Where's the justice in that, huh?"

"You're preaching to the choir," the detective said.

"Even if I had proof that Khadafi did this, you couldn't arrest him. He's smarter than y'all. Always has been. Brokering that deal with y'all in twenty-thirteen was probably his smartest move yet, and y'all just let him go free."

"Hey," the detective stated emphatically. "I had nothing to do with that deal. Maurice Tolliver was a friend of mine, not just a colleague. A friend that was something like a big brother. He was my mentor. He was a legend in detective circles. I was against that deal and everybody knew it. My boss, the Mayor, the US Attorney's office, the Maryland Officials—all of them knew I was against that deal. But it wasn't up to me, not then, not now. So, don't put that on me."

"Well, it doesn't matter who's to blame for Khadafi being home now. Does it, detective? I'm going home now. I need to gather my thoughts and prepare to bury my mother." I turned to leave, Cree by my side.

"Monica—wait, here take this," the detective said, handing me a card. "Please call me if you hear anything, see anything—Khadafi included. Call me, please."

I accepted the card from his outstretched hand, then walked away.

***

I couldn't sleep and neither could Cree. We both just laid in bed and remained silent. There was a lot to be said and nothing to be said. I was angry, I was hurt, I was in shock. I was in a deeply disturbed place, I was afraid. I turned my back to my husband and silently cried. There was nothing Cree could do to ease my pain and he knew it. Being a good spouse meant knowing when to just let the other spouse be. I was happy that our neighbor's daughter was able to babysit for us. I couldn't be a mother at the moment. I was too hurt. I felt like a child. A child that was being punished, eventually I found sleep.

***

"Do you know what he might've seen on your mother's phone?" Cree asked, sitting at the table feeding Creation food from his mouth.

"The only thing he could've seen were photos, her text messages and contacts. He could've accessed her social media—"

"There were photos of us in her phone. Of all of us, pictures in front of our house."

"So, you finally believe me when I tell you how dangerous this man is?" I asked.

Cree nodded his head. "I never believe it was this serious until now. But what if it wasn't him?"

"It was him!" I said a little too loudly.

It startled my daughter, Creation started crying. I walked over to the table and lifted her from her father's lap. I held her close to comfort her. But there would be no comfort for me. My eyes watered and tears ran down my face freely.

"He wanted me to know it was him. That's why he called—wait a minute. He saw the pictures of us. There were several pictures of you in her phone. Khadafi saw the photos and looked for information about you. He went into my mother's contacts. Somehow, he made the connection in the names. He wasn't sure about who you were. So, he dialed your number. Not mine. When you answered he hung up. Then he sat and waited to see what would happen. After you stopped calling, I started calling. That told him exactly who you were. It let him know that you were my husband. He has your name, all your numbers and your photo. He's looking for you, not me. Khadafi wants to hurt you."

"Hurt me? He bleeds just like I bleed, I bought the Taurus—"

"Cree, you don't have enough guns to challenge that man."

"Thanks for the vote of confidence," Cree said, wounded.

"This isn't about confidence or pride or who can piss the furthest. Khadafi is a killer, Cree. You're not!" I pleaded. "We have to get rid of your phone. We have to leave—"

"I'm not running from him, Marnie. Whether I am a killer or not. You can leave—take the kids and leave for a while. I want you, too. Until we know for sure whether or not it's really your ex doing this."

"What about my mother?" I asked.

"Your mother's gone, Marnie. You're alive. Go to North Carolina—to Wilmington with your family."

Silently, I acquiesced, Cree was right. I needed to go, to protect myself and my kids from Khadafi. "But what about you?"'

"I'm good, I'll be okay. If he comes anywhere near me, I'll kill him. No questions asked. Don't worry about me. Take the kids and leave. I'll come down and see y'all."

"Okay, but not until after I've buried my mother."

Anthony Fields

Chapter Forty-Two

Corey Winslow

I stepped out of the shower at Planet Fitness after a vigorous cardio workout. After drying off, I sat on a bench in nothing but boxer briefs and pulled out my cell phone. I dialed Rio Jefferson.

"Rio, sorry about the other night, I was a little under the weather."

"No, problem. Hope you're feeling better," Rio said.

"I am, a good workout always gets me back to where I need to be. So, listen, Doug brought me up to speed on the Tawana Curry murder. So, we think Khadafi did this one, too?"

"I know we've been throwing that name around a lot lately, but this might be him, too. I know how that sounds, Corey, but until we prove otherwise—"

"I get it. I talked to Fred Perry earlier. He pulled some strings and got that cell phone tested expeditiously for prints and DNA. He had to get some help from a buddy in forensics at the FBI on the DNA. He texted me while I was working out. The phone's prints came back to Tawana Curry only. And it was negative for any DNA match that remotely resembles Khadafi."

"I'm not surprised, Corey. In a perfect world, life would be that easy, but this ain't a perfect world. Khadafi's print on that phone or his DNA would be enough to charge him with murder and put him back in jail. I can never get that lucky. Getting something off that phone that matches Khadafi was a longshot. He's a smart sonuva bitch. Monica Curry said as much the other night. I hated to hear it, but shit, she was right. She said that Khadafi is smarter than us."

"He's had a good run of luck, but I wouldn't call that smart," I told Rio.

"Good luck is good luck. Wearing gloves while you search someone's home and make calls from their phone either before or after you killed them is smart, Corey. Crime scene search has been all over that apartment with a fine-tooth comb and can't find a trace of Khadafi being there. I talked to Monica Curry—I mean Monica

Summers, she got married. I talked to her earlier today, she's gonna leave town for awhile but not until after she buries her mother. I wanna see if Khadafi attends the funeral."

"And if he does? It doesn't matter because we can't touch him."

"I know that, I just wanna put my eyes on him. I also wanna see how he interacts with Monica. If he's hostile—if he tries to kill her—wait a minute," Rio said and paused. "I just remembered something else Monica said. She said that Khadafi went to her old job looking for her. There has to be camera footage of him driving and leaving. We need to see exactly when that was and what he was driving or riding in."

"The black van," I mentioned.

"Or a black SUV that matches the Meechie murder. I'm gonna be tied up on some other cases for the next couple of days. I need you to go to Forestville Health and Rehab Center in Marlboro Pike and get that camera footage."

"I can do that. Just so happens that I'm settling in the Planet Fitness on Silver Hill Road right now. I can go there as soon as I get dressed. When I get there, how far back do they need to go with the footage? Did she say when Khadafi went there? Who he talked to?"

"Good questions. Tell you what—I'll call her back and get the answers you need. Then I'll text you everything I get from Monica. How's that?"

"That's great, text me. Later!" I ended the call, put the phone down and got dressed. Twenty minutes later I was out the door.

***

In the lobby of Forestville Health, I flashed my credentials at the lady behind the counter. "I need to speak with Sherita Simms."

"That would be me," the woman said and smiled. "Marnie called me and told me that the police would be coming to talk to me."

"You called Marnie and told her that a man had come here looking for her?"

Sherita Simms nodded. "I thought it was strange that someone would come here looking for her and she'd been gone for almost two years. After he left, I called her and told her."

I spotted at least three different cameras in the lobby where I stood. Before entering the facility, I noticed cameras mounted all around the building. I looked at the text messages from Rio. "And that happened between the seventeenth and twenty-fifth of September, right?"

"Yeah, I believe so. Why? Did something happen? Marnie never told me what this was all about."

"Nothing happened, just need to see if the guy who came here is the same guy we've been interested in for some crimes."

"Who, the guy that came looking for Marnie?"

I nodded.

"Is he in trouble? Did he do something we need to know about?"

My curiosity pinged instantly. The woman in front of me seemed far too inquisitive and I couldn't understand why that was. Why all the questions? What was her invested interest? "Who controls security cameras around here?"

"Everything is operated and maintained by our security guy, Quan."

"Is Quan here now?" I asked.

"I think so." Sherita pushed a button on the phone near her.

Seconds later, a voice said, "Security. What's up, Rita? You need me?"

"I do. Quan, can you step up here to the front desk?"

"I'm on my way."

A Michael Clarke Duncan clone rounded the corner a few minutes later and walked directly up to me. He was dark-skinned, bald, muscular, and stood around six-feet-four or five inches tall. His uniform shirt was a size too small and looked like it would tear in half at any moment.

"You having a problem here, Sherita?"

Sherita laughed. "No, Quan. He's the police, needs to speak with you."

I flashed my badge on the big guy.

"You need to speak with me?" the man named Quan asked.

"Yeah, I asked to speak to you. In September, a man came here looking for an ex-employee. I need to see your camera footage from that visit here. To see if he's somebody we've been looking for."

"The guy came here looking for Marnie," Sherita said to Quan. "It was between the seventeenth and twenty-fifth, I remember because I worked a double shift that entire week. He came in—I wanna say it was in the afternoon. He asked some questions, looking for Marnie. I told him that she didn't work here anymore. The whole exchange lasted about five minutes."

"I need to see your video footage for that day. Can you help me, or do I need to get a bunch of people in here with warrants and bad attitudes?"

Quan threw up his hands in a mock sign of surrender. "You're the police. How can I deny you? Come on with me and I'll pull that footage for you." To Sherita he said, "You gotta come, too. You gotta point out the guy."

"Okay, let me get Tomecka to cover the front desk for me."

***

"That's him right there," Sherita said pointing at the screen.

I watched the encounter between Khadafi and Sherita Simms. There was no sound in the video. After a brief conversation, I saw Khadafi pull out a cell phone and slide it across the counter. Sherita picked it up and typed on it. That was her invested interest. Sherita had programmed her contact info into Khadafi's phone and never said a word about it to me or Monica. Sneaky bitch.

I wondered if she was in contact with Khadafi even as we sat here in front of the screens. I filed that in the back of my head and kept quiet about my general interest. Sherita Simms knew that me and the security guy saw the interaction with the phone, but still she said nothing. As if it never happened.

"That's him," I answered. "He's a little more muscular and he's grown a beard, but that's him. You're looking at Luther Khadafi Fuller, one of the most notorious killers of our era. He was just released from prison when he came here. Monica Curry—I mean Summers is the mother of his two children. While he was in prison, she cut off all communication with him. That's why he came here looking for her. Good work, Quan. Now I need to see how he got here. What vehicle he was in."

Quan, the security guy, manipulated the keyboard and controls until he had what I needed. My adrenaline pumped as I leaned forward and watched a black SUV pull off Marlboro Pike into the facility's grounds. A different angle showed the SUV cruising through the parking lot before finally parking. Then Khadafi exited the SUV from the driver's side. He walked through the parking lot and around a corner to the entrance of Forestville Health. I pulled my cell phone and dialed Rio's cell phone. He didn't pick up, I sent him a text.

//: Call me! It's important! Khadafi Has A Black SUV!

"I need you to zoom in and see if you can get a visual on that license plate. On the SUV he's driving."

Quan did everything he could, but the security equipment at Forestville Health was bottom of the barrel and antiquated. "Sorry, detective, that's about as good as it gets."

Standing, I patted the big guy on the shoulder. "You did good. Can you email me a copy of that video footage? I need everything we just watched."

"No problem, I got you," Quan replied.

I gave him my business card with my email written on the back. "I owe you one, big guy. If you ever need—"

"Don't trip, you good."

"Thank you, Sherita. Couldn't have done this without you."

"Anything to help the cops. Should I be afraid of him?" Sherita asked.

"Should you be afraid of him? Why would you have to be afraid of him? Is there something I should know? Do you know him?"

Sherita Simms shook her head. "Uh—no, I was just asking."

"I see no reason why you should be worried. But keep in mind that Khadafi has killed more people than any other person in this area—ever. He kills without remorse. Irrespective of who it is. If you ever see him again, get as far away as possible from him.

***

Back at the station, I watched the video footage Quan emailed me. My attention was on the black SUV. Whoever had killed Meechie on Half Street had been riding in a black SUV. On my computer, I pulled up the Half Street video footage of Meechie's murder. To my trained eye, the two dark colored SUVs looked identical. I forwarded both video footages to Martin Isle in our IT department, with a note attached.

Martin,

Are both of these SUVs the same? Check it out!

I called Rio Jefferson back again, no answer. I left him a voicemail. Then I sent him both video feeds to view, including the one of Khadafi inside the Forestville Nursing home. I sent him a text about Sherita Simms and her possible connection to Khadafi. A ping alerted me to an incoming text. I thought it was from Rio, but it wasn't. The text was from Ann Sloan.

//: My husband left this morning to go out of town. Want to reenact a scene from Power? Call me!

A smile crossed my face instantly. Several hours of Olympic style sex is exactly what I needed. I dialed Ann Sloan's phone.

***

Ann Sloan's house in Georgetown was straight out of the Architect Digest. It was a mini mansion in red brick. I pulled through the gate and drove all the way around to the side of the house as instructed. Ann met me at the door, dressed still in her work clothes, no shoes.

"Come in, come in," Ann said and hugged me in the doorway and then stood on her tiptoes and kissed me. Then she shut the door behind us.

"Your text was unexpected," I told her. "But well received."

"I bet it was." Ann grabbed my dick through my pants. "Later. First, I want you to taste something I made. Follow me to the kitchen."

***

"Well, how do you like it?" Ann asked.

"I love it. What is it?" I replied.

"Peach and Sesame crumble."

"It's delicious, I never knew you baked."

"I do a lot of things that you don't know about when I find the time. I'm glad you like it. I haven't tasted it yet."

"You haven't tasted it? Why?" I asked Ann.

"Wanted to wait until you got here."

Before I could say another word, Ann unzipped my pants and pulled my dick free. Then she stuck her fingers in the warm dessert and smeared it all over me.

"It's not too warm for you down there, is it?"

"Not at all."

"Good," Ann said before putting me in her mouth.

I stood there and leaned against the counter watching Ann Sloan lick Peach Sesame crumble off my dick, it was amazing.

***

"Oh, shit! Fuck me, Corey! Fuck me!"

My face was buried in Ann's neck. She smelled of fruits. Her shampoo or soap was berry scented. I laid between her legs in the missionary position and gave her the dick just the way she liked it. I cuffed one leg in the crook of my elbow and bent it back. That way I could force Ann to take more of me. Her toes curled in ecstasy as I guided myself deeply into her. I covered her mouth with mine and tasted the peaches in the crumble. I heard a small sound in the room but dismissed it quickly. What I heard next couldn't be dismissed.

"I gave you everything I had to offer, and this is how you repay me?" a deep male voice pierced the quiet in the room.

My head damned near rotated as if on an axel. I looked behind me and saw a well-dressed, silver haired, white man standing at the foot of the bed. I lifted off Ann and turned over completely. Ann drew the sheets over her body up to her neck.

"Ah—I see the object of your pleasure for so many years and now I understand your lustful behavior," the man said.

His eyes were on my deflating manhood, then our eyes locked.

"Solomon! What are you doing here?" Ann exclaimed.

"I live here, my dear wife. Or have you forgotten that?" Solomon Sloan said calmly. "Being as though, you're getting fucked in my bed, I think you may have forgotten."

Solomon Sloan moved his hand into view, and I saw that it held a gun.

"Put the gun down, Mr. Sloan." I sat up and said forcefully. "I'm a cop."

"Oh, I know exactly who you are, Detective Winslow. Corey Deshawn Winslow. Born and raised in Washington D.C. Mother was Carolyn Bright. Father was Malcolm Winslow, both deceased. Been on the Metropolitan Police Force for thirteen years. A detective in homicide for six of those thirteen. Thirty-five years old, pretty boy, athlete, ladies man. I know exactly who you are, and I've known about you for the last three years. I knew that my advanced age and vigorous schedule made for a bad husband. I also knew that my virility was not what it once was. So, I allowed your trysts with my wife to continue because I thought at some point, Ann would tire of this thing between the two of you. But it seemed that I was wrong. It has only grown stronger as my wife has grown bolder."

"Solomon, please, I can explain," Ann protested.

"No need to explain. I can see what's going on," Solomon answered.

"Mr. Sloan," I pleaded, "don't do anything that you will regret. Put the gun down!"

"The media will call this a crime of passion. I'll be arrested," Solomon Sloan said almost to himself. "I'll do some time in jail, but I'll get off light. After all, I'm wealthy, I'm a doctor, an exemplary citizen and I'm white."

"Solomon, what exactly are you saying?" Ann asked.

Solomon Sloan pointed the gun at Ann. "This is what I'm saying." He fired the gun, then he turned it on me.

"No," I gasped.

"Yes." He fired.

My whole world went dark.

Chapter Forty-Three

Nicole

"Breaking News—if you're just joining us here at CUS Fox News, the city of Washington D.C. is in mourning. The popular US Attorney for the District of Columbia, Ann Sloan and a D.C. homicide detective were slain today. D.C. Police are still at the scene, but sources close to the scene has told us at CUS Fox News that Ann Sloan and detective Corey Winslow were involved in an extramarital affair. Apparently, the US Attorney and detective Winslow were caught in bed at US Attorney Sloan's Georgetown home. Her husband, George Washington University Professor and noted Neurosurgeon, Solomon Sloan has been arrested for their murders. He has confessed to both murders.

My mother used the remote to change the channel. "Every time we turn on the news, somebody is getting killed. I'm sick of it."

Instead of responding, I closed my eyes and thought about what I had just heard. The top prosecutor in the city was dead. Killed by her husband for getting caught fucking a detective in their bed. I thought about all the times I'd seen Ann Sloan in and around the Superior Courthouse. Then the detective who had testified in Antonio's trial. He spoke about meeting Antonio at the morgue the day his daughter was killed. Antonio identified the body. Ann Sloan was the prosecuting attorney in that case.

I thought about the beautiful, Carmen Electra looking prosecutor and the handsome detective and shook my head. Both dead. The finality of death is what makes a person sad. The fear of the unknown. All I could think about was my son. How would he be affected by my passing? Tears welled up in my eyes, but I shook them away. I was tired of crying. I was bordering between sadness and anger. I was afraid of dying, but angry that death would visit me so soon.

I'd never get to see my son grow up. Never get to see him graduate high school or go to prom. I'd never get to see him get married or have children of his own. I couldn't figure out what I had done so wrong in the world for God to call for my soul so young. I wanted to know why life had dealt me such a cruel twist of fate. My tombstone would read that I had only lived for thirty-three years.

The questions in my head and the emotions on my face belied the story because my mother's eyes bore into mine and stayed there. Her tears matched mine.

"Nic, let's go to another hospital. One that specializes in Cancer treatment and get a second opinion. Maybe Dr. Chung is wrong. Doctors have been wrong about shit like this before. There has to be something else we can do. I think—"

I turned to face my mother. "Ma, listen to me. I have laid here in this bed for days thinking about what you just said, but that's false hope. Doctor Chung is one of the best doctors in the field, I'm told. If he says, I'm dying—then, Ma, I'm dying. Going to another hospital won't change that. We—you and I have to accept it and move on. We need to prepare for me not being here. I have several bank accounts. I've saved a lot of money. I want you to sell my condo, the cars and all my possessions. Then put all of the money in a trust for Antonio. He's my biggest concern—"

"My grandson will be taken care of far as long as I breathe—"

"And who knows for how long that will be? Longevity in life is promised to no one. I cannot and will leave you with the burden of raising a child at your age—"

"Burden? At my age? Nic, you—"

"Ma, just listen. I need you to listen to me. To understand something. I wasn't honest with you about Antonio's father. Why? I'm not sure. Maybe, I didn't want you to judge me. Or look at me in a bad light. Antonio's father's name is Antonio Felder, an older, married thug that I fell in love with. I knew Antonio from the neighborhood growing up. I had the biggest crush on him as a teenager.

He went to prison for murder when I was around fourteen. He ended up getting out on appeal. He got married to the woman whom he shared two daughters with. In 2013, Antonio's sixteen-year-old daughter was killed at a gas station in Northeast. Antonio responded by killing a lot of people. Anybody who he felt was responsible or complicit, he killed them. His wife found out that he was killing all the people she's been hearing about on the news.

She left him and took the remaining children with her. I don't know how, but Antonio found out that I was now an investigator. He hired me to find his wife and children. I ended up spending a lot of time with him as he grieved for his daughter and missed his wife and kids. Things between us turned sexual. I fell deeply for him then. He was later arrested and charged with sixteen counts of murder—"

"He's in prison?" my mother asked.

"No, Ma, just listen, please. While at D.C. Jail, I went there to help Antonio with his case and our sexual relationship continued there."

"At the jail—inside the jail?"

I nodded my head. "There were ways to get it done. I never thought about me getting pregnant or the fact that I was in love with a married man, seven years my senior. In fact, I didn't care about anything but him. In twenty-fourteen, he went on trial for the murders. The government's only witness was a guy that used to be with him named Khadafi. He got acquitted on all the charges.

One of the reasons he got acquitted was because I found his wife and convinced her to come back to D.C. She testified and lied to help her husband. Her husband, my lover. When he beat the murders and got out of jail, he went home to his family and I accepted that. Then one day, Antonio showed up at my office to tell me that he was leaving D.C. We had sex right there in my office and that was the day that my son was conceived."

"Nic, I hear you. It's an interesting story, but why tell me all of this now?"

"Because, Ma, I need you to understand that Antonio needs to be with his father."

"Does his father even know about him?" my mother asked with a look of sincere hurt on her face.

"No, he doesn't. But that's because I made the decision to keep Antonio a secret from his father."

"Baby, you're not thinking straight. How can you say that Antonio needs to be with a person that he doesn't even know over his grandmother? A grandmother that he loves and that loves him more than life?"

"Ma, you're making this about you and it's not about you. It's about Antonio and what's best for him. The decision I made almost three years ago was a bad one. It was the wrong one. I see that now as clearly as anything. Antonio needs to know his father. I'm gonna reach out to him and tell him to come here, back to D.C. from Florida. I'm gonna let him know that I'm dying and that he has a son. It's his choice to make, but I believe he'll make the right one and decide to raise Antonio"

"Are you insane? You want an animal—a thug, a murderer to raise your son? My grandson? That's what you think is best?" My mother grabbed her coat and put it on. She stood up to leave. "I can't deal with this right now. You are talking crazy. I'm about to lose my daughter and my grandson? I will never understand that."

I watched my mother leave the room in tears and it broke my heart.

***

The Next Morning

My hand shook but my resolve strengthened, I scrolled through my contacts until I found the picture of Antonio. I said a prayer that the number was still good and pressed send. The connection rang a few times and then I heard his voice. My heart melted and I knew it was Antonio.

"Hello?"

"Antonio, it's me, Nicole. Don't talk, just listen. I know you haven't heard anything from me in years, but I need you to get on a plane to D.C. No questions asked. I need you, it's an emergency."

After a slight pause, Antonio said, "I'll be there by tomorrow."

"Good," I said and sighed with relief. "This is my cell phone number, call me as soon as you get here."

Chapter Forty-Four

Khadafi

"That's what the fuck they get," I said to myself as I read the news about Corey Winslow and Ann Sloan on my phone. I couldn't believe my good fortune. "Saved me the time and effort of having to kill their stupid asses. Fuckin' homicide detective and the head prosecutor bitch probably been fuckin' the whole time. They at her house in her bed and the husband comes home, catches them, and smokes their asses. How cool is that?"

I put my phone up after texting Sherita and letting her know that I was outside. For some reason she'd called and texted me all day yesterday and most of today. I got out of the car, walked into her building, and climbed the stairs to her apartment.

Before I could knock on the door, it opened. Sherita stood in the doorway dressed in scrubs, hair down, feet bare, toes pretty, face not so much. "It took you this long to come and see what I wanted?"

"I was busy doing a rack of other shit. I'm here now. What's up? What's so important?"

"Come in here," Sherita said and stepped back to allow me entrance.

I walked over to her couch and removed my coat before sitting down.

"Why you cut your beard off?"

"Because I wanted to. You ain't call me here about my beard. What's up?"

"Why you ain't tell me that you're Marnie's baby's father?"

Smiling, I asked, "Would it have made a difference if I had? You loyal to Marnie or something?"

Sherita stood in front of me, hands on her hips and a serious look on her face. "I wouldn't say all that, but—"

"But what? Either you are or you ain't."

"She's cool. We worked together for years, but I wouldn't call us bosom buddies or BFFs. I guess it wouldn't have made a difference. I saw you, liked your style and said what I said. Straight like that, but you still could have told me."

"I could've but I didn't see the relevance. Who told you, though?"

"The detective that came by my job looking for you."

"Looking for me? A detective? At your job?"

"Yep. The same one that just got killed."

"The detective got killed?" I raised an eyebrow.

"Yes, the one that has been all over the news since yesterday. And it's crazy as shit because he must've gotten killed right after he left my job. But anyway, let me tell you everything, just so you'll know. The day you came to Forestville Health looking for Marnie, you told me you were a friend who just got back in town or some bullshit like that. I wasn't sure that you'd call me or not, so I called Marnie and told her—"

"You had a number for Marnie the whole time and didn't say nothing?"

Sherita nodded. "We worked together, covered shifts for each other and partied together before she got married and left Forestville. I called her and told her that you'd come looking for her. If she knew who you were, she never said shit. So, I left it alone and then you called. Yesterday, I get a call from Marnie telling me that a detective was coming by to talk to me. I'm thinking, what the fuck for? But I never tell her that. The detective comes by and tells me that he just needs to see the video footage of the day you came by because he wants to see if it's the same guy he's interested in for some crimes.

I start asking questions like, *'what did he do? Should I be afraid if he comes back?* Shit like that. He asks to view the security footage of you. Our security guy shows him the footage. I told him that you were the man I'd spoken to, but he already knew who you were. Said something about you being more muscular and that you'd grown a beard. Told us that you were Luther Khadafi Fuller, one of the most notorious killers of this era and all this and that. He said that Marnie was your two kids' mother and now she'd cut you off while you were in prison. And that you came to Forestville Health looking for her because of that. Then he wanted to see the footage from outside so that he could see what kinda vehicle you were driving."

"Did he see that? What vehicle I was in?"

Sherita nodded again. "Quan showed him everything. We saw you pull up in a black SUV and get out, then leave in the same SUV. He told Quan to email him the video footage. I started with the questions again. He told me that if I'd ever saw you again to stay away from you."

"And you never told him about us?" I asked.

"I never told him shit. I didn't want him to know I been with you."

"That's what's up. You did good then, baby girl. You are right to be concerned since that nigga told you all that bullshit about me. But I ain't on nothing. I haven't done nothing. The police stay on my line because I killed a cop years ago and beat that shit. That's why they looking for me, just being nosey. Tryna make sure I ain't doing nothing, illegal. I heard that Marnie's mother got killed recently. They probably tryna put that murder on me."

A look of genuine concern crossed Sherita's face. She went from looking like Ms. Piggy to the female troll on Shrek. "But why would they think you killed Marnie's mother?"

"Because of what he told you. Marnie cut me off while I was in jail. I been tryna find her to see my kids, but I can't find her. They gon' think I killed her mother to get to her."

"You haven't talked to her yet?" I shook my head. "Did you kill Marnie's mother?"

"Of course not. Why would you ask me some stupid ass shit like that?" A thought crossed my mind. "Are you wearing a wire or something?"

"Who me?" Sherita asked with a wounded expression on her face.

"Naw, the owl over there on the kitchen counter. Yeah, you."

"Khadafi, don't play with me like that. Are you serious?"

"Dead serious," I said and stood up. The gun in my waist visible. "Take your clothes off, everything."

"I can't believe this shit," Sherita said, but did as I commanded. Once she was completely naked, she said, "Satisfied? Told you I wasn't wired."

Relieved I told her, "Damn, cuz, you sexy as shit. Titties pretty, pussy pretty as shit. I knew you weren't wired, I just wanted you to take your clothes off. Come here." Sherita walked over to me. "Bend your sexy ass over, right here." I motioned to the couch.

Sherita sashayed closer to the couch and did as I instructed. She grabbed the pillow cushions. I got behind her, pulled out my dick and slid it into her. Twenty minutes later, I left her apartment.

***

"—the phone ringin/ said they rushing the spot/ the only time he play that crib is when he fucking a thot/ he was fucking with Kee and she was fuckin' an OP/ but he ain't never think about it she'll fuck with the cops/ she told them everything, nigga/ I know you thought that she would never sing, nigga/ rule number one, keep them bitches out of your business/ rule number two, better kill em, you know they snitching/ it's all fun and games until them bitches turn to a witness/ and know you in the courtroom waiting to get your sentence—" Meek Mill's song Tony's Story Part 3 blared through the speakers in the car.

I liked the beat, so I listened to the lyrics. In the song, he rapped about a girl named Kee becoming a witness against a dude named Paulie and I couldn't get the conversation I'd just had with Sherita out of my mind. The cops had video footage of me at the nursing home and knew that I'd been driving a black SUV that day. Even though the truck was gone, they would try and connect me to Meechie's murder because I was in the same SUV when I did that. I had an epiphany, immediately, I bust a U-turn and headed back to Sherita's apartment. I parked on the street and walked into her gated complex. Not long after, I was knocking at the door.

Sherita opened the door dressed in a bathrobe. "Hey, boo. I was just getting in the shower. You forget something?"

"Yeah," I replied and walked past her into the apartment.

"What did you forget?" Sherita asked and closed the door.

I pulled the suppressed Smith and Wesson. "I forgot to kill you."

"Khadafi, stop playing with me."

"I swear, I'm not." I aimed the gun and shot Sherita.

After wiping down everything I had ever touched in her apartment, I got a warm rag and soaped it up. I thoroughly cleaned Sherita's pussy, hands, and body to get rid of all fibers or traces of my DNA. I even washed her mouth out with soap. I laughed to myself at that. Once I was satisfied that all traces of my existence were washed away, I left, again.

***

Later That Night

"These crab legs are good as hell," Lisa exclaimed.

I cracked open an Alaskan king crab leg, got the meat out and popped it into my mouth after dipping it into melted, garlic butter. I had butter all over my lips and didn't give a fuck.

"It's been awhile since I had some of these joints. You right, they're good as a muthafucka. After I finish these joints, I'ma fuck them jumbo shrimp up."

Lisa looked across the table at her friend sitting with us. "Toya, you gotta excuse Khadafi, he been locked up for a—how long was you in jail this last time?"

"Just three years," I replied between bites of crab meat.

"Just three years," Toya repeated. "Just three? You say that like it was four months. Ain't no way I can be in nobody's jail cell for no three straight years. No seafood, no soul food, no Instagram, Facebook, Google, Siri, Facetime, or internet. No dick—drinks—"

"They got drinks in the joints. Might not be the Patron you want, but they definitely got drinks. Regular hooch and white lightning. And they got all the other shit you just named, too. Depends on where you locked up at. Niggas got cell phones, smart phones, and social media. Drugs, street food, all that shit. Niggas getting pussy, too. They fucking their bitches, C.O. bitches, education bitches. It's a prison, but it's still a world within a world."

Toya peeled the shell off a shrimp, dipped it into cocktail sauce and said, "Well, I guess that's why my brothers stay in and out of jail. I ain't know they were doing it like that."

"Your brothers?" I asked.

"Yeah, my brothers. I got seven of 'em. But only five of them is in the streets. One of 'em is a reverend, on church shit hard as shit and one of my brothers is gay as shit. The other five be in and out of jail like shit."

"Who are your brothers? I might know em."

"Shit—James they call him Lonnell or Doctor L, Antonio, they call him Black Clarence—"

"The Venables? I know them all," I told Toya. "Kilo your brother, too, right?"

"Yeah, Marquee, he's next to the youngest boy."

"That's my man, right there. Where he locked up at now?" I asked.

"He's in the feds, some wild ass joint in Kentucky."

I couldn't believe it I was batting a thousand. I'd already killed PeeWee and Meechie, the C.O. nigga Quebecky, Marnie's mother, then the detective and prosecutor who tricked me into turning into a rat got killed. I found Kito's family and smoked his aunt. Now I was sitting across from Toya Venable, Kilo's sister. Toya was still talking about her brothers, but my mind was elsewhere—

I was awakened by a bang on my wall, it was Kilo.

"Hey, Moe, I just got the Washington Post this morning. I got something you need to read. Send your line."

I fished the newspaper and read the article about me in the Metro Station.

"Aye, Moe," Kilo called out. "You got that?"

"Yeah, I got it, I got it!"

"Damn, Moe, kill my mother. You hot as shit. Hot bitch ass nigga."

I remembered how Kilo and all the *get with* niggas on the tier taunted me for the next two days nonstop until I got pulled off the tier. Before I left my cell, I kicked the wall and got Kilo's attention. I remembered what I told him as if I'd said it only hours ago.

"Aye, Kilo, for all the shit you been saying, keep up with the news. Condon Terrace ain't gon never be the same when I finish with your family."

A sly smile crossed my face as I looked over at the pretty, brown-skinned woman eating shrimp. Toya Venable was eating her last meal and didn't even know it.

"Khadafi?"

I looked over at Lisa, who'd just called my name. "What's up, Lisa?'

"Did you hear what Toya just asked you?"

"Naw, I didn't. What did you ask me, Toya?"

"Did you beat your dick all them years or did you get some sneaky head from one of them jail faggies? Tell the truth."

Deep down inside I was offended by Toya's question, but instead of checking her, I smiled. "I ain't never fucked with no faggies. I beat my dick a lot."

"What did you use to get your dick hard? Porn magazines, freak novels?"

"Mostly my thoughts but speaking of magazines they got these mags that I used to love to read. It featured real stripper bitches. The dude that put the magazine out always interviewed the strippers. Asked real good questions and had real good answers. Let me ask y'all some questions from the magazine."

"What magazine is that?" Lisa asked.

"Phat Puffs Magazine," I told her.

"Never heard of it, but go ahead and ask your questions," Toya said.

"Yeah," Lisa added. "Go ahead, I'm with it."

"A'ight, bet, but let me go to use the restroom right quick. I'll be right back."

In the men's room, I found an empty stall. I laced the bowl with toilet paper and sat down fully clothed. I pulled out my cell phone and called Lil Quette.

He answered on the second ring. "What's up, big cuz?"

"You. I need you, slim. You busy?"

"Naw, not really, just in the house playing video games and listening to Shakira get on my nerves about nothing. What you need me to do?"

"Test out that brand new four fifth you got."

"That would be good for me. Test it on who?"

"You know where Center City, D.C. at, offa H Street? Where the Gucci, Louis and Montcler shops at?"

"I'm hip to it," Lil Quette informed me.

"I'm at a restaurant down here called Del Fiasco's. I got the dyke broad with me that I told you about. Her girlfriend is the sister of an OP. I need you to get with her. I promised her brother that I'd make him cry when I got home. It's time to make his whole family cry. If I do it, I'ma have to crush Lisa and I ain't tryna do that. Come down here and park in the parking lot, near my Benz. You'll be able to see her and what she's driving when we leave here. Follow her somewhere and push her shit back. Can you do that for me?"

"Most definitely, I'm on my way. But big cuz, eventually we gon' have to hunt this nigga Cutty. He survived the hit—"

"I know that."

"Right, well, I don't think he saw me but like I told you the other day, I'm not sure. So, I gotta get him out the way. I been in the house cooling, but I'm tired of laying low."

"Say no more, we on it first thing tomorrow."

"Bet, I'ma text you when I get outside."

"Do that. One love." I disconnected the call.

***

"Who sexes y'all better? Men or women?" I asked Lisa and Toya.

"It all depends on my mood. Women make me cum more, but I prefer the dick. So, I'll have to say, men," Toya said and laughed.

The waiter brought their steaks and my stuffed chicken ravioli.

Lisa sipped her watermelon Patron, then said, "Some of the best sex I've ever had was with a woman. I like the strap-on joint, but the real thing is better. I think men fuck me better, but women give better head. So, I'll say both. I crave different things at different times. I can't choose."

"I respect that. Dick size. What's big and what's small to y'all?"

"That's easy, big is nine inches and better. Small is six or less. Anything between six and nine is average."

Toya appeared to be deep in thought. "Um—I had a nigga with a lil dick that used to work the shit outta that joint. Had me squirting all over the place. So, I'll say small is like five. Big is like eight and better."

"So, what's too big?" I asked.

"Too big is like ten or eleven inches. I want sex, not a pap smear," Lisa said.

Toya repeated what Lisa said, but added, "Gimme a real nigga with eight inches, a curve, and some girth I'm good."

"Okay, Toya since you brought up squirting, is that cum or piss?"

"Good question, it comes from pussy. Not the pee hole, so I gotta say that it's cum. But it's probably a mixture of both."

"I wouldn't know since I've never squirted," Lisa sulked.

"I think I might be able to help you with that. Next question, favorite sex position?"

"Back shots, for sure," Lisa answered.

"I like to ride, love being in control. After that face down, ass up."

"Anal sex?"

"Hell gawd daggone no! Not gon' happen," Toya stated emphatically.

"Depends," Lisa said. "On the dick size, the nigga and how many drinks I've had. Before I crossed over to bitches, I used to love that shit. I came automatically from anal sex."

Lisa was freaky as shit and I loved it. "When you came, was it a vaginal orgasm or did your ass cum?"

"Uh—never heard of an assgasm, so I'll say it was vaginal each time."

"A'ight ladies, last question. Be honest, too. After sucking a dick, do you spit or swallow?"

"You already know the answer to that, right?" Lisa asked me.

I nodded and me and Toya both laughed.

"Damn, bitch, you nasty as shit," Toya said to Lisa. "Eating that man's dick already. Your ass is confused like shit. And you making good, honest whores like me look bad." She eyed me lasciviously. "But you are kind of a snack, so I can't blame Lisa. To answer your question, I do both. Depends on my mood and who the nigga is. If I'm just fucking and sucking for coins, I'ma spit. If it's a nigga that I'm feeling, I'm swallowing all day, every day. Anything else you want to know?"

"Naw, I think that's it," I replied and started eating my ravioli.

***

I got the text from Lil Quette just as I was paying the bill for our food, drinks, and seafood. In the parking lot I glanced around furtively until I saw Lil Quette's Camaro.

"You going with me or Toya?" I asked Lisa, already knowing what her answer would be.

"After that conversation we just had, you better believe I'm going with you. Especially after you mentioned helping me squirt."

Toya laughed. "Damn, bitch, you pressed like shit."

Lisa turned and hugged Toya. "Naw, I'm just tryna squirt. Can I live?"

"Do you, baby. Do you. Bye, Khadafi, nice meeting you, and thanks for the food, drinks and good convo."

"Don't worry about it. It was fun for me. Let's do it again soon," I told Toya.

"Lisa, I love you, bitch. Call me!" Toya said and departed.

Lisa hopped in the Benz with me. I watched Toya climb into a beige Nissan. I watched her pull out of the parking lot. Then I watched Lil Quette pull out behind her.

Chapter Forty-Five

Lil Quette

"Shakira, I'm not gonna keep arguing with you about the same shit. I'ma hit you back. I gotta go." I ended the call with Shakira and pulled out of the parking lot behind the beige Nissan Altima Coupe.

Not to be obvious, I let it get about three or four cars ahead of me. Not long into the drive, the Altima pulled over and parked in front of a popular 24 Hour weed dispensary on H. Street. I debated whether to kill her there but decided against it. I needed the perfect blind spot to commit the perfect murder. I preferred a semi-deserted spot. At 5th Street, the Altima made a right and drove down by the court buildings. On Indiana Avenue, it turned left and headed for the 3rd Street tunnel.

I did the same just from a distance behind it. The Altima had no tints, so inside the well-lit tunnel, I could see that the woman was on her cell phone. I had no clue what her destination was, so I just followed her hoping for a break. The Altima kept straight on 295 until the exit for South Capitol Street on the Southeast side came up. The light where MLK Avenue ended was a good one. I thought about Lil Cee and V Dot in the G-Wagon, lingering at a traffic light before losing their lives on another part of South Capitol Street.

I watched as the light turned red and the Altima slowed. There were no other cars nearby. I pulled behind the car and hopped out. In seconds, I was at the driver's side of the Altima. The woman in the Altima, still on her phone, glanced at me with a look of confusion and surprise. I raised the gun and fired. Then I slipped my left hand into my sleeve and opened her car door. More shots followed to make sure that she was dead. I raced back to the Camaro and got the hell out of dodge.

***

The corner store on Talbert Street was closed for the night, but a small crowd of dudes still congregated there. I parked on the hill of Talbert and walked down to where everybody was. All eyes were on me as I approached. I could see dudes reaching for guns.

"Wayne," I called out to my man.

"Who dat, Lil Quette?" Wayne replied.

"Yeah."

"Ease up, that's my lil man," I heard Wayne say. "What's up, Quette?"

"You. I'm tryna get some of that new shit, I been hearing about."

"What? That gun smoke shit?"

"The shit that smell like gunpowder and taste like spices."

Wayne and his men laughed. "Y'all think I should sell him this shit?"

His men laughed again. I could tell they were all high as shit.

"That's what y'all smoking on?" I asked.

More laughter.

"Here, dawg, hit this," Wayne said and passed me the weed.

I inhaled the blunt, the acrid smoke made me choke instantly. I almost coughed up both lungs. "This shit tastes like chimney smoke."

Everybody busted out laughing again.

"You gotta get used to it," a light skinned, curly haired dude said and took the blunt out of my hand.

My head was spinning, my heart raced in my chest. "That shit gas."

"You still want some of this shit?" Wayne asked. I nodded. "How much you want?"

"Gimme an ounce."

Wayne ducked into a nearby vehicle and returned with the weed. "That'll be three bills, homie."

Counting out three hundred dollars, I paid Wayne and bounced. High as hell from that one pull.

***

I parked my car on N Street, not far from where I had killed two people. I reclined the seat and smoked the blunt I had rolled before leaving Talbert Street. I could only hit the weed a couple times before knowing I needed to put the jay out. For some reason, the surprised look on the woman in the Altima's face came to mind. In slow mo, I watched it change to confusion right before I blew her brains into the passenger seat. The four fifth was a dangerous muthafucka. I gripped the four fifth and ejected the clip. The large hydra shok bullets looked like circumcised dicks loaded in the magazine.

I thought about the mess they made and laughed. I didn't even know why I was laughing, just like I didn't know why I had just killed the woman in the Altima. Other than the fact that she was some kin to Khadafi's Op. I thought about my life and kept laughing. I couldn't stop, in an effort to find a new me, I'd completely lost the old me. Marquette Jennings was gone, replaced by Lil Quette the killer. Jomo's face came to mind next and the terrified look in his eyes before I killed him.

I saw him lying in a casket and then worms eating his eyes in the ground. Each face of a person I'd killed crossed the big screen in my mind and I still laughed. Suddenly, my stomach growled, reminding me that I hadn't eaten since earlier. I got out of the car and crossed N Street. A mint greet Cadillac XTS rode by. I saluted the driver and kept it moving.

There were several people inside Leo's when I walked in. I pulled my cell phone and called Shakira.

"What, Quette?" Shakira answered with a major attitude.

"Sha, you starting to really throw me off with your shitty moods. Fuck is wrong with you?"

"You are what's wrong with me."

"Fuck I do now? I just talked to you."

"I'm tired of muthafuckas calling me talking about you. All this wild shit been happening, and your name keeps coming up. In the last month, Meechie, Carlton, V Dot, AD, Big Pat, and Dooby done got killed. People saying that you and your cousin Khadafi is doing all the killing."

"For real?" I answered, suddenly very sober and attentive. "Who said that?"

My cousin Maureen and Den Den called me on the three-way asking about you. They said that word on the street is that some dudes named PeeWee and Meechie robbed your cousin's baby mother while he was in jail and that he snitched to get home. Since he been home, they say he killing everybody that was involved in the robbery. Your name is in the mix because you been seen hanging with him damned near every day."

"That's the word on the streets?" I asked. "That's just talk, Sha. Muthafuckas bored and nosey as shit. Ain't no truth to that shit. Fuck what they talkin' about. I ain't tryna hear that shit. I'm in Leo's about to order some food. You want something?"

"Hell, yeah! I want something. I want the platter. The number six with General Tso Sauce all over my wings and French fries. I want two steak and cheese egg rolls, a small chicken and shrimp lo mein and a Rock Creek grape soda."

"All that? Damn, you greedy as shit," I said and laughed.

"I'm eating for two, bae. Stop playing with me."

"Okay, let that be the reason, then."

"Quette, get my mother the orange Sesame Chicken with fried rice," Shakira said.

"She needs a soda with her food, too?"

"Naw, girlfriend probably got beers in her mini fridge in her room."

"A'ight, I'll be there in a few. I love you."

"Love you, too, bye."

I ended the call and shook my head. How in the hell did people in the streets know so much if Khadafi and I wasn't doing any talking? For the life of me, I couldn't figure that out. I made a mental note to bring that up to Khadafi the next time I saw him. I walked up to the glass and placed my order.

***

The lights were out inside Shakira's house, but I figured that she was somewhere by the door waiting for me. I climbed out of the car and saw Gunplay's green Caddy go by. I walked around the back of the car to the passenger side to grab the food. Out of nowhere a person appeared. I stood erect with the food in my hand about to speak when a gun appeared and fired. I dropped the food as the impact of the bullet knocked me back. I was suspended in time until I looked up and saw the moon lit sky. That's when I knew I was on my back. I could feel the blood and life leaving me. The person who'd just shot me stood over me. I looked into the face of my friend.

"Why?" I mumbled.

"Cutty saw you shoot Carlton and V Dot. He paid me to do this, I needed the money, bruh. Anyway, like I always tell you. I don't know what got into you, but I really did love it."

I saw the gun come up and I heard the gun fire. I saw the flash of light, then I could see nothing more.

Chapter Forty-Six

Khadafi

"Khadafi! Khadafi! Wake up!"

I felt myself being tugged. I opened my eyes to the sun shining brightly through the window, blinding me. I had to put my arm over my eyes to shield them.

"I'm up. What's up, cuz?"

"I'm about to leave. When you ready to leave, lock my bottom lock," Lisa said, her voice breaking.

Removing my arm from my eyes, I could see that she'd been crying. "What's wrong with you? Why you crying?" I asked.

"Somebody shot Toya last night. I gotta go and check on her mother. Ms. Brenda is like a mother to me."

I shot up in bed and sat back close to the headboard. "Somebody shot Toya? For what?"

"I don't know, but she's dead, Khadafi."

I feigned hurt and confusion. "Tell me who did it and I'ma crush—"

Lisa shook her head. "No, you not crushing nobody. Go back to sleep and I will call you later when I find out what really happened."

"Naw, I'ma go with you. Toya was your friend if somebody hurt her, that hurts you. If they hurt you, it hurts me. When I hurt, people die. Let me get—"

"No! Khadafi, no! Stay here, I'ma call you later."

"You sure?" I said.

"Positive, go back to sleep. I'ma call you later, bye."

Lisa hurried out of the room. Seconds later, I heard her apartment door open and shut. "Fuck Toya," I said aloud and laughed. "She better be lucky, I ain't kill her mother."

Swinging my legs over the bed, I reached down for my pants to get my cell phone. I wanted to call Lil Quette and thank him for murking Toya. I had several missed calls from Aunt Mary, Lil Quette, and a number I didn't recognize. I decided to call Lil Quette first.

After a few rings, a female answered his phone, "Khadafi?"

"Yeah, this me. What's up, where is Lil Quette?"

There was a long pause on the other end of the phone.

"Hello?" I bellowed into the phone.

"I'm here," the female said. "Quette—Quette—" I heard what sounded like crying from her and in her background.

A dark foreboding entered my gut and wrenched it, twisted it. "Where Lil' Quette at?"

"He's dead! They killed him last night—outside my house—"

At first, I thought I might still be asleep and that I was dreaming, but then I realized that I was wide awake. I dropped my head and cried. I couldn't believe it. In my haste to get rid of Kilo's sister to send him a message, I'd totally ignored Lil Quette's concern about Cutty and it had come back to haunt me. I was hurt beyond words, but I knew that I had to pull myself together. I had to, I needed to find out who was *they* and kill them all.

"Is this Shakira?"

"Uh-huh."

"Okay, listen, I need to talk to you, but not over the phone. Can you meet me somewhere now?"

"Uh-huh, I can drive the Camaro. But meet you where?" Shakira asked.

"Meet me at the Denny's on Benning Road."

"Okay, I'm leaving out now.

***

By the time I got to Denny's, Shakira was already there. I spotted Lil Quette's Camaro in the parking lot empty. I called Quette's phone. "Where you at?"

"In the Denny's, I'm in a booth in the back."

I walked into Denny's and saw Shakira sitting in a booth in the back just as she said. Her hair was pulled back into a ponytail. Her eyes were bloodshot red. I slid in the booth opposite her and sat down.

"I need you to tell me everything that happened. Talk!"

"Quette left me yesterday after you called him. He told me that he had to take care of something for you and that he'd be right back. Hours later, he called me and I kinda went off on him. My cousins Den Den and Maureen called me from two different phones, and I merged the calls. They both started telling me about somebody robbing your baby mother while you were in jail. That you snitched on somebody to get home.

After you got home, they said you killed some dudes named PeeWee, Meechie and his brother because they were the ones who robbed your girl. Then they said that talk had it that Quette was with you doing the killing. I argued with them for calling me with that dumb ass shit until I got mad and hung up on them. When Quette called me, I told him about everything they said. But they weren't the only ones who said some crazy shit about Quette and you. Carlton even confronted Quette—"

"Lil Quette told me about that," I interjected.

"Right but every time I said something to Quette, he denied everything and said that people were just talking and not to listen to none of that shit."

"He told you right. None of that shit you just said is true but go head. Then what happened?"

"Quette called me from Leo's carryout on N. Street. He ordered me and my mother some food." Tears welled up in Shakira's eyes. "That was the last time I talked to him. I went downstairs in my house to wait for him by the door." Her tears fell, she reached for a napkin and blew her nose.

I had to wipe tears from my own cheeks as well. All my tears were angry tears.

"I heard the gunshot but didn't know that it was Quette getting shot. I just got on the floor like I always do because bullets—stray bullets be killing people. Then I heard the second gunshot. After a while I got up and looked out the window. I saw Quette's car. The passenger side door was open. I saw bags of food on the sidewalk next to him.

I saw the body laid out on the ground. I knew that it was Quette. I screamed and ran outside. I lifted Quette's head and cradled it in my lap until I realized that he was gone. I knew I needed to call an ambulance because maybe they could save him. I searched his pockets and found his phone. I called nine-one-one, then I noticed the gun on his waist. I grabbed it and tucked it. Then I ran to my house and hid it. I still have it."

"So, you never saw who shot him?"

Shakira shook her head.

"On the phone you said they killed Quette. Who are they, Shakira?"

"I don't know, I swear to God I don't. If I said they, it was just a figure of speech. I never saw who shot him, I just heard the shots."

"You did good, Shakira, by taking that gun offa him. Did the cops question you a lot?" I asked.

Shakira nodded and wiped at her tears.

"What did you tell them?"

"What I just told you, minus all the stuff I talked to Quette about. I told them that I was at my door when I heard the gunshots and went from there. That's all I told them, nothing else."

"Good girl. Quette told me that you are pregnant?"

"I am," Shakira said, and her tears started anew.

"Listen, I need you to be strong for the baby. It's gonna be hard at times, but you gotta take care of the unborn child. And if it's a boy, name him Marquette."

"I will."

"I'm gonna come to your house later and get that gun. Lil Quette had another gun, a bigger gun. Way bigger, called a choppa. Do you know where it is?"

"No."

"Okay, don't trip. I got some money for you, too. For the baby."

"Quette gave me some money already. A lot of money."

"It doesn't matter, I'ma give you the money anyway. But I need to ask you something else. Do you know the dude Cutty that hangs in your hood?"

Shakira nodded her head.

"I need you to tell me everything you know and ever heard about him."

***

"Bet, big cuz, eventually we gon have to hunt this nigga Cutty. He survived the hit—"

I know that."

"Right, well, I don't think he saw me, but like I told you the other day, I'm not sure. So, I gotta get him out the way—"

"He saw you, lil cuz," I said to myself as I thought about Lil Quette's last words to me before I sicced him on Toya.

Life was a fickle bitch that didn't care who she fucked. She cared for no one. Another person that I loved was dead because of me. Had I left my younger cousin out of my shit he'd still be alive. He'd still be enjoying life, getting ready to be a father. Lil Quette's death brought up the question that I'd often asked myself time and time again. Why was I still here? Considering all the lives I'd taken, how was it possible that I outlived everybody around me?

I leaned on my car long after Shakira had left the Denny's and let my tears flow. People walked by me several times and saw my tears, my pain but I didn't care. I wanted the world to know how hurt I was because Quette was gone from here and I still remained.

"Why?" I looked up toward the sky and questioned Allah. "Why do you let me live to stay here and mourn all the people that have been taken from me? Why do you continue to spare my life?"

My tears bent me over. My hands on my knees, I found myself choking. My nose ran. I couldn't catch my breath. Images of my mother, my father, my uncle Marquette, Damien Lucas, Tee, Creeko, Wayne Wayne, Dion, Omar, Devan, Bean, T.J., Lala, Kemie, Reesie, Dawn, Esha, Boo, Umar, PeeWee, and now Lil Quette ran through my head in a taunting manor. They all laughed at me. I could hear their laughs. Those sounds filled my ears. I covered my ears to get them to stop. I stood up and shook my head. Trying to shake the images and laughs, I couldn't, I dropped to my knees.

"Sir, are you okay?" someone asked.

I looked up into the face of an old woman. Her car parked now beside mine. "No, I'm not okay," I muttered. "I'll never be okay."

***

I pulled into the driveway of Aunt Mary's house and expected her to be at work. But I was wrong, her car was in the garage. As I exited the car, she appeared in the doorway.

"You have a real bad habit of not answering your phone when I call you."

I looked at Aunt Mary and for the first time I noticed how old she looked. Loneliness, pain, and death had aged her beyond her sixty years. Her wrinkled skin stood out more now than ever. Her hair was grey and thin.

"Somebody shot Lil Quette last night. I been too distraught to talk. I was worried sick about you. Again! I can't go on like this, Luther. You are going to send me to an early grave. Marquette's mother called me after she identified his body. I thought the two of you might've been together when it happened. That boy was only seventeen-years old. And now he's gone, killed in the streets just like his father. His little girlfriend is pregnant, too. Did you know that?"

I nodded. "He told me."

"Are you next, Luther?" Aunt Mary asked as tears rolled down her cheeks. "Huh, am I gonna have to bury you next?"

I wiped at the tears in my eyes as I looked at my mother's only living sibling. The woman who loved me like I was her own son. "I don't know, Auntie. I just don't know."

Chapter Forty-Seven

Ameen

"Antonio, it's me, Nicole. Don't talk, just listen. I know you haven't heard anything from me in years, but I need you to get on a plane to D.C., no questions asked. I need you, it's an emergency—"

"Sir, I'm gonna need you to put your bag on the conveyor belt and remove your shoes. Thank you. Now step through, the machine right here," the TSA agent said to me. I followed all instructions. "You have to retrieve your bag at the other end. Enjoy your flight."

Nicole's words to me on the phone played over and over in my head. I grabbed my single carry on bag and filed into the line with all the other people boarding the plane. My bag went into the overhead compartment above my seat and then I buckled myself into my window seat that I'd paid extra to get. After reclining my seat, I closed my eyes. It was the same ritual that I'd been doing since flying with air marshals in Con Air while in the custody of BOP. I wouldn't open my eyes until the plane had taken off, then reached cruising altitude. That was when I felt most safe. Airplanes crashed on take offs and landings and if that was in the cards for me, I didn't want to see it. Once it was safe to open my eyes, I did. Staring out into the vast blackness of the heavens, the plane traveling at a speed too great to even imagine as it transported me back to Washington D.C. I thought about leaving D.C. three years earlier and moving to Florida. I thought I'd never go back until now, until that phone rang.

I had no idea why I was needed in D.C. but if Nicole called out of the blue, after so many years had passed and summoned me, it was for a good reason. One that made me do exactly what she said. Get on a plane to D.C. with no questions asked. I never asked her any questions, but I had several for myself. How did Nicole know that I was far enough away to where I'd need to take a plane back to D.C.? How had she gotten my cell phone number? It was a different number then I'd had three years ago.

"Sir," the stewardess got my attention. "Would you like something to eat or drink?"

"Nothing for me. Thank you," I replied and turned back to the window.

I thought about getting that call from Nicole and the lies that I eventually told my wife—"

"Why do you need to go to D.C.?" Shawnay had asked.

"To help Fargan with some things at the store. Inspectors and people from the Department of Regulatory Affairs are coming by and since technically, I'm still the owner of ISO, I need to be there. He said something about the manufacturers, too. I shouldn't be gone long, a day maybe two."

"I don't want you to go, Antonio. There's something you don't know."

"There's things I don't know like what?"

"Khadafi is out of prison. What if he has Fargan?"

"How do you know that Khadafi is out of prison?"

"Because Marnie called me and told me. She thinks Khadafi killed her mother."

"I didn't even know that you and Marnie kept in touch."

"We've spoken a few times over the years. She told me about other people that Khadafi has killed. What if Khadafi has Fargan under a gun telling him to call you back there?"

"That's not the case, Shawnay. Trust me."

"How can you be so sure?"

"Because I know Fargan, he'd rather die than betray me."

"I can't stop you from going, so I'll just beg you to be safe and cautious."

"I can take care of myself. Shawnay, you know that."

"And that's what I'm afraid of. You having to be Ameen instead of Antonio. Not him—"

I hated to lie to Shawnay but in some situations, a lie was better than the truth and it was safer. My wife didn't know anything about my affair with Nicole and I wanted to keep it like that. Then I thought about the lie I didn't tell but felt like I did. When Shawnay had mentioned Khadafi being home, I acted like I didn't know that when in fact I did. I never told her about the phone call I'd gotten from Fargan telling me about the youngin' who claimed to be my cousin looking for me at the store. After making some calls, I was able to confirm that Khadafi was indeed a free man. When I first got the call from Nicole, I entertained the thought of Khadafi being the emergency that Nicole spoke of.

I quickly dismissed that thought. Khadafi had no way of knowing the connection between Nicole and me. For all he knew, she was just an investigator who had worked on my case and Nicole would never put me in a kill or be killed situation. That I was sure of, if Khadafi had ever suspected a bond between me and Nicole, there'd be no emergency, Nicole would be dead, plain and simple. I thought about what Shawnay said about Marnie, Khadafi's baby mother.

She believed that Khadafi had killed her mother. Now that I believed, I didn't know why he did it, but he was definitely capable of doing it. Maybe that was Khadafi's way of expressing his displeasure about her helping me out in trial? I wondered who the other people were that Khadafi had killed. The next thing I knew, I fell asleep.

***

"It's forty-seven degrees in our Nation's Capital with clear skies. We hope you enjoyed your flight. Thanks again for flying American Airlines."

Minutes later, the wheels of the plane kissed the tarmac, and we exited the plane. After clearing TSA again, I stood outside of Reagan National and called Nicole's cell phone.

"Antonio?" Nicole answered.

"It's me, Nic, I'm here. Come get me."

"Antonio, I'm glad you came, but I can't come get you."

"You can't come and get me. Why not?"

"Because I'm in the hospital. I'm dying of cancer. That's the emergency."

The air left my lungs and I felt like I'd been punched, I couldn't believe what I'd just heard. "Nic—did I just hear you say—"

"Antonio, I'm at George Washington University Hospital. Come here."

"I-I-I'm on my way."

***

I walked into Nicole's hospital room, she laid in bed looking at me as I entered. Everything about her was different, her skin had no glow, no sheen to it. Her hair was thin but pulled into a ponytail. Nicole's eyes seemed hollow. Her weight, her thickness, gone. My eyes watered instantly. I stopped in my tracks and dropped my head. My tears fell and hit the floor.

"Antonio, please don't," Nicole pleaded. "Don't cry for me."

But I couldn't help crying for her. She was so frail. The room smelled of death and disinfectant. It smelled of medicine. My shoulders shook with grief as I tried to hold her eyes, I couldn't. All I could hear was her saying— *"I'm dying of cancer."* I was only feet away from her bed but I couldn't get there. My feet were heavy as if my shoes were made of lead.

"Antonio, come here."

I pulled myself together the best I could and walked the short distance to her bed. Nicole reached out and grabbed my hand.

"Go ahead and cry if you must. Get it all out because I need you to be strong and attentive, I need you to be brave."

"Nic, what happened? How did this happen?" I asked.

"Stage four Cervical Cancer, Antonio. It's terminal, it just happened. I didn't contract it. I didn't ask for it. It just happened. To me, and there's nothing anybody can do about it."

"I shouldn't have—left."

"Antonio, stop it. This didn't happen because you left. It would've happened had you stayed. This is my fate, my lot in life, my destiny. Once we're born, we are all living to die, right. My turn just came sooner than anybody expected. And there's no one to blame. I need you to pull yourself together. I need you to be strong. For you, for me and for our son."

I wiped at the tears in my eyes. "What did you just say?"

"You heard me correctly, Antonio. I need you to be strong for our son."

"*Our son?* Nic—what the hell are you talking about? Our son?"

Nicole squeezed my hand with tears in her eyes and said, "My death is not the only emergency I called you here for. I have to come clean to you. Tell you my secret and why I kept it from you. That secret is Little Antonio. My son, your son."

"But—how?"

"Do you really wanna ask me that? How are children usually created?"

"But it's been—years."

"I know exactly how long it's been since the last time we had sex. It's been three years and six months. Do the math, Antonio. Our son is two years and nine months old. He was born February fifteenth, twenty-fifteen. In three months, he'll be three. I have never been with any other man since the first time you and I had sex in my car. The day I picked you up from the cemetery. Do you remember that day?"

I nodded. "How can I forget it."

"You were a hard act to follow, so I never let anyone even try. I haven't had sex with anyone period since you. I haven't sex since the day you told me that you were leaving D.C. in my office. That was the day it happened I believe. When I found out I was pregnant, I wanted to tell you so badly, but then I thought that you wouldn't believe me. That you'd think I was trying to trap you. Trying to stop you from leaving or desperately trying to get you to stay. I thought you'd accuse me of trying to break up your marriage. So, I kept quiet. I never told anyone in my family who my son's father was, until now. Nine months after he was conceived, I had my son and named him Antonio after his father."

I dropped into the chair next to Nic's bed, let her hand go and massaged my head. I couldn't believe how things were unfolding. Learning that someone I loved was dying was a bombshell in itself but to hear that I now had an almost three-year-old son. That was breathtaking.

"Antonio, I know this is a lot to take in. It's a lot for me, too. And I never wanted you to find out like this. But to hear a doctor tell you that you only have weeks to live—is something that you can never imagine. It changes your perspective instantly, you know. I could've never contacted you and let my mother care for my son, but I can't leave her to shoulder that burden. She's almost sixty-years-old. My son needs his parents. But since I can't be here, that leaves you.

You have to step up, Antonio. And be the man that I know you are. Raise our son, you have to. It's my dying wish. Antonio, if you have ever loved me like you said you did, then prove it. Accept my truth. Our truth and do what needs to be done. I know you have a family in Florida. A wife and two children, I know this will cause a problem. But it's not an insurmountable problem. Antonio is your son, your blood is in him. He needs you and you need him. In time, you'll realize that."

I was suddenly a man on a surfboard caught between waves of indecision. Surfboard precariously slipping from under my feet. I was a traveler at a fork in the road, trying to decide what path to take.

Then I heard Nicole say, "Ma, bring Antonio in here."

My pulse quickened as my eyes found the door. A minute later, the hospital room door opened. An older version of Nicole stepped into the room, her hand behind her leading a small child. I stood up and saw him. Saw my son. A walking baby picture of myself in the flesh.

"Oh, my God," Nicole's mother exclaimed. Her eyes filled with tears. "They look just alike."

"Ma, this is Antonio," Nicole said. "Antonio, this is my mother."

"How are you?" I started, but Nicole's mother embraced me.

"Mommy!" the little boy screamed and lifted his arms in the air.

Nicole's mother let me go, then reached down and lifted the little boy and handed him to his mother. They hugged, the only eyes in the room not full of tears was the little boy.

"This little guy is Antonio. Antonio, say hello to your father. Say, hi Daddy!"

"Hi, Daddy," the little boy repeated.

Then to everybody's surprise he reached for me. I reacted instinctively. I picked him up and held him tight.

***

Hours later, when Nicole and I were alone again, we talked some more.

"You should've contacted me and told me about Antonio."

"Look, I already told you why I didn't. And had I never got sick you still wouldn't know. That's the reality of it, but we gotta get past that, Antonio. Past the why this and why that. I only have a few weeks left to live. I got a lot to do in that time. I need to hear you say it. Gimme your word that you'll raise Antonio."

"You got my word, Nic, but you don't need it. He's my son, there's no denying that. It's like looking back into time at myself as a child when I looked at him. I would never abandon a child of mine."

Nicole smiled. "I knew you'd say that, but it was good to hear. I have to get all the paperwork in order. Your name is already on his birth certificate and all his medical records. You're his biological parent, so things shouldn't be that complicated. I got a lot of money saved up and everything I own will be liquidated and put in a trust for Antonio. There are memories that I want him to have, things for him to see when he gets older. My mother's a great woman, Antonio and she loves Antonio, you have to make sure that they remain close. You two can work out the details of visits and all that. He loves—"

Nicole's words stopped abruptly. "Nic, what is it? Are you okay?"

"Antonio, what about your wife—your marriage?"

I hugged Nicole then kissed her lips. "My marriage will survive. It has to, it's survived losing a child. We lost Shawnay's grandmother and survived. My trial and possible life sentences. We've been through a lot and we survived. Shawnay has a son by my friend turned enemy and yet I love Kay Kay with all my heart.

I believe that Shawnay will do the same, eventually. I can't sit here and lie and say that things won't be difficult and awkward at first, but in time, it'll be okay. Lil Antonio is my responsibility, and I will never forsake him for anyone, Shawnay included. Wallahi.

You got my word as a Muslim man on that. As a matter of fact, I got some preparing I need to do. I'ma go and visit my daughter's grave, stop past my store, and then come back here in the morning. Then I'll fly home and break the news to Shawnay and my children. Once I do that, I'm coming back here to spend some time with you. Then if it's okay with you, I'll take Antonio home to Florida."

"Sounds good to me. Thank you, Antonio. I knew I could count on you. I love you so much."

"I love you, too, Nic. I love you, too."

***

My visit to my daughter's grave was as emotional as ever. I kneeled in front of her tombstone and wept like a kid. I missed my daughter more than I could ever express. Had she been alive, Kenya would be twenty-one-years old.

"Hey, baby it's me. I had to come and check on you. Everybody is okay. Well, as okay as we can be despite you not being with us. Kay Kay is boxing now and he's pretty good, too. His coaches think he can be a world champion one day. Asia is driving now, she's an honor roll student who thinks she's grown. Your mother is good, still working at the hospital. And here's some news I wish you were here to share in. You have a little brother, his name is Antonio—" My phone vibrated in my coat pocket, it was Shawnay.

"Hey, baby. What's up?" I said into the phone.

"I'm just checking on you. What are you doing?"

"I'm at the cemetery talking to Kenya."

"Tell her that I love her and miss her, would you?"

"I will."

"When are you coming home?"

"Tomorrow. My plane leaves Reagan at three p.m."

"Okay, I'll be at the airport to get you when you land."

"That's what's up. How are the kids?"

"They good, we miss you."

"Me, too."

"Have you seen the inspectors and all at the store?"

"Everything is good. I'll tell you everything when I get back."

"Alright, I love you, Antonio."

"Love you, too, baby. Talk to you later."

***

"Assalaama Alaikum," I said as I entered ISO.

Fargan came from around the counter to embrace me. "Walaikum Assalam. Ameen, it's good to see you, ock."

Angenic embraced me next. "Hey, Ameen, you look good."

"Thank you, baby girl. How's your father doing?" I asked her.

"He good, should be about to see the parole board soon."

"Get my new number from Fargan and give it to him. Tell him to call me."

"I sure will. This is my friend Crissy. She been here with us for a while."

"Hey, Crissy," I turned and said to the woman next to Angenic.

"Hi, Mr. Felder. I've heard a lot about you," Crissy replied.

"All good, I hope? Fargan, it looks good in here, ock. I love it."

"I knew you would. Let me show you all the new ISO gear."

***

I couldn't get the face of my son out of my head, my son. I couldn't believe it. I always wanted a son. Someone to carry on my name, my legacy, my bloodline. After so many years, I grew to accept the fact that me having a son wasn't Allah's will. I groomed

Kay Kay and lived my dreams through him. But now, in a twisted turn of fate, my dream of having a man child of my own has finally come true. I checked into the Radisson Suites a few blocks from Reagan National Airport. I Facetimed Shawnay and spoke to her and the kids, then I got some much needed rest. I closed my eyes knowing that tomorrow would bring a storm that would rival Hurricane Katrina.

Chapter Forty-Eight

Shawnay

Tallahassee, Florida

"Hey, baby, how was your flight?"

Antonio dropped his bag and embraced me, then kissed me. "Smooth."

"Glad to hear it. Let's get you home."

***

We were only in our house for a few minutes before Antonio said, "Bae, we need to talk."

"Sounds serious," I replied and hung my jacket up in the closet. "Something to do with the trip?"

"I need for you to sit down and try to open your mind. Go ahead, sit."

I kicked off my shoes and sat down on the couch. I tried to read my husband's face but couldn't. "Open mind, you're starting to scare me. What did you do, Antonio?"

"Look, there's no way to sugar coat this. So, I'm just gonna come right out and say it." Antonio paced the floor, then stopped directly in front of me. "When you packed up and left Arlington after Kenya's death, I was lost. I was grieving for my daughter. For your grandmother and upset with you for leaving. I started drinking and smoking. I—"

"Antonio, you've told me all this before."

"I know, but what I didn't tell you was that I had an affair."

"An affair? With whom?"

"With Nicole."

"The investigator chick, Nicole?"

Antonio nodded. "Yeah, her. I didn't think I'd ever find you and Nicole was there helping me find you. I spent a lot of time around her, drinking and smoking—"

"Please don't insult me by saying that you didn't know what you were doing."

"Never that, I knew exactly what I was doing. I was substituting the woman I loved for another who was there, who was available."

"And you're telling me this now, for what reason?" I was hurt and confused. "Does this have something to do with why you went to D.C.?"

"Yes, it does. Nicole called me and told me to come to D.C. immediately and that it was an emergency. I've known Nicole since we were younger growing up around Congress Park. I hadn't spoken to her in years, since the trial. I swear, so when she called me—"

"How did she get your cell phone number?"

"The same way she got yours over three years ago. Her friend in Quantico found me. Gave her all my information. She said she's had it for years but never used it until now."

"So, what did she want? What was the emergency?"

"Nicole is dying, Shawnay. Stage four cervical cancer. Doctors say that she only has a few weeks to live."

"Oh, my gawd! I'm sorry to hear that," I said sincerely, remembering the very pretty woman who found me in Texas and convinced me to go to D.C. to help Antonio beat murder charges. "That's why she asked you to come to D.C.? To see her on her deathbed?"

Antonio paced the floor again without answering, then suddenly he stopped. "No that's not why she wanted me to come to D.C. Nicole called me to D.C. to introduce me to her son, to my son, Lil Antonio."

I shot straight up off the couch and screamed. *"What! Your son, Lil Antonio? You have a fuckin' child with her?"*

"Apparently, I do. He's almost three and he looks just like me."

"Almost three? So, that means—wait a minute—he was born in what twenty-fourteen?"

"No, twenty-fifteen. He'll be three in February of next year," Antonio corrected.

"But how is that even possible? You were in jail for almost a year. Late twenty-thirteen until mid-twenty-fourteen. The math is off. And you said he looks just like you?"

"The math is not off Shawnay. I'm not gullible. When I was arrested for the sixteen counts of murder and housed at D.C. jail, the affair didn't stop. Nicole was a CJA investigator for the city which gave her access to D.C. jail twenty-four hours a day on any day she chose. We had sex in the legal rooms reserved for attorneys. We had sex a lot. All the way up until the trial. All the way up until she found you.

"What the fuck? I can't believe this shit! You was fucking this bitch the entire time I was gone, but you missed me so fucking much? And this bitch sat down in my living room and convinced me to come help you in court and she was fucking you the whole time?"

"Bae, chill out. You don't have to keep calling the woman a bitch."

"Are you defending this bitch in my fucking face!"

"Shawnay, the woman is dying," Antonio said.

"I don't give a fuck. At first, I did, now I don't."

"You don't mean that you're just upset."

"So what if I'm upset. I do mean it. Manipulative, scandalous ass—" my words got caught in my throat. My tears started then. The realization of what Antonio was saying hit me like a ton of bricks. "If she's dying—and called you to D.C. to meet him, she must expect you to raise him. Is that it?"

Antonio nodded and his eyes were wet with tears.

I collapsed to the floor. *"N-o-o-o-o! No! No! No! No!"*

"Shawnay, I have to take responsibility of the kid, he's my son."

I got up off the floor and ran upstairs. I locked myself in the bathroom and cried. The pain that I felt could only be rivaled by the pain of my daughter and grandmother's deaths. My heart was hurting. I cried loudly and for a long time, ignoring Antonio at the door begging me to come out of the bathroom. He said he was sorry over and over again. He told me how much he loved me repeatedly, but nothing could soothe my aching heart.

My life, my perfect life and storybook ending was about to change in a major way. I sat down on the toilet after putting the lid down. I wiped my eyes and tried to calm down. Images of Antonio with Nicole filled my head. His words about their affair narrated the images of them. I could hear her moans of pleasure. I could see them at D.C. jail. In one of the small legal rooms in the visiting hall, having sex. My stomach flipped, then I had an epiphany.

Right there on the toilet, images of Antonio and Nicole changed to images of me and Khadafi. The images that overtook my thoughts on too many occasions. Images that I'd blacked out completely, but they always returned. I could hear my own moans as Khadafi sexed me while Antonio was away, still in prison. I thought about the careless, spontaneous, and numerous sexcapades that I had shared with Khadafi. At my home, at my job, in his vehicles, and at hotels. I thought about my desire back then and my need.

I thought about how my love for Antonio never stopped me from giving myself to Khadafi orally or vaginally. I remembered the day I found out that I was pregnant after our affair had ended. I remembered my entire thought process that went into me deciding to keep the baby. I remembered explaining my infidelity to my girls. I had no communication with Antonio then and I feared the day he found out about my child and who his father was. I thought about when Antonio eventually found out and the day we sat in D.C.'s jail visiting hall and talked about it. I thought about Antonio coming home and how he never made me feel bad about Kashon.

How he always treated Kashon with love from day one. I thought about their bond today. If Antonio had forgiven me for my trespasses and sins and lived with the stain of my betrayal every day. How could I not do the same? I thought about everything that was just said in our living room and wondered if God was testing me. Was this God's way of balancing my scales? Or was this good old fashioned Karma coming back on me?

Whatever it was, I decided that losing my husband wasn't worth it. Losing the life that I'd grown accustomed to wasn't even an option. Like every other challenge in my life, I had to face it head on. I washed my face and brushed my teeth, then left the bathroom.

Antonio sat in the hallway with his knees drawn to his chest. He looked up at me as I stood in the hallway. His eyes found mine and held them. I smiled, then back away for him to come to me, he did. We stood in the middle of our hallway kissed for a long time.

"Karma's a bitch, huh?" I said, breaking our kiss.

"And then you die," Antonio replied.

"Well, life's too short and I refuse to let this break us."

"I agree."

"I guess we gotta figure out what to tell the kids."

"Again, I agree. But first, I need to see you in the bedroom."

"Uh—see me for what, sir?" I asked coyly.

Antonio lifted me off my feet and carried me to our bedroom. Then he undressed me, kissed me all over and made slow, passionate love to me.

Anthony Fields

Chapter Forty-Nine

Rio Jefferson

"Goddammit, Corey!" I said to myself as I touched the cold, hard head of Corey Winslow.

A tear escaped my eye as I walked away from the casket that held the shell of a man who was just so recently full of life. I thought about our public spat at the scene of the fire and murders at Imperial Autos. It was hard to believe that that had been over two months ago. I thought about all our recent conversations. I thought our comradery and desire to bring down Khadafi. It was sad that Corey wouldn't be around to catch the end result.

If there was such a thing as heaven, I hoped Corey was there watching over us with Moe Tolliver and that they'd both help us get Khadafi. I looked around the AME Church where Corey's funeral was being held and noticed that outside of the cops in uniform, the rest of the mourners were women. I allowed myself a small smile. Corey had probably been with every woman in the gallery. The police force in D.C. was a fraternity, a brotherhood that had lost one of its own in a dishonorable way. But with Corey, it would be overlooked as it always was.

It was common knowledge around the halls of 1st District that Corey was involved with the U.S. Attorney. He believed that they were being discreet. But when your city is only sixty-nine square miles in diameter, there was no discretion. My homicide unit was taking Corey's death particularly hard. To lose one's life in the line of duty was one thing, but to lose it in the line of booty was another heartbreak altogether.

Corey was headstrong, he was a way too handsome playboy that all the women fawned over. But nobody ever thought that he'd be killed by a jealous husband. Suddenly, the air inside the church became stifling and constrictive. I had to get some fresh air. In the parking lot, I found several members of the force gathered, most weeping. I embraced them all.

"Doug," I said to Detective Doug Davis. "Get Leo and Pete and meet back at the ranch in thirty."

Doug nodded and went about his task.

"Dammit, Corey," I said to myself again and headed to my car.

***

"The last case that Corey worked on was the Khadafi case. The last case that Moe Tolliver worked on was dedicated to bringing Khadafi down. I have always been dedicated to doing what they both died trying to do. Bring down once and for all Luther Khadafi Fuller," I announced to the three detectives in attendance for my impromptu meeting. "I need all of y'all to watch this video feed and tell me what you see."

I played the video that Corey emailed me of Khadafi at the counter talking to the woman at Forestville Health and Rehab. The video clip was a little under four minutes, everyone watched it in silence.

"Khadafi's grown a beard," Doug Davis said as soon as the video ended.

"Good observation, Doug, but not quite what I'm getting at. Anyone else?"

"Play it again, Rio," Leo Jacobs chimed in. I played the video again. "He booked her," Leo said. "Khadafi booked her."

"Booked her?" Pete Sandoval repeated.

"He means that Khadafi got the woman's number," I explained.

"Oh."

"That's what I saw. They talked and then Khadafi passed her his phone. She put her number in the phone and passed it back across the counter," Leo said.

I nodded. "Exactly what I saw, and Corey saw it, too. He sent me a text telling me that the woman, Sherita Simms—"

"Wait a minute—Sherita Simms? Is that Sherita Simms?" Pete asked.

"Yeah, the woman in the video at the counter is Sherita Simms."

"Rio, Sherita Simms was killed in her apartment a few days ago."

"Are you sure?" I asked Pete.

"Positive, I was with Willis when Smiley gave him the case."

"Shit!" I exclaimed. "Corey sent me a text. Well, let me say this, after Monica Summers' mother Tawana Curry was killed. She told me that Khadafi went to her old job at Forestville Health and Rehab looking for her. Sherita Simms called her and told her that a man had come looking for her. I wanted to get a look at the man and see if it was in fact Khadafi who'd come looking for Monica. I couldn't go, so I sent Corey.

He was able to talk to Sherita Simms as the security guy pulled the videos for him. Corey text me and told that Sherita Simms asked questions that a person not connected wouldn't have. He believed that there was something between Sherita Simms and Khadafi, which is what I was going to investigate before Pete just told us that Sherita Simms is dead. That's unfortunate and I'll get back to it, but right now I need you to see this second video that Corey emailed me."

It was the footage of the black SUV pulling into Forestville Health's parking lot. It showed Khadafi exiting the SUV.

"Rio, that looks just like the SUV that the killer got out of and killed Meechie," Leo Jacobs said as it played.

"I agree and Corey thought so, too. So, he forwarded these videos to IT. I spoke to Ivan Kellog who assures me that off the record the two SUVs are one and the same."

"Isn't that enough to apply for a warrant to at least search the SUV?"

I looked at Doug Davis and said, "Off the record, they're the same. But on the record, Ivan Kellog says that his conclusion is not based on scientific fact. He said and I quote, *"The black SUV in the nursing home parking lot footage is an old model Infiniti Ex sixty or sixty-five, depending on the year. The grill shows that Infiniti logo. The SUV from the Half Street murder is the same in all dimensions, but there's no good angle of the SUV's grill. No Infiniti logo and it's important to note that Nissan makes Infiniti, so the Armadas and Pathfinders look exactly like the Infiniti."*

"So, basically, we have nothing but speculation and conjecture," Leo Jacobs said.

"Pretty much," I replied. "Leo, get with Willis and see what he's found out so far about the Sherita Simms murder. Tell him about our Khadafi connection. They can look for his prints or DNA inside the apartment. Then talk to the owners of the property and see if they have surveillance cameras in and around the area. See if we can find that black SUV somewhere nearby. I think Sherita Simms told Khadafi that she was questioned by Corey and he killed her for it. This could be the—"

"Rio?" a female voice interrupted.

I turned to see one of the female detectives named Juanita Fleming standing there.

"What's up, Juanita?"

"Smiley wants to see you. Now, he says!"

"Thanks, Juanita. What the fuck?"

***

Smiley was the nickname given to Captain Greg Dunlop because he never smiled. Even when he was happy. But nobody on the force dared to call him that to his face. I walked into his office without knocking.

"You asked to see me, Captain?"

"Yeah, have a seat, Rio," Captain Dunlop replied, stood up and turned his back to me. "I've decided to retire early. Just wanted you to know and hear it from me personally. It's time, Rio. I've been in Homicide for far too long. I'm sixty-one years old and I been doing this shit for almost forty years. I've given way more than my pound of flesh. I think it's time to be granddad to my three grand babies. It's time to just be, Pop Pop."

"You can't leave, Captain," I said with sincerity. "This place needs you."

"No, it doesn't, Rio. It needs you. It needs Charlie Weiss. It's time for a new Captain to take the helm of the ship and I'm recommending Charlie. He's younger, charismatic, stern, yet fair—"

"But he's not you, Captain. And you know that," I argued.

"He doesn't need to be me to succeed. All he needs is your support. Nothing in this world lasts forever. The only constant thing in the world is change. I've lost five officers on my watch, Rio. Five! That's more than most Captains lose in their whole careers. Every one of them fucks with me. But this latest one with Corey Winslow hurts like a son of a gun. I always told Corey that he should've never been a cop. He was a smart kid, but God made him too goddamned handsome. He was banging the women around here like it was going out of style and thought I didn't know. I knew, I just never said anything, and I should have. Now look what's happened. That kid was like a son to me. I told him one day, *"Winslow don't let your dick make a bum out of you."* But he did it anyway. Him being killed by that bitch's husband who didn't do a day in jail so far, fucks with me, too much. That in itself tells me it's time to go."

"But Captain—"

"No buts, Rio, it's already decided. I didn't call you in here to talk me out of my decision. I called you in here to tell you that I'm promoting you. I already put the paperwork in, and it's been approved by Laney. My last day will be December thirtieth. Charlie Weiss will succeed as Captain and you'll inherit his job. It's not negotiable or up for debate. On December thirty-first of this year, you become Lieutenant and Charlie becomes Captain."

"I hear you, Captain—"

"Rio, just say thank you, would you?"

"Thank you, Captain. I promise, I won't let you down."

"Good. Do you have anything else on Luther Fuller, yet?" the Captain asked.

"We're following some good leads," I told him.

"I'ma need you to do what Moe Tolliver couldn't. Either put Khadafi away for life or kill his ass. Just that simple, I'd love to spit on his grave before I leave this office, for good. Do you catch my drift?"

"Drift caught, sir."

"Is it really? I told Moe Tolliver the same thing once and look what it got him."

"I won't make the same mistake, Captain," I assured him.

"Good. Now, get the fuck out of my office. I need to be alone."

***

"Rio, the ambassador of Southwest just came in. I think you need to hear what he's saying," Leo Jacobs informed me and led the way to one of the interrogation rooms.

I hated the smug look on Anthony Chandler's face as I entered the room. He looked like Master Splinter, the rat on Teenage Mutant Ninja Turtles. He sat in a chair, back up against the wall, talking to Pete Sandoval.

"Everybody here knows who Zinc is right?" Pete asked.

"Yeah," Leo and I said in unison.

"Good. Zinc, tell Detective Jefferson what you just told us."

Anthony Zinc Chandler smiled as if he'd just cracked the case of the century. "I checked on the black van. They say it was a work van, like them cargo types. One sliding door panel on the passenger side. One driver's side door. One passenger door. Double doors at the rear of the van. The van had paper tags, too, both of em. The one at the scene of AD's murder and the Carlton and V Dot murders. Sounds like the same van."

Pete Sandoval wrote down everything that Zinc said.

"And this is hot off the press," Zinc continued. "Word on the street is that the dude Khadafi came home and killed PeeWee for robbing his house like y'all said. PeeWee must've told Khadafi that Meechie was with him. Because he killed Meechie next. Okay, here's what y'all don't know. Khadafi had a younger cousin that grew up in Southwest. His mother Tasca was born and raised on Carrollsburg Street. His name is Lil Quette."

His father was Big Quette, Khadafi's uncle that got killed. Word is that Lil Quette aided and assisted Khadafi in killing Meechie. Lil Quette was allegedly driving the black SUV when Khadafi hopped out and killed Meechie. Somebody saw Lil Quette in the SUV a few times before the killing. They told Carlton, Meechie's brother.

Carlton approached Lil Quette after a crap game one day. The next thing you know, Carlton gets killed and V Dot too. But Cutty survives. Word is that he saw Lil Quette as he opened fire on the Benz Wagon. He's still fucked up from getting shot, but he put some money on Lil Quette's head, and somebody collected."

"Somebody collected?" I frowned. "Who collected?"

Zinc shrugged. "I don't know that, but I know that somebody killed Lil Quette a couple of days ago on Second Street."

Pete Sandoval pulled out a notepad and read from it, "Marquette Jennings, seventeen, shot and killed as he exited a vehicle in the one hundredth block of Second Street, shortly after midnight four days ago. Girlfriend Shakira Lennox called it in."

"So, Cutty had—paid somebody to kill Khadafi's little cousin?" I asked.

"It looks that way," Leo Jacobs said.

"Well, somebody needs to find Cutty before Khadafi does. Him and his entire family is in grave danger. Do we have an address for Cutty? It's our obligation to at least warn him."

"He's in our system listed as no fixed address," Pete added. "Zinc, do you know where Cutty lives?"

Zinc shook his head. "I don't have a clue."

"If Zinc knows that Cutty paid somebody to kill Marquette Jennings, you better believe that Khadafi knows it, too. And we all know how he's going to respond. Pete get some uniforms to shake up every corner of James Creek. We need info on Cutty. If we find Cutty, I'm willing to bet, we'll find Khadafi somewhere nearby.

Hopefully, in the black van and hopefully with a gun. Remember the van has paper tags on it. Get the word out, if anyone spots the van, call it in. No hot dogging or lone wolfing. Khadafi will be armed and considered extremely dangerous. We all learned from the Moe Tolliver situation that he'll shoot it out. Leo, get with Willis on the Sherita Simms murder. Hopefully, we can catch a break and connect Khadafi to that."

"Anything else?" Pete Sandoval asked.

"Yeah, let's pray that we're not too late. For all we know, Cutty and his entire family may be getting killed at this exact moment."

Chapter Fifty

Khadafi

Witnesses at the scene of A.D.'s murder and the G-Wagon massacre probably reported seeing a black cargo van involved in both situations. The police were probably looking for a black van with paper tags. My van was now silver with dark tinted windows and all the way around hard tags and racks on the roof and a ladder on the back door. There was an old lawn mower strapped to the roof of the van along with brooms, rakes, and other landscaping equipment. The uniform I wore was navy blue and smelled of all the weed I'd smoked all morning.

My eyes were bloodshot red from a lack of sleep and my heart was hard and cold. Murder ran through my veins like an aphrodisiac. I couldn't wait to kill Cutty. I'd probably bust a nut from killing Cutty. I want the streets to tell the tale of Cutty's murder for generations. That's how dirty I planned on doing him. I spotted a mint green Jaguar not far from where I'd killed A.D.

I remembered Lil Quette saying that Cutty had that exact same SUV. If his truck was nearby, so was he. I did what I did best, I waited. In the passenger seat across from me sat the Draco that I'd gotten back from Shakira. Lil Quette had hidden it in her bedroom closet. I figured that it would be only fitting for me to kill Cutty with the same choppa that Lil Quette shot him with. I looked for my prey walking with crutches or a cane. I crossed my fingers and hoped to see him soon.

***

I couldn't catch Cutty that day or the next. The unusual police presence made me paranoid, so I left early on both days. But on the third day, I got lucky. Cutty must've thought that he was in the clear because he surfaced. Shakira had gone on Instagram and screenshotted a picture of Cutty and texted it to me. I knew exactly what he looked like and I was looking at him now. A beautiful, burgundy Audi A7 pulled near the mint green Jaguar truck. I watched as Cutty got out of the Audi, leaned the seat back and retrieved a pair of crutches. I got out of the van and pulled my hat low. The mock turtleneck around my neck, I pulled up to cover the bottom half of my face. I walked around to the passenger seat of the van, opened the door, and grabbed the Draco.

Cutty eyed me coming but couldn't go anywhere. He reached in his waistband. I let the Draco go and lifted him off his feet. I ran up closer and filled his body with shells. Then I turned the Draco on the Audi, killing the female who was driving. I made sure to closed-casket her ass, then I ran back to the van and got out of there.

***

A gallon of unleaded gas cost two dollars and seventy cents a gallon. I paid for two gallons and filled up the plastic gas can. I climbed on the back of the van and pulled the lawn mower down. I left it on the side of the Amoco gas station on West Virginia Avenue. My destination came quickly afterward. Behind the Ivy City Masjid, there was renovation going on. There were old warehouses and deserted lots and a lot of woods.

I pulled off the uniform, underneath it I wore a Hugo Boss jogging sweatsuit. I pulled my New Balance 990s out of the van and switched them out with the boots I wore. Dousing the clothes, the Draco, the landscaping equipment, and the van with the gasoline didn't take long. I pulled the hard tags off the van and tucked them in my waist. Then I lit a match and watched everything burn. I stayed to make sure that the clothes burned, the choppa melted and then the van burned out. The smoke signals were tip drawing, so it was time to go.

I walked until I was back on West Virginia Avenue. From there I hit Florida Avenue and a liquor store. I purchased a gallon of Perch Ciroc and drank the bottle. The gun on my waist, my loyal companion. Across from the Langston Golf Course, near the old RFK Stadium, there was a small bridge surrounded by woods. The bridge overlooked the Potomac River. I leaned on the rail and poured half of the bottle of Ciroc in the dark brown water.

"Wherever you are lil' cuz, I pray that you can hear me. I should've left you out of my mess. In my hunger for blood and retribution, I never thought things all the way through. We should've never slept until Cutty was dead. That was my bad because I knew better. One of the laws of war is never stop halfway through total annihilation, because your enemy will recover and come back for you.

My mistake cost you your life. But you didn't die in vain. I got him for you, cuz. I nailed his ass to the pavement. Put that Draco on his ass. Fucked him around real proper. Him and the bitch he was with, fucked her up. All closed casket shit. I got him, cuz. I got him." I broke down then.

I allowed myself another five minutes of grief, then I pulled the license plates from my pants and tossed them. They landed in the murky water and floated. I watched the hard tags float downstream and let my tears flow. As always, I thought that killing my enemies would make me feel better, but it didn't. I still felt angry, I felt sad, I felt empty.

My cell phone vibrated in my coat pocket. I pulled it out and saw that the caller was Shakira. She still had Lil Quette's cell phone.

"Hello?"

"Khadafi?"

"What's up, cuz? It's me."

"Can I talk on this phone?" Shakira asked.

"I guess it's cool. I'm getting rid of it tonight anyway. What's up?"

Shakira paused for a moment and then said, "I heard about Cutty. It's all over the news."

"And?" I said ready to hang up at any moment.

"Cutty didn't kill Marquette."

"Is that right? How you know that?"

"I'm not trying to say all that over the phone."

"Respect, where you at?"

"I'm at home."

"Do you know where the DTRL is on Minnesota Avenue?"

"The one across from Shoe City?" Shakira asked.

"Yeah, that's the one. Meet me there in twenty-minutes," I instructed her.

"I'll be there. I'm leaving now."

***

I was trying on a pair of double sole butter Timberland boots when Shakira walked into Downtown Locker Room Shoe Store. She spotted me sitting on a bench and walked over. She sat down next to me.

"I always told Quette that he trusted too easily. It was easy for me to see that them niggas in the hood didn't really fuck with him. But I couldn't get him to see it. One of my friends be fucking one of Quette's friends named Delow. When he gets high and gets some pussy, he likes to talk. He told Simone, my friend, that Cutty put some money on Quette's head. He didn't say how much. He said something about Quette killing Carlton and V Dot. According to Delow, Quette's best friend, this ugly ass nigga named Gunplay collected the money on Quette's head. Gunplay killed Quette. Whoever did it, had to have known Quette. It makes sense to me. Gunplay did that with his crutty ass." Shakira's eyes watered and tears rolled down her cheeks. "I'ma kill his ass—"

"Nonsense," I said calmly. "Tell me everything you know about Gunplay."

***

The Next Afternoon

Lisa opened the door for me dressed in jeans that hugged her every curve. A Givenchy shirt hugged the top of her and looked painted on. I couldn't help but notice the new hairstyle. One side of Lisa's head was cut really low with designs cut into her head. The hair on her head laid down and fell to the opposite side. It was sexy as hell. Once I was in her living room, Lisa embraced me and held me tight.

"You smell good. You look so good. And you taste good." Lisa kissed my neck, then my ears, my cheeks and lastly my lips. "I'm addicted to you, Khadafi, but I gotta leave you alone."

I pulled back from Lisa's embrace until our faces were inches apart. I looked her straight in the eyes. "You gotta leave me alone?"

Lisa broke our embrace completely and walked away from me. She went to her couch and sat down, then pulled her legs up under her. "I just left West Virginia. Got back about thirty minutes ago."

"You went to see Bay One?"

Lisa nodded. "I needed to see her. Wanted to see her. Haven't been up there since I started fucking around with you. I love Bay One with all my heart."

"I know that and would never try to come in between that," I said and unzipped my Moncler coat and took it off. I tossed the coat onto the recliner nearest me.

"But you already are, Khadafi and you can't see it. I couldn't see it. Not until I sat in front of Bay. I felt fucked up, like cold blooded shit. Guilty as sin. Dick residue all over me, inside me, every orifice. Even my ass, I gave you my ass, Khadafi. I still can't believe it. I kissed that woman in the mouth and felt terrible. My ethers were off the whole time and I believe Bay picked up on it. She didn't say anything, but I think she knew my secret."

"So, you told her—about us?"

"Fuck no!" Lisa spat face screwed up. "And get myself killed in that visiting hall up there? I ain't that fucking crazy, or stupid. I will never admit to Bay what's been going on between us. Never, ever. I just know that I need to end this. End it now, before I can't stop."

"Whatever decision you make, I gotta accept."

"Do you really?" Lisa got up and walked up to me. She looked me in the eyes as she unzipped my jeans and pulled my dick out.

Lisa dropped to her knees and put me in her mouth. It felt so warm. She sucked me as if she was hungry, I closed my eyes and enjoyed the feeling, then she stopped.

"I gotta stop or I never will." Lisa went back to her seat on the couch, licking her lips. "See, I gotta get you out of my system."

I put myself back in my pants and zipped my zipper. "You want me to leave?"

"Yes," Lisa said and dropped her head.

I went to grab my coat and put it on.

"No."

I hesitated before getting my coat.

"Yes."

I picked up the coat.

"No," Lisa said, got up and snatched the coat out of my hand. "Not yet, take your pants and boxers down and sit on the couch."

I did as Lisa instructed. Lisa walked over to the couch where I sat, pants around my ankles, dick standing straight up. She wiggled out of her jeans and panties, then got on the sofa and stood over me. Her puss face to face with me. I went to lick it, but her hand pushed my head back. Lisa squatted on my dick.

"One last time."

I threw my head back and my mouth opened. I moaned in pleasure as Lisa's wetness coated me and her tightness gripped me. When she sat on me completely, Lisa hugged my neck and kissed me gently. Then I felt wetness on my shoulder, saturating my shirt and knew that it was her tears.

***

Sitting on my lap still, my flaccid penis having slipped out of her, Lisa never let my neck go. Her tears stopped but, no words passed between us for what seemed like an eternity. Then suddenly she spoke.

"I told Bay One about Toya getting killed. They met a couple times, but Bay said Toya and I were too close not to be fucking. She told me that Toya's brother, Marquee—Kilo took the stand in Ameen's trial as a defense witness, just like she did. I knew a little about the trial, but not the details. I knew that you and Bay One fell out about you deciding to be a prosecution witness.

I remember how fucked up Bay was about that. I watched her cry about it. That was the first time she told me that you didn't exist to her anymore. Bay told me that she didn't know Ameen at all, but she had to help him in trial because you were trying to get home off of him. She told me how Kilo also helped Ameen. You and Kilo were cellmates, she said—"

"He was never in no cell with me."

"My bad—he was next door to you when he found out that you were gonna snitch on Ameen. He contacted Ameen and offered to help him. After you got on the stand and implicated Ameen in a rack of murders, Bay and Kilo got up there and said you were lying on Ameen to get out of jail. Ameen ended up beating the case. Bay thinks you had something to do with Toya's murder to get back at her brother—"

"And you believe that shit?"

"That's the thing, I don't know what to believe."

"I was here with you when it happened. How could—"

"She talked to Marnie. Marnie told Bay that you killed her mother."

"Marnie don't know what the fuck she's talking about."

"She don't? You scare me, Khadafi. I remember the night you sat on this couch and looked at pictures of your children. You told me that Marnie's mother sent you the pics."

"She did. We talked, then she texted me the pictures. That means I killed her."

"Never said that. It's just the thought of you being capable— of—Marnie, who knows you better than me to even think you're capable of killing her mother. That's what scares me the most."

"Everybody's capable of murder, Lisa. Even you."

"I guess. Did you know that Marnie's mother's funeral is tomorrow?"

"Naw, I didn't know that."

"It's at the Pope Funeral Home on Marlboro Pike at like nine-o'clock, I think."

After saying that, Lisa got quiet. I thought maybe she'd fallen asleep.

"Bay also knows about your cousin getting killed. She was messed up about that. She said that your uncle Marquette was like a brother to her. And that Lil Marquette was his only child."

"I guess I did that, too, huh? Or had something to do with it?"

"Bay never said that. I never implied that. But she did say that it's strange how everybody around you ends up dying, everybody but you."

"Everybody, but me, huh? Damn that's fucked up," I said offended.

"That's what Bay said. That's not how I feel."

"So, how do you feel about me, Lisa?"

"I think I love you, Khadafi. That's why I gotta leave you alone."

I didn't say anything I was at a loss for words.

Lisa started grinding her pussy all over me until I rose. She lifted up and put me back inside her. "Just one more time, just one—"

Chapter Fifty-One

Rio Jefferson

Imagine being a cop, imagine being a cop that investigates homicides for a living. Imagine being a cop who investigates homicides for a living and knowing the one man who's responsible for the majority of the recent homicides. Then imagine being powerless to stop him.

"He's smarter than y'all—always has been." Monica Summers' words to me the night her mother was killed haunt me still. Not for the absurdity of them or the sheer audacity behind them. They haunted me because they were true.

The bullet riddled bodies of Marshall Cutty Summons and Yolanda Mock were found near N Street in Southwest. Cutty on the sidewalk, the woman in the car. Witnesses reported seeing a man dressed in some sort of uniform exit a silver cargo van and open fire on the two victims. A silver cargo van with a lawn mower attached to its roof, sliding panel door, one driver door, one passenger door, double doors at the rear of the silver cargo van. Silver! The whole police force was on alert about a black cargo van involved in at least two murder scenes, and Khadafi simply had the van painted silver.

"He's smarter than y'all—always has been."

I knew that Khadafi would kill Cutty and anybody close to Cutty. Yolanda Mock was the mother of Cutty's two children. She had dropped the children off to her mother's near Kentucky Avenue and was dropping Cutty off to his car when she was killed. A victim of circumstance, wrong place wrong time. Another young life lost. For no reason other than she was linked to the wrong man.

I pulled into the car wash parking lot across from the Pope's Funeral Home and parked, my eyes on the parking lot across the street. It was already filled with cars. People steadily strolled into the funeral home. The funeral service for Tawana Curry had been posted online. I knew that the service started at nine. I glanced at the time on my phone and saw that it was fifteen minutes after nine. As I looked up a car turned into the parking lot.

A silver Mercedes S550 with paper tags. The windows all around the Mercedes were tinted. I watched the Mercedes circle the lot and then park not far from the funeral home entrance. I waited to see who the people were inside the Mercedes, but no one got out of the car.

"That's strange," I said to myself.

I also noticed that the Benz had backed into the parking space. The windshield wasn't tinted but I still couldn't see the driver. Something inside me told me the driver was Khadafi. I needed to get a look at the driver without alerting him or her to my presence. I pulled my beanie down on my head and stepped out of my Impala. Adjacent to the funeral home was a small strip mall. There was a convenience store there.

I walked to the store and purchased a newspaper and chewing gum. Opening a section of the paper, I pretended to read as I walked down the sidewalk to Pope's. I walked onto its lot and journeyed past the Mercedes. The driver's eyes were in his lap. I stole a glance and realized that my premonition was right. Khadafi sat inside the silver Mercedes, now watching the entrance of the funeral home. His beard was gone, and he wore glasses, but it was him.

I kept walking, mind racing a mile a minute. Was Khadafi there to kill Marnie? Her husband? Or was he there to see his children? All kinds of questions entered my mind, but I had no answers for them. The only person who had the answers was Khadafi. Suddenly, I realized my dilemma. I had two options.

I could sound the alarm and have the entire area swarming with cops, but then look stupid if I found out that Khadafi only wanted to pay his respects to his baby's mother's mother. Or I could be cool, wait and see what he would do, then proceed accordingly. Walking around the building I headed back to my car. I chose the latter, I'd wait and watch, and at least warn Monica. I picked up my phone and sent her a text.

Chapter Fifty-Two

Marnie

"Like a comet blazing across the evening skies/ Gone too soon/Like a rainbow fading in the twinkling of an eye/ Gone too soon/Shiny and sparkly and splendidly bright/ Here one day/ Gone one night/ Like a loss of sunlight on a cloudy afternoon/ Gone too soon/ Like a castle built upon a sandy beach/ Gone too soon/ Like a perfect love that is just beyond your reach/ Gone too soon—"

Brenda Bryant covered the Michael Jackson song as if it was made for her. It was the same song that she'd sung at her daughter Kemie's funeral years ago. There wasn't a dry eye to be found. Oversized Chanel sunglasses covered my eyes and hid my pain. I held onto my daughter Khadejah as Cree held Creation. In the middle of us both sat my son Khamani. I wondered if his young mind really comprehended that his grandmother was gone, never to return.

Periodically, he'd point at the 10X12 photo of my mother that sat atop her casket and say, *"Gramma."* It broke my heart into a thousand pieces every time. Two TV monitors mounted to the wall behind the casket played a video montage of photos. Photos from every phase of my mother's life. I remembered crying the entire time I made the video.

After the song ended, my mother's best friend Sherry Battle walked up to the podium near the casket. "I was the last person to see and talk to Tawana. She was my best friend of over thirty-five years. So, it's only fitting that I eulogize my friend. Tawana Michelle Curry was born August forth, nineteen-sixty-two in Southeast, Washington D.C. The daughter of Lawrence and Tresilla Curry, sibling to Wanda, William, and James. Mother to Monica—"

My cell phone vibrating in my purse caught my attention. I fished the phone out and read an incoming text. It was from detective Rio Jefferson. It stopped my heart momentarily.

//: I'm outside of the funeral home. Khadafi is here. He's in the parking lot sitting in a silver Mercedes S550. He's here!

Khadafi was outside in the parking lot. Why hadn't he come inside? Did his guilty conscience keep him outdoors? Didn't he want to see me and his children? Was he here to see my husband and baby? Hadn't he killed my mother to get back at me? My stomach was in knots. I steeled my resolve and decided to confront my fears head on and get answers to my questions.

I lifted my daughter from my lap and sat her next to her brother.

"Dada, sit right here and watch your brother for me. Mommy gotta go to the restroom."

"Okay, Mommy," Khadejah replied.

"Cree, I'll be right back," I told my husband.

"You okay?" he asked.

"I'm good, just going to the restroom. I'll be right back."

I walked into the ladies room and looked at myself in the mirror after taking off my sunglasses. My mascara had run a little so I fixed it. My hands shook as I reapplied my make-up and checked my hair. I cupped my hands and drunk water from the faucet in the sink. I was ready to face the Boogeyman. I left the restroom and headed for the exit. Once outside, I spotted the silver Mercedes I could see the person sitting in the car. As I got closer, I faced Khadafi. I wished I had a gun. I swear I would kill his ass.

Chapter Fifty-Three

Khadafi

The door to the funeral home opened and a lone woman stepped out. As the woman headed in my direction, I realized that the woman was Marnie. Large frame sunglasses covered her eyes, but there was no mistaking that walk, that body. She'd grown more curvaceous over the years and even sexier. Her hair was different, long, and straight. How had she known that I was here? Who alerted her to my presence?

I glanced around the parking lot to see if I recognized the person who spotted me. I saw no one. I exited the car and leaned on the hood, just as Marnie walked up. Before I could utter a single word, her palm connected with my face, sending my Versace personality glasses flying across the parking lot. My eyes narrowed, my face stung and the beast inside me raved. I wanted to react, but instead, I remained calm. There were eyes on me that I couldn't see. I rubbed my aching cheeks.

"In your mind I guess I deserve that, huh?" I asked.

"You deserve more than a slap and you know it," Marnie spat.

"And what do you deserve for what you've done to me?"

"What I've done to you? I didn't do shit to you and neither did my mother. If you came here to kill me, here I am. I'm not afraid to die and I'm not afraid of you."

"Kill you, why would I be here to kill you? You too sexy to kill. I love that dress."

"You think this shit is a game? It's all a fuckin' game to you?"

"Cuz, you trippin' like shit. I'm just here to pay my respects to your mother."

"From the parking lot? Nigga, you lying. If you wanted to pay your respects, you would've come inside and done it. Not sit out here in the parking lot like a fuckin' pervert or something."

"I was going to come in, but before I could you came out. Speaking of which, how did you know I was out here?"

"What did my mother do to you? Why did you kill her?"

"I didn't kill your mother," I lied with ease.

"Lies," Marnie said, face twisted in anger. "All you do is lie, but you got me fucked if you think—"

"You got yourself fucked up, Marnie. And don't you ever put your hands on me again or I might change my mind about killing your pretty ass. Real talk."

"Do it then! Do it right now! Fuck you! Real talk, I'm not afraid of you."

"Yeah, right. That's why you left your job and moved wherever you live now, right? Because you ain't afraid of me. You know exactly what I'm capable of. You know what I am, who I am. How did you ever think that you could take my children away from me and get away with it? What did you think I was gonna do, huh? Just lay down and accept that? C'mon, cuz, you know me better than that."

"So, you admit that you killed my mother? To punish me, is that it? Because I kept my kids away from you?"

"My kids, cuz. All you did was birth them. You cut me off, got married, and had another child. I'm not fucked up about that. I'm fucked up about my kids. When I get fucked up, people die. That's how it goes, simple as that."

"Yeah, you did it," Marnie said with a perverse smile on her face. "You fucked up at me about the kids and I was protecting them from the fuck shit that you did. You know that I loved real niggas. Gangsta niggas like you used to be. I didn't tell you to become a fuckin' rat and put all your love ones under the gun.

As a matter of fact, I tried to talk you outta doing that shit. But you insisted, persisted. The day you took that witness stand against Ameen it was over between us. And it was my job to protect my children. I helped Ameen beat his case so that he wouldn't kill us. Every decision I made was for them. You endangered all of us with that rat shit—"

I struggled to remain calm. "You already know that it's not a good idea to disrespect me. Somebody called you and told you I was out here. They had to, and it gotta be the police. So, what does that make you, Marnie? Is that why you out here smacking me and talking reckless? Because you think the police can save you from me? Save your husband from me?"

"Save my husband?" Marnie's face changed to a look of pure hate. "Your beef is with me, not him. If you touch one hair on my husband's head, make sure that I'm dead, too. Because I swear on my mother's grave that I'ma kill your ass if you do."

"You know the old saying, be careful what you wish for?"

"I wish that you were dead. That's what I wish for. You killed my mother. I know it and you know it. You just ain't man enough to admit it."

"I admit it. You happy now?" I said with a smirk.

"What? What did you just say?"

"I said, I admit it. I killed your mother."

Marnie closed the space between us in seconds. Her face was inches from mine. "Every day that you live is too many. I pray that you die a terrible death. And you will never see your kids again after today. So, get a good look at 'em when they come out to the limo." Marnie reared back and hawk spit in my face, then walked away.

"That's a nice dress, cuz. You gon' be wearing it again real soon for that. You got my word on that," I called out after her, wiping spit from my face.

Before getting back in the car, I glanced around again. Then I spotted him, a man in a dark peacoat, hat pulled low, standing across the street next to an Impala. He stared right in my direction. My instincts screamed, *Cop*, I was right. Marnie had partnered with the police against me. As bad as I wanted to see Dada and Mani, I figured that it was time for me to leave. Before I did some goofy shit.

Calmly, I got in the Benz and pulled out of the parking lot. Dark peacoat was on his cell, I made it to Brooks Drive before the Prince George's County squad car got behind me and activated his lights. I pulled over to the curb and let my driver's side window down. Minutes later, there were at least ten cars surrounding me. I watched the scene unfold and smiled.

"Sir, we need you to step out of the vehicle," a white officer who appeared at my driver's side window said. "And keep your hands where we can see them. Do it, now!"

I noticed that all the cops' guns were drawn. The door to the Benz opened and I was pulled out and slammed to the ground. Seconds later, I was frisked roughly and handcuffed. What was crazy was that I could only think of my expensive clothes getting dirty as I laid on the ground. I watched as the officers converged on my vehicle, searching it. They looked like a pack of hyenas on a wounded gazelle. Then someone stooped low beside me. I looked up at him, it was the man in the dark peacoat. I could see his face clear it was the D.C. Detective that was outside my room at the hospital. He was at my trial and Ameen's trial when I took the stand. For the last five years or so, this detective was always somewhere near my life.

"It's been a few years, Khadafi. How are you?" the detective said. He leaned in close to me, almost to my ear. His voice a little bit above a whisper.

"I'm good, pig. And you?" I replied with a smile.

He put his hands on me, searched my legs all the way to my ankles and waist. Felt inside my pants around to my genitals.

"This is called sexual harassment, ain't it, pig?"

"You keep calling me a pig and you might as well be a cop. All that snitching you did against Ameen Felder. You might as well have been law enforcement. With your hot ass. Where your gun at? Where the choppa at, killa rat? Where the sound suppressors you been using? C'mon, tell on *yourself* for a change. The same way you did Ameen. And he was your fuckin' friend. I hate to see you tell on one of your enemies. The trial would be long as shit, because you'd probably never shut up, huh?"

Seething inside, I just kept quiet.

"Rat ass ain't got nothing to say now, huh? Well, keep it like that and just listen. I know you killed Cutty for killing your cousin Marquette Jennings. I can respect that. Cutty was a cold-blooded piece of shit that needed a killing. But his children's mother was innocent. Her name was Yolanda Mock. Say her name, Khadafi. Say it!"

No response.

"Everybody else you killed deserved it. We gotta solve the cases, but we ain't mad about the killings. Meechie, PeeWee, Carlton, V Dot, A.D. you did the world a favor by getting rid of them muthafuckas. Fuck em. Every last one of them. But PeeWee's sister didn't deserve that shit. Say her name, Khadafi. Jamya Smith. Say it for me, one time. Say it!"

I simply laughed out loud. "What did Tawana Curry do to deserve what you did to her? What did Sherita Simms do? Afraid she was gonna tell the cops something about you? It's a shame what you did to that woman. Her only sin was a good girl liking a bag guy. Where's your black SUV, Khadafi? Your black cargo van? The silver one that we found burning in Northeast, that was it, wasn't it? It's only a matter of time before you slip up and then we got your ass. No more sweetheart deals. No more Ann Sloan specials. Heard what happened to her, right? Shame, shame, shame! I'ma get you Khadafi. It's only a matter of time. You ain't gon' never stop killing until I stop you. Either with a life sentence or a bullet. And guess what? I'm up for the task. Are you?"

"It's clean, detective," a black PG Officer announced. "Nothing, no guns. No drugs, nada."

"You are one lucky son of a bitch, but your day is coming."

I was lifted off the ground and uncuffed. I could see Peacoat walking back to his Impala.

"Sorry for the inconvenience, sir. You're free to go," the black cop said.

I brushed off my Balmain jeans and Versace porka, got in the Benz and laughed out loud. My Spider senses had saved me again. The voices inside my head were real. When I decided to go to Pope's funeral home for Tawana Curry's funeral, my spider senses tingled, then my inner voice said, *'leave the guns at home.'* I never ride without my guns, but I decided to listen to my gut instincts and leave everything at home.

My guts and inner voice were on point. I reached for my cell phone and came up empty. I pulled over and checked my coat, my clothes, then the car. My cell phone was gone. I was on it right before my confrontation with Marnie. I remembered putting it back in my pants pocket before getting out of the Benz to face Marnie. I knew I hadn't dropped it, but yet, it was nowhere to be found. That meant that the detective who searched me while I was on the ground took it.

Again, I laughed, he could have the phone. He'd taken it illegally, the only thing in there were the photos of my children that I'd taken from Tawana Curry's phone. Good luck on trying to convince a jury that I committed murder with only pics from the deceased person's phone. The phone that he'd taken was a new one that I sent the pictures to. I'd just copped it that morning before coming to Pope's. So, there would be no sim card to trace to a certain cell tower that placed me at the scene of Cutty's murder. Or anybody else's. I thought about everything the detective had said.

He asked me about sound suppressors and a choppa. Mentioned me killing Cutty because Cutty killed Lil Quette. How in the hell did he know that? How had he known about Sherita so fast and connected that to me? What did they have? It couldn't be much because I would be in jail charged with something. It was as if they had an inside source telling them everything and that was impossible because my only sidekick to all my crimes was dead. I couldn't think of any other possible loose ends.

Had Lil Quette told Shakira everything? Was she the source of info to the cops? I dismissed that thought quickly before it started to sink in, and I got on her line and killed her ass. I couldn't bring myself to kill my little cousin's unborn seed. Was I just being paranoid? As I drove through the city with a destination in mind, my thoughts went to Marnie.

How had she partnered with the police? What had she told them? Or him, rather, Peacoat? I searched my brain for his name. Then it came to me. Rio Jefferson, Detective Rio Jefferson. In my state of anger about being smacked, I had allowed myself to get careless. I admitted to Marnie that I killed her mother. My word against hers. There was no physical evidence to prove it.

I thought about Marnie smacking me. I hadn't even recovered my Versace glasses. I had decided to leave her alone. I had decided to move on and let her do her. But I kinda liked them Versace glasses and spitting on me was a killing offense. His days were numbered. To my left, I spotted a Metro PCS. I pulled into the lot and in front of it, I need to buy a new phone.

***

I knocked on the door of the red brick tenement.

"Who is it?" a female voice called out.

"Khadafi," I replied.

Locks turned and clicked and then the door opened. Tasca looked terrible. Her hair was unkempt, her clothes were soiled and reeked of cigarettes. Images of a younger Tasca when she was gorgeous entered my mind.

"What do you want?" Tasca asked.

"Here, take this." I handed her a bag of money.

"What's this?" Tasca looked in the bag.

"That's to help with Lil Quette's funeral expenses."

Tears welled up in her eyes and fell. She looked at me with pure hate and malice in her expression. "He wouldn't need a fuckin' funeral if it wasn't for you! He's dead because of you! Get the fuck off my front!" Tasca bellowed. "And take your fuckin' money! I don't want it or need it!" She threw the bag at me.

The bag hit me in the chest and fell to the ground. Tasca slammed the door in my face. Slowly, I reached down and retrieved the bag. Then I walked back to my car. Pissed! I needed to relax. I needed to smoke. I needed some pussy. I pulled out my phone and dialed Lisa's number. She didn't answer. I sent her a text telling her that it was me calling from the number she didn't recognize. Still no answer. She hadn't answered any of my calls since I left her the day before. I dialed another number I knew by heart.

"Hello?"

"You still mad at me?"

"Who is this?"

"Khadafi."

"What do you want, Khadafi?"

"I wanna see you, I miss you."

"No, you don't, stop lying."

"E, I'm sorry for what I did. Real talk. I was fucked up about what Mousey said. I never should've put you in the middle of that. I never meant to hurt you. I wanted to hurt him. As bad as he hurt me with his words. Wishing death on me after all I did for him. I wasn't thinking straight, you gotta forgive me. I miss you like shit. I need to see you."

"I ain't gonna lie, I kinda miss you, too."

"What polish you got on your toes?"

"You'll see when you get here. Come on."

"You got weed?" I asked.

"You already know," Erykah answered.

"Cool, I'm on my way right now."

***

"I'm hungry as shit. What you got in here to eat?"

"A rack of leftover Thanksgiving food my mother made."

"A rack of pork shit, huh?"

"Naw, my mother fucks with a Muslim nigga. Ain't no pork in these. It's mac and cheese, sweet potatoes, greens with smoked turkey, stuffing, rice pilaf, chicken wings, barbecue and fried—"

I got up off the couch and walked into Erykah's kitchen. "E, come and navigate this shit for me. All I see in the fridge is shit in aluminum foil. Come make me a plate with all the shit you just named on it."

Erykah did as I instructed, then put the plate in the microwave. She made herself a plate as well. We sat at her dining room table and ate.

"Have you been talking to Mousey?" I asked, curiously.

"Naw. He hasn't called me since he told me he got the pictures."

"I'm sorry, E. No bullshit. I know y'all love each other."

"It is what it is. Mousey got sixty-three years."

"The Supreme Court just passed a law that you can't give juveniles that much time because their brains ain't fully developed at sixteen and seventeen. Cuz should be getting back in court soon. Did you know that?"

Erykah shook her head. "I wish him the best no matter what."

"If he do come home, you know I might have to—"

"We ain't even gon' talk about that."

"I'm just saying, cuz ain't gon' forgive me—"

"From now on, when we together, let's just talk about us, okay?"

"Respect, you got that. Only talk about you and me. I respect that."

"Yeah, but I do wanna ask you one question, though."

"Go ahead, ask me."

"Mousey said you sent a picture of me sleeping with cum on my face. Is that true?"

I nodded my head.

"How in the hell did you manage that? If I was sleep, where did the cum come from?"

I smiled a wicked smile. "I stood beside the bed and thought about us fucking, then I beat my dick and shot out all over your face."

"And I didn't wake up?" Erykah asked.

"Naw, you didn't even stir. You was knocked out," I told her.

"You beat your dick by the bed?" I nodded. "Do it again," Erykah requested.

"Do what again?"

"Beat your dick, I wanna see you do it."

"Are you serious?" I asked.

Erykah nodded. "Of course, I am. Do it."

"When?"

"Now."

"Right here?"

"Right here."

"When I'm about to cum, where do I cum at?"

"The same place you came at that night."

"On your face?"

"On my face."

I stood up, unzipped my pants, and pulled out my dick. I looked at Erykah's phat pussy print in her yoga pants she wore. I looked at her lips. I looked at her pretty feet, toes painted purple. I stroked my dick until I did exactly what Erykah wanted. I came all over her lips and face.

Chapter Fifty-Four

Khadafi

I had been to Mason's Funeral Home many times in my life and it hadn't changed much. I walked through the hallway and was met by an older man in a suit who introduced himself as the funeral director.

"The service for Marquette Jennings doesn't start until—"

"Ten, I already know that. I need to see my little cousin before everybody else gets here," I told the man, pulled out two-hundred-dollar bills and pushed it to him.

The funeral director pocketed the money. "He's in the last room down the hall to the left. Take as much time as you need."

It felt like I was walking the green mile en route to my own demise. I found the room where Lil Quette lay in a mahogany wooden casket with gold trim. The casket was open from the middle up, where only half of Lil Quette could be seen. He looked asleep, dressed in a solid black Givenchy form fitting sweater with the word Givenchy written in black letters on it. His jeans were black as well. One of the pairs that I had purchased for him when I first came home. His belt was Givenchy as well. Lil Quette's hair was perfectly cut in a low taper. Both hands were together resting over his stomach. Tears fell from my eyes. I reached out and touched him, he was hard and cold.

"Lil cuz, I promise you that your man Gunplay will die. I wish that you would have listened to me when I told you to keep your enemies close, but your friends closer. And I wish I would have listened to you when you spoke about getting Cutty out of the way. That was my bad. You paid with your life, but so did he. I just found out recently that Gunplay was the trigger man. He was paid to kill you. You trusted him and he killed you. Well, you know how I get down. He's on borrowed time. In the next twenty-four hours, he'll be joining you. I love you, cuz. Until we meet again."

I wiped my eyes, got myself together and called Shakira. "Meet me up the street from Mason's at the America's Best Wings on Alabama. I'm on my way there."

***

Courtesy of the drugs that I took from Fat Moochie and sold them to my old head Mumbo Scales, I copped Erykah a new car. My old friend Alex in Virginia gave me a good deal on a 2017 Mercedes Benz CLK 330. It was triple black with tinted windows. I was riding shotgun in the car with Erykah when we met Shakira. She pulled up in Lil Quette's Camaro and parked in front of the store. I got out of the Benz and walked over to the Camaro. The passenger window came down.

"I'ma get in and holla at you for a minute," I said then opened the car door and climbed inside.

"You went to see Quette already, didn't you?" Shakira asked.

I nodded. "It was tough seeing him like that, but I'ma make it right. I asked you to meet me here for two reasons. One, a couple of weeks ago, the cops pulled me over and searched my car. This detective that has been on my line for years showed up and started asking me about guns and choppas. He told me some shit that nobody knew but me and Lil Quette. I know that lil cuz never talked to the cops, so that leaves you—"

"Me?"

"Yeah, you. Did Lil Quette pillow talk with you and tell you—"

"Hold on, Khadafi—wait. You throwing me the fuck off. Are you accusing me of talking to Twelve about you and Quette? Is that what you saying to me?"

"More or less, yeah," I said, standing my ground.

"Let me say this to you so that we clear once and for all. Quette never pillow talked and told me shit about you. He never told me shit about what he did or what y'all did when y'all was together. Never, not one time. You didn't know him like I did. Quette knew not to tell me nothing. I kept hearing all this wild shit about you and

Quette killing people in the streets. Every time I confronted him about it, he denied it. I told you that at the Denny's. I was hearing so much shit about Quette that I was starting to believe it all. The night he died, we argued about what the streets were saying about him. That was the last argument we had—" Shakira's eyes watered. "I don't even remember telling him that I loved him before he hung up. But even if he did tell me something—which he didn't. Why the fuck would I tell Twelve anything? I hate the fucking police. I loved Quette with all my heart and he loved you. I would never go against him or you, for nothing or nobody. Does that answer your question?"

"I guess so. I had to ask you, though, cuz. The detective said—"

"He got from somewhere else, not from me."

"Respect, point taken. I need to find Gunplay and smoke his ass. Are you sure that he'll be at the funeral?"

Shakira wiped tears from her eyes. "I don't see why not. He doesn't know that I know he killed Quette. As far as he knows, he got away with murder. And him being so close to Quette, he knows that nobody will suspect him. Besides, it would look suspicious if he didn't go, given the so-called bond between them. He'll be there. Watch what I tell you."

"I hope you're right, cuz. I hope you're right."

***

From my position in the car, parked on T Street, I could see Mason's and all the people lined up to get into the service for Lil Quette. I sent Shakira a text.

//: *Do you see Gunplay around? Is he there?*

A few minutes later, I got a reply text.

//: *He's here. I'm looking at his ass right now.*

//: *What does he have on? Describe him.*

//: *He's brown-skinned, about my height, dreads pinned up on his head. He's wearing black jeans, black Gucci shoes, black and gold Gucci logo belt. A black Gucci sweat hoodie trimmed in green and red. A black, bubble Montcler vest, black Gucci shades.*

I read Shakira's text and quickly sent her a reply. *//: Thank you.*

***

"E, listen, the dude that killed my cousin is in that funeral home. When he comes out, I need you to follow him. When we get somewhere that I like, I'ma bake his ass. Are you down for that or do I need to drive, and you catch an Uber back home? Your choice?"

"I'm with you," Erykah said looking me straight in the eyes.'

"Are you sure?" I asked.

"Positive."

"That's what's up. That's why I fuck with you."

"What does this nigga look like?"

I showed Erykah the text I got from Shakira."

***

"That's him right there," Erykah announced.

I looked up from my place and saw a dude that fit Shakira's description to a tee. I watched him walk down to 16th Street to a parking lot. I had to get out of the car to see what vehicle he got in. I got back in the car with Erykah.

"He's in a metallic grey Charger. Go down by sixteenth street and wait for him to pull out of that parking lot."

Erykah followed my instructions to the letter. We were a couple cars behind Gunplay, and he didn't know that death was lurking. He went up 16th Street to Hunter Place, then hit Morris Road. Morris Road ended at the top of the hill and turned into Ainger Place. From there he went to Langston Place and double parked near the entrance to Langston Home projects. An ice cream truck was parked in front of him. I watched Gunplay walk around the car to the ice cream truck.

"Pull over right here," I told Erykah. "I'll be right back."

I hopped out of the Benz and walked over to the ice cream truck. A crowd was gathered on the side, mostly kids but I didn't care. I pulled my gun as I walked. Gunplay never knew what hit him. I upped the gun, got right up on him, and blew his brains out. People screamed, everybody scattered. Calmly, I shot Gunplay in his swollen head as he laid on the ground. Then I spit in his face and walked away.

I looked up at the sky. "I got him, cuz. Rest in peace."

***

"I love that gangsta shit! Oohhh—I love it!"

I stood behind Erykah who was bent over with her upper half inside the driver's side of the Benz. Her pants and panties huddled at her ankles. My pants were around my knees. I held onto Erykah's waist and pounded myself into her. The garage parking at Pentagon City Mall was nearly deserted early in the day.

"You love that gangsta, shit, huh, cuz?" I asked and slammed back and forth into Erykah. "That shit turns you on?"

"Yes! Ohh—yes! Yes! Yes! Yes! Yes!"

The cold air coming into the garage from outside didn't deter me from what I was trying to get from Erykah. It didn't deter her either. She came all over me and then minutes later, I followed suit.

***

Later that night, I couldn't sleep for shit. Now that I had avenged Lil Quette's murder, my thoughts shifted back to Marnie. I thought about the story that Erykah had told me earlier about when her and Marnie clashed in 2013. I already know that they bumped heads, but I never knew the details.

"I was filling out the visiting form and told the CO behind the glass that I was there to see you. She was in the line behind me and I didn't know it. Had I known it I would've just left. She walked up to me and asked me did I tell the CO behind the glass that I was

there to see Luther Fuller. I told her that I had said that. Then she went off on me.

She asked me who I was to you. I got mad and told her that I was your woman. That pissed her off. She told me to go ahead and visit you but afterward when I came outside that she was gon' fuck me up. I thought she was bullshittin, she wasn't. I left the facility and drove home. She followed me here. I was walking down the street when she popped up outta nowhere and whipped my ass. I ain't gonna lie, she fucked me up."

I had forgotten all about the incident between Marnie and Erykah and I never thought about how it contributed to Marnie fucking with another dude after that. Was that the day that Marnie met Cree? Was he the man that she ran to? The more I thought about it, the angrier I became. I turned over and reached into my pants pocket. I grabbed my phone, the photos of my children and all the contact info I'd taken out of Tawana Curry's phone were there.

I laid in bed next to Erykah and looked at my children. I looked at Marnie, her toddler daughter, and her husband. I looked at the pecan-skinned man with dark, curly hair and grey eyes. Imagined him sexing Marnie as I had done for years. Imagined their happiness, their laughter, their love. I became even more disturbed. I put the phone down and tapped Erykah awake.

"What?" Erykah mumbled groggily.

"Where are the keys to the Optima?" I asked.

"Uh—they on the kitchen counter by the microwave."

***

Waller And Ingram

I Googled the name on the sign that I now stared at and read everything that was online about the accounting firm where Marnie's husband worked. I sat in the small coffee shop directly across from the building and eyed the entrance.

I didn't know what kind of vehicle Marnie's husband drove, but I had his place of employment and at some point, I'd see him going and leaving work. I just had to wait and be patient. Waiting and patience was my strong suit. I ordered another cup of coffee and a pecan, hazelnut hot buttered croissant. I looked at Cree Summers' photo on my phone and etched his face into my memory. Then I focused on the entrance to Waller and Ingram. It was 7:15 a.m.

***

Having seen Marnie's husband appear out of nowhere and enter Waller and Ingram, I decided to leave the coffee shop and return later that day. At a little after 4:00 p.m. Cree Summers exited the building. I followed him down 14th Street. He walked all the way to 7th Street Shaw-Howard University Subway Station and disappeared inside. I wasn't far behind him. He never paid me any mind as I stood on the same platform as he that was crowded with people enduring the rush hour traffic.

On the train, I kept my head low and pretended to read a book, but kept my eyes glued to my target. At Eisenhower Avenue Station in Alexandria, Cree left the train and so did I. A parking garage was adjacent to the subway station, his car was parked there. I watched as he entered a white BMW and pulled out of the garage.

***

The Next Day

Parked on Eisenhower Avenue, I waited for the BMW. It didn't take long to leave the garage. I got behind it as it found the 295 South exit and merged onto it. I stayed several cars behind in traffic but never took my eyes off the BMW. About forty to fifty painstaking minutes later, the BMW took the Woodbridge exit off 95 South. I took the exit as well. Twenty minutes later, it pulled into a driveway in front of a beige, brick house on Evergreen Court, 5507 Evergreen. There was a beige Buick LaCrosse Sedan parked in the driveway as well. I typed the license plate number into my phone and the home's address. I saw Cree Summers exit his BMW, pull out keys and open the front door.

"Got you, cuz," I said to myself and left.

***

Erykah's Kia Optima also had tinted windows, so I was able to drive to Woodbridge and periodically stake out 5507. I learned that the Buick Sedan belonged to Marnie and that she still had the Mercedes that PeeWee bought her, although she never drove it. After taking a much-needed walk through the neighborhood disguised as a sanitation worker, I saw the Benz parked in the rear of the house. The house 5507 had a space between it and the next house and there were no gates or fences to separate them. I also discovered that I could get to Marnie's house from an alley that ran directly behind all the houses on Evergreen Court.

Routine is a muthafucka and it didn't take but a few weeks to learn that Cree Summers spent every Saturday afternoon at the gym. The Christmas Holiday came and went, and I decided that I wanted Cree Summers dead before the New Year. I wanted Marnie to ring in 2018 in a whole lot of pain. I could have easily disposed of Marnie's husband at any time, but I wanted to do it where she lived. I wanted her to know that I knew where she lived, no matter how hard she tried to hide from me. I wanted her to know how vulnerable she was the entire time and that I could've killed her at any time as well. I decided to bring death right to her front door.

Chapter Fifty-Five

Marnie

"Miles, you have to find the balance between the growth, then value the stock. Growth stocks have outperformed value stocks since two-thousand-six."

"I get that part, Cree," Miles Jerome replied. "But what exactly makes a stock a value stock or a growth stock? Is Apple for example a value stock or a growth stock? Because I would argue that for the past ten years it's been both. The same could be said about Microsoft over the past twenty years."

"Perhaps, it's more about not worrying about categories and more about buying great companies. Warren Buffet had it right when he said, *"It's far better to buy a wonderful company at a fair price, than a fair company at a wonderful price."*

"So, what actions should I take, if any, when it comes to balancing growth stocks versus value stocks in my portfolio?"

"First and foremost, don't split the difference. When unsure, investors tend to over diversify. If one home improvement stock is good, two is better. Equally weighing value and growth is akin to buying the SP500. Save your time and buy an index fund. I recommend as your accountant that you—"

As I put milk into my daughter's bottles and filled her diaper bag with jars of baby food, I ear hustled Cree's conversation with his client. His business acumen and intelligence were powerful and exhilarating. I loved to listen to my husband talk shop because it was sexy to me. Everything about Cree Summers was sexy to me. I glanced back at him as he walked back and forth while video chatting with his client. His height, his weight, the all-black sweatsuit he wore, his curly hair, pecan-complexion and light grey eyes. Whew! I couldn't get enough of him.

"How do we anticipate the relative out performances of value versus growth?"

"Miles, how did we get back on that again? I told you, it all depends on how you view our current economy. If you believe that the United States will face a protracted recovery, you might want to consider overweighting growth stocks in your portfolio. When economic growth and earning growth become scarce, investors are generally willing to pay up for growth characteristics. If a company is trading at a multiple of twenty-five times to thirty times earnings, but is growing earnings at twenty to thirty percent, most would call that a fair trade. Much more attractive than, say, a company trading at six times earnings with no growth."

"Semantic. You still haven't answered my question—"

"Miles, buddy, I gotta run. We'll talk again on Monday. I have to get my daughter to my mother's house and then go to the gym. I'll call you when I get in the office first thing Monday morning, okay?"

"Okay, I'll be expecting your call."

"Bye, Miles. Have a nice day."

Cree walked toward me, pocketing his cell phone. He kissed my cheek. "Miles Jerome again, I see."

"Driving me nuts," Cree commented and opened the refrigerator. He took out a carton of orange juice and drank from the carton.

"Uh—cup, please, sir."

"My bad, baby," Cree replied with a sly grin.

After putting the orange juice back in the fridge, Cree leaned down and kissed Creation. "You ready to go, princess?"

Creation stirred in my arms, smiling, and talking gibberish to her. Her light grey eyes were just as mesmerizing as her father's.

"Here, take her and put her coat and hat on while I get the rest of her stuff ready." I handed Creation to Cree.

Khamani raced into the kitchen and saw Cree putting Creation's coat on. "I wanna go! Mommy, I wanna go with Cree'a and Daddy!"

"Next time, lil man. I promise. Not today," Cree told Khamani.

"But how come Cree'a gets to go?"

"Cree'a's going to her grandmother's house," I told my son.

"Can I go to my grandmother's house?" Khamani asked.

Cree looked at me and I looked at him, but neither of us said a word. Cree leaned in and kissed me. His kiss saying, I'ma let you deal with that. I grabbed Khamani by the hand and led him upstairs with me.

"You wanna play the video games with me?"

"Yeah, mommy. Wanna play the game."

I knew exactly how to get my son's mind off his grandmother. "Let me get the baby's bag and then I'll hook up the game and you can play Mommy, okay?"

"Okay."

I tossed the rest of Creation's things into the bag and then ran the bag to Cree. I kissed him and then my baby girl. "Drive safe. Call me after you drop Cree'a off. I love you."

"You got it," Cree responded. "Love you more, bye."

Upstairs, I connected the PlayStation 4 in Khamani's room. Was just about to pop the Assassin's Creed game into the console when the unmistakable sounds of gunshots rang out. My heart stopped momentarily as I prayed that what I heard was kids playing with fireworks in anticipation for the New Year. I left my son there, raced down the stairs and threw open the front door. I saw Cree's legs protruding from the rear seat of the BMW.

"C-r-e-e-e-e!" I cried out and ran to him.

Cree lay on top of Creation. I grabbed his body and turned him over to grab her. I could see the holes in Cree's coat, feathers floated around the air. Quickly, I scooped up my daughter and shook her.

"Cree'a wake up, baby! Open your eyes! Open your eyes!" I held her close as tears cascaded down my cheeks. When I pulled my daughter away from my chest, it was then that I noticed all the blood. Blood stained her soaked coat and now my shirt. Right then, I knew that her and Cree were dead.

***

When my eyes opened next, I noticed the faces of my neighbors and several police officers, plain clothes and in uniform.

"Where am I?" I asked.

"Monica, you're at the hospital. You passed out and an ambulance brought you here. Me and Derek rode here with you," Malinda Shafer, my neighbor said.

"My children?"

"They're with Chavon and Malika at my house. They're safe. I called your cousin Danielle in Washington, just like you told me to do in case anything ever happened to you or Cree—"

"My daughter, Creation—Cree—where are they?"

Malinda's silence spoke volumes, it was real—true. I was not inside of a nightmare waiting to wake up. My husband and my daughter's bloodied bodies filled my head. They were dead. I looked down at my bloodstained shirt and lost it.

"N-o-o-o-o! N-o-o-o-o-o!"

"Get a doctor or somebody in here now!" I heard a male voice say.

I kicked and squirmed and hollered and fought all those trying to restrain me. *"Please—God—noooo! T-a-k-e Me!"*

Chapter Fifty-Six

Rio Jefferson

"Do you want gravy on these turkey chops, Rio?"

There was a commercial on, so I got up and went to the kitchen. My girlfriend, Tonya stood in front of the electric stove and cooked for me. I kissed her neck until she faced me, then I kissed her lips, her sweet soft lips. Tonya was two honey buns away from being declared a fat chick, but I didn't care. She was pretty, with silky dreads, white teeth, and flawless caramel skin. Tonya was a good person, great cook, and an uninhibited lover.

"It's up to you, bae. Gravy or no gravy it don't matter."

"Okay, no gravy. I'll just add onions, peppers and mushrooms. Let them sautee in the turkey chop juice. Bread, Texas toast, garlic bread or croissants?"

"Texas toast," I called out over my shoulder, heading back to my favorite recliner. The college football playoffs were on and I didn't want to miss a snap. Alabama versus Georgia had turned out to be a pretty good game. The quarterback for Alabama, Jalen Hurts was dynamic.

"Rio, you left your phone in here and it's vibrating again," Tonya announced.

Georgia's quarterback, Jake Fromm had just moved his team to the 17-yard line in the red zone. I was on the edge of my seat.

"Fuck that phone," I muttered.

"Your phone is about to vibrate off the counter and I can't grab it because my hands got all kinds of stuff on 'em. Come and get your phone!"

Reluctantly, I got and walked backward to the kitchen, my eyes still on the large screen T.V. I wasn't thinking about the phone. I just wanted Tonya to shut the fuck up and stop worrying me about it. It was now third and three for Georgia, with Alabama up seven. Jake Fromm dropped back and got sacked. Georgia sent its field goal unit in. I picked up my phone and it started to vibrate again. The caller was Doug Davis.

I answered it, "Yeah, Doug? What's up? I'm a little busy."

"Are you near a T.V.?" Doug asked.

"Yeah, why? I'm watching the Alabama—Georgia—"

"Put the T.V. on the news, Rio. CUS FOX News."

The sense of urgency in Doug's voice, coupled with the melancholy tone let me know that whatever he wanted me to see was serious. I grabbed the remote and put the news on.

"Those of you who have just tuned in, a massive manhunt is underway in Woodbridge, Virginia. Virginia police are looking for a man, a lone gunman who opened fire on a father and child. Fox News correspondent, Alyson Chaney is live at the scene. Alyson, tell us what you've learned."

"Martin this situation is heartbreaking. While loading his one-year-old daughter into his vehicle. Creemont Summers who was still holding his daughter Creation was shot and killed. Authorities here at the scene believe that bullets passed through Creemont Summers and fatally struck his one-year-old daughter. Both father and daughter were pronounced dead at this scene. Local authorities are pouring over video feeds from the houses nearby and we're told that the hunt for the killer is on.

The investigation here is ongoing, but sources close to the scene tell us that Creemont Summers was a native Washington who worked at the prestigious accounting firm Waller and Ingram. His wife, who found him and the child after the shooting had to be rushed to a nearby hospital for unknown reasons. Officers from Woodbridge, Del Ray and Virginia State Troopers are involved in the hunt for this killer—"

"Muthafucka!" I threw the remote across the room. "Fuck! Fuck!"

Tonya came rushing into the room. "Rio, what's wrong? What the hell happened?"

"I swear to God, I'ma kill this muthafucka!"

"Kill who, Rio? Who are you gonna kill?"

Ignoring Tonya, I put my cell phone back to my ear. "Doug, do you know what hospital she's in?"

"I knew you'd ask that, so I took the liberty of finding out before I called you. She's at WMHC—Woodbridge Memorial Hospital Center. She works there. She's probably in bad shape, maybe you should wait—"

I disconnected the call and went to get my coat and hat. "Keep the food warm for me, I gotta go. But I'll be back soon."

***

Monica was in a recovery room near the Hospital's emergency room. Outside her room door, I encountered homicide detectives assigned to her husband and daughter's case.

I introduced myself to them and filled them in on what the police in D.C. already knew.

"These murders were committed by a sociopath, uncaring, unforgiving, ruthless killer. One, the state of Virginia hasn't seen since Conrad Muhammad. He's thirty-seven years old, recently released from prison and he's the father of Monica's other two children. His name is Luther Fuller, but he goes by Khadafi on the streets." I went on to give them Khadafi's history up until the present day. "We predicted that he would go after her husband. I spoke to Monica myself several times. She knew that he was gonna come after them. That's why they moved to Woodbridge in the first place. He killed—well, we suspect that he killed her mother Tawana Curry, not less than a month ago. It was him, I'm sure of it."

Detective Marshall Bell spoke first, "No disrespect to you, but you being sure doesn't help us here in the Commonwealth. We need some type of proof that this guy Goddafi—"

"Khadafi. K-H-A-D-A-F-I."

"Whatever, we need something tangible to take to a judge here. He's facing two counts of capital murder and because one of the victims was a one-year-old child, he'll get the death penalty for sure. So, until we find something—anything that connects Luther Khadafi to our shooting here, there ain't nothing we can do."

"Even if I had proof that Khadafi did this, you couldn't arrest him. He's smarter than y'all. Always has been—"

"He's a smart son of a bitch. I'll send you fingerprints, DNA and the file we have on him. Maybe you'll connect something from the scene to him. A cigarette, a piece of gum, something. Has Monica talked to you guys, yet?"

"Hasn't been in any shape to talk," Detective Tom Cross answered. "She's in shock and I can't blame her considering what's happened and all. We talked to her neighbors. They say that they sat with her until the uniforms arrived. According to them, Mrs. Summers didn't witness the actual shooting. She came outside after hearing the gunshots. That's when she found them. The husband and little girl were already dead."

"Is she awake now? You say she passed out, right?"

"Yeah, at the scene. Don't know if she's awake. Haven't looked in in a minute."

"Well, I'm gonna go in and see if she wants to talk. She knows me."

"Fine by me," Detective Bell said.

"Be my guest, just be sure to let us know if she says anything useful," the other detective added.

When I walked into the room, there were two people seated near Monica's bed. A black couple, they both stood as I entered. "Hello, my name is Rio Jefferson, I'm a detective in D.C."

"D.C.?" the man repeated.

"Yeah, D.C. I'm one of the detectives working the case of Monica's mother's murder. We believe that the same person who killed her mother, killed her husband and daughter. And you are?"

The man was a little taller than me with a dark complexion and a head that looked to be too large for his body. He spoke first, "I'm Derek Shafer and this is my wife Malinda. We live in the house next door to Monica."

"Does she know that you're here?" I asked looking at Monica who appeared to be sleeping.

"She knows," Malinda Shafer said and looked at her husband, then back at me. "We've been here with her. We rode in the ambulance with her. We found her outside her house crying—we saw the bodies."

"Did you see anything else that might help us find the man who did this?"

"We already told the other police that we didn't." Malinda Shafer's eyes filled with tears. "Derek was asleep in the basement when I heard the gunshots. I was in the bedroom upstairs separating laundry. I'm from D.C., detective. Sursum Cordas, I know what gunshots sound like, and I know that stray bullets don't have eyes. They'll kill anyone. I got on the floor until they stopped. When I got up, I glanced out the window. I could see Cree's BMW and his legs protruding from the passenger side door. After quickly checking on my kids, I ran to the basement and woke up Derek. Together we went outside and discovered the carnage—" Malinda's voice broke and she started crying.

Her husband consoled her as best he could. Then she said, "All we saw was the aftermath, detective."

I saw Monica stir and figured that she was awake. "Can I try to talk to Monica alone, please?"

"We don't mind. We're about to leave anyway. Go and check on the kids. Her two kids are with our kids. We need to go and make sure everything is okay. It's sad. How's she gonna tell her other two kids that their baby sister is dead?" Derek Shafer asked, but didn't wait for an answer. He led his wife out of the room.

I stood beside the bed and looked down at Monica. I couldn't imagine the pain she must be in. In the span of thirty-days, the woman had lost her mother, husband, and baby daughter. Her eyes were still closed, and her chest rose and fell rhythmically. She looked to be at peace, and I hated to disturb her, but I needed to talk to her.

"Monica, can you hear me?"

"I hear you, detective. I've been listening to you talk for the last ten minutes. What do you want?" Monica said, then opened her eyes.

"I'm sorry, Monica—so—so sorry."

"Sorry doesn't bring my husband back. Doesn't bring back my little girl."

"No, it doesn't but—"

"But what, detective? Then again, it doesn't matter."

"Monica, what can I do to make—"

"Khadafi told me that he was gonna do this. He told me that nobody could save us from him," Monica interjected.

"He said that to you?" I asked incredulously.

Monica nodded, her eyes flooding with tears. "He was right, too."

"If he said that to you, we can arrest him for felony threats—"

"I accused him of killing my mother and told him to just be a man and admit it. He admitted it and smiled at me."

I pulled out my notepad and wrote down everything Monica said. I couldn't believe it. Khadafi had confessed to killing her mother knowing that she could be a witness against him. *Leave no witnesses.*

"I need you to make a full report—"

Shaking her head vigorously, Monica looked at me. "No reports. No testifying. No jail. No courts."

"Please, Monica," I begged. "This is what we need—"

"To what, detective? Put Khadafi in jail again? You tried that already, remember? It didn't work. He went to prison for three years and got out. He got out and took three people that I love away from me."

"I'm sorry, Monica. About what happened. I've told you that several times. The deal he made with Ann Sloan—he should have never been allowed to snitch to get home. He should have never gotten out after killing Moe Tolliver."

"But he did!" Monica yelled. "He got out. I never should have betrayed him. All over a stupid street code that he violated. I never should have married Cree. I always knew that Khadafi wouldn't accept what I did to him. I knew it, I never should have gotten pregnant—"

"Monica, stop it. This is not your fault," I told her.

"It is my fault. If not for the decisions I made, Cree would still be alive. My mother would be alive and my daughter—"

"Monica, stop it! Stop it! You are not in your right mind—"

"I'm in my right mind, detective. But I wasn't before. After Khadafi admitted to killing my mother, I threatened him. I spit on him. I was hurt and upset. I told him that he would never see his kids again. He told me that the dress I wore that day, I'd be wearing it again soon. And I didn't listen, I didn't listen."

"It's not your fault that Khadafi is a psycho.

"It's not, but I'm the woman who fell in love with him knowing full well what he was. I had two children by him knowing who and what he was. I knew that he would kill Cree. I told Cree that. I begged him to run. I begged him to move all of us away from here. I told him that Woodbridge wasn't far enough.

I told him about the time Khadafi went all the way to New York and killed a dude because of something the dude's brother did to Khadafi in prison. But Cree wouldn't listen. The man in him wouldn't accept what I was saying. The man in him couldn't take running from another man. A monster like Khadafi. His pride and ego got in the way. He told me that he would kill Khadafi and I believed him. I believed that he'd be our protector." Monica sat up in bed. "I believed that we'd be safe. I was wrong, but I know how to make it right." She swung her legs over the bed and stood up. Then she found her shoes and put them on.

"Monica, lie back down. You've experienced a lot of trauma. You need to rest," I implored her. "I'll leave, so you can sleep. I should've never disturbed you."

"I will never rest again until Khadafi is dead. And I'm gonna be the one to kill him. I promised him that. I owe him that. I gotta make things right."

Monica walked past me and out of the room. Her words before she departed had me riveted to my spot for a moment. I got my head together and went after her, calling her name. But she ignored me. The two homicide detective's eyes were on me as I raced to catch up with Monica.

"Monica, stop! Listen to me," I said.

"I'm done talking, detective," she replied.

"I can help you. As a matter of fact—would you stop and listen to me. Please, one more minute. Give me one minute."

Monica Summers stopped in her tracks, turned, and faced me. "You've got one minute."

"The day of your mother's funeral, I had P.G. Police pull Khadafi over. While they searched his car, I slipped a tracker under the front bumper. If Khadafi's driving the Mercedes, I can find him. Anywhere."

"What do you mean, if he's driving the Mercedes?"

"He's had access to multiple vehicles. When he went to Forestville Health and Rehab looking for you, he was driving a black four door SUV. He's been in at least two different vans and who knows what else. The Mercedes is leased to his aunt, Mary Henderson. Whatever he drove out here—"

"Is abandoned somewhere or on fire by now," Monica finished my sentence.

"I have the aunt's address, but I'm not sure if he's staying there."

"Knowing Khadafi, he's not there. He's somewhere shacked up with a bitch. And that could be anywhere. I need to find him, detective. I need to find him and kill him. Then and only then, I can grieve for my loved ones."

"Monica—I hear you loud and clear, but—"

"No, buts, detective," Monica stated emphatically.

"What I was gonna say is, but you have to let me do it. I'm gonna kill Khadafi. I'm a cop, I'll get away with it. I can say it was justified. No court in the country will even try to convict me. Let me kill him for you."

Monica shook her head. "Not gon' happen. Either you help me, or you don't. It doesn't matter. I'll find him without your help. He's mine. I have to do it for my mother, for my husband, for my daughter."

"Do you have a gun?" I asked her.

"My husband brought one, it's at home."

"Do you know how to use it?"

Monica nodded. "Khadafi taught me how. Isn't it, ironic?"

"Okay, I'm in. Let me find him. When I do I'll call you. You'll come to wherever he is and if the scenery is okay, you kill him.

Then you walk away, and I'll cover for you. You'll never do a day in jail."

"Thank you, Rio."

It's the first time that Monica ever called me, Rio. "Don't thank me until after he's dead. Stay by the phone." It was my turn to walk past her.

***

Two Days Later

"Monica, he's driving the Mercedes. I'm about three cars behind it right now. He's not in it, so he has to be in one of these three buildings on Galveston Street."

"Galveston Street? A small street with a few houses and three buildings? One building faces the street and the other two face each other?"

"Yeah. How did you know that?' I asked her.

"Khadafi has a problem with fucking all of his friends' girlfriends. The bitch that lives in that middle building, her name is Erykah. I followed her to that street one day and whipped her ass. Apparently, she's still fucking him. Do you see a black Kia Optima parked somewhere?"

I looked all around. "Naw, no Kia Optima."

"It was probably her car he used when he came here. You don't see it because he got rid of it. I'm on my way there now. Call me immediately if he leaves."

"You text me immediately when you're pulling up. I need to talk to you, but not over the phone."

***

"When he comes out—if he comes out tonight. I'll walk up and distract him. You'll have to get up on him from behind. So, you park up there. That way, you can approach without him seeing you."

"That makes sense," Monica agreed.

I turned and walked away from her car, then stopped and turned back around. "And do me a favor. Make sure you kill him and not me."

"I promise, I'll only kill him."

***

I sat in my car and wondered if I was doing the right thing. Then I thought about the family of Moe Tolliver and the families of Emily Perez, Jamya Smith, Yolanda Mock, Sherita Simms, and countless others. I thought about Monica and all the loved ones that she'd lost. I thought about all the collateral damage that Khadafi had left behind in his killing sprees. My anger at the senseless and innocent lives lost stiffened my resolve and quieted all voices of doubt in my head.

I was conspiring to commit murder and didn't feel bad at all. I had taken an oath to protect and serve and that's exactly what I was doing. Serving the community by protecting it from Khadafi. He needed to be stopped. He had to be stopped. An intense calm washed over me. I was doing the right thing.

Chapter Fifty-Seven

Khadafi

The murders I had committed blanketed the news non-stop for the last two days. Even though I felt that Erykah could be trusted, I never breathed a word to her about my savage act. I watched every news cycle since the murders to see what the police had. There were no witnesses to the murders, no suspects, and no motive. There was no mention of the black Sedan that sped away from the scene immediately after the shooting. That black Sedan was now scrap metal at the junkyard in Fort Washington, Maryland.

I told Erykah that her Kia Optima was gone, and she accepted that with no questions at all. She didn't give a fuck about the Kia since she now owned the CLK 330. I thought about Marnie and the pain and grief she had to be experiencing. That brought a smile to my face every time. To lose her mother last month and now her husband and daughter, that was enough to push anybody over the edge.

"Kill yourself, bitch," I muttered to myself.

I thought about the photo of Marnie's daughter that the news stations showed with every mention of the toddler's murder. I never meant to kill the baby girl, only the husband Cree. Moments before I ran up on Marnie's husband, I had reached down to tie my boots, then adjust the mask I wore. So, I never saw the baby in his hand. I didn't know that he was strapping the baby girl into a car seat.

I saw his body ducked into the backseat of the BMW and assumed that he was tossing a gym bag inside. The powerful hydra shok ammunition must've traveled straight through him into the baby girl. Every time my conscience bothered me about the baby, I thought about Marnie smacking me and spitting on me. I thought about my Versace glasses she had ruined. Although, the news reports said that the Virginia police had no suspects, evidently, some other police agencies did. They suspected me.

My aunt's house had been raided and searched twice. But nothing had been found. A large bag of cash was hidden in Erykah's closet. All my clothes had been destroyed already. The duffle bags full of guns and ammo now resided at the storage unit where my other things were.

There was no van, either black or silver to be found. No black SUV, no paperwork for any other vehicle besides the Benz. The police didn't have shit on me. I knew it and they knew it. I got up and walked out to the living room in Erykah's apartment. She sat in her lazy boy chair, eating a bag of caramel popcorn while watching T.V.

"What you watching, cuz?" I asked.

"Love and Hip Hop," Erykah answered.

"Which one?"

"What you mean, which one?"

"Which one you watching? They got them weak ass joints in a rack of different places now. Miami, Hollywood—"

"Oh—yeah, this is Love and Hip Hop New York."

I snatched the bag of popcorn from her and stood next to the recliner, watching the show. "You know what I hate about this shit?"

"No what? And gimme my damn popcorn back. Greedy ass!"

I handed the bag of popcorn back to Erykah. "I hate the fact that this shit is called a reality show and ain't none of it real. All that shit is scripted—"

"No, it ain't," Erykah remarked.

"It is, that shit fake as shit. And then they always wanna show all types of gay shit. Niggas kissing and shit on everyone. Miami's got Trina's gay ass cousin Bobby always in some extra flaming shit. Hollywood joint got the faggie ass nigga Zell and Jason. Then Love and Hip Hop Atlanta got Mimi, Stevie J's baby mother fucking with a basketball player chick. The New York joint you watching now got that Puerto Rican faggie—"

"Bae, don't let the LGBTQ community hear you. They gon' say you hating like shit. And you better be cool before them *check it mob* dudes fuck your ass up, gay people bashing."

"I'll kill everyone of them check it mob niggas. Kill my mother. I wish them niggas would. As a matter of fact, fuck them niggas. Come here," I said and pulled Erykah up off the recliner.

"What, Khadafi? Leave me alone. I'm tryna watch my show."

"Your show? I told you that shit fake as shit." I pulled Erykah's sweatpants down.

"Stop it, bae! I'm tryna see when Yandy saying Mendecees gon' come home from the feds."

"Fuck Yandy and Mendecees."

"That's probably how they feel about you, too."

I put my finger inside Erykah's panties and rubbed her clit.

"Khadafi—stop!" Erykah protested.

"Fuck that show. We gon' play some Hip Hop and make love."

"Khadafi—leave me alone! Stop! Don't do—that!"

A few minutes later, Erykah was back on the recliner, legs wide open. I was on my knees, rubbing caramel popcorn all over her wet pussy and then eating it.

***

"Now, you gotta go and get us something to eat," I told Erykah, later.

"How the fuck I'ma do that and my pussy and legs hurt?" she replied.

"You faking like shit. I didn't even have your legs pinned back that long. You on some lazy shit."

"I'm not, my legs hurt for real. All the acrobatic fuckin' you be doing. All them damn pushups you been doing over the years done made you too strong. I ain't playing, bae. You be fucking the shit outta me."

"Your pussy is a torch, so blame you, not me. I'ma go get the food. What you tryna eat?" I asked and sat up on the couch.

Erykah wiped her hair outta her face. "Uh—the steak and shrimp combo from Hanabis."

"The Japanese Steak House on Donnell Drive?"

"Uh huh. Their food good as shit, bae. You gotta get the Teriyaki grilled chicken and grilled salmon combo. It comes with grilled vegetables, lo mein noodles, fried rice, and salad. Shit bomb. You gon' love it. Get that for me."

"I'm sold on it," I said and got up off the couch naked. I grabbed my clothes. "They do take out, right?"

"Uh-huh."

"Call it in while I'm in the bathroom so it'll be ready when I get there."

"I'm on it. And while you in there, you need to shave all them red hairs off your ass. That shit ain't cute," Erykah said and laughed.

"Your two baby toes ain't cute, either. Both of 'em look like tootsie rolls and shit."

"They must taste like tootsie rolls, too, because you keep my toes in your mouth."

"I do that just so I can keep my dick in yours."

"Bae, kill yourself," Erykah joked."

"You, first."

***

It was dark outside and cold as hell. I zipped my coat all the way up and walked down the pathway to the sidewalk. The street was clear except for a lone man who exited a vehicle down the street. He headed my way, I reached under my coat and gripped the handle of my four fifth, ready to pull it. As the man got closer, I recognized him.

"Shit!" I muttered but kept walking.

How in the hell does he always know where I am?

The gun on me was clean, but it would get me at least five years in prison. I wasn't going out like that. I remembered the vow I made to myself about not going back to prison. I looked around to see if he had other cops in cars I didn't see. I saw no one, no one, but him.

The detective smiled as he approached, hands in his pockets. "Khadafi, my man. Fancy meeting you here."

"Not again," I said aloud.

"Not again, what?" the detective asked.

"This whole impromptu meeting between us sorta feels like the one I had with your partner Moe Tolliver that night out Maryland. Behind my aunt's house. I walked out of the house and there he was, alone. Just like you are now."

"I guess great minds really think alike."

"Great minds can also die alike, too, cuz. Are you here to search me again? Because I know you didn't come to arrest me by yourself. You know damn well, I ain't going out like that."

"Naw, no search, no arrest. This visit is friendly."

"Friendly? Stop it, cuz. We ain't friends and you know that."

"I'm offended."

"You're like a gnat buzzing around my ear, irritating."

"I know you killed Sherita Simms. You're on video—"

"We already went through all this before, remember? You told me everybody that you think I killed while P.G. was searching my car. Did you get anything out of the phone you took from me?"

"Nope. But you already knew I wouldn't. Gotta hand it to you, Khadafi, you're one smart muthafucka."

"Listen, cop, I'm tired from fuckin' all day and I'm hungry. I don't know how the fuck you keep popping up wherever I am, but it don't matter. If you got something on me, arrest me. If not, leave me the fuck alone."

"After tonight, nobody's gonna ever bother you again."

"What's that supposed to mean, cuz?"

Before my sentence completely left my mouth, I heard a gunshot pierce the silence of the night. At the same time, I felt the hot bullet enter my back and explode. I turned around and looked into the face of the person who shot me. A look of confusion crossed my face. The gun fired again. I saw the sparks leave the barrel. I felt an instant pain in my chest. I felt myself drop to the ground. I felt sleepy, I felt winded, I was in pain. My eyes closed but I could hear more gunshots. By then I couldn't feel a thing.

Chapter Fifty-Eight

Marnie

I stood transfixed to my spot and watched Khadafi fall. I watched him take his last breath. Then I watched the short woman drop the gun and fall to her knees. I watched Rio Jefferson kick the gun away from her and then handcuff her. He kneeled over Khadafi and checked for a pulse. He looked at the woman who had just killed Khadafi and then at me. His eyes dropped to the gun in my hand.

"Leave now," Rio said to me.

But I was too in a daze to move.

"Leave!" he shouted.

I turned around then and walked back to my car, confused as to what had just happened. I felt like I had been robbed. Killing Khadafi was my destiny. It was my defining moment. His life was mine to take for the lives that he had snatched from me. Opening the driver's door, I glanced back one last time. Rio was putting the woman in the back seat of his Impala. I stare at Khadafi's body askew, sprawled on the sidewalk. Blood congealing beneath him and getting cold on the pavement.

The Boogeyman was dead. Gunned down on a small street by an unknown woman. Who was she? What had Khadafi done to her to make her kill him? I sat down behind the wheel of my car and thought about all the times Khadafi had been shot or injured. I thought about the times I'd patched him up or pulled the bulletproof vest from his body to massage the places where bullets were supposed to have been. I thought about all the times Khadafi had escaped death.

All the instances where he survived his wounds. Superman is what I used to think he was. The weight of the gun still in my hand reminded me of its presence. It was a large gun for my small hand. Tears welled up in my eyes and fell. I cried for all the people that Khadafi had hurt or killed. I cried for my daughter. I cried for my husband. I cried for my mother.

"Khadafi's dead but where does that leave you?" a voice said.

"Oh, my gawd. Not you again," I replied.

To my right, sitting in the passenger seat was my pain. It had been years since I'd last seen it.

"Leave me alone," I mumbled and put my head down on the steering wheel.

"I will never leave you alone again. I'm here to stay."

"No, you're not. You're not even real. I can tune you out."

"Stop acting childish."

I put both of my hands over my ears after letting the gun fall to my lap. I closed my eyes. "I can't see you or hear you."

"But I'm still here," my pain assured me.

Despite having covered my ears, the voice was loud and clear in my head.

"Listen to me, Marnie, I'm here because of Cree. Because of Creation, they're both gone, and you're hurt too deep to feel anything else. Here I am. We are forever linked, you and I. I can imagine what the rest of our life will be like. You'll never smile, never laugh again. We'll be miserable the rest of our days. You and me, together. Dada and Mani will never have a normal life again, because you'll be too messed up in the head to be a good mother. As much as you love them, even they will never make you happy again. They'll be around us and their lives will be miserable, too. One big miserable family. Killing Khadafi wasn't your destiny. Loving him while hating him is your destiny. Forever missing Cree and Creation is your destiny.

"You're wrong," I said to my pain.

"I'm right and you know it," my pain replied.

I opened my eyes and looked at the gun in my lap, I reached for it.

"What are you going to with that, kill yourself?" I nodded. "You tried that before, remember? Twice and never went through with it. You are not strong enough to get rid of me. To get rid of us. Face it, Marnie, we are one, you and I and nothing can separate us. Not even death." My pain started laughing.

"Don't laugh at me, ain't shit funny," I hissed.

"You are funny, always threatening us."

"This is not a threat." I put the gun to my temple and pulled the trigger.

Anthony Fields

Chapter Fifty-Nine

Rio Jefferson

Bok!

I was on the phone with Doug Davis when I heard the single gunshot. In the still of the night, it reverberated loud and clear. My head jerked in the direction of the sound. I lowered the phone from my ear as the feeling of impending doom gripped my stomach. MPD Police cars swarmed Galveston Street from both ends, an ambulance and fire truck in tow. I exited my car and walked down the street. Monica Summers Buick Sedan in sight. It was located not far from where Khadafi's body lay. As I slowly approached the vehicle, I knew what I would find. But deep inside, I hoped that I'd be wrong. I wasn't, I peeked inside the passenger side window and my heart broke.

"Damn, Monica!" I muttered and signaled to some uniformed cops. "Over here!"

Monica Summers' head rested on the driver's window. Her blood and brain matter coated the glass in a grotesque creature of some kind. Like ink splattered onto a white canvas. Like paint that stained the wall before a mural. I backed away from the car as it became inundated with cops. All I could do was shake my head. Monica Summers had decided to take the easy way out. Her grief was too much to bear. It wasn't a decision that I could have made, but I understood it.

"Damn!"

***

The woman who had killed Khadafi looked up at me as I entered the room. Her left wrist was cuffed to the wall as she sat on a metal bench. I uncuffed her.

She rubbed her wrist and said, "Thank you, that cuff was starting to hurt."

"You have the right to remain silent," I said and read her, her Miranda rights. "Anything you say can and will be used against you in a court of law. You have a right to an attorney. If you cannot afford an attorney, one will be provided for you—yada, yada. Would you like to speak with me without an attorney present? Answer a few questions for me?"

"Sure. Why not?" the woman replied.

"First, I need to know your name. Second, why did you kill Khadafi?"

I sat down at the table I was across from the woman. I pulled out a pen and my notepad. The woman was beautiful, and she looked young. Her long, doe like eyes had long lashes. Her eyebrows were thick and dark. Her latte complexion was flawless. Her lips were luscious and painted with pink gloss. The hairstyle she rocked reminded me of a young Toni Braxton. Standing she was no more than five-feet tall, but she was thick and sexy. She leaned back until her back touched the wall and closed her eyes.

"My name is Lakia Ransom. Why I killed Khadafi is a long story."

"I've got nothing but time and so do you," I told her.

"This is my first time in jail. Can you tell?" Lakia asked.

I shrugged. "Haven't really been around you long enough."

"I knew exactly what I was doing when I shot Khadafi. I'm confessing to that."

"Did you use to mess with him or something?"

Lakia Ransom opened her eyes. "Never that, he wasn't my type."

"So, tell me, why did you kill him?"

"In twenty-ten, I was a correctional officer at Hope Village halfway house. It was there that I met Charles Gooding. The streets called him Lil Cee. He had just come home from the BOP and for some reason I really liked him. Luther Khadafi Fuller I later learned had killed Charles' mother and—"

"Three-year-old sister on S Street in Southeast, the same day that he was released from prison in two-thousand-eight."

Lakia nodded her head. "You're familiar with the situation, I see."

"Was one of the homicide detectives that worked the case."

"Charles was forever heartbroken about what happened to his family and why. You see, he never did what Khadafi and the others thought he did. He never snitched about the murder at Beaumont Pen and they believed he did. That's why Khadafi killed his family. Anyway, when Charles got home, he wanted revenge. He searched for any of Khadafi's family members that he could find, but he couldn't find them. He also looked for Khadafi and couldn't find him. Then one day he found Khadafi. He tried to kill him but Khadafi was armed, saw Charles, and shot back. Then one night, they bumped into each other at a hotel party. They tried to kill each other—"

"The Omni Shoreham Hotel parking lot. Five people were killed that night. One guy even jumped off a bridge that night, I remembered it well."

"Right after that Charles and I left the city. I quit my job and we left. Ended up in Norcross, Georgia. I was also pregnant by then. Months later, I gave birth to our daughter. We named her Charity after his little sister that Khadafi killed. We settled into a slower life in Norcross and I thought that Charles had forgotten about Khadafi after a while.

He spent a lot of time with me and our daughter, but Charles couldn't quell his desire for retribution. His hunger for revenge burned so hot inside him that he couldn't be the man that he wanted to be. For himself or for us. Thoughts and dreams of Khadafi consumed Charles. In his life, his scales were unbalanced. His desire for Khadafi's head outweighed his need for love. The night he told me that he was going back to D.C., I cried. I knew that if he came back here, he would die. I felt it. Dream it.

I pleaded with Charles to stay in Georgia. I told him about my dream. I told him, *"If you go back to DC he's gonna kill you."* I had already seen it. My tears, my words, nothing was enough to change his mind about what he wanted—what he needed to do. He left us that night and I never spoke to him again. Months later, I got the call that Charles had been killed outside of the D.C. jail. The same night that Khadafi was released from jail again.

I flew back here and gave Charles a proper funeral and burial. Then I went back to Georgia and raised my daughter, trying to act as if Charles never existed. But I couldn't do it. My life wasn't the same. I moved back here and gave my daughter to my mother to raise. I started using drugs. The drugs led to a lot of other shit I'm not proud of.

In twenty-fourteen, I read online about Antonio Felder being charged with Charles' murder. I found it interesting that his accuser was Khadafi. I couldn't believe it, how everything had come to a full circle right before our eyes. The notorious killer, who killed snitches had become one himself. In two-thousand-seven, at Beaumont Pen, Keith Burnette, a guy who'd snitched on one of Khadafi's friends was stabbed to death by Khadafi and dismembered. Khadafi, Antonio, a guy named Boo, one named Umar and Charles were all locked up for that murder.

For reasons only known to the executive and correctional staff at Beaumont. They separated Charles from the other four. Why? He never found out. But since he wasn't around Khadafi, Umar, Boo and Antonio assumed he was a snitch. In twenty-ten, night before Charles was released from prison, Antonio Felder went on trial for Keith's murder because he told prison officials, he'd committed the murder.

By then Khadafi had been released and for some reason both Boo and Umar got themselves killed not long after coming home. Antonio beat the Beaumont murder and ended up getting back in court on appeal. Charles wanted to kill him, too, but not as much as Khadafi. He believed that Antonio had ordered Khadafi to kill his mother and sister. I attended Antonio Felder's trial—"

"I never saw you there, I was present every day," I said.

"I was there. I just didn't look like this. I was still on drugs real bad. Anyway, I sat in that courtroom and listened to everything. I heard Khadafi testify that Antonio killed Charles. Then that lady got on the stand and said that some unknown person killed Charles.

They both lied. Khadafi killed Charles that night. I don't know how he did it, but he did it.

I saw it happen in my dream. It was then that I had another dream. I saw myself killing Khadafi. When I woke up that morning, I knew that I had to do it. I had to find Khadafi and kill him. I got myself together and shook the drugs. I've been sober three years now. I know Khadafi got sentenced to three years in Maryland. I was in the courtroom in Montgomery County when it happened.

I kept up with him until he was transferred to Western Correctional in Cumberland. I waited patiently while he did his time, his three years. He was released on September seventeen of this year. I didn't know where he lived or who he lived with, but I knew that he was here in the city and I knew that you were obsessed with finding him—"

I leaned forward in my chair. "Me? You knew I was obsessed with finding him?"

Lakia nodded. "Yes, you have always been my ace in the hole. I knew you'd find him. I knew that you hated him for killing your friend Maurice Tolliver. I knew that you'd been investigating Khadafi. All I had to do was follow you around. I knew that a month ago, you put a tracker on Khadafi's Benz after seeing him at his baby mother's, mother's funeral.

I've been behind you, Rio Jefferson every step of the way. You just didn't know it. I didn't know when you'd find Khadafi, but I knew you would. Today, I sat and waited to see who you were meeting. Who you were waiting for. Then I saw Khadafi walk out of that building and my prayers were answered. I saw you get out and confront him. I gave myself a pep talk and then I handled business. End of story."

"Hold on," I said and stood up. "What're you talking about? Me being obsessed with finding Khadafi? Me, hating him for killing Moe Tolliver? How in the hell do you know about the tracker I put on Khadafi's Benz? Talking about I was always your ace in the hole. Who the hell are you and how do you know me?"

"Temper, temper. Did Alabama win the football game? I like the Georgia Bulldogs, myself. Who won?"

"What?" I exploded confusion etched all over my face.

Lakia Ransom leaned a little closer in her seat. "Haven't made the connection yet, detective? Well, let me help you out. My name is Lakia Ransom, but everybody in my family calls me Kia. I talk to my aunt all the time and apparently, you do, too. Your girlfriend Tonya—"

"Latonya Ransom," I said in disbelief.

"My favorite aunt. I love her to death and vise versa. Everything that you talk about on the phone, I knew. Everything you've ever said about Khadafi, I knew. Small world, huh. Thank you for everything, detective. I couldn't have killed Khadafi without you. And I think, I'll take that lawyer now."

The End

Note from The Author

No matter what we do right, some people can only see the wrong in it. There are going to be people who read this book and say, "He's glorifying or glamorizing rats." That was not my intention. My intent was to tell this story as real as it could possibly get. There are Khadafi's in every city, every state, and every neighborhood. Dudes who were gangstas, then turned rat. But just because they turned rat doesn't change the fact that they kill.

Off the top of my head, I know several dudes in my city who are just like Khadafi. Cold blooded killer rats and nobody is trying to oppose them. These dudes I know will kill everybody in your house including all the pets, but they are rats. It's the way of the world. Just wanted to say that to the loyal Sacrifice readers and all my critics who'll drag me through the mud because Khadafi a rat killed all the good men in the book.

Lastly, I wanna shout out my celly, Leshawn Kool Elijah for putting up with me during the writing of this book in the midst of a global pandemic. I wanna shout out my son Kevin Grover in USP Big Sandy and let him know that I'm proud of the man he has become. To my cousin Joseph Ebron in ADX who was sentenced to death in 2008, I love you, lil cuz with all my heart, hold your head.

To my man Pretty B, to Trey Manning, Donzell McCauley, Chew, Dog, Buck, Big Mac, Griff, Eight L, Veedo, Rico Suave, Rock, Enjoli Gaffrey, Thurman Parker, Kevin Atkins, Big Vee, Nitty (WV), Smiz (from the Ville), Tommy (Louisville), Jug (Ohio), Roc (New Orleans), Fat Rat, Delmont Player, Cheri Johnson, Nickey Foots, Anette Snyder, Tontieta Virgil, Tina Grover, Willie Scooter Hill, Mumbo Scales, Gary Butler, Kevin Devonshire, Dink, Antwan Thomas (LA), Cinquan Blakney (Chez), Tony Roy, Steve Crockett, Deon, Tarzan, Ronald Randolph, Erick Hicks, D.C., Marcus Martin, and Lil Jihad. All the good men.

Lastly, again, all the men who know and love Buck, I remain firm, unbroken, and unblemished. Never let suckas get in your ears with vile slander and lies. Go check out the book before this one, entitled If You Cross Me Once. It's a good one. Up next is Angel 3 You'll Cross Me Twice and Blink 2 Times and You Missed It. Hopefully, the TV series, 69 Square Miles will come to the screen one day. Stay Tuned.

One Love

Buckey Fields

Death Before Dishonor

P.S.

Thanks a million, to every person that has supported the Ultimate Sacrifice Series over the years.

Submission Guideline

Submit the first three chapters of your completed manuscript to ldpsubmissions@gmail.com, subject line: Your book's title. The manuscript must be in a .doc file and sent as an attachment. Document should be in Times New Roman, double spaced and in size 12 font. Also, provide your synopsis and full contact information. If sending multiple submissions, they must each be in a separate email.

Have a story but no way to send it electronically? You can still submit to LDP/Ca$h Presents. Send in the first three chapters, written or typed, of your completed manuscript to:

LDP: Submissions Dept
Po Box 944
Stockbridge, Ga 30281

DO NOT send the original manuscript. Must be a duplicate.

Provide your synopsis and a cover letter containing your full contact information.

Thanks for considering LDP and Ca$h Presents.

Anthony Fields

Coming Soon from Lock Down Publications/Ca$h Presents

BOW DOWN TO MY GANGSTA
By **Ca$h**
TORN BETWEEN TWO
By **Coffee**
THE STREETS STAINED MY SOUL **II**
By **Marcellus Allen**
BLOOD OF A BOSS **VI**
SHADOWS OF THE GAME II
By **Askari**
LOYAL TO THE GAME **IV**
By **T.J. & Jelissa**
IF LOVING YOU IS WRONG… **III**
By **Jelissa**
TRUE SAVAGE **VIII**
MIDNIGHT CARTEL III
DOPE BOY MAGIC IV
CITY OF KINGZ II
By **Chris Green**
BLAST FOR ME **III**
A SAVAGE DOPEBOY III
CUTTHROAT MAFIA III
DUFFLE BAG CARTEL VI
By **Ghost**
A HUSTLER'S DECEIT III
KILL ZONE **II**
BAE BELONGS TO ME III
A DOPE BOY'S QUEEN III
By **Aryanna**

COKE KINGS V

KING OF THE TRAP II

By **T.J. Edwards**

GORILLAZ IN THE BAY V

3X KRAZY II

De'Kari

THE STREETS ARE CALLING II

Duquie Wilson

KINGPIN KILLAZ IV

STREET KINGS III

PAID IN BLOOD III

CARTEL KILLAZ IV

DOPE GODS III

Hood Rich

SINS OF A HUSTLA II

ASAD

KINGZ OF THE GAME VI

Playa Ray

SLAUGHTER GANG IV

RUTHLESS HEART IV

By Willie Slaughter

THE HEART OF A SAVAGE III

By Jibril Williams

FUK SHYT II

By Blakk Diamond

TRAP QUEEN

By Troublesome

YAYO IV

GHOST MOB

Stilloan Robinson

KINGPIN DREAMS III

By Paper Boi Rari

CREAM II

By Yolanda Moore

SON OF A DOPE FIEND III

By Renta

FOREVER GANGSTA II

GLOCKS ON SATIN SHEETS III

By Adrian Dulan

LOYALTY AIN'T PROMISED III

By Keith Williams

THE PRICE YOU PAY FOR LOVE II

By Destiny Skai

CONFESSIONS OF A GANGSTA III

By Nicholas Lock

I'M NOTHING WITHOUT HIS LOVE II

SINS OF A THUG II

By Monet Dragun

LIFE OF A SAVAGE IV

MURDA SEASON IV

GANGLAND CARTEL III

CHI'RAQ GANGSTAS II

By **Romell Tukes**

QUIET MONEY IV

THUG LIFE II

EXTENDED CLIP II

By **Trai'Quan**

THE STREETS MADE ME III

By **Larry D. Wright**

IF YOU CROSS ME ONCE II

ANGEL III

By **Anthony Fields**

FRIEND OR FOE III

By **Mimi**

SAVAGE STORMS II

By **Meesha**

BLOOD ON THE MONEY III

By J-Blunt

THE STREETS WILL NEVER CLOSE II

By K'ajji

NIGHTMARES OF A HUSTLA III

By King Dream

THE WIFEY I USED TO BE II

By Nicole Goosby

IN THE ARM OF HIS BOSS

By Jamila

MONEY, MURDER & MEMORIES II

Malik D. Rice

CONCRETE KILLAZ II

By Kingpen

Available Now

RESTRAINING ORDER **I & II**

By **CA$H & Coffee**

LOVE KNOWS NO BOUNDARIES **I II & III**

By **Coffee**

RAISED AS A GOON I, II, III & IV

BRED BY THE SLUMS I, II, III

BLAST FOR ME I & II

ROTTEN TO THE CORE I II III

A BRONX TALE I, II, III

DUFFLE BAG CARTEL I II III IV V

HEARTLESS GOON I II III IV

A SAVAGE DOPEBOY I II

HEARTLESS GOON I II III

DRUG LORDS I II III

CUTTHROAT MAFIA I II

By **Ghost**

LAY IT DOWN **I & II**

LAST OF A DYING BREED

BLOOD STAINS OF A SHOTTA I & II III

By **Jamaica**

LOYAL TO THE GAME I II III

LIFE OF SIN I, II III

By **TJ & Jelissa**

BLOODY COMMAS I & II

SKI MASK CARTEL I II & III

KING OF NEW YORK I II,III IV V

RISE TO POWER I II III

COKE KINGS I II III IV

BORN HEARTLESS I II III IV

KING OF THE TRAP

By **T.J. Edwards**

IF LOVING HIM IS WRONG…I & II

LOVE ME EVEN WHEN IT HURTS I II III

By **Jelissa**

WHEN THE STREETS CLAP BACK I & II III

THE HEART OF A SAVAGE I II

By **Jibril Williams**

A DISTINGUISHED THUG STOLE MY HEART I II & III

LOVE SHOULDN'T HURT I II III IV

RENEGADE BOYS I II III IV

PAID IN KARMA I II III

SAVAGE STORMS

By **Meesha**

A GANGSTER'S CODE I &, II III

A GANGSTER'S SYN I II III

THE SAVAGE LIFE I II III

CHAINED TO THE STREETS I II III

BLOOD ON THE MONEY I II

By J-Blunt

PUSH IT TO THE LIMIT

By **Bre' Hayes**

BLOOD OF A BOSS **I, II, III, IV, V**

SHADOWS OF THE GAME

By **Askari**

THE STREETS BLEED MURDER **I, II & III**

THE HEART OF A GANGSTA I II& III

By **Jerry Jackson**

CUM FOR ME I II III IV V VI

An **LDP Erotica Collaboration**

BRIDE OF A HUSTLA **I II & II**

THE FETTI GIRLS **I, II& III**

CORRUPTED BY A GANGSTA I, II III, IV

BLINDED BY HIS LOVE

THE PRICE YOU PAY FOR LOVE

DOPE GIRL MAGIC I II III

By **Destiny Skai**

WHEN A GOOD GIRL GOES BAD

By **Adrienne**
THE COST OF LOYALTY I II III
By Kweli
A GANGSTER'S REVENGE **I II III & IV**
THE BOSS MAN'S DAUGHTERS I II III IV V
A SAVAGE LOVE **I & II**
BAE BELONGS TO ME I II
A HUSTLER'S DECEIT I, II, III
WHAT BAD BITCHES DO I, II, III
SOUL OF A MONSTER I II III
KILL ZONE
A DOPE BOY'S QUEEN I II
By **Aryanna**
A KINGPIN'S AMBITON
A KINGPIN'S AMBITION **II**
I MURDER FOR THE DOUGH
By **Ambitious**
TRUE SAVAGE I II III IV V VI VII
DOPE BOY MAGIC I, II, III
MIDNIGHT CARTEL I II
CITY OF KINGZ
By **Chris Green**
A DOPEBOY'S PRAYER
By **Eddie "Wolf" Lee**
THE KING CARTEL **I, II & III**
By **Frank Gresham**
THESE NIGGAS AIN'T LOYAL **I, II & III**
By **Nikki Tee**
GANGSTA SHYT **I II &III**
By **CATO**

THE ULTIMATE BETRAYAL

By **Phoenix**

BOSS'N UP **I , II & III**

By **Royal Nicole**

I LOVE YOU TO DEATH

By Destiny J

I RIDE FOR MY HITTA

I STILL RIDE FOR MY HITTA

By **Misty Holt**

LOVE & CHASIN' PAPER

By **Qay Crockett**

TO DIE IN VAIN

SINS OF A HUSTLA

By **ASAD**

BROOKLYN HUSTLAZ

By **Boogsy Morina**

BROOKLYN ON LOCK I & II

By **Sonovia**

GANGSTA CITY

By **Teddy Duke**

A DRUG KING AND HIS DIAMOND I & II III

A DOPEMAN'S RICHES

HER MAN, MINE'S TOO I, II

CASH MONEY HO'S

THE WIFEY I USED TO BE

By Nicole Goosby

TRAPHOUSE KING **I II & III**

KINGPIN KILLAZ I II III

STREET KINGS I II

PAID IN BLOOD **I II**

CARTEL KILLAZ I II III

DOPE GODS I II

By **Hood Rich**

LIPSTICK KILLAH **I, II, III**

CRIME OF PASSION I II & III

FRIEND OR FOE I II

By **Mimi**

STEADY MOBBN' **I, II, III**

THE STREETS STAINED MY SOUL

By **Marcellus Allen**

WHO SHOT YA **I, II, III**

SON OF A DOPE FIEND I II

Renta

GORILLAZ IN THE BAY **I II III IV**

TEARS OF A GANGSTA I II

3X KRAZY

DE'KARI

TRIGGADALE I II III

Elijah R. Freeman

GOD BLESS THE TRAPPERS I, II, III

THESE SCANDALOUS STREETS I, II, III

FEAR MY GANGSTA I, II, III IV, V

THESE STREETS DON'T LOVE NOBODY I, II

BURY ME A G I, II, III, IV, V

A GANGSTA'S EMPIRE I, II, III, IV

THE DOPEMAN'S BODYGAURD I II

THE REALEST KILLAZ I II III

Tranay Adams

THE STREETS ARE CALLING

Duquie Wilson

MARRIED TO A BOSS… I II III
By Destiny Skai & Chris Green
KINGZ OF THE GAME I II III IV V
Playa Ray
SLAUGHTER GANG I II III
RUTHLESS HEART I II III
By Willie Slaughter
FUK SHYT
By Blakk Diamond
DON'T F#CK WITH MY HEART I II
By Linnea
ADDICTED TO THE DRAMA I II III
IN THE ARM OF HIS BOSS II
By Jamila
YAYO I II III
A SHOOTER'S AMBITION I II
By S. Allen
TRAP GOD I II III
By Troublesome
FOREVER GANGSTA
GLOCKS ON SATIN SHEETS I II
By Adrian Dulan
TOE TAGZ I II III
By Ah'Million
KINGPIN DREAMS I II
By Paper Boi Rari
CONFESSIONS OF A GANGSTA I II
By Nicholas Lock
I'M NOTHING WITHOUT HIS LOVE
SINS OF A THUG

By Monet Dragun

CAUGHT UP IN THE LIFE I II III

By Robert Baptiste

NEW TO MONEY, MURDER & MEMORIES

THE GAME I II III

By **Malik D. Rice**

LIFE OF A SAVAGE I II III

A GANGSTA'S QUR'AN I II III

MURDA SEASON I II III

GANGLAND CARTEL I II

CHI'RAQ GANGSTAS

By **Romell Tukes**

LOYALTY AIN'T PROMISED I II

By Keith Williams

QUIET MONEY I II III

THUG LIFE

EXTENDED CLIP

By **Trai'Quan**

THE STREETS MADE ME I II

By **Larry D. Wright**

THE ULTIMATE SACRIFICE I, II, III, IV, V, VI

KHADIFI

IF YOU CROSS ME ONCE

ANGEL I II

By **Anthony Fields**

THE LIFE OF A HOOD STAR

By Ca$h & Rashia Wilson

THE STREETS WILL NEVER CLOSE

By K'ajji

CREAM

By Yolanda Moore

NIGHTMARES OF A HUSTLA I II

By King Dream

CONCRETE KILLAZ

By Kingpen

Anthony Fields

<u>BOOKS BY LDP'S CEO, CA$H</u>

<u>TRUST IN NO MAN</u>

<u>TRUST IN NO MAN 2</u>

<u>TRUST IN NO MAN 3</u>

<u>BONDED BY BLOOD</u>

<u>SHORTY GOT A THUG</u>

<u>THUGS CRY</u>

<u>THUGS CRY 2</u>

<u>THUGS CRY 3</u>

<u>TRUST NO BITCH</u>

<u>TRUST NO BITCH 2</u>

<u>TRUST NO BITCH 3</u>

<u>TIL MY CASKET DROPS</u>

<u>RESTRAINING ORDER</u>

<u>RESTRAINING ORDER 2</u>

<u>IN LOVE WITH A CONVICT</u>

<u>LIFE OF A HOOD STAR</u>

CPSIA information can be obtained
at www.ICGtesting.com
Printed in the USA
LVHW020818070521
686660LV00002B/14